FATAL FEAST

A MERLIN MYSTERY

FATAL FEAST

JAY RUUD

FIVE STAR
A part of Gale, Cengage Learning

GALE
CENGAGE Learning·

Farmington Hills, Mich • San Francisco • New York • Waterville, Maine
Meriden, Conn • Mason, Ohio • Chicago

GALE
CENGAGE Learning®

LIBRARY OF CONGRESS CATALOGING-IN-PUBLICATION DATA

Ruud, Jay
    Fatal feast / Jay Ruud. — First edition.
        pages ; cm. — (A Merlin mystery)
    ISBN 978-1-4328-2987-2 (hardcover) — ISBN 1-4328-2987-4 (hardcover) — ISBN 978-1-4328-2980-3 (ebook) — ISBN 1-4328-2980-7 (ebook)
    1. Merlin (Legendary character)—Fiction. 2. Guenevere, Queen (Legendary character)—Fiction. 3. Knights and knighthood—Great Britain—Fiction. 4. Murder—Investigation—Fiction. 5. Great Britain—History—Medieval period, 1066–1485—Fiction. I. Title.
PS3618.U88F38 2015
813'.6—dc23   2014031305

First Edition. First Printing: January 2015
Find us on Facebook– https://www.facebook.com/FiveStarCengage
Visit our website– http://www.gale.cengage.com/fivestar/
Contact Five Star™ Publishing at FiveStar@cengage.com

Printed in the United States of America
1 2 3 4 5 6 7 19 18 17 16 15

For Stacey, my own Rosemounde

CHAPTER ONE:
THE APPLE OF DISCORD

"Pin him down!"

"He's choking! Pound his back!"

"It's the falling sickness! Open his mouth! Don't let him swallow his tongue!"

"Loosen his clothes!"

"Give him some wine!"

The din became so confused that no one could hear what anyone else was shouting. I looked to the queen, who sat amazed with her jaw clenched tight and a look of horror in her eyes. Suddenly, Sir Patrise gave a terrible shudder and then abruptly stopped moving altogether. By now Sir Mador was cradling him in his arms as Sir Tristram bent over him, feeling the pulse in his neck. Tristram stood up, looking around at the crowd that now listened expectantly. Sir Tristram merely shook his head.

"The apple!" came a cry from behind me, where Florent stood gaping at the floor. Every eye followed his gaze, and indeed there was the apple, lying on the floor next to Sir Patrise's now immobile right hand. Two large bites had been taken out of it. Now all eyes turned accusingly to the queen.

When her pleading eyes met mine, all I could do was sputter incoherently. How had it come to this? And the banquet had started out so well for her, so triumphantly.

When she had entered the great hall that evening, every jaw had dropped. She was always a striking beauty: Guinevere, princess of Cameliard, Queen of Logres, chief jewel in Arthur's crown. But today she was extraordinarily magnificent; her gown was bright red samite, interwoven with gold filigree, and she wore a high headdress embossed with pearls. If I were a wandering troubadour, I'd have sung that her bare neck and bosom heaved white below her radiant countenance like freshly fallen snow. But for me it was her ironically arched right eyebrow and the smirking lips that always seemed on the brink of laughter that made her herself, that made her Guinevere.

Sir Bors's eyes bulged wide when he saw her, and Sir Agravain cleared his throat and licked his lips. Not one of the twenty-four knights seated around the elaborately set table even remembered at first to rise in her presence. Finally, after several seconds of stunned silence while the queen stood framed in the open doorway, Sir Gawain leapt to his feet and bowed low in her direction, stammering slightly as he blurted out "My lady . . ." It was the most tongue-tied I'd ever seen Sir Gawain, that paragon of chivalry and courteous speech, and his face was flushed as red as his flowing hair and mustache.

Fair-haired and fair-tongued, Sir Gareth was not far behind his brother in demonstrating his civility, and the other knights all stood en masse, all mumbling courteously things like "Your highness . . ." and "My queen . . ." Guinevere nodded benignly and then seemed to float into the room. As she approached the head of the table, to sit with Gawain at her right and Sir Bors de Ganis at her left, I held her chair and she inclined her head toward me, whispering conspiratorially "*Mon dieu,* young Gildas, do you think they're expecting someone important?"

I stifled the chuckle and maintained my formal composure as I pushed in her chair. She did that kind of thing to me all the time. As a page in her household, and undoubtedly her favorite, I knew she felt comfortable letting her hair down around me— more comfortable than she did with a lot of other people, even her husband. Even her ladies-in-waiting. Even her husband's nephew and heir apparent, Sir Gawain. But not, I admit, more than Sir Lancelot.

Though even that relationship seemed strained. I didn't really know why, but Lancelot was apparently out of the queen's good graces of late, and last week had gone off on his own to seek honor and glory and all that. The queen seemed somewhat put out by his going, and that's why this dinner was so important to her. It was her way of announcing to the court, "I do not need Sir Lancelot around to make me happy. I am the queen and I am the social arbiter of this kingdom, and I'm going to throw this feast for Camelot's best and brightest, and at the same time show them what a queen should look like and act like, by God!" Not that she'd ever say it out loud, but I knew what she meant.

My first task was to serve the claret. I poured it into the queen's glass, then in Sir Gawain's, then in Sir Bors's. Other pages around the table did the same for the other guests. Now Sir Kay, the king's foster brother and seneschal, stood up. Fat and blustering, he thought a lot more of himself than anyone else did, but tended to be the first to speak anyway, no matter what was going on. Normally this feast would have been his charge—and he did such things well—but Guinevere had insisted on seeing to every detail of this one and invited Kay to sit at the foot of the table, opposite the queen herself. He had risen to give the toast.

As he lifted his glass of spiced, sweetened wine, the others followed suit. "To our gracious sovereign lady," he intoned through his nose. "The kingdom's most beautiful woman, and the world's most generous queen." He finished the toast with a smile that parted his thick lips and showed a set of yellow teeth that looked a little too big for his mouth. I wondered how long Kay had lain awake last night to come up with that toast. "Hear, hear!" came the answer from twenty-three other knights, followed by the clanking of glasses and a number of healthy gulps.

Now the party settled into comfortable chatter and I retired to my post behind the queen's right shoulder and well back from her chair. I would be called upon later to carve the meat and to pour the wine. But for the moment, I let my gaze wander over the assembled worthies and let my mind drift along with them. Servants began bringing in the first course, consisting of fresh white wastel-bread, assorted cheeses, *mortreux* served as a pate, and a dish of *blancmange*—chicken in a thick white sauce. As the guests helped themselves to these appetizers, I mentally took attendance, in case the queen needed some help later on remembering exactly who had been there and what each had done and said. On Kay's right at the foot of the table was Sir Palomides, the Moorish knight, sitting opposite Sir Bors. To Kay's left, opposite Sir Gawain on the other end of the long table, sat Sir Pinel le Savage, a knight of Wales.

Down the side of the table to my right sat, first, Sir Gareth, then Gawain's other brothers: Sir Gaheris, fair-haired like Gareth; and Sir Agravain, a redhead like Gawain. On Agravain's right was Sir Galihud, once rescued by Sir Lancelot; Sir Galihodin, whose father was a king; Sir Bedivere, one of Arthur's oldest knights; Sir Patrise, a knight from Ireland; Sir Mador de la Porte, cousin of Patrise; and finally, to the left of Sir Pinel, Sir Breunor, whom Kay in his scathing wit nicknamed "La Cote Male Taile" (the "Ill-Tailored Coat"), a name that stuck.

I had just finished memorizing that side of the table when the queen gave a signal to the servers that they were to bring in the second course, and I knew that was my cue to pour wine for the guests. I stepped to Gawain's right and began pouring a lusty red Bordeaux in the glasses of Sir Gareth and Sir Gaheris, overhearing as I did so—how could I help myself?—snatches of their conversation:

"He deserved what happened to him."

"I won't argue with you, Gaheris. You are my closest brother. But I still say it was treacherously done."

"Gareth, he would make our mother a whore."

"She needed no help in that department."

Gaheris clicked his mouth shut and stared ahead darkly, and I couldn't hear any more of the conversation without appearing to be listening, which I really wasn't. Really. But the queen would be interested in what I had overheard. She did trust me to be her ears as well as her eyes at these kinds of affairs, and nobody ever notices the page pouring his wine.

By now the second course had appeared. A large platter of chicken with marybones and a dish of walnuts was making its way down one side of the table, and up the other side were being passed a large plate of pike in a galauntyne sauce and a platter of pease and worts. I stepped back to observe—and memorize—the guests again.

On the other side of the table, beginning to the left of Sir Bors, sat his brother, the burly Sir Lionel—after Sir Bors the cousin Lancelot loved most. Next to Lionel sat Lancelot's brother Sir Ector de Maris, and then more of Lancelot's kinsmen—Sir Blamor de Ganis and his brother, Sir Bleoberis de Ganis. For someone who wanted to show the court that she didn't care a fig whether Lancelot stayed or left, the queen certainly had invited the greater part of his family to the party.

To Bleoberis's left sat Sir Ironside, otherwise known as the Red Knight of the Red Lands. His color suited him—many a knight had been bloodied at his hands. Sir Tristram de Liones came next, nephew of King Mark of Cornwall and one of the greatest of Arthur's knights. Sir Brandiles was next to him—another one of the knights that Lancelot had saved from the renegade Sir Turquin. Next sat Sir Ywain, Gawain's friend and cousin whom people knew as the "Knight of the Lion." Finally next to Sir Palomides, sat his brother, Sir Safer. That was all. A worthier assemblage of knightly flesh I don't think anyone has seen outside of a great tournament, but here the only weapons they were wielding were the knives they ate with.

"Sir Bors, what will your kinsman Sir Lancelot du Lac say when he finds he has missed the most magnificent feast of the season?" Sir Gawain asked, sucking on a chicken bone and eyeing the stolid Sir Bors mischievously. The queen's lips pursed as she fought back a smirk.

"My lord Gawain, Sir Lancelot enjoys a courtly feast as much as any man," Bors answered with all appropriate formality, though his lip quivered slightly under his well-trimmed mustache—he was a man who knew when he was being played with, but also knew how to behave courteously in every social situation. "But it will be no hardship for him to miss a meal. He hungers more for honor, and therefore rides now to achieve it where God gives him the adventure. His only true regret"—and now Bors inclined his close cropped head toward the queen— "would be in missing the unutterable beauty of my lady the queen as she appears before us tonight."

After what sounded like a snort, I heard Guinevere mutter "Yes, I dare say," as she dipped a piece of pike lightly into the galauntyne sauce with her fingertips.

"Boy! Some of that wine!" came the call from Sir Bleoberis. Dutifully I stepped behind his seat and poured some Bordeaux into his outstretched glass, then filled the empty glass of Sir Ironside beside him.

"If I had my way, we wouldn't let any of them into the country, damned foreign savages," the Red Knight was saying. Sir Bleoberis grunted noncommittally through his food. "I mean, look at them. Like a pair of graceless beasts. It's a dishonor to us to be seated at the same table with them." He glared across the table and toward the left.

Bleoberis followed his gaze. "What," he asked, "you mean the

Saracens? Why, they're all right. A little strange in their ways, of course, but as fine as any knights in Camelot. What's your problem with them?"

Sir Ironside shook his head in irritation. "No, no, not the Moors. Next to them. I'm talking about the Irish. That silly young dog, Sir Patrise, and his villainous cousin, Sir Mador. Look at the buffoons—they haven't the first clue how to act in a civilized setting."

I glanced down the table myself to the two Irish knights. They were chatting quietly and sipping their wine. I saw no particular difference between their behavior and that of any of the other knights at the table. But then, I did not have the refined social sensibilities of the Red Knight of the Red Lands, so I would have to defer to his judgment. I shrugged in silence.

"Bleoberis!" Sir Ironside continued as he stuck a piece of his own fish into the galauntyne sauce, soaking his fingers up to about the second knuckle. "Do you know why the Holy Land got all of the Moors and Logres got all the Irish?"

"Hmm?" Bleoberis answered through a mouthful of chicken, adding a shrug of his own.

"The Holy Land got first choice!" The Red Knight stopped for a moment, looking at Bleoberis in silence. Bleoberis shook his head and returned to the important matter of eating. Sir Ironside let out a huge guffaw in response to his own joke, so that it took a stern look from the head of the table to get him to settle down and behave in a manner more appropriate to the occasion. At that point the Red Knight glanced up in my direction and stopped. "Well, boy? Can I help you?"

"No, sir. Thank you, sir." The servants were beginning to bring in the main course, and so I made my way back to my place behind the queen's chair. She met my eyes and shared a bemused look with me. She knew I would have some juicy gossip after the dinner.

The third course was the pièce de résistance. First, plates of more nuts and cheese were brought, along with some root vegetables. But these were followed by two huge platters each bearing an entire roasted swan, with neck and head still attached. Amid an audible gasp followed by enthusiastic cheers from the guests, four servants brought the first platter to the head of the table, and four others brought the second to the foot and set it before Sir Kay.

As guest of honor, Sir Gawain had brought his squire, his son Florent, to carve the roast at his table. Florent, a few years older than I, would soon be Sir Florent. He had his father's fiery hair but not his temperament, inclining in that way more toward the milder and fairer qualities of his uncle Gareth. He took his role as carver very seriously, and priggishly cut into the steaming brown bird with a look of high solemnity.

My own job, as the queen's page, was to carve the other roast. I strode to the foot of the table and squeezed in between Sir Kay and Sir Pinel. As I took up the oversized knife and began beheading the great fowl, as a prelude to cutting off its wings, I couldn't help but overhear the less interesting conversation going on between Sir Kay and Sir Palomides.

"In my country," Sir Palomides was droning, "a good dash of fenugreek would have been used on that chicken we had earlier. It has a sweet and savory taste and would have added a great deal to the dish. That and perhaps some cumin, ground into a fine powder and sprinkled throughout."

Sir Kay, as seneschal of the king's household, had a special fondness for new kinds of spices for the cooks to try. "Cumin we have had here, and should have again. The fenugreek I am not familiar with." But his eyes said he would very much like to find out more about it.

Sir Safer leaned in with the intent of building up his brother. "Sir Palomides," he confided to Kay, "is learned in all the lore of herbs and spices in our country. He can tell you the properties of any plant you find."

Palomides scoffed a bit in his humility. "Certainly not every plant, brother, but I do make a point of learning herb-lore—it can be very valuable. Now coriander seed—that would be quite useful in the roasting of this great swan. It has a light, almost citrus flavor."

"Coriander seed, yes." Kay looked as if he were trying to memorize the names of these herbs so that he could try to purchase some from those involved in the trade routes to the Holy Land.

"But more than anything else, the perfect spice for this kind of meat—or for almost any, truth be told—is saffron."

"Saffron! Yes, I've only heard of it, but I understand it is as valuable as gold!"

"True," the Moorish knight nodded. "Saffron is a rare and valuable commodity. Very labor intensive. An entire field of saffron might yield only five pounds of the spice as its whole crop. Very rare. Very expensive. But the king of all spices."

"And should not the greatest king in Christendom possess the world's richest spices for his table?" Kay asked "What is the best way to go about . . ."

By now I was done with the carving, and, stifling a huge yawn, I set down the knife and began to circulate again, refilling wine glasses, beginning with Sir Pinel's to Kay's left. He seemed as bored with the conversation as I was, and was staring absentmindedly across the table toward Sir Gawain on the other end. He was so much in his own little world that he didn't seem to notice his glass had been filled. I continued my rounds, and the soft buzz of muted conversations, all drifting from full-bellied guests, surrounded me as I circled the table, so that I caught only snatches from here and there.

". . . But Sir Ywain, you don't mean to say the beast actually

15

sleeps with you?"

"Only when I am traveling. My lady, alas, waxes uncomfortable with a full-grown lion in the bed . . ."

". . . Who made that new hauberk I saw you with at the Winchester tournament? My own armor-maker disappointed me with my new greaves and I think overcharged me as well . . ."

". . . Pass me some of those nuts, will you, Sir Breunor . . . ?"

". . . Isolde of the White Hands? Kind of a coincidence, isn't it, that you and your uncle married women with the same name?"

By now I was back behind my lady's right shoulder, leaning against a great unicorn tapestry that covered the wall and, like many of the guests, nearly dozing. Their weariness was from eating themselves into a stupor; mine was from running around and waiting on them, but there would be plenty of leftovers in the kitchen once this was over, and it promised to be over before too long. The servants at last were bringing in the voide, the final course.

A great bowl filled with fruit—large red apples and yellow and green pears—was brought in and set before Sir Gawain. Smaller bowls of honey were placed strategically around the table so that the guests would have something sweet to dip their fruit into. But Gawain, normally a ravenous eater of fruit, was looking a little green himself by now.

"My lady," he begged off. "Tempting as this dessert is, in truth I could not possibly swallow one more morsel. Please forgive my rudeness. After any other meal, I would gladly take that huge red apple on top of the bowl, as you have seen me do on other occasions. But the magnificence of this meal is already unparalleled, and I could not forbear eating too much of every course to allow me to save room for any of this one. Please, pass it to Sir Bors."

The bowl of fruit accordingly began to make its way down Bors's side of the table. A few of the knights picked off small pears but most passed it on, bloated by what they had already eaten. When the bowl had reached Sir Patrise, the queen in her graciousness deigned to recognize him.

"Ah, Sir Patrise. I invited you here to recognize and welcome a foreign visitor, and for the sake of your kinsman, Sir Mador, already a knight of my husband's table. I know it is commonly spoken that I harbor no love for the Irish because of their war with my father and later my husband many years ago. But that is past and I hold no grudges. We hope to be good hosts to you during your stay in Logres, and dare to think that you may, like your cousin, find the climate to your liking. Perhaps that you will even strive to become a member of that most exclusive of chivalric orders, the Knights of the Round Table. Please accept our good wishes, and take if you will the prize from that dish, the great red apple on the top."

Engorged as he was, it would still have been the nadir of churlish manners for Sir Patrise to refuse an offer so courteously tendered, and so with a silent and deferential nod of his head, Sir Patrise took the apple. As the bowl continued to make its rounds, Sir Kay stood up once again at the foot of the table and raised his glass—a final toast to balance the one he had made to open the feast.

"And now," he droned, "I think I speak for every knight here present when I say that never, since the day I was made knight, have I been entertained by so magnificent a meal provided by so munificent a queen." Oh, Kay must be proud of that one, I mused. I tried to catch Guinevere's eye with a preemptive smirk but she was adamant in her avoidance of my look, gazing politely at Kay with the sincerely enthralled look on her face that I'd often seen her practicing in the mirror.

"Raise your glasses, gentlemen," Kay continued, "to the fairest . . ."

A sudden movement and a loud crash to his left stopped Kay in mid-sentence and he turned to look, then stared open-mouthed. Sir Palomides was standing and shouting excitedly. Sir Pinel sat thunderstruck and pale as a ghost. I looked in time to see Sir Patrise, his wine knocked over and spilt across the table, his chair fallen over backwards on the floor, and himself writhing on the floor in apparent distress, or perhaps agony. His hands were grasping at his throat and his face was turning purple. Was he choking? His cousin, Sir Mador, was attempting to hold him and find out what was wrong, but Sir Patrise was thrashing about so violently that no one could pin him down. Some of the knights stood aghast. Others raced to the side of Sir Patrise or shouted advice to Sir Mador. But by then Sir Patrise was clearly dead—poisoned at the queen's banquet.

That was what had brought us to this—the queen broken, her eyes pleading toward me, her terrified hands shielding her quivering lips.

The quiet in the great hall was deafening. Not a soul there had missed the insistence with which Guinevere had offered the apple to Sir Patrise. And no one was likely to forget it now.

Sir Mador stood slowly. Holding himself perfectly, almost exaggeratedly erect, he spoke in a quiet voice that grief and shock had muffled. "My Lady Queen Guinevere," he began with utmost formality. "I have here lost a knight of impeccable nobility and one of my own blood. This is a grievous wrong and a shame to my house, and this thing does not end here. I will have revenge for this vile act of treachery. I hereby accuse the queen of treason in this death, and I demand the utmost satisfaction for this deed!"

The queen was too weak to rise, and tears were forming in

her eyes, but through a great effort of self-control, she was able to will herself to answer in a composed voice. "You have spoken, Sir Mador. Is there no knight present willing to take up my defense against these charges?"

The twenty-two other knights present all became suddenly very interested in the floor of the room, or glanced furtively at each other before quickly averting their eyes. All had seen what the queen had done, and even Sir Gawain was not willing to stake his reputation in defense of the queen. In the end it was Gawain who said "My lady, the charges are severe that Sir Mador has brought against you. The only thing to do now is to take the matter before the king. I will go to him and request an audience. I suggest that some two or three of you carry Sir Patrise to a more seemly place of Sir Mador's choosing, and after preparation, he will lie in state in the chapel. The queen may stay here or retire to her chambers, whatever pleases her. The servants should put off cleaning this place until the queen retires. All others should void the great hall for the evening."

And immediately knights began to leave. They couldn't get out of that room fast enough, and there was little order or ceremony to their leaving, not one remembering to take his leave of the queen. Not that she would have noticed. She sat thunderstruck, staring blankly at nothing in the room. Sir Tristram, Sir Ywain, and Sir Lionel picked up the body of Sir Patrise and began making their way out of the hall, followed by Sir Mador, his head bowed and his tears flowing unabashedly. Sir Gawain had turned to leave, but then paused and turned back. "Wait. One more thing. Sir Gareth and Sir Gaheris, stand guard at the door here. Follow the queen when she leaves to go to her chamber and guard the door there."

He glanced toward Guinevere, whose face had clouded, and whispered to her, "For your protection, my lady. I have faith in your honor, but I fear for your safety." At that he turned on his heel and marched out of the room, followed by his two fair brothers, who stationed themselves outside on either side of the door.

When all others had left and the room was empty save for the queen and me alone, her poise finally gave way and she collapsed, sobbing onto the table. With a great inarticulate wail of pain she raised her streaming eyes to the sky and then, seeing me close by her chair, my own tears pouring from my eyes, she gripped the front of my tunic and, with pleading red eyes, asked me hoarsely, "My God, Gildas, my God, what is going to become of me now?"

CHAPTER TWO:
THE WEIGHT OF THE CROWN

The throne room was only about half as large as the great hall, but was far more impressive, intended as it was to inspire awe in visiting dignitaries who came to court the favor of the greatest monarch in Europe. The throne itself was placed on a dais on the north end of the hall, four feet above the floor from which all suppliants were forced to stare upwards at the stern visage of the lord of the realm. The throne was an elaborate seat of ornamented cherry wood. The armrests sported the carved, serpentine heads of dragons and the back, rising high above the crown itself when the king sat in his thickly cushioned seat, bore a deeply engraved facsimile of the three crowns that formed Arthur's coat of arms. Each crown was bedecked with inlaid gems, any one of which was worth the bride price of another Guinevere. The entire throne was gilded with gold leaf. One look at that throne, and you knew you were in the presence of real power. And that was before anyone even sat in it.

Behind the throne hung a large banner of woven scarlet thread, decorated with three rampant dragons in gold—the coat of arms of Arthur's father, Uther Pendragon, carried by Arthur's army before every battle to trumpet to the world the legitimacy of his claim to that golden throne. Everyone remembered how Merlin had spirited the child Arthur away to have him raised secretly under the fosterage of the good Sir Hector, Kay's father, only to produce the fifteen-year-old boy again upon the death of Uther in time to claim the throne.

The triumphs of Arthur in the twenty-five years of his reign were proclaimed in magnificent tapestries that lined the walls of the throne room, covering each of the three walls nearly to the floor. On the east wall was depicted Arthur's early triumph over King Lot of Orkney, Sir Gawain's father. In life-sized poses, it presented a bloody and battle-weary Lot kneeling and swearing allegiance to a young Arthur, who stood like a colossus and held high the sword Excalibur. On the south wall were two tapestries, one on each side of the large doors. The first showed the united armies of Arthur and King Lot charging up Mount Badon to defeat the invading Saxon army. Nine hundred of the enemy lay strewn about the slope of the mount, all laid low by Excalibur in a cavalry charge as Arthur carried high his shield on which was an image of the blessed Virgin. On the other side of the door King Arthur was shown leading his cavalry against the Irish, led by King Rience, who had thought to strip Arthur of his conquests. The tapestry depicted Arthur with his mouth opened, frozen in a silent war cry. In the background Merlin himself was portrayed, enchanting the great Irish ring of stones in order to carry them back to Logres, where they would be set on Salisbury plain to be renamed Stonehenge. On the west wall the tapestry told the story of Arthur's greatest victory, over the army of the Emperor Lucius. Here King Arthur and Sir Gawain could be seen, larger than life, doing battle in Gaul and laying low huge numbers of the Roman army, while the emperor was shown fleeing in terror. In the heavens were the likenesses of Belinus and of Constantine, Arthur's ancestors whose claim to the Roman throne legitimized his own.

Without doubt, the throne room was consciously designed to cow the haughtiest of visitors into awed submission. And I was far from the haughtiest.

I accompanied the queen only to give her an arm to lean on. She was so weak from stress and grief that she could scarcely stand. Her hair had fallen and had gone askew, but she took no heed of it. The roses had faded from her cheeks, and her face now looked ashen and sickly. What red there was surrounded her eyes in raw circles of care that weeping and rubbing had made. She had removed her gown since leaving the great hall and stood before Arthur in a simple linen shift, as if to show her repentance.

"He will be merciful," she whispered to me in a shaky voice, intended more for herself than for me. "He is a merciful king. He will pity my sorrow." It seemed an odd comment for a woman to make about her own husband. But maybe not so strange when that husband was her king. For a moment I wondered why Arthur had not been at the banquet himself. But then, when had he ever taken much note of those things that interested the queen?

She stood on wobbly legs, clutching my shoulder, and flanked by Sir Gareth and Sir Gaheris, standing rigid and stony faced on either side. Sir Gawain stood closest to the throne, with Sir Mador on his other side. Finally the king entered from behind the arras of dragons, and mounted the dais to the throne. He stood a moment and looked at us before he spoke.

"If I understand Sir Gawain correctly," King Arthur began in a calm, stately manner, "we have had a grievous incident in the great hall." He did not sit, but rather stood before the throne, so that he towered over us more than ever. He wore royal blue robes of state, with an ermine collar and cuffs. His hose were a similar blue color, and his silver-brocaded tunic was an imperial purple. For this solemn occasion, he had elected to wear his crown—heavy silver encrusted with rubies and a huge star sapphire centered over his brow. His gray eyes looked weary, and the crows' feet at their edges tokened a man much older than his forty years—as did the gray in his trim black beard and the temples of his shoulder-length hair. But when Sir Mador answered, the eyes flashed at his boldness.

"Call it by its true name, Sire. It is outrageous murder. My cousin, Sir Patrise, is dead, and he is dead at the queen's urging. Every knight at the banquet heard her entreat Sir Patrise to eat the fruit, and as soon as he had taken a bite of that cursed apple he fell dead. It was the queen's table, it was the queen's fruit, and it was at the queen's insistence that my kinsman ate the apple. And he died from the queen's own poison." Sir Mador was a young knight, and he was unable to keep his tears from flowing as he made his accusations. The brown curls on his head shook with emotion, and his lip quivered beneath his long brown mustache as he continued. "I formally accuse the queen of treason in the shameful death of my kinsman, and I demand satisfaction."

Sir Gawain glanced back at Guinevere and responded to Sir Mador's charges. "There is no doubt some justice in Sir Mador's accusation. It is certainly true that every knight at the table heard the queen's command to Sir Patrise to eat the poisoned apple."

At this Guinevere moaned audibly and hung on to my arm with both hands so that I thought she might swoon on the spot. But she took a deep breath and held on.

"But I can't see why my lady the queen would harbor any ill will toward Sir Patrise," Gawain continued. "There must be some other explanation for this terrible crime. Queen Guinevere could have no reason to want the Irishman dead."

"No ill will? It is well known that the queen resents my countrymen because of the war King Rience wrought upon her father in the old days. She has never forgiven us for that!" Sir Mador responded, and continued with a mounting fury in his voice. "She must stand trial to answer for her treachery. My cousin's blood cries out to me for justice, and I will have it, or let it be known there is no justice in Arthur's kingdom."

The king spoke, as always, in measured tones, but there was no mistaking his meaning. "Threats have no place in our throne room, nor are we moved by them, except to the extent that we will brook no further such comments, no matter who makes them. Being wronged does not annul the obligations of courtesy."

His eyes seemed to pierce Sir Mador to the core, and the knight calmed himself, though not willingly. But the king's eyes softened again as he looked toward Guinevere and continued: "There will be justice in the kingdom of Logres as long as I am king. Nor is any person, regardless of rank, immune from our laws. Those laws make treasonous murder a capital offense. Nothing we can do can prevent the queen's forfeiting her life, if . . . I say *if*"—his eyes flared as he rounded again on Sir Mador—"she is proven guilty of these charges."

Now the queen, strong as she was, began to sob and dropped to her knees on the floor. She was beside herself, and there seemed to be nothing I could do to console her or to make her speak coherently. She only muttered continually "I did not know . . . I could not know . . ." And to her I whispered meaningless consolations. "Your name will be cleared; you will be safe," as, meanwhile, I only half heard the rest of the conversation.

"My lord," Sir Gawain was saying, "in these kinds of matters, trial by ordeal or trial by combat is the usual option."

At the first option Arthur winced. I knew that he could not abide the idea of Guinevere walking over hot coals, or being forced to hold in her hands an iron bar directly out of the fire. The thought of her fair flesh being burned and marred, the thought of her agonized screams, was more than he could bear. At least that's what I thought I saw in the wince. I know that the thought was too much for me to bear. Besides, I had never seen a trial by ordeal in which the accused was proven innocent. The idea that God would prevent any harm being done to the guiltless did not seem to me a sound legal position. The innocent suffered every day and God did not prevent it. Wasn't Sir Patrise himself innocent, and had God prevented his death?

"It must be combat," Arthur finally said. "But it is an unusual case. What is the law concerning trial by combat when the accused is a woman?"

"My lord, there are precedents for such a situation," Gawain replied thoughtfully, his face betraying his tacit understanding of where the king was trying to go with this. "There are two possibilities in such a case. In the first, the woman is allowed to do battle herself. She is fitted with armor and a sword as best suits her, and the knight with whom she battles is placed waist-deep in a hole in the ground, and must fight her that way. The other possibility is that the lady find a champion who will do battle in her place. If her champion wins the battle, then the lady is proclaimed innocent. However"—and at this Sir Gawain's ruddy face grew redder yet and his voice grew more strained—"if the lady's champion is defeated, then she is pronounced guilty and must be burned at the stake for her treachery. So says the law."

"I am ready to fight any champion the queen may send to the lists!" Sir Mador exclaimed, his jaw jutting forward defiantly. "My cause is just, and God will uphold the right!"

For myself, I was relieved. Just as I was skeptical concerning trial by ordeal, my experience with trial by combat was that God invariably favored the side with the better champion, so that innocence depended mainly on muscle and skill of arms. Now if only Lancelot were not away from court, the queen stood a good chance of being acquitted of all charges.

Arthur's head hung low as he thought deep before replying. "My lady, and my lords," he began slowly. "This is a difficult situation, particularly for me. As husband of the accused, I am honor bound to defend her innocence, and take upon me the role of her champion. That is what any other man would do."

At this the queen lifted her head and, through her tears, I saw her eyes brighten faintly. Sir Mador blanched. Evidently he had never considered the possibility of doing battle with his own sovereign lord, and the idea shook him to the core. But his discomfort was short-lived.

"However, as king, I cannot do as other men do." Guinevere's head fell forward again, and the color returned to Mador's face. "My duty compels me to act as true and fair judge in this case. None other can do it. I would dare stake my life that my wife is innocent of the crime you accuse her of. For that reason I am certain that one of my knights will take up her cause and agree to defend her in the lists. It would put my whole court to shame if one knight will not step forward to defend the honor of his queen. Now therefore, Sir Mador, name your day of battle. But let it be no sooner than a fortnight hence, so that the queen is able to find a suitable champion to represent her in the trial."

A fortnight. The king was clearly considering all the angles. In two weeks' time, there was every chance that Lancelot will have returned to Camelot. If not, we might have time to prove by some other means that the queen was not guilty of this murder.

"My gracious lord," Sir Mador replied cautiously, averting his eyes from the king's. "I beg you not to be angry. But the fact is all of the best knights in your kingdom were present at the queen's table tonight, and all of them witnessed what I did. I would swear that not one of the twenty-two knights who sat at that dinner with me would stake his reputation and honor on the queen's innocence. They all saw what I saw. The apple was poisoned. She made Sir Patrise eat it."

The king raised questioning eyes to Sir Gawain, who blushed again and muttered, "What he says is true, Sire. None of those knights is likely to volunteer." And that included, by implication, Sir Gawain himself.

Gareth and Gaheris looked first at each other, then looked to the king and shook their heads. The queen let out an audible sob and clung to my arms with a death grip.

"My lord," the queen pleaded, rolling her eyes between Gawain, Mador, and Arthur, "I intended no evil by this feast. It was only to celebrate, to recognize the greatest of our knights. I swear to God Almighty that I never meant for anything like this to happen. That I'm innocent of Sir Patrise's blood."

"Of that we'll have proof. My lord the king," Mador continued, straightening up into a formal pose again. "I demand my day of justice to take place according to your word, two weeks from today."

"Very well. On Wednesday two weeks hence, see that you are well horsed and armed and ready for combat, in the morning just after prime, in the lists outside of Camelot. If a knight appears that day to champion the queen by challenging you, then you are to do your best to defeat him and defend your charges. The queen will be there as well, ready to face her judgment depending on the outcome of the combat. May God speed the right."

"I am answered," Sir Mador responded, and with a bow to the king, he turned on his heel and strode purposefully out the door opposite the throne.

After a moment of silence, Arthur nodded to Gareth and Gaheris, and told them to wait outside the door to escort the queen to her chambers. Obviously she was to be under what amounted to house arrest as long as she stood accused of this high crime. The two brothers stepped out, and then the king came down from the dais and approached the queen. His face was haggard and gray, and he had abandoned the imperial air he had put on for the formal hearing.

"Guinevere, my lady," he said in what was almost a whisper.

"How in God's name did you get mixed up in this?"

"So help me, I haven't got a clue. It was just . . . just a party. I can't imagine how the apple was poisoned."

"Well we've got to find you a champion. Where on earth is Lancelot when we need him?"

"I don't know, I don't know . . ." the queen moaned, and her tears overcame her again. She tried to say through her sobs, "Bors and Ector and his other kinsmen don't know where he is. They think he's left the country."

"No! Why now? If we could get word to him . . . but we can't count on that. Listen: what about Sir Bors?"

"My lord, Sir Bors was one of the knights present at the dinner," Gawain reminded him. We had almost forgotten he was there.

"Doesn't matter, doesn't matter." The king shut his eyes and shook his head. "He'll do it. He'll do it if Guinevere begs him to do it for the sake of Sir Lancelot. We all know that Lancelot would do this battle for the queen if he were here, and Bors knows it too."

I looked at the queen. Guinevere had her secrets, and I knew what I knew, and by the look on Sir Gawain's face, he knew something or other as well concerning Lancelot and his sovereign lady. And right now we were all wondering what it was the king knew. But he continued, "Bors loves Lancelot like his own life, and is as loyal to him as any vassal ever was to his liege lord. If we make Sir Bors understand that Lancelot would be devastated if he returned from his adventures to find that the queen had been burnt for lack of a knight to defend her, he *will* take up the challenge."

The wisdom of that was undeniable, and the queen concurred. "I shall go to Sir Bors tomorrow," she said. "And now, my lord, it has been a very difficult evening for me, and I feel I need to sleep. If you will excuse me." She was incredibly composed. Perhaps the king's sensible plan to save her from the stake had calmed her, or perhaps she was now so exhausted that she was beyond further weeping, but I followed her closely as she began to make her way slowly to the doors—close enough to hear her mutter under her breath, "And yet, he would not champion me himself . . ."

"Gildas!" I turned to see the king himself calling and beckoning me back. The back of my neck exploded in a thousand pinpricks and I felt a sudden throbbing ring in my ears as I turned back to approach him. He had never really spoken to me before, and I had not realized that he even knew my name. But in case you have never had the experience yourself, let me tell you: when your sovereign beckons, you damned well better go to him.

As I stood face to face with the king, I could see over his shoulder the image of the young Arthur, standing victorious on the field of battle while King Lot and other combatants knelt in homage before him. His young face shone with promise, vigor, and authority, and his gray eyes sparkled.

Before me, in the flesh, stood a pale imitation of the tapestry's figure. His shoulders sagged with the burden of responsibility, as if the crown had never weighed so heavily upon him. Here was a situation where the responsibilities of the king as Law must override those of the king as Man, and the resultant inner turmoil showed in a face twisted by anguish. The king seemed a broken man. He clutched Sir Gawain's arm and looked into his face with pleading eyes.

"Find Lancelot," was all he said.

Sir Gawain's eyes widened. Without a word he turned and marched out the door. Then the king's weary gaze fell on me.

"Merlin," was his only word. I understood, and followed Gawain out the door.

CHAPTER THREE:
THE CAVE OF MERLIN

Merlin was besotted. At least that's what people said. Personally, I preferred to think of him as just plain nuts.

Years ago he had completely lost his head over a "Damsel of the Lake," one of the retinue of the Lady of the Lake. They were nymphs or virgins or I don't know what, but they lived in their own community in the woods outside Camelot, and rumors said they had magical powers, or worked witchcraft at least. But Merlin didn't care; he just had to have this Nimue, and there he was, a foolish old man following this young nymph wherever she went and basically making a big nuisance of himself. So she locked him in a cave.

I don't mean to say that she had rolled a large boulder before the cave's entrance. What she did was cast a spell on him to keep him in the cave forever. So the rumors said. At least it kept him from harassing her constantly. It couldn't have been much of a life for him, though.

When Arthur spoke that one word, "Merlin," I knew right away what he wanted. Merlin was the wisest man Arthur had ever known. He was probably the wisest man who had ever set foot in the kingdom of Logres. He was said to have great powers, but I think mainly he was just able to figure things out better and faster than anybody else, and when he did, what he had come up with seemed miraculous—as, for instance, had the transportation of those stones from Ireland portrayed on the king's tapestry. His wisdom had shown him the way to keep Arthur safe during his childhood, and that made him Arthur's most valuable counselor in his early years as king. That was what Arthur missed now. Merlin would know what to do. Merlin would see a way out of this disaster for Arthur and the queen.

So it was Merlin I needed to find, and tonight.

I had a pretty good idea where to find his cave, in the wild woods a mile or so north of the castle. But finding it in the dark would be tricky, and it was dark by the time I crossed the main courtyard, the lower bailey, toward the barbican and gatehouse. I was surprised to find the great wooden doors open and the iron portcullis raised.

"Gildas! About the last person I'd expect to see out and about so late."

I recognized the voice, coming through one of the many arrow slits in the gatehouse walls as I neared the great doors. Young Robin Kempe was one of the king's valued foot soldiers and commanded the garrison that manned the barbican. I knew him well enough to exchange a few rough words with him in jest from time to time.

"Just checking up to see whether you're doing your job, Master Kempe. I'll tell the king he can rest easy tonight, seeing that you've left the main gate to the castle wide open. Planning to invite a few Saxons in to tour the place, are you?"

"Mind your tongue or I'll put an arrow through your eye." I heard him twang his bowstring to punctuate his threat. "You're hot on the heels of my Lord Gawain. He just rode through here at a pretty brisk pace, like he had somewhere important to go. Wouldn't tell me anything but 'king's business,' and I could tell by his tone he was in a hurry. Haven't even had time to lower the portcullis since he left."

"Well, he *was* on important business for the king," I confirmed—as if Robin needed my confirmation. But I was quite surprised that Gawain had moved so quickly. He must have had

32

a horse saddled already to have left so fast. All I had stopped to do myself was grab a woolen cloak and hood to keep off the October chill in the night air. But the knight had ridden off before me.

"And I'm on important business for the king myself," I added, trying not to sound pompous but failing miserably.

"Right, and I'm the Emperor Lucius of godawful Gaul. I see the king's fitted you out with one of his finest corsairs for your urgent business?"

Realizing how foolish I sounded, I continued, "Nevertheless, I really am sent by the king—to try to fetch the enchanter Merlin from his cave. My Lord Arthur has need of him, and so does the queen. Since his cave lies only a short way off, I'm in need of no horse, and besides"—I lowered my voice to a confidential tone—"the king is in too agitated a state to worry about trivial matters like a horse. Let me through the gate. I should be returning before long. See to it you've got the gate closed by then, or I'll report your incompetence to Sir Kay."

"And I'll report to the queen that you're prowling the countryside at night rather than attending her as you ought!"

The mention of Guinevere sobered me again, and I proceeded through the gate and across the drawbridge without more words. The bells of the Convent of Saint Mary Magdalene to the southeast were chiming compline as I reached the path on the other side of the moat. Southwest of the castle lay the city of Caerleon, a thriving town of a thousand inhabitants who depended for their livelihood on the castle and the king's business. I turned the other way and hiked along the path that led northward from the castle through the plowed fields of the king's estate. Harvest had finished a few weeks ago, so there was little left standing in the fields.

After some six or seven furlongs the path plunged into the wood. It was too dark to see the bright colors of the leaves, and

a cold breeze made the branches shudder as I passed beneath them. The signs presaged a dip below freezing tonight. A furlong deep into the forest the path ran into a shallow brook. I turned right—upstream—and began to walk more cautiously along the brook's edge. Not that there was any danger. The water was only about a foot deep and the stream perhaps ten feet across. But the grassy slope that led up from the creek was wet and slippery, and I didn't feel like falling into the cold water on such a brisk night.

I followed the bend of the stream for some five hundred paces, the swoosh of running water and an occasional cricket my only companions, until I had almost reached the wide, cool source of the brook, Lady Lake—so named not in honor of the Blessed Virgin, though many in the area liked to think so, but rather for the mysterious Lady of the Lake, whose secretive sorority lay somewhere on the far shore.

Here on this shore, the lake splashed against a tall rock wall of dolomite and limestone into which, over the long years, the waters of the brook and underground streams had eaten a honeycomb of caves. Which of these caves housed the old enchanter?

I stood on the lakeshore and looked up at the rocky shoreline to my right and my left. Should I go to each hole in the rocks I could find and peer in, looking for the magician's hoary head to stand out in the dark? I was about to give up all pretense that I actually knew what I was doing and to begin shouting Merlin's name all up and down the shoreline when I noticed it.

I smelled it first: unmistakably the smoke of a wood fire that had been lit, surely for warmth, on this chilly night. It was coming from my left, and as I strained my eyes in the shadows I could see a thin line of white smoke rising on the other side of the brook and down the shoreline a good hundred paces. Grimacing, I removed my shoes and waded through the water,

taking quick steps that kept my feet in the cold stream for as brief a time as possible, and punctuating every step with a different epithet: "Ah! Ow! No! Damn! Cold! Mother! Of! God!"

My feet were stinging when I reached the other side and re-shod myself. I figured that if I had had any notions of coming upon Merlin quietly, they were pretty much defunct. I ran over to where I saw the smoke coming up through what seemed solid rock, and looked into the first opening I saw that faced the lakeshore. A red light glowed from within.

I don't know what I expected. I knew Merlin by reputation only, since he had been trapped in Nimue's cave well before I arrived at Camelot two years past. Maybe I thought I'd see an old fellow with a pointed wizard's hat and black robes decorated with signs of the planets and the zodiac. Maybe I thought that, since his father was reputed to be an incubus, Merlin would take after him and possess fiery, demon eyes and horns on his head, and carry a great staff that symbolized his allegiance to the black arts and was an instrument of great power.

What I saw was a man with gray-white hair and beard, neither of which had been trimmed or combed in recent memory. His head was uncovered, and his robes were brown, worsted, and threadbare. He did not look terribly old. That is, he appeared to be vigorous, but sat in a small wooden chair in a posture of apathy and dejection. The only really remarkable thing about him, as far as I could see by the red firelight, was the length of his eyebrows. They were the same color as his mustache and rivaled that formidable bush in length and wildness. Then I noticed that those brows were aimed in my direction, and saw beneath them flashing eyes, glowing red with the fire.

"Get out," came a voice rusty with long disuse.

I thought at first I had startled him, and that if I only explained myself, he would be more accommodating.

"I . . . I'm Gildas of Cornwall, page in the household of her

35

majesty Queen Guinevere. King Arthur has sent me to you. He needs your assistance in a matter of the most extreme urgency. Will you speak with me?"

The shadow of the body lit flickeringly by the fire's light still sat motionless, and the black eyes beneath those ponderous brows still stared blankly out at me, or at least toward me. I waited for my words to have some effect. Ten seconds. Twenty seconds. Thirty. "Will you help?" I finally added.

"Go."

I took this lethargy, this dark motionless stupor, to be an aspect of the enchantment that the damsel of the lake had wrought upon him. I didn't know whether the spell could be broken, whether I could in any way rouse him, but I did know that without his help, the queen might be as good as burnt. Therefore, I needed to do what I could in spite of my less-than-courteous welcome.

"Your king needs you. Would you deny Arthur, after all he has been to you?"

At that I saw the smallest twitch of an eye. Something had struck him, if only slightly, and I followed up with more, talking so quickly I hardly had time to think. "The king you put on the throne, the king you helped to defeat the Saxons, and the Irish, and the Romans. He mourns your long absence and now needs your counsel in the direst of circumstances . . ."

"And so he sends a page to me, on foot, in the dark of night."

All right, it wasn't exactly the most encouraging reply, but it was a reply. I was getting to him; somehow I had broken through the gloomy curtain that had seemed to separate him from the world.

"I was all he had with him at the time, and I was one person he knew he could trust with any task that concerned the queen. And the task was too urgent to wait. I came immediately and didn't think to take the time to saddle a horse from the stables and . . . listen, don't you want to hear what the king needs from you?" The old enchanter was beginning to irritate me. Spell or no spell, my lady the queen needed him, and by God, I was going to get him to listen to me.

"I'm coming in there," I said, stooping down to enter the cave.

"Beware!" the stern look under those stormy brows stopped me in my tracks. "The spell that Nimue has put on this cave seals me forever inside. I have no doubt that it will incinerate anyone trying to enter without her leave."

Skeptical as I was about things supernatural, the possibility of instant annihilation, no matter how remote, was enough to make me reconsider my priorities. But I was on the king's own mission. And without my help the queen Guinevere, my sovereign lady, was very likely going to be incinerated herself, not by supernatural means but by very real, man-made and tormenting flames. I took a deep breath, crossed myself, and plunged through the opening.

"Damn," Merlin said as I stood directly before his chair. "That one usually works."

"No more tricks, old man. Listen to me now. The queen is in grave danger. She is to be brought to trial for treason and is likely to be burned at the stake. The king has asked for your help to save her."

"King Arthur no longer has need of me," Merlin answered, finally warming slightly to the conversation, though still talking in a slow, half-audible way, as if it burdened him to speak. "He will find his own way out of this dilemma. He is a grown man. He outgrew the need for my counsel years ago."

"Not for this. This is nothing that he can control. The queen has killed a knight with a poisoned apple at a banquet she was hosting. Sir Mador de la Porte, the knight's cousin, has demanded justice. The queen must find a champion to defend her in the lists, or face burning."

"She will have Lancelot."

"Lancelot is gone—out of the country. Even Sir Bors doesn't know where he is. He'll never get back in time, and none of the other knights will defend her because they were all at the feast and saw what she did. The king is beside himself with grief and worry. You're the only one he can turn to." I had said it to flatter the old enchanter, but after it came out of my mouth I realized how very true the statement was. Arthur's closest counselors—the queen, Sir Gawain, Sir Lancelot—were all for one reason or another unable to help with this situation, and I knew it was true: Merlin was indeed the only one the king could ask for help. But could the spell of Nimue be broken?

Merlin now closed his eyes and sighed deeply. "When the weight of the black cloud comes upon me like this, I am only good for hiding away in dark places. It has been upon me like a lead weight on my heart more and more often these five years past. I cannot move to help the king."

"Is that the spell of Nimue, this black cloud you speak of?"

Merlin actually permitted himself a grim half-smile. "The black cloud is the creature of my own mind. It cripples me more than any nymph's spell. But Nimue is the most immediate cause. That much is true."

"How do you mean? Then you are not trapped here by enchantment?"

"Only in a sense," the old man replied. "I was enchanted by the beauty, grace, and quick mind of that most gentle of damsels, my Lady Nimue. I had never been enchanted in that way before. For surely you know, I had never married, never had children of my own. It may be because I feared what my progeny would be. My mother always said I was fathered by an incubus, a devil of the air. Of course, I knew how likely that was. No doubt I was a bastard and she could not, or would not, name the father. Still, what if the story were true? What kind of children might I engender? Would they inherit demonic powers from their grandfather's stock? Besides, I had Arthur, who was more than a son to me. But he has outgrown the need of me—or had until now."

"And Nimue?" I wanted to get him back on track. It seemed his mind was wandering, and I still hadn't got him to agree to help the queen.

"My desire for her was mere dotage," Merlin declared. Whether he believed it or not I couldn't tell by his voice. "I was thirty years her senior. When she finally told me in no uncertain terms that she could never love me and that I was merely a foolish old man, I realized everyone else saw things just as she did—that I was the only one who had been blind to my own idiocy. The shame was enough to bring on the black cloud again."

"You mean to say," I said, the light finally dawning, "that there is no spell, as has always been rumored? That Nimue is not holding you? That you are here of your own accord?"

"Hiding away from the world. Crippled . . . held prisoner by the binding spell of my own depression."

"Then you're saying you could walk out of this cave right now?"

The old man shuddered visibly and shrank back into the chair, even lifting his legs into his body in a fetal position. He turned away from me saying "No. I could not."

Exasperated, I took a moment to try to collect my thoughts and to look around the cave, now that my eyes had adjusted to the dim light put off by the fire. I could see that the old enchanter was not living in some dark dungeon-like hole in the ground. For one thing, there was the fire itself. I realized that it was not filling the cave with smoke. Looking closer I saw that it was contained in a stone structure like a fireplace, and that a hole through the roof of the cave was drawing the smoke up and out of the room. It was a fairly comfortable room some twenty feet square, with a dry stone ceiling perhaps ten feet high. Glancing around, I saw also that the bare rock was almost nowhere directly exposed, and that the cave walls were actually lined by woven tapestries, of the same quality as those in the king's throne room. Possibly they were made by the same hands, but these, as best I could tell in the gloom, all depicted supernatural kinds of scenes—dragon slayings, fairy mistresses, and on one the image of the elusive Holy Grail. Beside the wooden chair on which the old enchanter sat was a small table, where, perhaps, he took his meals when he remembered to have them. There was a smaller table a short way across the room and another chair. On that table was a chess set, with the pieces set up as if ready to play. Back against the far wall was a straw mattress and a headboard holding some fifteen or twenty ancient books—thick volumes containing, no doubt, all the secrets of Merlin's necromancy.

"If you've got to escape from the world," I ventured, "there are certainly much worse places. What is the chess set for? You play against yourself, or maybe some visiting incubus?"

"Do you play?" Merlin asked, with the first real interest I had heard in his voice. But the interest faded quickly as I shook my head. His bushy brows glowered and the old man murmured, "I don't think I want to talk to you anymore. Go away."

"No, wait, maybe you could teach me?" I was grasping at anything, trying to prevent him from shutting down completely again. "I'll bet you're a great player, a great strategist. You could probably teach me well. When was the last time you played?"

Now the old enchanter looked almost pleasant as he remembered. "It's been perhaps a month. Oh yes, I do have visitors. Or rather, a visitor. Nimue comes to see me every month or so. She brings me food to stockpile, and will always take the time to play a game of chess with me." He took on a confidential tone. "She's really not much of a chess player, so once in a while I have to let her win just to make sure she'll keep playing with me. But I enjoy the distraction. She is really a wonderfully kind maiden, is Nimue. Not very yielding, but always kind. Listen, I have no idea why I am telling you so much. If you are in fact from the king, then I know you are to be trusted. If you are close to the queen, then I know you can keep secrets well. And aside from all of that, I have spoken to no one other than the Damsel of the Lake for five years, except to shoo away some unwanted visitors. So unburdening myself to you is something of a relief, even if you are nothing but a child, and a foolish Cornish one at that."

I bristled, but realized that Merlin was having a little joke with me, and that I knew was a real breakthrough, a minor miracle.

"We need to talk about the queen," I began, softly but resolutely.

"Ah, yes," the old man agreed. "The lesson will have to wait for another day. But as for the queen, what can I do? I am no champion to defend the queen's honor in the lists. And from what you've told me, her role in the knight's death is unmistakable. Arthur was grasping at straws when he sent you to me. I have nothing to offer. Perhaps after all it is better if you return to the castle and leave me to my shadows. I can wait in silence until Nimue visits again."

Searching for something to break his lethargy, it came into my head that the chess set was my way in. "Merlin," I asked coyly, "what is it about playing chess that amuses you, even now in your doldrums?"

"The contest, of course. The strategy involved. The challenge to work out a puzzle that the opponent has created for me. It's the one thing that frees my mind from the numbing shackles of darkness. My mind works the problem and forgets the slough it wallows in. The—"

"What the king asks of you is the same!" I pounced. "A puzzle has been laid for you: the queen did not commit this murder. Somehow she was compromised because it occurred at her banquet. Someone else was responsible for it. But it's someone who assumes that no one, not even the great Merlin, can work out the truth of his crime. He thinks to escape detection and so checkmate your inquiries. But he cannot be allowed to do it. What do you say? Will you take up this challenge for the king?"

The old man cast a wary but appreciative eye on me. "You have the makings of an excellent chess player," he said.

He rose from the chair, showing more interest and energy than I would have thought him capable of. He began to pace back and forth, moving from me toward the fire and back again in quick, jerky motions. "Tell me the details!" he barked, head down and hands behind his back. "Don't leave anything out, no matter how trivial it seems."

"Well," I said, taking his place in the vacated chair and trying to reconstruct the events in my mind. "It was the dessert course. A bowl of fruit—apples and pears, basically. The knights had all finished three courses and none of them had much room for the fruit."

"The knights! Start there. Who were they?"

"Well, there were twenty-four of them. Sir Patrise, of course, who was killed. Sir Mador, his cousin. Sir Kay, of course. Uh . . . Sir Gawain and his brothers, who sat to the right of the queen. Sir Bors and Lancelot's other kinsmen. The Moorish knights, Sir Palomides and Sir Safer. There was Sir Tristram and Sir Ywain. Sir Ironside—"

"The Red Knight of the Red Lands?" Merlin's head popped up.

"Yes. Why?"

"Nothing. Go on, go on," he waved his hand at me and continued pacing.

"Let me see . . . Sir Pinel, Sir Galihud, Sir Galihodin, Sir Breanor—"

"La Cote Male Taile?" Merlin's head popped up again.

"Yes! Yes! Uh . . . that was all. There were squires and servants around the room . . ."

"I'll want their names as well. For now, though, go on. The fruit came to the table?"

"And the queen passed it to her right, to Sir Gawain. He declined it, and sent it to the other side of the queen, to Sir Bors. Some of the knights took pears, but not all."

"Who ate the pears?"

"Why, that's hard to remember. Uh . . . let's see . . . I believe Sir Bleoberis had one, and Sir Ironside, oh, Sir Palomides . . ."

"None of them took an apple?"

"No. The apple on top of the bowl was tempting, but so huge that nobody had the appetite for it."

"Perhaps."

"But when it reached Sir Patrise, the queen made a special request that he eat it. She complimented him and welcomed him here from Ireland, and made as if to say that the beautiful red apple was meant just for him."

"So he took it and bit into it? And then fell over?"

"I'm not sure how much he had eaten before he began to react," I said honestly. "All eyes had turned to Sir Kay, who had begun a toast thanking the queen for the meal. Sir Patrise knocked over his wine in the middle of Kay's toast and then fell. We thought he was choking, or that he had the falling sickness, but soon he was dead, and the apple at his side half-eaten."

"So you deduced he was killed by the apple. Was there anything else he had eaten that might have caused this? Was anyone else taken ill?"

"All of the knights were eating heartily. I'm pretty certain that, except for the apple, others would have eaten the same things he did. But whether anyone else felt ill, I can't say. We dispersed almost immediately. My Lord Gawain took charge of the situation. He had everyone exit the hall, had Sir Patrise taken to the chapel to lie in state awaiting the funeral, and had Gareth and Gaheris bring the queen to the king's throne room."

"Then the servants left as well following the incident?"

"Everyone left at the same time."

"No one has been back to clean the room?"

"My understanding was that it would wait until morning, after more pressing matters had been dealt with, and that all were to stay out of the hall until it had been cleaned."

"God's toenails!" he said. He stopped his pacing, and looked at me with some excitement. Then, with a shout of, "Come on!" he grabbed me by the shoulder and began pulling me after him, out the cave's door.

"What?" I managed to gasp as he pulled me along.

"We've got to get a look at that apple!"

CHAPTER FOUR:
IT WAS HERE A MINUTE AGO

It took a lot less time to get back to the castle than it had taken me to find Merlin's cave to begin with. Still, I thought it must be approaching midnight as we tramped back through the fields toward the gate. There was enough of a moon out to allow us to see the road and where we were going, but it was difficult to make out much other than shadows in the distance. I was glad we didn't have far to go, since traveling at night could be dangerous, even in Logres—but this close to the castle we should have been safe.

Of course, Sir Patrise had been murdered tonight, *inside* the castle itself. Perhaps there was no real safety anywhere.

A rather sleepy voice called to us as we approached the moat.

"In the name of King Arthur, who goes there?"

"Robin, you great ox-brain, can't you see it's just me again?"

"It's the middle of the night. What kind of ruffian would be gallivanting about like this in the dark? I don't think I can open the gate to the likes of you. I was warned just a few hours ago by a personage of very high nobility that I had better have the gate closed before he returned from his vital mission for the king. I'm just doing as I'm told, mind."

Merlin stood behind me, almost as if he wanted my protection against other human contact. His hood was pulled far up over his head so that even if it were not the middle of the night, his face would have been invisible in shadows. "What kind of imbecile does Arthur have in charge of his barbican these days?"

he muttered.

"Oh, it's all right. Our Robin just likes to have his jest." And I could see that the drawbridge was already lowering, and the portcullis was being taken up. But suddenly I heard Robin's voice call out with sincere concern.

"Hold on, Gildas. You're not alone! Who is that tall figure with you?"

"Why, it's Merlin. I told you I was on the king's business to fetch Merlin to the castle."

"What, is the old necromancer there with you?" Robin let out a soft whistle of astonishment. "You mean you really were out on the king's business? I thought you were off to meet some loose wench in the woods, and were having me on about the Merlin thing."

The night hid my blush. Robin often chided me about wenches and that sort of thing. But in spite of his jibes, that was not my way. The queen, you see, would not approve. And I was devoted to her. As my sovereign lady, I mean.

"No, of course it's Merlin, as you see," I called up to him as we walked noisily across the drawbridge and into the castle gate. "Now see that you treat me with more respect in the future, my good man!" I snapped my fingers at him as we passed through the great doors.

But as we hurried away, I heard him call after me, "Oh, I regard you with the utmost respect, young Gildas. The other day the queen told me that you weren't fit to eat with pigs. I told her you were so!"

Merlin's hood moved side to side as we made our way across the lower bailey toward the doors into the great hall, and I knew by that motion that he was shaking his head. "Interesting friends you have, Gildas of Cornwall, page to the queen." He had a disapproving tone, but I thought I heard a small snicker as he said it.

The great hall was pitch-dark when we entered. No candles had been left burning when the servants exited the room. Next to me, the voice of Merlin chanted, *"Fiat Lux!"* and suddenly I saw fire appear in the old enchanter's hand. It lit up the room enough for him to find a candelabrum on the table, and he lit the candles with the fire he held.

At my astonished expression, Merlin let out a short laugh. "It's not magic, you know. It's just a bit of sulfur and some other ingredients I carry with me." Seeing my disappointment, he added, "Thought I was giving you proof of that incubus story, didn't you?"

"No . . . uh . . . aw, you're joking." The old man was actually rather pleasant when he wasn't suicidal. But I guessed it was the challenge of the hunt that was raising his spirits—the quest for the solution to the puzzle of who killed Sir Patrise. Assuming always that it wasn't the queen.

Merlin held the candelabrum close to the table and looked over the dishes that still lay around the table. "Now at which place was Sir Patrise sitting? You do remember?"

"Of course," I answered. I had memorized the whole seating arrangement before the catastrophe. We were standing at the foot of the table near the spot where Sir Kay had been seated. I pointed to our left side and counted three spaces down. "There," I said. "The third seat on that side of the table was Sir Patrise's."

Merlin brought the light around to that area and began to look closely. "Yes, here, as you said, the wineglass has been knocked over, and wine has been spilt across the table. And the chair is lying here on its back, though farther down the table. Obviously in his death throes Sir Patrise keeled over backwards in his chair, but rolled or writhed out of it as his seizure continued. He must have kicked the chair, or one of the other knights moved it as they gathered around him."

Merlin knelt down next to the chair and began looking closely at the floor. He swept the light back and forth, and began crawling around on his knees, making a loud "tsking" noise with his tongue as he did. He continued this for several minutes until I finally asked him what he was doing.

"It's gone," was all he said.

"What?"

"The apple. Gone. You said that he had dropped it on the floor when he fell?"

"Yes. Everyone saw it. It was next to his right hand, with a couple of large bites taken out of it. So it would have been right"—I pointed to an empty spot on the floor, and said with a subdued voice—"there. It must have been kicked as well, like the chair."

"Not by Sir Patrise, certainly, if it was next to his hand, and if you saw it after he was dead."

I tried to remember exactly. It was indeed after Patrise had been pronounced dead that everyone started to shout about the apple. "That's right, of course," I said. "Unless maybe somebody kicked it when they were lifting Sir Patrise's body to take to the chapel."

Merlin shook his head. "Do you remember seeing the apple there after the body was carried out?"

I couldn't be sure. But Merlin, giving one more sweep with the light across the floor, seemed uninterested in my opinion. "I don't think it matters. Because I am sure the apple is no longer here. We can come back to look in the morning light, but I'll wager my head we'll find nothing. Someone came back into this room after the banquet and picked it up."

"But who? Why?"

"Don't be a dunce of a Cornishman. The murderer, of course. Or an accomplice. Whoever poisoned the apple didn't want us to learn how."

"Well, then, the queen could not have done it, since she was in custody from the time she left the hall. She certainly could not have come back here to pick up the apple."

"Unless, of course, *she* had an accomplice."

"Oh," I muttered, deflated.

"Well then," Merlin continued, as if, having established one point, he was ready to move on to what naturally followed upon it. "I assume the fruit bowl is still somewhere nearby on the table." He began slowly to sweep his candelabrum across the tabletop, moving left from Sir Patrise's place at the table.

"The bowl? Why do you want to find the bowl?"

"Gildas of Cornwall." Merlin straightened up and glared at me. At least I felt the glare. The light was too dim to see anything but the reflected candle flame in his eyes. "You have *got* to start asking more sensible questions than this. When Arthur was your age, he was already King of Logres. How do you think he was able to do that?"

"Well," I replied, stung a bit by the rebuke, mild as it was. "He was King Uther's only son, and he had *you* to help him with that sword-in-the-stone enchantment."

"Wha . . . I . . . that . . ." the old man sputtered with no small degree of exasperation. "He might never have become king, and certainly not at fifteen, nor would he have stayed on the throne, if he hadn't thought to ask the important questions, like how do you rule with justice, or for what reasons do you wage war on your neighbors."

"Humph," I grumbled a bit under my breath. "Maybe that made him a *better* king, but it didn't make him king."

"Don't burn me with the facts when I'm pontificating, boy!" Merlin shot back. I could tell by his self-mockery that he was really in a good mood. The challenge of the quest had quite invigorated him—I could see it by his energetic posture as he leaned in to study the items remaining on the table. About

49

three places down from Sir Patrise he found what he had been looking for.

"Aha!" He picked up one of the yellow pears from the bowl and held it to his nose, then touched it gingerly with the tip of his tongue. "Now you said that several of the knights ate pears, and so far as we know all are still alive and none suffered any ill effects."

"At least not right away. Sir Patrise died almost immediately, so it seems that none of the other fruit was poisoned."

"Precisely. Or rather I should say, more precisely, that none of the *pears* was poisoned." He then picked up one of the apples still left near the bottom of the bowl. He carefully held it close to his nose, then recoiled in disgust and hastily dropped the apple back into the bowl as if it had been a viper ready to strike. "Foxglove!" he cried.

"Foxglove?"

He looked at me a bit impatiently. "A plant that will kill with ease if the victim ingests enough of it. It causes the heart to cease beating. Sir Patrise died from a poison that stopped his heart. The apples in this bowl were treated with, perhaps soaked or smothered in, a large concentration of that poison. Whoever did this deed was an expert in herbs and their uses."

"But why?" I asked, pondering his revelation. "Why would the murderer come back to this room, take away the apple that killed Sir Patrise to hide the evidence, but leave the other poisoned apples in the bowl?"

"*Now* young Gildas," Merlin cried, sounding almost over-joyed. "*That* is a good question! Can you imagine an answer?"

"Um, perhaps," I said slowly, "the murderer didn't think that anyone as brilliant as Merlin the necromancer would be investigating the crime, and so he took away only the most obvi-ous piece of evidence."

"Stop trying to flatter me, boy, and think about it again. Why leave evidence that was truly just as obvious as the other apple?"

"Because," I said, dimly seeing the point, "maybe the person didn't know that the other evidence was there!"

"Which means . . . ?"

"Which means that it wasn't the murderer who came back to take the apple."

"Absolutely right. An accomplice—someone who knew who the murderer was and wanted to protect him . . ."

"*Or*," I added triumphantly, "someone who had a hand in the crime and was afraid the evidence would lead back to himself."

"You amaze me, young Gildas," Merlin said. He sounded less amazed than amused. "See what kinds of fascinating answers you get once you start asking the right kinds of questions?"

"All right," I conceded. "But I haven't a clue what the next question ought to be."

"The next question," Merlin replied as he straightened up and looked toward the door, "is where do I sleep? It's quite late and I'm tired. And I would venture to say that you are a bit exhausted yourself after the day you've had."

Now that he had said it, I realized that it was only the stress of the murder and the excitement of the chase that were keeping me awake at this point. I was sure the queen would have me up early in the morning, and realized that I had better get some rest, since tomorrow promised to be another bone-wearying day.

"Come," I told him. "You can sleep in my quarters. Give me the candelabrum and follow me."

We had to make our way through the stone passageway, past the throne room to the door of the queen's chambers. I admit to feeling a little nervous walking those dark corridors with only the dim, flickering light of the candles, knowing that at least two people involved in a fiendishly premeditated murder were sleeping—or perhaps still awake—in all probability within the walls of this castle. The long shadows that Merlin and I cast behind us only added to the eerie atmosphere. There was some comfort, however, in the bells of matins that I heard coming from the convent south of the castle walls.

"My, it *is* late!" Merlin yawned from behind me. "Tomorrow morning will come all too quickly. I assume the queen will have work for you in the morning?"

"The queen will have her ladies dress her and then will want me to accompany her to visit Sir Bors immediately."

"To find whether he will consent to champion her in the lists."

"Yes. The king believes that he will do so for Lancelot's sake."

"It may be so, it may be so," Merlin responded thoughtfully. "Well, when you are about those duties, I will make another visit to the great hall, to see whether anything can be found that may have escaped us in the dark. But I doubt I shall find anything more."

"Still," I said as we passed by the door to the throne room, "we have learned a lot tonight, haven't we?"

"God's eyelids, yes!" the old man cried, a bit too loudly in those dim shadows to my liking. "We know that there were two killers involved. We know that one of them poisoned the apples and that the other tried to destroy the evidence. We know that one of them was expert in the lore of herbs, and skilled in the extraction of poison. We know a great deal that we did not know before."

"And we know that the queen is innocent!"

"No," Merlin said quietly. "That we do not know."

"But why? She couldn't have come back to destroy the evidence, because she was being guarded by Sir Gareth and Sir Gaheris. And she knows nothing of herb-lore. Of that I can assure you." I was pretty sure that the queen had never set foot in an herb garden in her life. She might walk in a flower garden, but could barely tell one flower from another. She just liked to pick them for nosegays.

"But remember, there is an accomplice. It is still possible for the queen to have poisoned the apples with a poison concocted for her by the accomplice, and for that accomplice, fearing his own detection, to remove the evidence after the feast."

"Oh, that's right, of course," I said glumly.

"Cheer up, Gildas of Cornwall," the old man said, putting his hand on my shoulder. "I do not believe your queen is guilty of this deed. But we must look only at what the facts tell us, or at what we can deduce from the facts. That is how this chess game works."

We had reached the door to the queen's chambers, where Gaheris stood guard. I assumed he and Gareth must be splitting up the night guard, and that Gaheris must be due to be relieved soon, judging by the bleary red around his pale blue eyes. He was leaning casually, arms crossed, against the stone wall next to the doors when we came upon him.

"I can't accuse you of trying to sneak up on the queen's rooms, young Gildas," Gaheris said as we approached. "You make as much noise as a shipful of Saxons drunk on mead . . ." But when the dim light of the candelabrum revealed my companion, Gaheris's mouth fell silent and his jaw . . . well, it just fell. Those blue eyes grew as round as apples.

"Good evening, Sir Gaheris of Orkney," Merlin said, a twinkle under his unruly brows. "You are well, I trust?"

Now I knew, and so did the old man, that Merlin was the last person anybody expected to see in the castle. He hadn't been seen in five years and all those, like Gaheris, who had known him in the old days thought he was enchanted forever in the cave. Those who were new to Camelot, like myself, knew the legend, but if we thought of him at all, believed he was simply a myth. That is, until tonight.

"Hello, old seer," was all Sir Gaheris was able to choke out. He stood back as the two of us entered through the door.

The outer chamber was my own quarters. It measured some fifteen feet wide by ten feet deep and contained three beds. At present, however, as I was the only page her highness was able to put up with, I had the room to myself. It was divided from the inner chamber by thick curtains that ran the width of the room, both on my side and on the other side, which was occupied by the queen's four ladies-in-waiting—mostly silly young things who spent time with the queen during the day. There was Anne, Elaine, Vivien and Rosemounde—the silliest of all and just my age. But as far as I could tell, her entire conversation consisted of giggling behind a nosegay. The queen outshone them like the sun outshines the lesser planets, and whether they were with her or no, I could not see how anyone with eyes could *have* eyes for anyone but Guinevere.

The queen herself slept in a private closet some twelve feet square accessed through a door from within the inner chamber. She slept by herself. So far as anyone knew.

"Choose any bed you like. I'm the only one who sleeps here these days," I told Merlin.

"Thank you for your hospitality, Gildas of Cornwall." The old man sighed wearily as he took off his dark hood and outer cloak and lay down on the bed. "It's been a very long day. You are a kind boy, and the gods always reward hospitality. Good night, my boy, and sleep well."

I blew out the candles in the candelabrum, lay down myself, and closed my eyes, trying to block out all the events of this impossible day and to drown myself in forgetful sleep. But after a few moments I opened my eyes again. It was no use. Something that Sir Gaheris had said when we met him at the door had been working at my brain.

"Merlin?" I called cautiously.

"Be quiet, I'm asleep."

"But what Gaheris said . . ."

"Yes?" he responded, with something in his voice suggesting that he had expected this.

"He called you 'old seer.' What did he mean by that? I thought you were a magician, a worker of wonders—or at least, someone who, as you say, knew how to figure things out so that when you were able to do them and nobody else could, people called them wonders. But what is this about being a 'seer'?"

"Yes, it's true," came the voice from the darkness after a long moment's pause. "It's true that I have a certain gift. Or perhaps I should call it a curse."

"Well, if you have this power," I said, getting excited now, "can't you just use the sight and see who plotted to kill Sir Patrise? Can't you solve this crime now?"

"The sight does not work in that way," Merlin explained patiently. "For one thing, it comes upon me unbidden and unawares, like a thief skulking at midnight. It may be months between visits, or only days. I never know. It begins as a dull throbbing in one of my temples. At that point I have visions of white lights, spinning and flashing before my eyes. I begin to feel nauseated, and the throbbing in my temple becomes worse and spreads to my right eye, which seems to bulge from my head, swollen and throbbing. When this occurs, I need to avoid all light, and lie down in a dark and quiet room. That is the point at which I seem to hear, in the throbbing, dark voices, and I try to make out the words."

"And you remember the words after the pain has subsided?"

"I write them quickly, before I forget. They take the form of riddles or odd symbolic oracles—'the red dragon will eat the two horses for dinner' and such nonsense. But those oracles have been called the 'prophesies of Merlin' by some. When Arthur and I put our heads together, we could see that there was

Jay Ruud

some sense to them as predictions. But that was usually after the fact. Although the one about the dragon and the horses was pretty easy to figure out: it had to be referring to Arthur's defeat of the Saxons. The red dragon, of course, is Arthur himself, son of Uther Pendragon. The chiefs of the Saxons when they fought Arthur at Mount Badon were Hengist and Horsa, names that both mean 'horse' in the barbaric yelping of the Saxon tongue. But most of the time, the oracles are incomprehensible until someone sees a connection long after something has happened."

"How do you mean?"

"Well, one of my prophesies was that four French poodles would bite a giant who wore a fake beard. How were we to know that the Irish king would demand Arthur's beard for his collection from those who paid him homage? And that four French knights—Lancelot, Bors, Ector, and Lionel—would come to Arthur's aid in the war? So you see, the gift of sight is very inexact and unreliable. Besides that, it's very painful. It takes me days to recover from one of these attacks of seeing. Facts, my boy, facts are what we need to solve this crime. Now be quiet and let me sleep, or I'll turn you into a toad."

"Ha!" I laughed at the joke. For a moment. Then I wondered whether he was really joking. I decided it was time to sleep.

CHAPTER FIVE:
THE CHAMPION

The great horse shook his head and grunted, stamping his foot impatiently as he waited for his bucket of oats. His great brown coat glistened from the brushing he had just received, and his huge muscles bulged on his flanks. His front hoof left marks from the sharp nail heads protruding from his shoes, designed to trample any unfortunate foot soldiers who might get in his way. He stood some fifteen hands high and weighed a good ton, probably twice as much as a palfrey, rouncy, or other riding horse that a lady or one of the lesser folk might own. He was a destrier, a full-grown warhorse from far off Tuscany, bred specifically to carry an armed knight in combat and to give force to the blow of the knight's lance with his own speed, weight, and power.

Such a horse cost a fortune to buy and to maintain. Only a wealthy knight could afford such an animal, and even then it generally cost a quarter of the knight's annual income to keep the horse. Without his warhorse, a knight was not a knight. Certainly that was why Sir Bors de Ganis, the son of a king, was so very careful about his investment, and made a point of visiting the stable daily to brush his horse and feed him his special bucket of oats. Sir Bors's horse, Pegasus, was his most prized possession, and had helped him through as many tough situations as his mythical flying namesake had ever done for Bellerophon. Only rarely did Bors allow his squire to take his place for the morning ritual, and on those days Pegasus pouted and stomped and was generally out of sorts until he could see his master again.

It was in the stable that we found Sir Bors on the morning after the notorious "banquet of death," as the knights were beginning to refer to it. It was a measure of the queen's desperation to find herself a champion with a good chance of defeating Sir Mador de la Porte that she ventured into the stable area. When she rode her own palfrey she always had a page—usually yours truly—bring it out to her since she wasn't fond of the smell of the stable. But this morning, armed with a fresh nosegay and accompanied by her most faithful servant—also yours truly—she had made her way down, across the upper bailey, to the stable area and found Sir Bors about to feed Pegasus his oats. A grumbling Sir Gaheris, not yet relieved by his brother Gareth, dragged slowly behind.

Bors glanced up from the horse to see our approach, then looked back to his horse. Suppressing the irritation in his voice as much as he could so as not to appear discourteous to Her Royal Highness, if he could help it, he greeted us a bit coldly:

"Good morrow to you, my lady. Had I been informed you wished to see me, I would have come to your own chambers, rather than making you come to the stable. Or you might have simply sent me your page."

Sir Bors was himself a good-sized animal, as solid as his horse and as valuable to his king as any knight in Camelot. His brown face was broad and oval, with a small pointed beard at the chin and thin, short-cropped hair on his head. He had large dark eyes and a determined jaw, and had never been known to take one drink too many or to dally with any wench at all. He was virtuous, chaste, and dull, and I had on more than one occasion heard my Lord Gawain joke to his brothers that Bors was well-named, "Because he bores the hell out of me!"

Next to his horse, he loved Lancelot the best of any living

creature, and lived to serve him as his liege lord. And Lancelot depended on him in any situation, trusting him with his life. Bors may have been colorless, but he was true, and there was no other knight in Camelot whom you would rather have on your side when it counted. And that was what the queen was counting on now.

"Sir Bors, I beg you," Guinevere said, curtsying with bowed head. "Grant me the favor I will ask you."

Her deference clearly made Sir Bors uncomfortable. "My lady," he answered, "please do not do me these courtesies. It is not seemly."

At this she raised her head and looked him in the eyes. Her beauty should have been enough to move the stoutest heart. Even today, with a face worn from weeping most of the night, her fair eyes rivaled the sun for brightness. Her hair sparkled in the morning light as it lay across her shoulders topped only with a small white headdress. Her gown was simple, for a queen, being a light blue silk that matched her eyes and showed off her magnificent white bosom. *Look at her, Sir Bors,* I said to myself. *Fall into the deep wells of her eyes and lose yourself. Be her champion.*

But this was the chaste Sir Bors I was talking about. He was, I thought, not much like other men—at once more courteous, more precise about the chivalric code, and at the same time colder, less passionately involved with life, but more one who seemed to observe it from above.

"But will you not say that you will grant me what I ask?"

"My lady, at the risk of seeming discourteous, I cannot promise to grant your boon without knowing what it is you request, for fear that I may be agreeing to something that I am unable to do. Please ask me plainly your will. I give my word as a knight that it shall not go undone if I can in good conscience carry out your wish." As polite a "maybe-I-will-and-maybe-I-won't" as I've ever heard. I had to give Bors that.

"Then know," the queen continued, her head bowed again as if she realized her eyes were having no effect on Sir Bors's resolve, "that Sir Mador de la Porte has accused me before the king of treason in the death of his cousin Sir Patrise. The king has ordered the charges to be defended in the lists a fortnight hence. Sir Mador will appear to uphold his charges, and I must produce a champion to defend my case or forfeit my life as a condemned murderer. I am here to plead with you, Sir Bors de Ganis, to act as my champion in this case. Defend me, and save my life."

The grimace on Sir Bors's face said more clearly than words ever could just what Sir Bors thought of the request. Obviously this was precisely the favor that he had expected, and dreaded, from the moment he had seen the queen approaching.

"Madame," he began, looking through her with those dark, honest eyes. "What can you expect me to answer? I cannot have anything to do with this matter, for the sake of my own reputation. You know very well that I was at the dinner. I sat at your left hand. What would people say if they knew that I had taken up your cause and pledged to be your champion?"

"That you are the most courteous of knights, faithful to your queen." Guinevere, fearing to see her cause slip away, hid her face in the bouquet she held so that the knight could not see her tears.

He closed his eyes and shook his head. Behind him Pegasus could be heard chomping his oats.

"My lady, you know that many of the knights, perhaps all of them, who attended your banquet would hold me in suspicion. They would say that I conspired with you in the death of Sir Patrise, and therefore stood with you for your defense against these charges. Everyone saw the murder. There is no doubt that if you had not insisted on Patrise's eating that apple, he would be alive this morning and we would have no reason for this conversation."

The queen had no answer but to sob into her nosegay. "Lost!" she whispered. "Lost."

But Bors was not yet finished. He was growing red in the face, and I could tell there was something else bothering him that was behind his refusal. "If Lancelot were here," he continued, taking his volume up a notch, "you would have no need of me. He worshipped you, and you know it. He would never have failed you in any situation, right or wrong. But you've driven him out of the country, and I marvel that you have the effrontery to ask me, of all people, to be your defender now. How can you, for shame, come to me after what you did to my Lord Lancelot?"

It was not merely a discourteous outburst. It was downright insulting. Apparently Bors knew more about what had happened between Lancelot and the queen than I did, or than anyone else in the castle did, but he seemed to have no qualms about shouting it out now, in front of me and God and everybody. Sir Gaheris looked more puzzled than surprised, but fixed his gaze on the stable floor to avoid looking into the queen's eyes. It was not like Sir Bors to lose his composure in any situation, which made this outburst all the more disturbing now.

The queen's sobs reached a crescendo of their own as she listened to Bors's upbraiding her, and I thought she, too, had lost all reason, for, abandoning any hope of keeping her dignity or even her propriety in this situation, she flung herself to her knees on the dirt floor of the stable and grasped Sir Bors by the legs. Gaheris gave an audible gasp.

Horrified, Sir Bors reached down to try to pull her to her feet. "No, my lady," he cried, "for the sake of your worship, do not do this! You dishonor me!" The horse behind him stomped his foot and whinnied at the impropriety, but the queen would not budge.

Still grasping the knight's knees, Guinevere moaned, "I will neither rise nor let go until you have agreed to champion me. I have nowhere else to turn!"

"My lady, I dare not—"

"You said that Lancelot would be my defender, if only he were here!" she sobbed desperately. "If I am in any way to blame for his long absence, I surely repent it now. But you . . . you are his man, you say, faithful to him in any cause, right or wrong."

A flustered Sir Bors, now red in the face and looking about, shamed that Sir Gaheris and a lowly page were witness to this pathetic scene in which he appeared to be cast as the villain, responded in the only way he could. "My lady, as to that, I do not presume to say that my Lord Lancelot would ever be involved in a wrong cause. I serve Sir Lancelot because he is a courteous knight devoted to right. Therefore, I can say that I follow him in all things because in all things he defends the right."

"And yet you say he would most assuredly defend me."

"But he is not here."

"No, he is not here, but *you* are here, Sir Bors. You are his man, his chief vassal, his right arm. Defend me for the sake of the good Sir Lancelot! Defend me because he is not here, and in his absence you protect his interests! Defend me because he would ally himself to my cause. You know this is true! And you have said he will only promote the cause of the right. Defend me because I am lost without you!"

With that the queen flung herself down bodily onto the dirt floor of the stable, her arms covering her head, her flowers dragging in the filth.

The sight of her groveling before him in the dust was too

much for Sir Bors. "All right! All right!" he blustered. "I'll do it!"

"Do you swear?" The queen lifted her head, her face brightening.

"Yes, I promise by my faith that I shall not fail you. This is the hardest thing I can think of that you could have asked me to do. It's going to make a lot of my fellow knights angry with me, especially the ones who were at the banquet. They'll call me a recreant knight, they'll think I was a party to the poisoning, they'll shun my company when they find out. But I'll grant this to you for the sake of my Lord Sir Lancelot, and for the sake of the king. I will be your champion on the day of your trial. That is, unless a better knight than I appears to champion you on that day, and then I will gladly step aside."

Now tears of joy ran down the queen's face. "Oh thank you," she said, weeping. "Thank you, my lord. You are a saint—a true saint on earth. I will never forget this. The king will reward you handsomely no doubt—"

"I seek no reward, nor do I ask for one. It is my master who lacks the reward—from *you* my lady. Now rise and comfort yourself. I shall be your champion. And may the right prevail."

With that, he helped her to her feet and the queen, still murmuring a thousand thanks to her new champion, brushed herself off as best she could. Sir Bors, with a distinct air that the interview was now ended, returned to his horse, stroking Pegasus's long head as he finished his bucket of oats, and whispering soundlessly in the horse's ear something, no doubt, about the fickleness of women or the capriciousness of queens.

Guinevere leaned on my shoulder as we exited the stable, bending, like Sir Bors, to whisper in my ear. "Well *that's* a load off! But I knew I had him as soon as I knelt down. He didn't know how to handle that one!" She winked at me, and I noticed that all trace of tears was gone from her face. She had an amazing resiliency, did my queen.

We stepped out into the sun—it was well past prime and certainly time for my breakfast—and nearly ran into a pair of knights coming toward the stable. Sir Kay and Sir Pinel nodded coldly to the queen, though they greeted Sir Gaheris warmly enough. No doubt what Sir Bors, and Sir Gawain before him, had said was true: the knights present at the banquet were all of a like mind concerning Guinevere's guilt, and were not about to show her any more than the most mandatory of courtesies. "Your highness," they mumbled incoherently as they passed us by, while the queen returned the greeting with a haughty nod and a perfunctory "My lords."

She walked forward without breaking stride, and I began to follow her, but then turned. I realized I was lucky to have run into Sir Kay in particular. He was Arthur's seneschal and so keeper of the kitchen. I realized that it was entirely possible he might have information valuable to Merlin and his investigation, especially given what we had learned last night. Merlin wasn't here now. Wouldn't he want me to take advantage of the opportunity to find out everything I could when adventure threw the chance in my path? Wouldn't he be proud of me if I thought to ask intelligent questions at this meeting, instead of just letting the opportunity pass me by?

I called to Guinevere "My lady! I beg your leave to converse with these gentlemen briefly."

She looked over her shoulder at me with her left eyebrow raised questioningly, but after a short pause she simply said, "Very well. I shall continue back toward my quarters. Don't be long, and catch up quickly!" As she began to make her way across the courtyard, Sir Gaheris yawned an incoherent farewell to the other knights and dragged himself after her.

"Yes, madame," I answered, and turned sharply to catch Sir Kay before he got away. "My Lord Kay!" I called just as he was about to enter the stable door. "A word, if I may beg your indulgence!"

Kay turned back, his arrogant eyes scowling down at me and a sneer curling his lip. "Make it quick, boy. I have more important things to do than spend my time conversing with upstart pages."

I was used to Sir Kay's attitude, and knew that he was simply the sort of person who would treat you like pig droppings purely because he could. But I had also learned long ago how to get what I wanted out of him.

"Good sir, please bear with me. I am on the king's business. He told me last night that I was to assist Merlin, the necromancer, in a quest to discover the truth of what occurred yesterday evening at the queen's banquet." All right, so I stretched the truth a tiny bit. It was for a good cause, and Merlin himself seemed to think of me as his assistant, so why not take the title officially?

"Merlin! That old charlatan? Hah!" Sir Kay guffawed at the idea. "I thought he'd been locked away for good by that little tart of the lake. What's her name? Anyway, he's imprisoned in a cave somewhere, so how can he be on this quest of yours?"

"On the contrary, my lord, Merlin is even now within the castle walls. He would certainly have wished to speak with you himself, knowing how competently you oversee every detail of the castle's administration. But as I happened to run into you, I thought I would perhaps anticipate his questions and speak with you myself. In the interest of saving your valuable time," I added hastily. "And in the interest of expediting the king's investigation." Flatter him while at the same time showing him your own authority. That was the way to get Sir Kay to cooperate.

"So Merlin is actually here?" asked the voice from Kay's left. I had nearly forgotten Sir Pinel, but he looked at me with some interest. I recalled he had come to Camelot only within the past two years from somewhere in Wales, though I didn't know what his parentage was. Thus, like me, he had probably heard only legends of the miraculous feats of Merlin the Magician. Sir Pinel turned toward me, his fists on his hips and his thin, pinched face inclined toward me. He had small, beady eyes that seemed set unusually close together, and had long sandy hair that hung almost to his shoulders but in very thin strands. But his expression was kindly and manifested a real curiosity. "Tell me, what kind of man is he?"

"Sir Pinel, he is a puzzle," I answered truthfully. "One minute immobilized by gloom, the next animated by fire. But he has a mind that seems full of wisdom, and full of questions, and eager to discover new truths."

Sir Pinel nodded and smiled. "I have heard so much about him. I earnestly hope I shall be able to meet him while he is here."

"Yes, yes, yes, I'm sure we're all very impressed by Merlin the Mage," Sir Kay interrupted. "But what is it you want of me? I am in a hurry to inspect the stables and don't have all day to chat about besotted necromancers. Your business, boy!"

"Just one question, sir. I know that you have as part of your charge the kitchen and kitchen staff. Yesterday they spent much of the day making ready the queen's banquet. Now I understand she oversaw most of that herself, but it is still your kitchen, so I am certain you kept a close eye on what was happening."

"Her majesty occasionally takes charge herself, for events that are special for her. But my assistance is generally required to ensure that things run smoothly. If a problem comes up that is beyond the capacity of the kitchen help, for instance, I may need to step in to solve it."

"And yesterday? Did anything unusual occur yesterday that required your attention?"

"Nothing. Things went quite smoothly. Oh, the kitchen came up short of dill, which we wanted to help season the fish, and I sent a kitchen boy out to the convent to borrow some, but nothing important to speak of."

"What about . . . visitors? Did anyone make a visit to the kitchen who wasn't expected?"

"Stupid question. Why would anyone . . . hold on, I do recall that Sir Palomides came by, but that was just out of curiosity."

"Curiosity? Why would a knight of the round table harbor any curiosity about the workings of the kitchen?" Then I remembered myself and qualified that comment. "That is, unless it was his appointed task, as it is your grace's."

But Sir Kay was too interested in defending Sir Palomides's honor to notice the insult to his own, and he rushed to the Moorish knight's defense. "He does come by occasionally, because of his strong interest in herbs and spices. They are, you know, the chief export of his native land, and he takes a keen interest in our cooks' use of them to prepare meats, fish, and fowl. He was especially interested yesterday because of some of the unusual dishes that were being prepared—the swans, you know, and all."

"Sir Palomides knows more about the uses of herbs than anyone else I have ever met," Sir Pinel added. "Truly, he regaled us last evening for over an hour about the little-known qualities of every herb, spice, and plant you can imagine, those that grow in Logres and those that are found only in his own lands. The man is a walking volume of herbology. To tell you the truth," he said in a low voice, "I was awfully bored by it."

"Quite so, quite so," Sir Kay continued, now in a dismissive tone. "As I say, it was not unusual to see him in the kitchen. He has visited at least two or three times before. Now that's all the time we have for you, young Gildas. Come, Sir Pinel." He turned, and with a nod to me, Sir Pinel turned to follow him.

"Thank you, my lord," I said, though he was already deeply involved in ignoring me altogether.

"Taber!" Kay called, and a slouching stable hand poked his head out from one of the stalls, leaning on a pitchfork. "Bring out those three new Belgians that I wanted to show Sir Pinel. Take them out to the corral."

Sir Kay having left no doubt that I had been dismissed, I looked up to see that my lady the queen and her reluctant escort were only about halfway across the open courtyard. Other folk were starting to stir now, particularly groups of squires and pages going about their masters' early morning business. I sprinted to catch up to Guinevere and Gaheris, going over in my mind what Sir Kay and Sir Pinel had told me.

If Sir Palomides was such an expert on the culinary virtues of herbs, why, then, wouldn't he be intimately aware of the poisonous properties of other herbs? Wouldn't that make him a prime suspect in this particular murder? Wouldn't Merlin think I had done well to make this discovery? I couldn't wait to speak with him about it.

When I caught up to the queen, she was looking back over her shoulder, watching Taber and another stable boy lead three large warhorses out of the stable to the corral outside the walls of the castle. "Look at that ugly horse," she observed as I fell in beside her, speaking as if she were continuing a conversation we had been having all along.

"Which one?" I asked, following her gaze.

"The ugly one," she answered, turning back to continue her walk with an air that said another matter had been settled satisfactorily.

CHAPTER SIX:
IF YOU CAN'T STAND THE HEAT

When Merlin scowled, his eyebrows made a giant hedge through which his blazing eyes pierced ominously. And he was scowling now.

"Nitwit of a Cornish dunce! Who gave you permission to start bouncing off on your own investigation, willy-nilly? God's teeth, I hope you haven't muddied the waters permanently. If Kay knows I'm investigating the murder, you can wager your father's farm that by this time every knight in Camelot knows it. They'll all be on their guard."

"Um . . . my father is an armor-maker, my lord . . ."

"I don't care if he's a carpet-maker to the sultan of Baghdad, that's not the point. What was going through that thick skull of yours, other than the west wind?" He leaned over to knock playfully on my forehead as if it was a door. "Nobody home?" he queried. I could tell he was not so angry as he was at first. He was already thinking about making use of whatever information I had gleaned from my brief interview with Kay and Pinel.

"I saw the opportunity to ask Sir Kay about the kitchen. I didn't know when we . . . that is, *you* would have the chance to catch him alone again."

He sat upon his bed in the outer chamber of the queen's quarters while I stood before him, fresh from my excursion of the morning. We had agreed to meet back here once our morning tasks were done. Guinevere had passed through to the inner chamber, where she planned to spend the morning spinning with her ladies-in-waiting, muttering as she left Sir Gaheris at the door. "Since I'm to be guarded like a prisoner in my own chambers, I may as well make the most of the time and do some useful work."

Merlin had been up and about for some hours, gone to explore the great hall by the morning light to see whether any new evidence could be gleaned. When I returned, I could tell by looking at him that the missing apple had not been found.

"Come, my boy." The old man sighed as he leaned back on the bed and stared at the ceiling. "It can't be helped now. Let's hear what you found out from the seneschal. I found nothing more in the great hall, so your morning is bound to have been more fruitful than my own."

"Well, I figure that whoever poisoned the apples must have had access to the kitchen, and so must have visited it while the preparations for the banquet were taking place, some time yesterday."

"A logical assumption, to be sure." Caught off guard by Merlin's congratulatory tone, I allowed myself a bit of selfish pleasure and puffed my chest out, just a little bit. But the old man was baiting me and snapped, "Unless, of course, the murderer was in fact someone who regularly worked in the kitchens—like Kay himself. Or unless the apples were poisoned when they arrived in the kitchen, in which case we must suspect the fruit peddler who sold them to the castle. But if he were still around, you can wager all of your father's Persian carpets that he's run off now."

"Oh."

"All right, go on, go on," he urged me irritably. "What did you find out?"

"Well," I continued sheepishly, "the queen, of course, was there a great deal. But that was to be expected, since she was overseeing the banquet. Sir Kay was there much of the day as well, and he mentioned that Sir Palomides had wandered by for a short time."

"Sir Palomides? The Moorish knight?"

"The same."

"And he was at the banquet as well, was he not? Now I wonder what a knight of the round table would be doing hanging about with kitchen wenches and cooks? What could Sir Palomides possibly find to interest him in a scullery?"

"Sir Pinel pointed out Sir Palomides's interest in herbs and spices. To tell the truth, at the banquet last knight that's all he and Sir Kay talked about. I found it awfully boring—as, I take it, did Pinel."

"Herbs? Spices? The properties of rare plants?" Merlin mused. "This is becoming more and more interesting. I think we will need to pay our Moorish knight a visit. But first, perhaps we had better make our own investigation of the kitchen itself, and see what the cooks and maids remember about yesterday. Let's go!" He leaped up with such spontaneous energy that I was knocked off balance.

"I, uh . . . I need to request permission of the queen before leaving her, my lord. Let me just step in to get her leave. I don't think she will need me today, with her women to keep her company. But just a moment."

The mage folded his arms and began tapping his foot impatiently. "Well, well, go on. Make your farewells. We haven't got all day."

I quickly darted through the space between the curtain and the near wall to enter the inner chamber. There sat the queen and her maids, each spinning away solemnly with the exception of Elaine. That young lady was reading aloud from a large, expensively illuminated manuscript in French. From what I could gather as I walked in, it was a romance telling the story of Troilus, a prince of Troy, and his love for the beautiful widow

Criseyde. Elaine broke off when she saw me, though, and the queen glanced up from her spinning. "Yes, Gildas?" she demanded. "What is it?"

"My lady." I bowed courteously. "The Lord Merlin requests that I accompany him today as he continues to investigate last night's unfortunate . . . accident. And I thought that, since you have your maids here and you seem to be intent on staying in . . ."

"The king seems to be intent on my staying in," Guinevere corrected me. "And since I am to be caged like some dangerous beast in this bare cell"—I looked around discreetly at the rich tapestries that adorned the walls of the inner chamber, at the velvet-covered chair on which she sat to spin, and at the gold leaf illuminating her Troilus romance—"it doesn't mean that I need to torture my poor page as well. Go, then. Leave me to my ascetic dungeon." She waved me off with one hand while with the other she held a silver cup from which she sipped a fine French wine.

Rosemounde had begun to giggle uncontrollably at her spinning wheel in the corner, and put her hand in front of her face as she bowed her head, looking up at me through her long, dark eyelashes. I shook my head at the distraction and focused again on the queen.

"Then with your leave, my lady." I bowed again and backed out of the room.

As soon as I had cleared the curtain, I felt a strong, gnarled hand grasp me by the collar. "Let's go, then, boy!" an impatient Merlin boomed as he pulled me through the door. But when we had passed through the queen's heavy outer doors, it was Merlin who paused.

"My Lord Gareth, so you really have grown up! And very like your father, I see. Just like your brother Gaheris."

"Old trickster!" cried the knight with unfeigned joy as he

reached out to embrace Merlin. "Then it's true you're still walking this earth! I had feared that you'd left us long ago to join your own father somewhere in the spirits of the air!"

"When that happens, you'll be the first to know it, Beaumains. I'll haunt your sleep until you cry me mercy. Then we'll see who has the last laugh."

"Beaumains?" I asked tentatively.

"The name Sir Kay gave me when I came to Camelot in disguise, and worked for a year as a scullery boy in the kitchen, young Gildas." Sir Gareth had always treated me like a fellow gentleman, but he was equally at ease with peasants and kings. His own self-confidence sustained him in such a way that he had no need to dominate others or to flatter them in order to keep it. His genuineness and his good humor made him the favorite of his brothers, of his king, and of the other knights, especially Lancelot himself.

"A job," Gareth continued, "that builds character. If I had my way, I would require it of every ambitious page in the kingdom."

"That you should mention the kitchen, Sir Gareth, is ironic, and it comes in good time. Gildas and I are on our way even now to visit the kitchens, to find—"

"To find out if anyone there can give you evidence of what happened yesterday evening. It's logical, of course, since what killed Sir Patrise came from the kitchen, though it came by way of the queen's hand. But I wish you luck. More than anything I would wish to see the queen cleared of these charges, though her guilt seems pretty clear just now."

"Come with us, Beaumains!" Merlin said suddenly. "You know the kitchens better than any nobleman in Camelot except for Sir Kay. Perhaps better, since you know the cooks and scullery maids personally, and on their own level. You can help us find the truth better than anyone else."

Sir Gareth was tempted—I could see it in those pale blue eyes—but he shook his head somewhat reluctantly and said, "Old man, I truly would like to help you, I'm sure you know. But I am here by order of the king. The queen is to be guarded twenty-four hours a day, and at this point only I and my brother Gaheris are assigned the duty. I hope we will be relieved or at least reinforced soon, but the king's orders stand."

Remembering Guinevere's bitter words as I left the inner chamber, I ventured, "And you have a rather unpleasant task, I'm afraid. The queen is more resentful of her imprisonment than of anything else I can remember."

Sir Gareth shook his head and looked at me sincerely. "The king trusts the queen," he said slowly. "He doesn't suspect her of any foul play. What he is concerned about is the feelings of the knights. With all of the resentment after the banquet of death, the king fears that my Lady Guinevere may be in danger. We are not imprisoning her, we are protecting her."

Say what you will, I thought, but that isn't what the queen sees. But I kept my mouth shut.

"Listen, here is what I advise," Gareth continued thoughtfully. "Find Roger. He is one of the cooks, usually the one responsible for stews, soups, and sauces. But he knows everything that happens in that kitchen. Nothing gets by him. Anything unusual that might have happened in the kitchen yesterday, Roger would know about it. Just tell him that Beaumains sent you to him, and he will know that he can trust you."

"Ah!" Merlin agreed. "Sounds like just the sort of man we need to talk to. We'll look him up immediately. Adieu, Sir Gareth. I'll see you again before long."

"Well, let's hope it's before another five years goes by. Good luck, old man."

We swung out into the courtyard and began to cross it toward the kitchen. The kitchen was just west of the great hall along the castle wall. It was a single story, since any rooms above it would run the risk of being set on fire. But a covered passageway led up a flight of stairs from the kitchen directly to the great hall on the second floor, so that food being transported from the kitchen to the dining area would not get cold.

As we walked purposefully across the castle's lower bailey, my curiosity got the better of me and I needed to find out just exactly what Merlin was thinking about what we'd found out so far. "Merlin," I asked, "do you believe Sir Palomides might be guilty of this crime?"

"Believe?" He drew the word out as if it were a note of plainsong. "Eradicate that word from your vocabulary, boy, if you're going to begin looking into crimes. Not that I can say I know a single sheriff or other investigator who wouldn't say the same. But they're all wrong, you see. Facts. Find all the facts available. Then make logical deductions based on the facts. Only that will lead you to the truth. At least, the truth as we can know it in this world here, this thoroughfare full of woe."

I could tell by his tone he was having some fun with me at the expense of the castle chaplain, Father Ambrose, or perhaps of those in religious occupations in general. But most of what he said was serious, and I continued to try to pin him down. "Then don't tell me what you believe, tell me what you think. Based on the facts so far, can you make any deductions about Sir Palomides and his possible guilt?"

"Ah, now you ask the right question, boy! Sir Palomides had the opportunity to do this deed. That is certain. He was in the kitchen at the time the feast was being prepared. Of course, so were all the cooks, scullery maids and other servants, Sir Kay, and the queen. None of them can be ruled out.

"But Sir Palomides also had the means to commit this crime. By all accounts he is a wizard with herbs. He knows more about them than anyone else in the castle according to common gossip. The truth of that you say you witnessed yourself at the table last night. So, means and opportunity. That is a hard combination to ignore.

"But as yet we lack the most crucial element: means, motive, and opportunity, young Gildas, and never forget it. Means, motive, and opportunity are the three ingredients in a murder. Find someone with all three, and you most likely have the killer, or at least a very good suspect. And what we don't have for Sir Palomides is motive. What possible reason would he have had to hate Sir Patrise? Answer me that, Gildas of Cornwall, and I'll go to the king right now and have the Moor arrested!"

I didn't know either of the knights well enough to give him any kind of answer, and besides, we had come to the doors of the kitchen. They were open wide, for even on very cool late autumn mornings like this one, the kitchen felt like an inferno for those inside.

One heard and smelled the kitchen before ever arriving at the doors. To the left of the entrance was a pen where five goats, a cow, three sheep, and several chickens were kept. These poor beasts were blissfully ignorant of the fact that they were on tomorrow's menu. But to the right was a small herb garden cultivated by the cooks' servants for spices that could be grown locally. There was a larder off the kitchen where spices of a more exotic nature were kept.

"Ready for a foretaste of hell?" Merlin asked as we plunged through the door into the heat.

I never thought the kitchens were a bad place to visit at all. Sure, the outside smells were never very pleasant, and the heat was like a palpable force that had to be cut into when you entered the room; but inside, the smells were truly savory, and the bustling to and fro of many bodies busy with the life-sustaining business of food always made me feel there were worthwhile things being done down here.

As we entered, we stood a moment to let our eyes adjust to the light. To our left was the larder, a separate room where wine, beer, and mead were stored, as well as spices, flour, yeast, and other essentials. There were slabs of meat hanging there as well, awaiting their turn at the fire. Directly before us in the kitchen space was a sink, in which two scullery maids were busy cleaning several pots, knives, and large spoons. Directly to the right was a large counter where four butchers could be seen carving up the remains of what looked like it might have been a sheep at one time. Along the wall to our right were four brick fireplaces and, closest to the door, a brick oven, from which I could catch a whiff of the new baking bread. A baker was just opening the oven to check on the progress of his loaves. In two of the fireplaces, young kitchen boys were turning whole pigs on spits over the open fire. They looked nearly ready to eat. It was, after all, nearing sext when we came to the kitchen, and the late morning meal was the chief meal of the day at Camelot.

In the last fireplace, a huge bronze cauldron hung suspended on a hook over the fire. A hearty stew bubbled in the cauldron, and standing over the cauldron with a long three-pronged meat hook he was using to spear the meat in the stew stood the cook that I guessed must be Roger.

"Roger!" Merlin called to him as we made our way through the hubbub of the kitchen workers. "Are you Roger? Sir Gareth told me to seek you out. Do you mind if I ask you a few questions?"

"Looks like you already 'ave," Roger observed in a slow drawl, without taking his eyes off the meat he was stirring with his long hook.

"Look, Roger." Merlin approached him, ignoring his remark. "Beaumains would have come himself, but he's tied up with guarding the queen—"

"A dame what needs a good bit of guarding these days, from

what I 'ear." The cook pronged a chunk of what looked like beef with his hook and took it out of the cauldron, examining it to see how well done it appeared.

"Precisely what I need to speak with you about," Merlin continued. "You have heard, then, that the queen is accused of willful murder in the death of the knight Sir Patrise. On behalf of the king, I am investigating the knight's death. The queen protests her innocence. The king, as is to be expected, believes her. But we need to discover the truth of what happened in order to clear the queen's name—or to establish her guilt conclusively."

"What good's that gonna do, then?" Roger returned, eyes still on the stew. "Ain't there gonna be a trial by combat? Ain't the queen already got 'er champion in Sir Bors? What can you do about that, old man?"

Clearly Gareth had been right in his choice of a witness. Roger seemed to know everything that went on in the castle, even including private conversations that had occurred that very morning. He must have a direct connection to every gossip in the castle. And maybe some from outside, as well.

"We hope," Merlin continued, "it will not come to that. If we can find the truth before then, we may need no trial by combat at all. But the first thing we need to find out is what was going on yesterday here in the kitchen. Did anything unusual happen? Did anybody spend time here who didn't really belong?"

"You mean like you fellows?" Roger asked, finally turning from his boiling pot and resting his meat hook on his shoulder like a spear. His broad face was red as raw meat—singed, I supposed, by constant proximity to the fires of that place. His brown hair was pushed back on his head and seemed to be held there in place by the thick layer of grease that appeared to cover his entire body. He wore a large apron that at one time might have been white, stained now by smoke, blood, and a variety of sauces. His eyebrows sloped upward toward the center of his forehead and his gray eyes squinted at me—wondering, perhaps, what business any of this was of mine.

"Look," he said, " 'ere's the story. I reckon I can trust you well enough if Beaumains sent you. I know you've already 'ad some of it from Sir Kay as well. That's all right, though," he said over the murmured protest that had begun to issue from Merlin's mouth. "I like to double-check on things myself. Now let me say right off that none of my boys 'ere could 'ave been in on this thing, nor any of the scullery maids neither. First off I watch 'em like an 'awk and they can't get away with nothing 'ere. Besides that, they're all good kinds and none of them ever 'ad anything to do with this Sir Patrise bloke. Didn't even know who 'e was. Sir Kay would 'ave known 'im, of course, and I don't watch Kay, 'im being my boss and all. I figure 'e'll do whatever 'e wants and damn anybody what stands in 'is way. Know what I mean?"

"Right," Merlin agreed. "So you're saying it's unlikely any of the regular kitchen workers had anything to do with the crime. You don't seem so sure of Sir Kay."

"Ain't my place to be sure or not sure." Roger shrugged. "Just saying I didn't watch 'im close. The queen neither, for that matter. But the queen, now, she pretty much kept talking to me the whole time she was 'ere, and followed me around too, looking over my shoulder at everything I did. It woulda been pretty 'ard for 'er to 'ave done anything I didn't notice, since she stuck so close. Too bad your young page there wasn't with 'er that day. Most days she's got 'im tagging along like 'er puppy dog."

I'd thought myself that it was unfortunate I had been busy with other tasks most of the day yesterday. If I had been with the queen more, I could have been certain of her innocence. Not that I wasn't, you understand, but I could have given evidence for her that she had never come near those apples.

Which reminded me. "Where was the bowl of fruit yesterday?"

Merlin gave me a sharp look, to the effect that I was there to be seen and not heard—and if the truth were told, preferably not seen either if it meant drawing attention to myself. But it was a significant question I thought. And the answer proved to be interesting as well.

"We didn't make up the bowl till it was almost time to serve it, so the bowl didn't sit there at all. We did 'ave a small basket of apples and another one of pears sittin' yonder at the end of the counter nearest the door there." He nodded toward the door we'd just come in. "The queen never touched either of them baskets, that I saw. But you know who made a big issue out of 'em was that black fellow, that Sir Palomides."

"What can you tell us about Sir Palomides?" Merlin took the opportunity to ask. "How long was he here?"

"Oh, no more'n about a quarter of an hour. 'E never stays too long when 'e comes, but it's always the same. 'E comes in with a big smile and keeps lookin' over my shoulder to see what kinds of spices I'm puttin' on the meat or in the sauces or whatever. Kind of makes 'imself a nuisance, is what 'e does, an' 'e's always got advice. 'Why don't you use such and such in that?' or 'When I cooked fish in my country, we always had it with thus and so.' Pretty annoyin' if you know what I mean. But 'e's a good-natured bloke."

"He comes often then, does he?"

"Oh, I dunno," Roger reached up with the hand that was not holding the meat hook and scratched himself absently under his chin. "Once a week maybe 'e'll be down. No set day or anything, just when the spirit moves 'im. Pretty much always does the same thing, like I tol' ya."

"So did he do anything unusual yesterday? And when you say he made an issue of the apples, what exactly do you mean?"

"Went on about 'ow in 'is country they got all kinds of great fruit, and 'ow it's so unusual a treat for 'im to have fruit here in Logres, so 'e picked up one of them apples and started eatin' it here. I told 'im to 'old 'is 'orses on account those apples were for the queen's big feast an' he just said well, 'e guessed 'e wouldn't 'ave one at the feast then if 'e was gettin' 'is fair share now. But 'e did make a big deal out of them apples. Even gave one to the nun."

"The nun?" Merlin raised his shaggy brows.

"Yeah, yeah, Sister Agnes what works in the convent kitchen over to Saint Mary Magdalene's. She showed up 'ere for a minute or two, brought over some dill from the convent garden when we came up short."

"And Sister Agnes ate one of the apples as well?"

"Seemed pretty glad to 'ave it, too. Treats like them is rare in the convent, I'm bettin'. But I shooed Sir Palomides out after that. Escorted 'im out the door meself. Told 'im to quit messin' with the victuals for the queen's feast or I'd tell 'er all about it and 'e'd have 'er sharp tongue to deal with. 'E just laughed. So did I, for that matter. 'E's an amiable devil of a black Moor is Sir Palomides."

"And the nun?"

"Oh, she come out eating the apple while I was standing there with Palomides. Said she 'oped we'd return the favor if they ever run out of anything over in their own kitchen. Went back the way she come. And that was it. Those are the only folks who visited the kitchen all day yesterday. For whatever good it does ye."

Roger turned back to his stewpot and began stirring things with his meat hook again, and Merlin thanked him in the name of the king and queen. "Sure, sure," he replied, "but if I don't get this midday meal up to 'em right quick, their thanks will be pretty short-lived. Boy!" he called at one of the boys who was running back and forth with bowls and spoons. "Come 'ere and get this stew ready to serve upstairs. Quick now, or I'll sell your liver for dog meat."

As the boy came running with some large bowls, Merlin murmured "Right. We'll be off then," and pushed me ahead of him out the door.

The cool breeze felt like new life as we emerged from the heat of that kitchen. We both breathed in some of the refreshing air and then looked at one another.

"Walk with me," Merlin told me, and he began to stroll slowly across the green toward the barbican. "What have we learned?" He challenged me.

"Well, Roger says that the queen never went near the apples. So we've cleared her of guilt, then, yes?"

"The accomplice, Gildas. Don't forget about the accomplice. But I admit, the queen looks better and better the more we find out. What else do we know?"

"We know that Sir Palomides did indeed have the opportunity to poison those apples! Doesn't he begin to look more and more guilty the further we look?"

"Sir Palomides may have slipped poison onto those apples, though he doesn't seem to have had much time. He also ate one of the apples. And lived. And he gave one to the nun, who also survived. So if he did the poisoning, it would have been after that happened, and so he must have done it right under Roger's nose. No, Sir Palomides may be our most likely suspect, but his guilt is far from established."

"Then what do we do now?" I wondered aloud.

"Clearly we need to interview Sir Palomides. Even if he is a suspect, we still have no motive. But I don't know. First I think I will go back to my cave to think. You call on me there tomorrow."

"Your cave?" The thought made my stomach drop like a

stone. I was worried that once he got back there I'd never get him roused again. "Why don't you just go back to my chamber and rest?"

"Not the same, boy," Merlin answered. "I need my familiar surroundings. Just come to me there."

"But Merlin, tomorrow is the day set aside for Sir Patrise's funeral. I thought that maybe I should go to that, you know, for the queen. I don't think she'll want to go herself."

"Yes, yes," Merlin said tiredly. His head was down and he already looked to me to be slipping into a dark mood. "By all means. Go to the funeral. Come to me when you can. Tomorrow. Or the next day . . ." his voice trailed off. I bade him farewell as he walked, now almost mechanically, through the gate to the drawbridge. I heard him say one more thing as he was leaving, perhaps to me, or perhaps he was just thinking out loud.

"Who was that nun?"

CHAPTER SEVEN:
REQUIEM AETERNAM

The funeral procession for Sir Patrise of Ireland was as elaborate as any that had been seen at Camelot. After all, it was not often that a knight of the round table was murdered, or was interred here in Logres rather than in his home country. But Sir Mador de la Porte had insisted that his cousin's funeral be here, and that it be conducted with all due ceremony, as if to underscore his loss and the queen's guilt.

The body had lain in state in the castle's chapel since the death occurred. Now the remains, placed in a leaden casket, would be taken from the chapel to the cathedral in Caerleon, where the bishop would preside over the requiem mass and interment, and the casket would be placed in a tomb within the church.

The funeral was a communal event for the castle, and I too had my place in the procession. The queen, however, had begged leave to miss the ceremony, and wisely too. How much would her presence at the rites have angered and antagonized Sir Mador? How could the mourners have conducted themselves with courtesy if the perceived murderer walked in the procession for her victim? But I was there, and, as so often in the past, I would be the eyes and ears of my queen.

A lowering sky threatened rain as William of Glastonbury, Bishop of Caerleon, led the procession in full ecclesiastical regalia, crossed and mitred as befitted a lord of the Church. Behind him walked the king's personal chaplain and confessor,

Father Ambrose, who also conducted what services were required at the chapel. It was he who had given Sir Patrise his last rites after that unfortunate dinner. He was followed by twelve canons attached to the cathedral, marching in line two-by-two. They began the march slowly and deliberately from the door of the palace chapel, and were to proceed along a route across the castle courtyard, over the drawbridge, along the road into the city, and on into the cathedral in the center of town. It was an elaborate ceremony that would entertain the peasants and artisans of Caerleon as well as any theater they had seen.

The king himself came next. With the queen as *persona non grata* and his eldest nephew and heir apparent, Sir Gawain, still not returned from his quest for Sir Lancelot, Arthur walked alone. He wore a long gown of black satin, trimmed on the sleeves and around the hood in richest sable. His coat of arms with the three crowns was emblazoned on the robe and his head bore his ceremonial crown. He walked with head bowed and a pained expression on his face. I suspected no small part of that pain was caused by the weight of the heavy crown, but I knew that part of it was for the death of his knight, and perhaps the greatest part was fear for his wife, and helplessness at having to rely on others to rescue her from her distress.

The king was followed by his nephews, Sir Gareth and Sir Gaheris, relieved of their guard duty for the duration of the funeral and replaced by a pair of royal archers. Behind them were the king's other nephews, Sir Agravain and Sir Yvain, Gawain's closest cousin and famous as the "Knight of the Lion." Following them were some sixty more knights of the round table—all those who were present in Camelot—marching two-by-two, and wearing long black gowns, though reaching only to mid-calf so as to be shorter than the king's.

Members of the king's household followed the knights, as well as squires and pages attached to the company, all walking, again, two-by-two. I walked at the end of this contingent, next to Florent, Sir Gawain's squire. We all marched in black tunics and hose, with the coat of arms of our masters' houses emblazoned on the black. Mine bore the king's insignia. Since I assumed the king had provided the mourning garments for all the retinue, it must have been his decision not to dress me with the queen's family coat of arms, the red leopard of Cameliard. I was thankful for his prudence, since it would have been very awkward for me in that procession to have borne that crest.

Behind the eighty or so squires and pages and other household retinue came, at last, the leaden coffin bearing Sir Patrise's earthly remains. Twelve green-clad archers of the palace guard carried the casket, led by Robin Kempe as chief pallbearer. The casket was draped in a cloth of white velvet with a gold cross stitched on it that ran the whole length of the coffin.

Following the casket was the last cortege, the chief mourners. There were but three: Sir Patrise's squire, Patrick; his page, Michael; and, behind them and walking alone, the darkly countenanced Sir Mador de la Porte.

It was about the hour of none when the long procession left Camelot chapel and marched slowly over the drawbridge and took the road that led southwest of the castle into the city of Caerleon. Townspeople lined the main street of the city to watch the pageant. It was not often that they had a chance to see so many noble folk dressed in such finery, and most of them looked appropriately sad as they watched the elaborate procession; though some viewed the whole affair with an ironic gleam in their eyes, reflecting that, despite the elaborate sendoff, Death the Great Equalizer would ultimately treat Sir Patrise no better than it would any of them.

"Why in bugger's name the casket had to be *lead* I'd like to know. Really. Somebody tell me, eh?" Robin was grumbling in a voice audible only to me as the solemn procession made its way to the cathedral.

"You like a good challenge, there's a nice lad," I whispered back to him. "How else could you show off your great swelling muscles for all the ladies if they gave you some sissy wooden casket?"

"Oh, no. Wooden caskets are only good for the likes of you and me, and these poor buggers watching from the sides. Our noble Irish knight can't have any of that, can he?"

By now the procession had reached the doors of the cathedral, and it was beginning to rain. The whole ceremony was turning into one bad cliché. It was going to be gloomy enough in the church, but now we were going to be gloomy *and* wet.

We all filed in to a church whose nave and apse were hung with black velvet draperies. Along the processional aisle of the nave stood several dozen candelabra, and candles burned in the choir and the apse as well. They glowed like a thousand stars flung across a welcoming heaven. Or perhaps it was more like a thousand little burning fires of hell. I really didn't know anything about the state of our good Sir Patrise's soul when he bit un-shriven into that fatal fruit. In the front of the church, as focal point for the ceremony, a black lattice-work catafalque stood on top of a bier on which Robin and the others placed the coffin when they entered the church.

Everyone now stood back, surrounding the draped casket in rows two-dozen deep as the bishop and other priests prepared to say the requiem mass. Sir Mador stood closest to the front, flanked by Patrick and Michael, while King Arthur and his nephews stood slightly to the side. Robin and the other royal archers who had served as pallbearers stood in a line behind that group, and the rest of us filled in as space provided. I found myself standing directly behind Robin as the Introit began.

"Requiem aeternam dona eis, Domine," chanted Bishop Wil-

liam. *"Et lux perpetua luceat eis."*

Eternal rest give unto them, O Lord. And let perpetual light shine upon them.

"How he can rest I don't know," I whispered in Robin's ear. "His killer is uncaught, and the queen wrongfully accused."

"You and your Merlin will fix that, eh? You'll get to the bottom of all this, I'm sure." I was taken slightly aback. I had never told Robin why I was sent for Merlin, or what he was doing here in the castle. That Robin knew all about it suggested the word was circulating all over Camelot that the great mage Merlin was investigating the circumstances of Sir Patrice's murder, assisted by a certain young Cornish page.

"Old Merlin is the wisest man in Logres. Or so he's let everybody know." Robin, in his early twenties, was not old enough to remember the days when Merlin was the mainstay of Arthur's court and his chief adviser. But he certainly knew the old necromancer by reputation.

"Mind your tongue or I'll have him turn you into a newt. That old man is the cleverest fellow I've ever met. If anybody can shine some light on this mystery, it's him."

"Kyrie, eleison!" came the bishop's chant. *"Christe, eleison! Kyrie, eleison!"*

God have mercy on us. Christ have mercy on us. God have mercy on us.

"Mercy is what the queen needs now, especially if we fail, me and the old man."

Robin nodded. "But justice is what they're planning for her, eh? Sir Mador and the court and even the king."

"Not justice. Vengeance. Vengeance at the first object they can find. But the king is trapped. The law requires him to put the queen to trial, and Sir Mador has demanded trial by combat. The king must act as impartial judge. How he can be impartial with his wife facing the stake I can't imagine. But he is also the

Law in Logres, and the Law can't be biased."

"Shouldn't be, you mean. It certainly can be. What if it were some peasant suspected of killing old Patrise, eh? You think we'd be waiting around for a trial in his case? Pshaw. Sir Mador would have gutted him on the spot, and no questions asked."

"Maybe so," I admitted. "But not if Arthur had been there. He really does want justice and truth. And Merlin too. Merlin will find the truth of what has happened here, I'm sure of it. But for now the king's hands are tied."

"Dies irae," Bishop William continued, *"dies illa solvet saeclum in favilla."*

This day, this day of wrath shall consume the world in ashes.

"You've got to untie them." Robin was seldom serious, especially with me, but he seemed so now. At least I knew that everybody in Camelot had not already found the queen guilty as charged and condemned her to the fires.

"Mors stupebit et natura, cum resurget creatura, judicanti responsura."

Death and nature shall be stunned, when mankind arises to render account before the judge.

"Even if we fail to find the truth, Sir Bors has promised to act as the queen's champion. It won't be easy for Sir Mador to beat him. Especially if the queen's cause is right. Or, I mean, especially *because* the queen's cause is right."

"You can't help doubting a little, can you, Master Gildas? Remember, Sir Mador will be fighting savagely for his family and his honor, and he'll put all of his rage and grief into the battle. Sir Bors is fighting because the queen asked him to. He neither believes in her cause nor even likes her all that much. And even if he does beat down Sir Mador's attack, there'll still be doubts about the queen's innocence. You have them yourself, as you've just shown with that 'if.' "

"Ingemisco tamquam reus; Culpa rubet vultus meus; Supplicanti

parce, Deus."

I groan as one guilty, my face blushes with guilt; spare the suppliant, O God.

"Well, I pray she will be spared." I began to look around the nave to the other mourners. Remembering that I was to report back to the queen whatever I observed, and remembering too that anything interesting that went on among those present ought to be reported to Merlin as well when I went to meet him, I thought it might behoove me to make my way unobtrusively among the rows of standing mourners. I whispered a brief farewell to Robin as I stepped away. "I'm going to spy a little bit. Keep your eyes open, too, will you? Let me know if you see anything strange or unusual going on, either here or afterward when things break up."

"The strangest thing I've seen here is you. But that probably won't help your investigation. So I'll keep my eyes and ears opened and my mouth closed, and anything I find out goes straight in your ear." He winked and I silently slipped off.

"*Domine, Jesu Christe, Rex gloriae,*" the bishop droned on. "*Libera animas omnium fidelium defunctorum de poenis inferni.*"

Lord Jesus Christ, king of glory, deliver the souls of all the faithful departed from the pains of hell.

Personally, while I was feeling fairly charitable toward the faithfully departed Sir Patrise, I wouldn't have minded if the souls of those responsible for his death were consigned to the pains of hell, if only for the pains they were causing my queen.

I searched among the crowd in what I hoped was a subtle way, my head bowed and my eyes peering from beneath my lowered brows. Soon I caught sight of what I was looking for: standing out conspicuously from among the sea of white faces was the dark visage of Sir Palomides, close by his brother, Sir Safer, a row or two behind the king. Slowly and reverently, I began to make my way toward him. He was still our prime suspect. If I could observe him, watch his reactions, listen to anything he might say during the service, perhaps I could find what Merlin had called his motive.

"Hostias et preces tibi, Domine laudis offerimus."

Lord, in praise we offer you sacrifices and prayers.

Head bowed, I eased my way behind Sir Bleoberis, Sir Lionel, and Sir Kay, until I stood directly, but inconspicuously, behind the Moorish knight. He did not notice me behind him, but seemed to be praying. But he appeared to be agitated, and began rocking impatiently back and forth.

He shifted in what I interpreted as a guilty manner. He turned to his brother on his right, but Sir Safer's head was bowed and his eyes piously closed. He glanced over to Sir Kay on his left and spoke in low tones into his ear, but not low enough to escape my hearing.

"Sir Patrise, he was on the crusade, was he not?"

Kay, who made it his business to know the gossip on every knight in Camelot, whispered back, "True. He was retainer to a French lord who went to Jerusalem under the banner of God-frey of Boullion. They say he distinguished himself against the infidel."

"Ah. I had thought it," replied the former infidel.

"Sanctus, sanctus, sanctus Dominus Deus Sabaoth! Pleni sunt co-eli et terra gloria tua. Hosanna in excelsis!"

Holy, holy, holy Lord God of hosts! Heaven and earth are full of your glory. Hosanna in the highest!

It took a moment for the implication of what I was hearing to sink in. Sir Patrise had been a part of the great heaven-blessed host that had descended upon the lands of the Saracens and won back those holy places for Christ. Was this what I had been looking for? Could it be that Sir Palomides's quarrel with the dead Irish knight had been not personal but communal? That it had to do with Sir Patrise's participation in the crusade that may have ravaged the Moor's homeland? Was that participation enough to murder him for?

"*Benedictus qui venit in nomine Domine. Hosanna in excelsis!*"

Blessed is he that cometh in the name of the Lord. Hosanna in the highest!

An army had marched on Jerusalem in the name of the Lord. Savage fighting with the Moors of those lands had finally wrenched Jerusalem and the rest of the Holy Land from Saracen hands. Where had Sir Palomides been? Had he taken part in the fighting on the side of the infidels? Or was he already converted to the true faith by then? When and how had he been christened? I didn't know the details, but perhaps Merlin did. I couldn't wait to find the old man and tell him what I'd learned.

"It was his wife, you know," came a voice from behind me, apparently attempting to be quiet but loud enough for me to hear it clearly. I glanced very cautiously over my right shoulder, keeping my head bowed the whole time, and saw Sir Pinel speaking in private with Sir Breunor, "La Cote Male Taile."

"Suspected? Or confirmed?" Sir Breunor wanted to know.

"I had heard that he was seen leaving her rooms when Sir Ironside was away from the castle."

"But rumor is not necessarily truth."

"I only repeat what I heard. I do not say it is the truth. But if you ask me"—Sir Pinel le Savage now had a confidential tone in his whispering—"the Red Knight believed it."

"Of course he believed it. The man sees everything as a threat. Ask Sir Gareth."

"Nevertheless, the Red Knight has made no secret of his hatred for the Irish."

"Hush now, he's reached the *Agnus Dei*."

"*Agnus Dei, qui tollis peccata mundi dona eis requiem.*"

O Lamb of God, that takest away the sins of the world, Grant them rest.

Sir Pinel's comments gave me such a start that I wanted to smack myself in the head and rail on my own stupidity. How could I have forgotten? Sir Ironside, the Red Knight of the Red Lands, had spent much of the time at the queen's feast—at least much of the time I was around him—complaining about the Irish in general and Sir Patrise and Sir Mador in particular. If there was bad blood between the Red Knight and Sir Patrise, that was definitely motive for the murder. Jealousy over his wife?

Men had killed for less. And been killed. The wife may have been innocent as a lamb, as La Cote Male Taile implied, but that was never proof against jealousy. I was certainly not as clever as Merlin, but it looked to me as though we had two clear suspects now, and two pretty good motives. Sir Palomides still had the means and opportunity, though, so he remained chief suspect to my mind. But those sins of the world that our bishop was suggesting had been taken away certainly seemed all around me at the moment.

"Lux aeterna luceat eis Domine cum sanctis tuis in aeternum: quia piuses."

Let everlasting light shine on them, O Lord with your saints forever: for thou art merciful.

Now I could barely wait for the service to be over, so that I could get to Merlin's cave and share with him what I had found out. I started to gaze around the nave impatiently, to see whether perhaps there was something else I had forgotten about that unpleasant banquet. That was when I noticed them, standing in the back among a group of artisans from the town of Caerleon that had crowded into the rear of the church to witness the noble's funeral rites. I would have failed to see them altogether if it hadn't been for a beam of light from outside that must have broken through the clouds and shone through a stained-glass window.

From the window in the side aisle, depicting Jesus with Mary Magdalene in the garden after his resurrection, light burst through the glass and cast a blue glow on four nuns in Benedictine habits bowed in prayer in the rear of the church.

Nuns! Sisters, no doubt, of the Convent of Saint Mary Magdalene. Had they some acquaintance with Sir Patrise? Or were they sent by the convent as a public sign of sympathy and support for the castle in its time of mourning? Or did they merely happen to be in Caerleon that morning and decided to come in to see the spectacle of this elaborate funeral? Whatever the case, I couldn't help remembering what Roger had told Merlin and me yesterday about the nun who had brought the dill from the convent kitchens the day of the feast. Sister Anne? Sister Agatha? Anyway, that one. Perhaps one of these nuns was the one. Perhaps the one that seemed the most moved. The nun second from the left as I looked at the group was younger than the others, no more than nineteen or twenty I calculated, with a narrow aquiline nose and large, dark brown eyes that seemed lined now heavily with red. Her head was bowed and she seemed to be praying earnestly and with great vigor. I was intrigued.

Sister Agnes! That was what the name had been. Was this Sister Agnes herself in back of the church? I had to find out, but I had a huge crowd of bodies to weave my way through before I could get near to those nuns. As I began working my way to the rear of the nave, I could hear the final words of the mass leaving the bishop's lips:

"Tremens factus sum ego et timeo, dum discussion venerit atque venture ira: quando coeli movendi sunt et terra."

I am seized with fear and trembling until the trial is at hand and the wrath to come: when the heavens and earth shall be shaken.

Amen and amen, I said to myself. The queen's trial was getting closer by the day. The wrath to come, in her case, was most certainly Sir Mador's. And she needed delivering, badly. Were these nuns a key to that deliverance? Was anything I had heard or seen today a key? I felt a kind of slow panic rising from my guts. There were too many clues, too many things to sort out. Maybe none of them was pointing to the real killer. A picture flashed in my mind unbidden of the queen tied to a stake screaming in agony as flames engulfed her beautiful flesh. The press of people was making it hard to breathe. I grew light-headed.

I began shoving people discourteously to make my way to the door and into the fresh air. After what seemed an eternity I reached the portal and stumbled out into the sunshine.

At last! I could breathe again. I leaned back against the archway framing the church's main doors and drew in deep breaths as I looked about. The streets were wet and muddy from the rain, but the sky was clearing, and everywhere I could see bright sunlight reflected off tiny puddles like so many mirrors reflecting back the eye of heaven. Nothing could escape that all-penetrating eye. There was for me some comfort in that.

I realized then that people had been steadily trickling out of the church. I had no desire to go back in, knowing that the only thing I would be missing now would be the actual interment, the lowering of the lead casket into the vault in the floor of the cathedral. I had no desire to be reminded that such a fate could well be Guinevere's in just over a week's time.

But I did want to catch those nuns if I could. I looked back through the open door to see nothing but a crowd of people on its way out. As they poured forth into the street I was swept along with them, looking about all the time to see whether I could spot the Benedictine habits. But it was no use. I couldn't see them anywhere. I was just about ready to give up, and had convinced myself that what I needed now more than anything was to find Merlin and to share with him what had been going on. But just as I had determined to start for the woods, a hand grabbed my elbow.

"Not so fast, Gildas, my lad," Robin urged. "You told me you wanted me to tell you if anything strange was happening."

My eyes widened at that. Something else was going on that I had missed? I didn't know if I had any room in my head for any more clues, but asked him anyway, "You've heard something? What is it?"

"I don't know whether it means anything or not," Robin confided, "but it struck me as odd. Nearly everybody has left the church, but me and the lads had to finish lowering that godawful lead casket into the ground. So I'm late coming out but I pass Sir Ywain and he's talking to Sir Agravain. And he seems pretty stressed, you understand? Like he's really worried about something. And he says 'the horse was ready and he left right away. I told him I'd go with him but he left too soon, and he hasn't come back.' And that's when Agravain saw me, and he puts his hand on Ywain's arm like this, you know." Robin touched my forearm. "Like as if to say keep still, the walls have ears, you know? Now what do you suppose that was all about?"

"Don't know," I admitted. "I can't see that it has anything to do with Sir Patrise. But I'll tell Merlin. Maybe he'll be able to figure it out."

"Well, you'd better be right about him, that's all I can say. Now I've got to bugger off. The archers are supposed to march in formation back to the castle. You help that old mage to get it figured out, will you? We're counting on him."

"That I will," I answered, and turned to find the way back to Merlin's cave. I hoped he would be somewhat easier to rouse this time around.

CHAPTER EIGHT:
DEATH TO THE INFIDEL

"Yes, we were most assuredly present when Jerusalem fell to the Franks—both my brother and myself," Sir Safer confided to us. The solar in the castle was dimly lit by flickering candlelight. It reflected off his shining mahogany face and made his eyes sparkle, two points of mirrored fire against a field of black. "I only wish he were here to tell you the story himself, for he feels it deeply."

When I had finally been able to rouse Merlin, we had dropped in at the knights' rooms in the castle around compline two days after the funeral, thinking that might be the best time to find Sir Palomides at home, but we were disappointed in that. His brother was available, however, and seemed more than willing to talk to us. Word had obviously got around that Merlin had been set the task of investigating the untimely death of Sir Patrise. Everyone involved in the incident seemed more than willing, under the circumstances, to help out, if for no other reason than to broadcast their own innocence. Sir Safer had invited us in and treated us with all courtesy. Whether he knew why Merlin might be asking questions about the siege of Jerusalem I don't know, but it was a subject he seemed to warm to.

"We were new to the profession of bearing arms at the time. I don't know whether you are aware that Sir Palomides and my humble self were born in Ethiopia, but our parents emigrated to Egypt when we were young. The Fatimids were a powerful dynasty and we believed able to withstand any kind of threat.

We were disturbed when the Seljuk Turks took possession of Palestine, for we—that is, my brother and I—believed the holy places there should be in the hands of those who would treat them with respect and allow open access to pilgrims, whether Muslim, Jewish, or Christian. And so we were glad when the Fatimids regained control of Jerusalem. We subsequently went to the holy city as personal bodyguards in the service of Iftikhar al-Dawla, governor of the city on behalf of the Fatimids."

"And you were there, then, when the crusading army laid siege to the city?" Merlin prodded. He was back in one of his overexcited moods, in which he was avid to learn everything he could from any source, and learn it quickly. When I had stopped in at his cave that morning, he was ready to go and eager to hear about any information I had gleaned from my eavesdropping at the funeral service. He agreed that we must find out whether Sir Patrise's involvement with the crusading army was motive enough for Sir Palomides to commit murder. But he also wanted to interview the Red Knight of the Red Lands, and to visit the Convent of Saint Mary Magdalene to talk to Sister Agnes. And he wanted to do it all today.

Unfortunately, Sir Ironside was on a hunting trip, and a trip to the convent had to be arranged in advance, the abbess being rather strict about visitors. We sent word to Madame Hildegard, prioress of the convent, that we would like an interview next Tuesday, and she had graciously consented. So by default we were only able to focus on Sir Palomides for the time being.

"We were indeed in the city when the Frankish army came," Sir Safer answered. "Actually, we had felt no fear. The Fatimids were on good terms with the Byzantine emperor, and he was Christian. We assumed the Franks would be under his direction, and expected no trouble—especially when al-Afdal (that is, the vizier) promised to allow two hundred pilgrims at a time to visit the holy places.

"But we were wrong. The Franks kept coming. We expelled all Christians from the city in anticipation of the siege, for there would be fewer mouths to feed. We filled all the cisterns with water. We had herded all the sheep and cattle from the surrounding countryside into the walls of the city to provide us with food. And we had word that an army of reinforcements was coming from Egypt if we could hold out that long. We had every confidence that we could.

"Al-Dawla ordered all the wells around the city poisoned, so that if they attempted a siege they would be unable to sustain it for lack of water. The surrounding countryside was denuded of any trees as well, in order to prevent the Franks from building siege engines. But it was all to no avail. The Franks brought water in from the Jordan River. And two Genoese galleys arrived in the port of Jaffa bearing wood for the building of machines. The Franks brought that wood in, and they also had the luck to find the caves where the Fatimid army had hidden the wood from their own siege engines used the year before when they freed the city from the Turks. That gave the Franks both water and wood, and that meant we were in for a terrible siege."

"What happened to you and to Sir Palomides when the fighting started?" Merlin asked, encouraging him to go on, though Sir Safer needed little prompting.

"The Franks laid siege to the city for six weeks. They tried an assault on the walls with scaling ladders during the first week, but we repulsed them fairly easily with stones and boiling oil. So they retreated and bided their time. Still we were confident that the Egyptian army would reach us in time.

"But as the month of *sha'bān* wore on, we were shocked one day to see two great wheeled siege towers appear. We had no idea they had got the wood together to construct these, and the Franks had kept them hidden until they were complete. One tower was brought in to face the north wall of the city, the other to the south wall near Mount Sion. Iftikhar ordered those sections of the city reinforced, and ordered a steady bombardment of the towers with stones and with Greek fire."

"And where were you and Sir Palomides in all of this?"

"We were, as I have mentioned, personally attached to Iftikhar, and so we went wherever he went. He himself commanded the garrison set to defend the south wall, that being deemed the weaker. The attack began in earnest on the evening of 20 *sha'bān*. The Franks endeavored first to bring the wooden towers right up to the walls. Count Raymond of Toulouse commanded the Franks attacking the south wall, and we hammered his forces continually with great stones and liquid fire to keep them from the walls. We kept them thus at bay for a whole day, and into the next—they were never able to establish their position on our side of the city. At last, we succeeded in setting the tower itself on fire, and cheered as it burnt down, killing all of the Franks inside.

"But it was not enough. No sooner had the tower burnt than we heard a greater cheer coming from the direction of the north wall—and the cheer was coming from Frankish throats. A messenger arrived, breathless and exhausted from the heavy fighting, and begging for our help. The wall had been breached, he said. The Duke Godfrey had used the north wind to his advantage. He had ordered his troops to set stacks of straw ablaze and let the wind carry the black smoke into the faces of the defenders on the north wall. So thick was the smoke that the defenders had to abandon their positions on the wall in order to breathe.

"That was when the Duke Godfrey's men succeeded in placing long wooden beams from the siege engine to the top of the wall. It was enough to hold them as they rushed across the bridge and into the city.

"Iftikhar sent half his troops to reinforce the north wall. But by then it was truly too late. The Franks coming across the bridge, along with the black smoke, had scattered the defenders on that side of the city, and that allowed more and more of the enemy to breach the wall with scaling ladders. So many had entered the city, and so routed were our forces before Iftikhar's reinforcements arrived, that a group of Franks was able to throw open the North Gate—the same that the Franks named the Gate of St. Stephen—and at that all the army rushed in, infantry and cavalry alike. Knights on horseback were riding down the citizens, mutilating them with swords and great war-axes, and sparing no one—not women, not old men, not babes in arms. The streets ran with blood."

"What did you do? How did you escape?" I piped up. Merlin, caught up in Sir Safer's account, did not even bother to glare at me.

"When we saw how things stood, Iftikhar led us to the Mihrab Dawud, the Oratory of David you would say, a strong tower in the citadel. It guarded a substantial treasure, something that Iftikhar must have had in mind when he chose that place of defense. We barricaded ourselves in the tower and we fought on. The Franks could not penetrate that stronghold. But from there we could see the horror that was taking place in the streets. Marauders from within the city had now opened the South Gate and let in the Count of Toulouse and his army, so that the citizens who fled from the north now encountered more merciless Franks pouring in from the south. The people ran in panic in every direction, screaming in terror and in agony as they were pursued and hacked to pieces by Frankish swords.

"That all took place on *22 sha'bān* of the year four ninety-two—what you would call July fifteenth of ten ninety-nine. Over the next few days, we held out in the tower, but the Franks pillaged the city. They entered into every private home, slaughtering anyone they found hiding, whether man, woman, or child. Having dispatched the occupants and thrown their mutilated bodies into the street, a knight would set up his shield and coat of arms before the house, claiming it as his own residence by right of conquest.

"I understand, though of course I could not see it from the tower, that the Franks defiled the Mosque of Umar, that is, the Dome of the Rock from which the prophet Muhammad is said to have ascended into heaven. It is said that they stole some forty great silver candelabra, another hundred and fifty silver candelabra, plus a magnificent silver lamp that weighed more than forty pounds. A fortune in silver and a profanation of the mosque.

"But that was not the greatest enormity committed in those days. The citizens of Jerusalem, those who had not been cut down on the streets or slaughtered in their homes, all fled for the most part to the Masjid al-Aqsa in what you would call the temple district. That part of the city was protected by walls and towers, but the Franks forced their way in and massacred everyone they found, slaughtering indiscriminately. I have heard that ten thousand souls were sent to Allah on that day, speaking only of those in the temple area. These included those who fled there as well as those pious souls who had moved to the holy place to live an ascetic life as imams or religious scholars. No one survived."

"No one but you, it seems." Merlin looked at him with curiosity from under his bristling tangle of eyebrows.

"We fought on from the tower. Our arrows kept the Franks from storming the barricade, and if any got close we had stones enough to discourage them. But we did not have food and water enough to hold out indefinitely. Eventually we would be too weak to fight. But what was our alternative? We saw from the tower citizens of the place begging for mercy one moment and lying decapitated the next, their severed heads bouncing in the blood-soaked gutter. Nor could we hope to hold the tower against an onslaught of the entire Frankish army. There were perhaps a score of us and many thousands of them. Our only comfort, if comfort it was, was to resolve grimly that we would not be taken cheaply—that each of us would take several Franks with him to meet Allah.

"Iftikhar had another hope, though. He still commanded some respect even from the Franks, as the representative of the Fatimid Empire. And he understood, as well, the twisted Frankish concept of honor, which would allow them to dismember a child barely weaned from the breast, but would never under any circumstances allow them to go back on their word. And he understood greed.

"He appealed to the knight who seemed most honorable of all those commanding the southwest part of the city, the one who appeared to him to be in command of that army, Count Raymond.

"The Tower of David contained a fair amount of treasure. Since such booty seemed a major concern of the Franks, Iftikhar promised Count Raymond to surrender to him the tower and all its treasures in exchange for sparing his life and the lives of his retainers within, and a promise of safe passage out of the city. Raymond agreed, and pledged his truth that no harm would come to us. At that word, we surrendered the tower and received an escort from Count Raymond out of Jerusalem and through the enemy lines.

"How shall I describe to you the carnage that polluted the streets of that holy city? We walked out of the tower into a street littered with pieces of bodies—limbs, severed heads—and mutilated torsos in unrecognizable condition. There were places we could not step without treading on some human body part, and the blood was ankle-deep in some areas. And this was before

Jay Ruud

we knew of the even greater slaughter in Masjid al-Aqsa. Nor did we know, then, that all the Jews in the city, who had run to their synagogue to escape the brutality of the Franks, had been slaughtered without mercy as well when the Franks set fire to the building. They died in agony in the flames. We were the only ones of all the thousands of souls in that holy place to escape alive.

"I was sick at the sight of those corpses, as was my brother, and half of the guard. We added our vomit to the filth filling that street. But my biggest shock was not the extent of the slaughter. It was in seeing the Frankish knights when they knew that the battle was over and that the holy city was in their hands unchallenged. For they were embracing each other and weeping tears of joy. Some were on their knees in the blood-soaked earth praying with ardent fervor.

"That was when it hit me. I understood now. This was for them *jihad*—a holy war. Their holy men—their Peter the Hermit and the others—had whipped them into a frenzy. They believed with all their hearts that their God had sanctified this war and more, sanctified the punishment of the citizens who dared live in their holy city. If any of those knights felt horror or shame at that abomination, they did not show it then. Perhaps later, in the cold light of reason, some might see the enormity of their crime—"

"Your sorrow at what you saw there must have smoldered in you for years," Merlin finally interrupted. "How could you remember that day without rage?"

Sir Safer shrugged. "It changed us, both my brother and me. We mounted our horses and were led out of the city and through the Frankish lines. We followed Iftikhar to Ascalon, where there was an Egyptian garrison. By then it was night, and we rode in silence through the dark, thankful that no one could see our tears. But we no longer had a taste for war. We left Iftikhar's

104

service soon after that, and began our long wandering as knights-errant, which eventually brought us to this place. But it was not rage we felt. It was bewilderment. We could not understand the ways of Allah. We could not penetrate the mysteries of those horrors. At least that was my feeling. My brother perhaps felt more strongly . . ."

"Strong feelings of hatred for any Christians involved in the conquest of the city? Hatred strong enough to kill any one of those knights he felt deserved his rage? Would your brother resort to murder if he felt it was just punishment for the massacre?"

"Why don't you ask him yourself, old man?" Sir Palomides's booming, low voice spoke from the doorway. He stood poised, a green cape pushed back by one arm on his hip and the other on the hilt of his sword. The hood lay pushed off his head as well, so that his glaring eyes that fixed Merlin in their gaze stood out all too sharply beneath his dark, lowering brow.

He was a formidable figure, and at the sight and sound of him I took a step back and swallowed audibly. Merlin, however, was not easily intimidated, nor was he ever at a loss as far as I had seen. His reaction to Sir Palomides was congenial and welcoming and, I hoped, disarmingly courteous. "Ah, Sir Palomides, how fortunate that we have been able to find you. You know my young companion, Gildas, I assume?"

"I know you, old man." Palomides brushed aside the common niceties. "We have not seen you in Camelot for some five years or more. Now you come only to pry into the private lives of good knights? Go back to your water-wench. Or go bother only recreant knights. We have no guilty secrets here, and that cannot be said of some of your other Camelot elite."

I felt my ears turning red. He was striking close to home, implying something about the queen perhaps? I bit my tongue. Sir Kay, Sir Gareth, Sir Bors, even Sir Gawain—all who had been present at the banquet—were suspicious of the queen because of the murder. How could I have expected anything else from the Moor?

"You know, my lord," Merlin continued, as usual undeterred, "I have been entrusted by the king to find the truth behind the sudden and unlooked-for death of Sir Patrise. Because of that you will understand that I am speaking to the knights who were present at the queen's banquet. I must say, I do not believe that the queen is guilty of this crime. The queen had nothing to gain from the death of Sir Patrise, does not seem to have known him other than by name and by sight, and had no apparent reason to hate him or want to harm him. Therefore I am trying to determine what relationship the various knights had with him."

Palomides snorted, relaxed his aggressive stance, and strolled more casually into the room. "As to that, there's not much I can tell you. I hardly knew him myself. He was, as you know, fairly new to Camelot. He was Irish, I had heard. But I had scarce spoken to him before he died."

"It's the truth," Sir Safer said, nodding. "He had befriended a few knights. His cousin Sir Mador, of course, and Sir Dinadan—who was not at the feast—and, oh, I believe Sir Bedivere as well. But he was not close to any whom we call good friends. It was only yesterday, at the requiem, for example, that we learned he had been at the siege of Jerusalem."

"And how did that make you feel, Sir Palomides? I should think had I been through what you experienced in the crusade, there must have been some resentment."

"One cannot resent the dead," Sir Palomides said matter-of-factly. "I was not aware of his service to Duke Godfrey in that campaign until yesterday, as my brother says. Still, that would not have been my feeling. I heard Sir Safer telling you as I came in that we both felt bewildered and lost after the massacre of Jerusalem. That is most true. We saw to what extremes religious fervor could push people in the faces of the crusaders at the slaughter. And we saw how little our faith in Allah protected the women and children of Jerusalem. We felt lost and empty. We did not hate. We were dead inside. We wandered aimlessly until we found a home under King Arthur, and found some meaning to our existence in the idea of arms used only in the service of right.

"And as for me, I have even regained a kind of faith again. In any case, as you well know, I have been baptized. I cannot answer for my brother in that area . . ."

Sir Safer shrugged. It was clear that his own faith in anything other than the ideals of Arthurian chivalry was still dead, or at least largely unconscious.

"But why, after what you saw Christians doing at the siege of Jerusalem, would you convert to Christianity?" Merlin asked, honestly confused.

Now it was Sir Palomides's turn to shrug. "I do not think of the men who committed those atrocities as Christians," he answered. "They were fanatics. Fanatics can appear in any faith. Besides, I could not hate all Christians and want them dead because of the actions of a few. I had seen enough killing to resolve that I never wanted to see killing ever again. Even now the thought makes my gorge rise, as it did that night I saw Sir Patrise fall.

"Besides," he added. "I discovered yesterday that I had more reason to love Sir Patrise than I ever could have imagined."

"Really?" Merlin's curiosity was piqued now. "Why on earth do you say that?"

Instead of answering immediately, Sir Palomides strode purposefully to a small writing desk in the corner of the room. Without saying a word, he took up a piece of parchment and placed it into Merlin's hands. I looked over his shoulder as he began to read aloud:

107

To Isolde

When the winter melts away
And spring is at hand
Then small birds sing sweetly in every tree
And Love's force renews itself in me
As well as in the land,
And to my lady-love I pray.

Alas! She will have none of me
And yet I serve her will.
My lady will not deign to look my way
Nor will she hear a single word I say
I sit in sorrow still,
Her Daunger won't let my true love be.

My sickness seems to have no cure,
My wound will not be healed.
Have mercy on my pain or I must die!
But I cannot bear the look in my Love's eye,
My fate has been sealed.
Without her love my death is sure.

When I lie dead inform my Love
"Here lies the truest heart
That ever served you faithfully and true.
For his death all the world throws blame on you.
Death had to be his part,
The only way his love to prove."

I scratched my head, failing to see what exactly this poem had to do with Sir Patrise, or anything else we had been talking about. But Merlin seemed a few steps ahead of me.

"Isolde?" he asked. "Wife of King Mark of Cornwall? That Isolde?"

"The same." Sir Palomides's dark cheek grew darker as the blood rushed into it. "I know that it is not customary to name one's lady in poems written to her, but my love is not secret and besides, the poem is not likely to be delivered. I have written her dozens over the years, but she will not acknowledge me. She loves Sir Tristram. It is common knowledge to all but King Mark. But she is true to Tristram. How could I want my love to be untrue? I love her because of her virtues, and her truth is a virtue.

"When I first came into this country, I did great feats of arms. I entered tournaments and even unhorsed Sir Tristram himself, to try to get her to at least notice me. I was baptized more for her sake than for any other reason. I've told you my feelings about religion, but if faith in her God will win me her heart, I am willing to try it. But clearly I am frustrated. You, old man, must understand my pain better than anyone. Your own frustrations in love with the maid Nimue are legendary in Camelot."

"Frustrations? Dotages, I believe, would be the word more commonly used when that affair is spoken of. But I understand you, certainly, and can sympathize as well as anyone with your lovesick pain. But tell us, what does all of this have to do with Sir Patrise? You spoke of having reason to love him."

"Sir Patrise was of Ireland, as you know. And of a noble family. The youngest son of a noble family. His eldest brother inherited the lands and estate of their father, while the second son made a career in the church. Sir Patrise joined the army of Duke Godfrey in hopes of carving out for himself some new estate in the Holy Land. Like most knights, he returned from that place without achieving that dream. But the Lady Isolde . . . as you know, she is the daughter of the king of Ireland. Sir

Patrise's father was nephew to the king. That is, Sir Patrise is the near kinsman of my beloved lady. I could no more have harmed him than I could make a river run backwards. I only wish I had more opportunity to know him.

"I hold no rancor in my heart for any man. It is true I lost any meaning my life had when Jerusalem fell and I saw the carnage that was the price paid for the conquest. But I have a new lord in King Arthur and a new lady in my Queen Isolde. The ideals of chivalry and of love give me reason to go on in life."

We walked silently down the passageway in the castle that led to the queen's quarters. Merlin was pensive and walked with his head bowed, and I ached to find out what was going on behind those bushy eyebrows. I was about to take the chance of interrupting his thoughts when that became unnecessary.

"God's bodykins," he blurted out, stopping in mid stride and shaking his head. "He's an inscrutable devil, this Palomides. Pulled that love poem out of nowhere. That threw me, let me tell you."

"Do you buy it, Merlin? You think he wouldn't have harmed Sir Patrise because of his Irishness and all, being related to his lady-love?"

"But he said himself, or his brother said, that he didn't know anything about Sir Patrise until the funeral. If it's true, as I have no reason to doubt, that Patrise was indeed kinsman to Queen Isolde, Palomides would not have known about it before the murder. So it doesn't excuse him."

"Good Lord you're right. I didn't even put that together."

"The story of the siege of Jerusalem seems motive enough for anyone who had been there to hate the crusaders who committed the atrocities. Sir Safer's account of the battle was vivid enough to show that no matter how much time has passed or how much his circumstances have changed, he has neither forgotten nor forgiven what happened in those days."

"But by the same token," I put in as we resumed the walk, "if Palomides did not, according to his word, know Sir Patrise had been in Godfrey's army, then there was no motive for him there."

"And for that, we have not only the testimony of him and his brother, but also the fact that you yourself heard him asking about it at the funeral. However"—Merlin stopped to consider—"how certain can you be that you were not marked? Think of it. Sir Palomides had to know that you were helping me with the investigation into the murder. Sir Kay would have been sure to tell him, and as you say, he was talking there with Kay. Now let's say he observes you as you slip behind him. What better opportunity for him to stage a question to which he already knew the answer, in order to throw us off from suspecting him of the very motive that drove him to the murderous act?"

My mind boggled at that. The observer of the suspects—that is, me—creates a situation where nothing he sees can be believed because he affects all of the suspects' actions. How could I trust anything to be real? How could Merlin?

"So everything we just heard—or everything I've heard in the past three days—could be false?"

"False, or at the least colored for our benefit. We need to be very careful of what we believe and what we do not. But as for Sir Palomides, my gut feeling is that he can be trusted. Isolde or no Isolde, the long years since Jerusalem appear to have mellowed him, and I have not known him to be violent before, except in the tournaments. He came to Camelot too late to fight in any of Arthur's wars. And besides, Patrise was not the only knight in Camelot who was at the siege of Jerusalem. There are perhaps three or four others whom he must have known about long ago who have never been harmed. I don't believe we can drop Palomides from the list of suspects altogether, but we certainly need to check other possibilities."

"I hate to say it, but what about Sir Safer?"

"The two are close. If one is guilty, then the odds are very good that both are. But we need to look farther afield."

"And that would mean . . . Sir Ironside?"

But when I looked up at Merlin, I was shocked by what I saw. The old man looked pale and sickly. He reached out to me to lean on my shoulder as he sank to the floor, breathing heavily. His hands moved up to cradle his forehead, and I noticed his eyes for the first time. One was nearly closed, but the other bulged out like an egg, almost a thing with a mind of its own. He was moaning softly as he sat, weak and slumped on the stone floor of the castle.

"Merlin! Are you all right? What is it? Are you ill? Shall I get the king's physician?"

"Listen," came a voice from deep in his throat that hardly sounded like his own. "These things must come to pass. The great bear is brought down by the pack of curs. But that is long past. Listen to the lion."

"What? What are you saying? I don't underst—"

But now he had passed out altogether, and slumped down on the cold floor. No one else was around, and I ran down the hall for Sir Gareth.

CHAPTER NINE:
THE TALE OF SIR GARETH

Sir Gareth sat resting comfortably with his back against the closed door of the queen's quarters. He had taken his sword out of his sheath and placed it by his side so that it was within easy reach if he needed to be suddenly on his guard. Also, to tell the truth, it was a lot more comfortable to sit on the floor without his sword getting in the way.

He had a bottle of Flemish wine that his brother Gaheris had brought him to help him pass the time during the long watch. The bottle was almost full, but my guess was that Gaheris had taken another, empty bottle away when he had brought this one to Gareth. The long hours of standing guard on a woman who refused to leave her room were beginning to seem quite dull, and Gareth welcomed the opportunity to spend some time talking to another human being.

I sat on the floor myself, leaning against the door next to Gareth, crossing my legs in front of me. A candelabrum stood on the floor in front of us, creating a little island of light in the dark corridor. Gareth tipped the bottle up and took a long drink of the wine, then passed it to me with a great show of camaraderie, patting my back with the close friendship of a new-found drinking buddy.

When Merlin had collapsed with the pain in his head, Gareth, leaving Gaheris to guard the queen, had come back with me and together we had carried Merlin into my room in the queen's quarters. We had lain him down and made him as comfortable as he could be, and then left him to try to sleep through the pain.

"So the old man has these kinds of attacks often, does he?" Gareth asked me as he took the bottle back from me and held it up for another swig.

"Well, he told me they come upon him. And he said, too, that they pass again after a few hours, maybe. It's the headaches that gave him the reputation of being a seer."

"How so?" Gareth snuggled his back comfortably into the door, as if he was settling in for a long chat.

"He sees things, hears voices, when he has these spells. He speaks the words but doesn't always know what he's saying, and it's never anything stated clearly. It's always some cryptic message that nobody can figure out until after it happens, and then they say 'Ah! Merlin foresaw this! See how his prophecy fits the events now?' "

"So did he see anything this time?"

"I guess he must have. He muttered something about a bear and a lion and some wolves or dogs or something. It sure didn't mean anything that I could understand."

"Lions? Bears? Sounds like a bunch of gibberish to me."

"Yes," I answered. "So it was something like 'the dogs attack the bear, and the lion is talking.' "

Sir Gareth scratched his head and twisted his face up as if in deep thought. "So the lion is the king of beasts, right? Suppose old Uncle Arthur is the lion, then. The dogs are attacking the bear. Well, everybody's attacking Guinevere, right? Maybe she's the bear, and everybody's supposed to listen to Arthur and leave her alone."

"So the queen is the bear, then? Why would the queen be symbolized by a bear?"

"Maybe because *bare* is how the king likes her best!" Gareth collapsed into writhing laughter at his own witticism. Okay, he was kind of drunk and getting drunker; otherwise I wouldn't have let him get away with that kind of insult to the honor of my lady the queen.

"Look, my young friend Gildas of Cornwall." Sir Gareth now put his arm around my shoulders and pulled me to him in a conspiratorial manner. "Tell me, how's this 'secret' investigation going? You and the old necromancer finding out any dirt on any of my fellow paragons of chivalry? Got the murderer dead to rights yet?"

Now Gareth, like every other knight who had been at the banquet, was probably a suspect as far as Merlin was concerned. And from what I had heard around the castle, our investigation was not exactly a popular one. So just how much I could trust Sir Gareth of Orkney was a difficult question at the moment. But the king trusted him with the honor and safety of the queen. And Merlin himself seemed perfectly comfortable with him, calling him by that fond nickname—what was it? Beaumains? Pretty hands? What was that all about? In any case, I decided it couldn't hurt to let Gareth know whom we had been thinking about as possible suspects at least. Perhaps he could even shed some light on some of them. He certainly knew them better than I did, and perhaps better than Merlin did. So I took a chance and cautiously told Gareth what we had been doing.

"We kind of had an idea that Sir Palomides, the Saracen knight, might have been involved. I'm not so sure that's going anywhere, though. Then there's Sir Ironside. There's a chance he might have had something against Sir Patrise, but we're not really sure what. I guess you could say we haven't ruled anybody out."

"Including me I suppose?" Sir Gareth's eyebrows lifted and his face opened up into an even more innocent look. It was hard to imagine he was anything but what he appeared to be: an open and sincere devotee of the chivalric ideal. Who was, at the moment, letting his hair down a bit.

But his face darkened and his blond eyebrows lowered over his now thoughtful blue eyes. "Sir Palomides is a noble knight. I have never known him to act dishonorably. Oh, I've seen him display his anger and frustration on occasion, especially in tournaments and specifically against Sir Tristram . . . Oh yes, their rivalry is not exactly a secret among the knights," he said with a short laugh at the surprise my face must have portrayed. "But Sir Ironside—the Red Knight of the Red Lands—*he* is a different story altogether."

I remembered now hearing something about how Sir Gareth knew things that could discredit Sir Ironside. Where had I heard it? It didn't matter. Now, in preparation for questioning the Red Knight, I wanted to learn everything I could about him. And Gareth seemed to be in a mood to talk, so I encouraged him. "What is his story? And how do you know it?"

"It's a well-known story. Others could tell you as well, but it's true that I was most directly involved. But there was a time—oh, some ten years past I suppose it must be by now—when the Red Knight of the Red Lands was a notorious renegade knight. My wife, the Lady Lyonesse—you have not met her I suppose? She lives in our castle, a fine castle that has been in her family for generations. It is our home. I live there most of the year, when I am not in attendance on the king, my uncle. But what was I saying? Oh, Sir Ironside." His lip curled into a sneer of disgust. "Sir Ironside had besieged my lady Lyonesse's castle. He insisted that she must marry him and waged war on any good knights who tried to come to the lady's rescue. He fought and defeated forty knights in single combat who came to deliver her. And he treated them shamefully, without pity or mercy. Once he had defeated them, he hanged them by the necks like dogs, would hear no pleas for leniency, and would not kill them honorably on the field of battle. When I saw them, their bodies

116

hung like dead branches from the trees around the castle, food for the carrion birds. He had hung their shields from their necks so that the corpses could be identified by those who knew the coats of arms. The man was said to have the strength of seven knights, and his skill at arms was unsurpassed. But he was a brute without the slightest idea of the meaning of courtesy."

"But why would he do that?" My head was spinning with the drink and with the new brutalities that had been laid open to me. It had truly been a day to speak of horrors.

"Jealousy. The Red Knight of the Red Lands was consumed by it. He wanted Lady Lyonesse and would not hear of any other man rescuing her. To him she was a beautiful object that he must possess or die in its pursuit—a beautiful object that no other man must ever have."

"Then Sir Ironside is quite capable of murder, you would say?"

"Capable? Hah! He's had more experience than anyone else I ever heard of, and takes great enjoyment in it."

"Why was he never brought to justice? If he could be held accountable for forty murders, shouldn't the law have dealt with him?"

"According to the laws of chivalry, he was quite within his rights," Sir Gareth explained. "He fought his challengers in broad daylight, and they fought him of their own free will. Their entering into single combat with him meant they knew what they were risking. Their lives were at his mercy if he defeated them at arms. And mercy he had none. Every knight after the first he killed must have been aware of that from the start, because of the bodies—the bodies they would have seen hanging from the trees."

"But all this for a woman?"

Gareth snorted at my naiveté. "The lengths a knight will go to for a woman are far beyond your ken, master Gildas of

117

Cornwall. But I'm sure you will learn that soon enough. In fact, though, you're right about Ironside in this case. There was more to it than his desire for Lyonesse. His jealousy was a bottomless pit of rage. For he also had an insanely virulent jealousy of Sir Lancelot and of my brother Sir Gawain, and he believed that if he kept killing good knights, and his reputation became powerful enough, King Arthur would have no choice but to send out either Lancelot or Gawain to fight with him."

"But why? Why was he so intent on fighting one of those two?"

Sir Gareth looked down, as if unsure of the answer. "He gave out that it was a request from a woman he had loved before, one whose brother had been killed by a knight of the round table. According to his story, this brother had been killed by Sir Lancelot or Sir Gawain. She did not know which. And therefore Sir Ironside had set his trap to catch and take revenge on one of those knights. So what he was saying was that no matter how churlish his behavior was, it was excusable within the code of chivalry because he was doing it for a woman.

"But I was never aware of any other woman in the picture beside Lady Lyonesse, and he surely wasn't doing all of this as something she wanted. And if he were a true knight, he would have treated all women courteously for the sake of his own beloved. No, I think what he really wanted was to beat one of those two great knights to make his reputation. Everything I ever knew him to do, he did out of jealousy: jealousy for Lyonesse, and jealousy of my brother's reputation, and of Sir Lancelot's. Oh, yes, I'm pretty sure he made up that revenge story on the spot when I had him at my mercy, to spare his own worthless life."

"You defeated him, then, after he had killed all of those other knights?"

Sir Gareth smiled with a bit of embarrassment. I could see

that he didn't want to boast, that being unbecoming a knight's courtesy, but that he really did want to tell me the story. So I coaxed him on. "Tell me about it. You won the Lady Lyonesse that way? Is that what happened?"

Gareth smiled coyly and took another swallow from his bottle. "It was when I first came to Camelot. Now keep in mind I was just a small toddler when my oldest brother, Gawain, first came to serve our uncle at the royal court. And he was in every way the premier knight of his time, before Sir Lancelot arrived. Gawain had not been home since, and wouldn't have recognized me when, fifteen years later, I decided to follow him here to Logres. My other brothers were in Arthur's service by then, except for Mordred, of course. He's still at home. But Agravain was not in the court, and Gaheris was off with him looking after the king's interests in Scotland, as I recall, so they were not here to recognize me or spoil my plan."

"What plan was that?"

"Getting to it, getting to it." Sir Gareth chortled and patted my shoulder. "I knew, you see, that if I arrived as the king's nephew and Gawain's brother, things would be easy for me. They'd make me a knight right away and everybody would give me all this respect and I wouldn't have done a blessed thing to earn it. So here was my plan, see? I'd come to Camelot as a stranger, and ask the king to take me in. Then I'd bide my time until some adventure or other presented itself, and that's when I'd take it on as a task, you know. And prove myself. Prove I was worthy of the knighthood and the respect, and then tell them who I was. You understand? I wanted my honor to come from my deeds, not from my parentage."

"That's true courtesy!" I chimed in, taking the bottle from him and having another swallow.

"True courtesy, by God, if ever I heard of it," Gareth agreed. "So I arrive at the court, see, and Arthur says to me, 'What is it

I can do for you, forsooth,' and all that. So I say to him, 'Oh, great lord and king of all chivalry, grant me three requests,' and I kneel there in front of him right there in the throne room. Well, you know, since the king started it by asking me what I wanted and all, I knew that if I asked him anything within reason, he'd have to grant it to me or lose face, right? So I ask him this, I say, 'Oh great and wise and glorious King Arthur,' and all that, 'first I ask that you give me food and drink and lodging for a year. And I reserve the right to make my other two requests some time during that year.'

"Well what can the king do? I've got him now, right? There's no way he can turn down a simple request for room and board, and now I've got the right to ask him pretty much anything I want later on. And of course what I'm going to ask him is for the right to take on the first big request that comes to the court. And the other thing I'm going to ask for is to be knighted, at the same time I take on that quest."

"Sounds like a good plan, I guess," I said to keep up my end, while I passed the bottle back to him again.

"I thought so. But you'd think I'd asked for the moon or something, because all hell broke loose in the throne room. Quite a few knights were in attendance on the king at the time. As soon as he granted me the food and lodging for the year, Sir Kay chimes up, and he starts talking through his blubbery fat lips like he does." Gareth thrust out his lower jaw and curled his lips up ape-like and imitated Kay's droning voice:

" 'This boy is nothing but a churl, to ask for something so ignoble. He sounds like a beggar at our door.' Well, Sir Lancelot, God bless him, and my brother Gawain, who must have seen some kind of family resemblance, they jumped on Kay right away and told him to stop it, because they thought this young man looked like he had some noble blood in him. Well, Kay kept after me, and swore if I'd been noble or had any true courtesy in me, I'd have asked for armor or a warhorse or something like that from the king. So Kay ends up doing this. He grabs me and says if I'm going to stay there for the year, I'm not going to loaf, and he says he's going to make me work in the kitchen."

"No! So that's where you learned all about our kitchens, eh? But what did the king say?"

"Well, Kay's his seneschal, and he's the one who runs the household, so he's the one who had to arrange for my room and board. And that was the way he wanted to do it. That's when he gave me the nickname 'Beaumains'—beautiful hands. Kay thought my hands showed I'd never worked a day in my life, and he was going to correct that problem. Gawain and Lancelot warned him it wasn't a good use of my qualities, but Kay just likes to be in control, you know?"

"Oh, yes, I know. That's his way. A kind way of saying he's a bully and nobody can stand him."

Gareth burst out laughing, so that wine started coming out of his nose. That must have burned a bit because his eyes teared up and he had a coughing fit. I was having trouble controlling my own laughter, but finally Gareth was able to continue.

"But let me get to the story," he finally choked out. "So I've been working in the kitchen for almost a whole year, and then one day I'm serving dinner at one of Arthur's feasts, and in comes this damsel. She's just arrived on a white palfrey and she comes into the great hall straight from leaving the horse with a groom outside. She's dressed in an expensive blue velvet gown, so I know that whoever she is she's got some wealth behind her. She breaks right in to the meal and demands that Arthur send somebody to rescue her sister, and I mean right now. The Red Knight of the Red Lands, she says, is besieging her sister in her castle and he's killed every knight who's come to rescue her. But she refuses to tell anybody her name or her sister's. She just demands that Lancelot or at least Gawain be sent to dispatch this Red Knight. Well, Arthur doesn't really like her tone or her manner, and he says he can't really help her if she won't even tell us her name. Now that's my opportunity."

"The quest you've been waiting for."

"Absolutely. I jump up and I remind Arthur that he's promised to give me two more boons, and I ask that he give me this quest as one of them. I'm pretty sure Arthur couldn't see that sending me to face a knight who had already killed a whole pile of others was much of a favor, but he'd promised long before and he couldn't back off now. And I also gave him my third request: to be knighted, and specifically by Sir Lancelot. I'd been in Camelot long enough to know that Lancelot was the greatest knight, the most courteous and the noblest, as well as the strongest in battle. Nobody had ever beaten him. Only a couple of knights—Sir Tristram and Sir Lamorak—had ever even unhorsed him."

"And were you knighted then and there?"

"Well, things got a little crazy then. The damsel—my loving sister-in-law Lynette—throws a tantrum about Arthur's insulting her by sending a kitchen boy to take care of her poor sister. So she stalks out of the great hall and gets on her horse and rides away. Well, all the time I've been in the kitchen, I've had a servant from back home standing by in Caerleon with a horse and armor for me, so I have to send for him really quickly so I can get armed and mounted and chase after Lynette, who's riding off in a huff. Now Sir Kay decides that he can't let me go because if I do succeed in this quest, he'll look like a fool because Lancelot and Gawain told him so when I first came to Camelot. So he calls for his horse and mounts up to chase after me. And now Lancelot, who the king has promised is going to knight me, is left standing there in the great hall wondering what it is he's supposed to do. So he figures he needs to come after me as well so as to do the knighting."

"But you did catch the sister-in-law?"

"Oh, yes. I caught up to her just about the time that Sir Kay caught up with me. And the first thing he does is challenge me, and tells me I need to acknowledge him as my master and get back to the kitchen or he's going to thrash me to show me some manners and teach me not to get all uppity and copy my betters. Well I tell him that I don't know him as my master but only as a rude, churlish knight who wouldn't know courtesy if it came up and bit him in the arse."

Now it was my turn to burst out laughing with my mouth full of wine. I'm afraid I spat it out into the king's passageway, but there was nobody around to notice, and Sir Gareth just went on with his story.

"Kay put his visor down and came charging at me without another word. I was armed, but I didn't have a shield, and didn't have a lance either, so I had to do some fancy dodging when he came roaring by. But I had my sword out and took a swing at him. He missed but I struck and he flew off the horse so hard that it knocked him out when he hit the ground. By then Lancelot had got there, and he figured that if I could unseat one of Arthur's knights and knock him cold, I was worthy to be knighted, and he did it right there in the field. So I became Sir Gareth of Orkney, knighted by the greatest knight in all the world.

"Not that Lynette was impressed. I jumped back on my horse, took Kay's shield and lance, and galloped after her while Lancelot returned to Camelot to tell the king what had happened and to send somebody to bring Kay in. But Lynette kept snubbing me and saying as how I got lucky that Kay's horse stumbled, and that I smelled too much like the kitchen so I needed to ride several steps behind her."

"But she changed her tune after awhile, didn't she?"

"Here's what I did: Sir Ironside had found out that Lyonesse had sent to Camelot for one of Arthur's knights. He sent his four brothers to guard the road between Caerleon and Lyonesse's castle, spaced a few miles apart. So I'd have to fight one of his brothers every few miles until I reached him. He must have figured that if they didn't kill me, at least I'd be worn out by the time I got to him. And I think he also figured that there were only a few knights—Lancelot and Gawain, Lamorak and Tristram—who could possibly get through all four of his brothers, so he'd end up getting his wish and fighting one of the greatest knights, and killing him most likely, because he'd be worn out by the time he got there to fight Ironside. Or at least that's what he figured.

"But as it turned out, I made short work of the Black Knight, the first brother to challenge me. I ended up running him through with the lance and killing him on the spot. I defeated the Green Knight and the Gold Knight pretty handily, and made them promise to come to Camelot and swear fealty to Arthur. All this time Lynette is nagging me to go back home because I'm useless. I'll tell you, that was a greater test of my knighthood than the battles—keeping a courteous tongue in my mouth all the while her tongue was lashing me like a whip.

"But by the time I got to the Blue Knight, Lynette was starting to realize that maybe I could help her sister. She warned me that the Blue Knight was the strongest of the four, and wished me good luck with him. I won't bore you with the details, but it took me a whole afternoon to beat him. I was pretty exhausted. Not really in the best shape to take on the Red Knight that same day."

"But you did anyway?"

"I didn't have a lot of choice in the matter. Lynette went riding ahead of me with her big mouth and started yelling 'Beware, Sir Ironside, you Red Knight of the Red Lands, for here now is a champion from Arthur's court who has come to destroy you!' "

"Kind of took away any advantage you might have had with the element of surprise, didn't it?"

"Did it ever. Sir Ironside was mounted and ready when I arrived before the castle of Lyonesse. There was a treeless field before the gates of the palace that was obviously the Red Knight's preferred arena of combat. And I need to tell you that I smelled the place before I saw it, for from the branches of trees surrounding the area hung forty rotting corpses, the bodies of unsuccessful knights who'd been slain mercilessly by Sir Ironside and then mocked in death in that villainous manner."

"But you obviously beat him. How, when you were already exhausted from fighting all of his brothers?"

"I had two advantages that I hadn't counted on. For one thing, remember I was carrying Sir Kay's shield. When the Red Knight saw that, he was just enraged. He thought it had to be Lancelot or Gawain, but it turns out to be Kay that beat up all his brothers. Or so he thinks. And so he's thinking all the time that he's sizing me up that I'm probably not even worth his trouble and he just needs to brush me aside like a pesky fly and Arthur will have to send somebody better.

"The other thing I had was Lyonesse. When I got to the clearing, Lynette was already there, and she shouted at me to look up to a window in the castle tower that faced the field to receive the blessing of her I had come to rescue. Let me tell you, Gildas old boy, when I saw her eyes, those two dark beauties gazing helplessly from a face so fair it took my breath away. It was like two smoldering coals on a field of fresh-fallen snow. It was as if a lance sharper and more potent than any Sir Ironside wielded had pierced my heart and driven it straight out of my body."

I scoffed. These courtly knights were always talking this way.

I had seen Sir Palomides's lyrics just recently as more evidence. But I knew it was only rhetorical hyperbole. Women were nice to look at, certainly, especially those as beautiful as my lady the queen, but these kinds of exaggerated metaphors I found pretty amusing.

"Mock all you want, my young Cornish friend, but someday you'll see what I mean. I tell you, when I saw the Lady Lyonesse pleading silently with those dark pools of her eyes, all I knew was that nobody, not Sir Ironside or any of his brothers nor Sir Kay nor Sir Lancelot himself, would ever get past me to harm her as long as there was breath in my body. I charged the Red Knight with all my power, and he, thinking it was Sir Kay, got a rude shock when my lance shivered in his side.

"We fought for a long while, but he never really recovered from my initial onslaught, and, not to bore you with the details, he eventually had to yield. Lynette, of course, was on the sidelines cheering me on to cut his head off, but I let him live as long as he took an oath to leave his siege, to give up all claim to the Lady Lyonesse, and to offer himself in the service of King Arthur. Which is how he got here.

"As for Lyonesse, I married her soon after. I've never had a moment's regret, either. I still get weak in the knees just thinking about her." He smiled a kind of sappy smile at me and I just shook my head.

"What happened to the nag, the sister?"

"Oh, Lynette?" Now the smile turned mischievous. "I got her married off to my brother Gaheris. It couldn't have happened to a nicer guy. And that's how I got to be a knight of the round table. And that's the story of Sir Ironside, and why I don't put anything past him. He's murderous and he's jealous, and he doesn't scruple to kill good knights. Oath or no oath, I don't trust him. But he's a doughty fighter, respected throughout the world of chivalry. I made my reputation when I beat him. After that they ranked me with the three great knights—Lancelot, Tristram, and Lamorak."

All right, this was the third time I'd heard the name, and I was overcome by my curiosity and had to ask. "Gareth, I know Sir Lancelot of course, and Sir Tristram. They stand out as the greatest knights in Camelot. But I don't know this Lamorak. He's not a knight of the round table? Where is he?"

"Dead." Sir Gareth's face turned a sickly gray. He took the last swallow from his bottle and leaned his head back so that it rested against the doorjamb. Gone was his easy smile and his spirit of play. Perhaps he was the sort of person whom drink made lively, but more drink turned morose. But it was clear that the thought of Sir Lamorak was unpleasant, even painful, for him. He began speaking, not with the affable banter of before, but in a flat, expressionless tone.

"Sir Lamorak de Gales was the son of King Pellinore. Lamorak was one of the greatest knights of his time, and with Sir Tristram one of the only knights ever to unhorse Sir Lancelot himself. Lamorak won many tournaments and seemed invincible. He was known throughout Logres and all of Europe for his worthiness and his courtesy.

"Now Pellinore, you may already know, was the man who killed my father, King Lot, in single combat. It was a fair fight, but the feud between the house of Pellinore and the house of Lot has continued. Sir Lamorak, however, was not interested in feuding.

"After my father's death, Sir Lamorak developed a lust for my mother, the queen Margause of Orkney. And she, it seems, was all too willing to give him the opportunity to act on that lust, though she was twice his age. It was shame to her, shame to the family, and I am ashamed to say, it was not the first time she had engaged in such behavior. But those older indiscretions are not the point of this story. Lamorak began to visit her discreetly. But as the affair went on, the two lovers became less careful about their liaisons. It happened that one day, when returning home to the castle at Orkney, my brother Gaheris came upon the two of them in bed together. Imagine his blind rage. Here was the son of his father's murderer fornicating with his mother, the victim's own wife. Gaheris drew his sword and with one stroke beheaded his own mother.

"That act seemed to have sobered him. Sir Lamorak had sprung from the bed and was poised to attempt to defend himself, naked and unarmed as he was. But all of Gaheris's wrath seemed to have oozed from him as my mother's blood turned the bed crimson. He told Sir Lamorak to dress himself and leave his home, saying he would not kill an unarmed knight. But he warned Lamorak that he would not forget and that he must expect a challenge."

Horror upon horror had assaulted my ears today, and now, most terrible of all, the image of Sir Gaheris covered with the blood of his matricide burned itself into my mind. "Then Gaheris challenged Lamorak?" I prodded Gareth. "Is that how he died?"

"No. Gaheris wanted to, but Agravain and Mordred were afraid that Lamorak would be allowed to get away with the crimes of his lust, and Gawain himself was intent on revenge. One night, as Lamorak rode alone through a forest not far from Camelot, all four of my brothers waylaid him. They killed his horse first, and then all four attacked him at once. He held them off valiantly, I am told, until Sir Agravain stabbed him from behind. When he fell, the others all hacked at his body. All but Gaheris, I'm told, who still would have liked to have had a fair fight.

"When the bodies of horse and rider were found the next day, it was strongly suspected that my brothers had committed the murder. But there was no one who could prove it. And there still isn't. If you ask them, they will deny it. But I know what the truth is."

"You? How would you know?" A voice came from the darkness and then the formidable figure of Sir Gaheris appeared in the ring of candlelight that surrounded us as we sat against the queen's chamber door. Gaheris had his foot on Gareth's sword so that he could not have gone for it if he had wanted to. "Brother, you aren't keeping your watch. An enemy could have come upon you and caught you unarmed. You must be more careful of your safety."

Brother or no brother, I couldn't help thinking that it sounded like a warning. But when Gaheris turned his face to me, he was all smiles and pleasantry. "You should excuse my brother, my young friend. When he drinks too much, he is prone to run off at the mouth, and his imagination gets the better of him. You really can't trust anything he says after he's had too much wine. His fancy so muddles his reason.

"Go to bed, now, little brother." He helped lift the groaning Gareth to his feet, and handed him back his sword. "Get some sleep so that you're more alert when you come to relieve me. I'll take the watch now."

At that Gaheris turned to me and gave me a curt nod. "Good night, Gildas," he said, as Gareth stumbled off through the dark. And then he added, "Sleep well."

CHAPTER TEN:
THE CONVENT OF
SAINT MARY MAGDALENE

Merlin was still sleeping when I woke up the next morning, so rather than wake him I left the queen's quarters to go down to the kitchen and grab a bit of bread and cheese to break my fast. I passed Sir Gaheris standing at attention outside the door, and he nodded to me, but I found it difficult to look at him in the same way as I had before. Gareth had indeed been drunk last night, but I trusted everything he had told me. And looking at Gaheris in the harsh light of day was disturbing to me. His calm demeanor now belied the mortal fury that had driven him to take his own mother's life in a mortified frenzy. I didn't want to know about it. I wished I didn't. But that didn't make it go away.

I was gone for a good hour or so, but when I returned to the room, Merlin still had not arisen. And he remained in that condition for the rest of the day, and on into the next. I was aching to talk to him about the things Gareth had told me on Sunday night. Surely Merlin knew the story of Sir Lamorak. I wondered if he knew the truth as I had heard it, straight from Gareth's mouth. I supposed he knew the story of Beaumains and the Red Knight, which had certainly convinced me that Sir Ironside was capable of murder. But what did Merlin think?

I was anxious to get on with the investigation. The fortnight's leeway we'd been given by the king's decree was fast melting away. Today was Tuesday. The queen's trial by combat was set to take place on the following Wednesday. With our interview of

Sir Palomides proving inconclusive, we seemed to be back to the beginning again. But certainly Sir Ironside seemed to have motive, if what I had overheard about his wife and Sir Patrise was to be trusted. And he had already killed forty knights and treated them villainously. He looked like a pretty strong suspect to me. But Merlin wouldn't wake up.

I kept staring at him, and suddenly realized that he wasn't asleep at all. He was awake, but lying with a blanket pulled up around his neck as if the bed were a refuge from the world. His eyes were open.

"Merlin!" I pounced on the opportunity. "Come on, get up! I've got to tell you about Sunday night!"

"Go away," was all he said, and he turned to face the wall, curling up in a fetal position and pulling his blanket with him.

"What? No, you can't do this. There isn't time! We've got to talk to Sir Ironside, and see what he knows. The queen's judgment gets closer every day. Get up!"

"Not enough time," the old man replied with gloomy annoyance.

"Don't say that. Are you joking? Look, we know a lot already about what happened. We just need to find out who's behind it. Come on. It's got to be Sir Ironside, right? Or do you still think it's Palomides?"

Merlin answered only by pulling the blanket up over his head so that he couldn't see me at all.

Frustrated, I snatched the blanket in my hand and pulled it off him. Sure, it was disrespectful and discourteous, but I didn't know how to rouse him from this mood. I had succeeded the other night in shaming him with his duty to the king, but that didn't seem to be working this time, and I was afraid we might lose another whole day's investigation when there were precious few days left. "The Red Knight!" Now I was shouting at him. "I know he's a killer. I'll swear he did this murder as well."

But Merlin only shivered, and curled into an even smaller ball. "I've failed my king," he managed to croak out. "I want to go back to my cave."

I was on the verge of tears with frustration, but I couldn't help pitying the old man. I did not know the depths of his darkness, but I could see there were times when he was in a place in his mind that would allow no light in. I covered him again with the blanket. Speaking mostly to myself, I sighed, "What can I do? I don't want to waste the day, but I sure don't want to go talk to Sir Ironside by myself."

"The nun," Merlin responded from his protective ball.

At that I looked down at him with mild surprise. He was not so far engulfed in darkness that he could not still respond rationally. And that gave me hope he would come out of this soon. I decided to leave him to his bed and trust that by tomorrow, he would be ready to continue the quest. I left him, after exerting some mild pressure: "Very well, I'll go to the convent and let you know what I find out. We can go to see Sir Ironside tomorrow. Rest well."

I turned to leave the room, but then caught myself. There was one more stop I should make before I left the castle.

My main business in Camelot, though I may have forgotten it this week past, was to serve as page in the household of Queen Guinevere. While that lady had been confined to her quarters since the unfortunate dinner, she had not needed my services much, except in the way of being her eyes and ears. And my main business of late had been snooping around to try to find the murderer, so I hadn't been doing much reporting to the queen. I felt it would behoove me to get the queen's permission before I left the castle again.

It was with a bit of trepidation that I poked my head through the curtain into the queen's outer chamber. Her ladies were already in attendance, and I noticed someone had brought in a small breakfast tray that was as yet untouched. The women were bustling about, entering the queen's private chamber with clothing, jewelry, and headdresses to dress her for the day. All, that is, except for Rosemounde, who greeted me as I came in.

"Yes, Gildas?" She stood directly in front of me, hands folded at her waist. She was far less giggly than usual, but still looked up at me with a bemused expression twisting her mouth and her head tilted a bit mockingly to one side. "What can we do for you at this *early* hour?"

Oh, come on, I thought, it's not all that early. It was certainly well past prime, though I'm sure it had not yet struck terce. "I, uh, I'm wondering if the queen is stirring yet? I need to take my leave of her, since I need to be about Merlin's business this morning."

Rosemounde closed her dark brown eyes and shook her head in an exaggerated dramatic style. "Oh dear, oh dear, how shall we ever force ourselves to endure your absence again today? What business can we contrive for ourselves today to keep us from pining for your pretty face all the day long?" She put her hand to her forehead in a kind of mock despair, and then came pouring out the all-too-familiar rash of giggles. Then she backed away slightly and covered her small, pink mouth demurely. And she glanced up at me, suddenly shy again, her long eyelashes slowly opening to reveal those large, dark brown eyes that fixed me for a moment in her gaze. And I suddenly realized that they were like . . . well, like two smoldering coals on a field of fresh-fallen snow, and it was truly as if a sharp lance had just pierced my heart, and driven it straight out of my body. Where had I heard that before?

Very well, maybe it sounds cliché, but there she was, and I had never noticed it before, but she was a beauty more rare than I had ever imagined. How could I have been blind to it before?

133

Jay Ruud

Her hair hung down in dark, flowing tresses that cascaded around her shoulders. It was parted in the middle and confined by nothing but a small gold circlet around her head that partly covered her broad, white forehead. She wore a simple gown of emerald green serge, fastened in front by a small gold brooch. The gown was cut tight in the sleeves and across her bosom as well, showing the contours of her soft and petite body. It was gathered at the waist and flowed out into an ample skirt that reached to her shoes of embroidered green velvet. She wore no surcote, but her gown was decorously confined at her hips by a jeweled leather belt that buckled in front and had a long tongue hanging down to her knees. She was the prettiest picture I'd ever seen.

"So . . . has the cat got your tongue, young Gildas of Cornwall?" Rosemounde's brow was lowering with irritation over those smoldering dark eyes, and I realized that I had been standing there for some time, staring at her without saying anything.

"Yes," I said, feeling the hot blood rushing into my face and bowing awkwardly in an attempt to regain some semblance of courtesy. "I mean, no. I mean, pardon me, good Lady Rose-mounde, I did not wish to appear discourteous. Please understand that I was distracted by thoughts of this quest that we are on, Merlin and me." Regaining my composure, and hoping I was impressing her, I continued. "The strain of this investigation is sometimes distracting. There are so many things to try to sort through . . ."

"Oh, I dare say," she said, turning from me with that impish look in her eyes again. "Things like your laundry." Walking away and giggling again, she called back. "I'll inform Her Royal Highness that you are here to wait upon her."

She ducked her head into the queen's closet and then turned back to me after a moment. "She says come on in," she told

134

me, jerking her head toward the closet door. She watched me as I came through the outer chamber, her hands on her hips. I felt as though my face was on fire, yet my hands were cold and I was weak in the knees. But I held my composure. The last thing I wanted to do was to give the Lady Rosemounde more ammunition for her chronic giggling. She seemed to think I was nothing but a clown, which made the way I suddenly felt under those eyes all the more hopeless.

But it was the queen I needed to focus on. Stick to the business at hand. Rosemounde would, well, work herself out one way or another, but the queen commanded my allegiance now, and she needed me to work for her and to prove her innocence. That was what I was going to do. With Merlin's help, of course.

The queen sat before a large mirror while the Lady Elaine stood behind her braiding her hair. Usually, Queen Guinevere went about with her hair unbound and flowing in great blond cascades down past her shoulders. It was only on very formal occasions that the queen would wear her hair braided with a headdress. I wondered what she might be up to.

When Guinevere glanced up at me she seemed to read my thoughts, and then gazed before her again into the mirror. "It's the king," she explained. "My presence is requested—read 'commanded'—at a royal dinner this afternoon, in the great hall. Scene," she added with a sardonic laugh, "of my murderous past. There are ambassadors from Norway come to court last evening to kiss the king's arse, so he must needs release me from my cage and air me out a bit. You know, so as to make all appear fine and dandy in our little Eden of a Camelot. Except someone's eaten the forbidden fruit, hasn't he, my good Gildas?" This time her laugh was a bit more mirthful, as she surprised herself with the joke she had just unintentionally led herself into.

"Oh well, at least it will give those two bookend nephews of his a bit of a rest. They can't be having much fun planted in front of my door like blond shrubberies twenty-four hours a day." At that I nodded and suppressed a smile. Gareth and I had had a bit of fun Sunday night, at least. My head the next morning had throbbed a dull reminder of it in my ears all day, and I could only imagine what Gareth's head must have been like.

"My lady," I told her, "I've come to take my leave of you for the day. I must be about the business of finding the killer of Sir Patrise and saving your reputation." I knew it wouldn't do to speak any too seriously with the queen. There was almost always an edge of irony in her own speech, and she distrusted anyone who was not at least to some extent jaded and sarcastic. That's one of the things I liked about her. But now she turned to me a pair of pale blue eyes that were dead serious, and filled with real fear.

"Do so, my young whelp. You find that killer and get me out of this mess. Do you think the old man will solve it in time?"

I thought of Merlin curled up on his private hell in the outer chamber and lied the best I could. "Absolutely, Madame. We have a number of important leads, and even now he is spending time thinking through the clues we've already found. Meanwhile, I must go off today to Saint Mary Magdalene's, by your leave, to follow up on one of the leads we have."

A curious look replaced a part of the fear in the eyes that stared back at me. "The nunnery? What in heaven's name could you find there?"

"I hope an answer or two, my lady. There was a nun present in the kitchen the day of the unfortunate dinner who might have seen something or know something that nobody else does. Anyway, it's worth following up on."

"Well, follow up, by all means," the queen said, waving me off. She seemed to have regained some of her flippancy. "But

Gildas, come back to see me this evening, please. I'm certain I'll want a venting period after my Norwegian dinner, and you know that I particularly enjoy venting to you."

I bowed and mumbled a farewell, and by then Guinevere had turned her mind to other things. "Elaine," I heard her saying as I backed out of the room. "I really miss my dogs. When we're done here, send down to the kennels, and make sure that a boy brings Aeneas and Dido to me after my dinner. I want to take them for a walk."

I turned on my heel and started out for my own walk, nodding politely but, I thought, noncommittally to the other ladies, paying no more attention to Rosemounde than to either of the others. I left without a word but heard an explosion of giggling behind me when I'd come through the curtain. I shook my head, wondering what on earth could possibly be so funny so much of the time to girls that age. And as I headed out the door, my eyes lit on the motionless form of Merlin curled under my blanket. I shook my head at that as well. Once out the door, I murmured some polite leave-taking to Sir Gaheris the matricide as I started down the hall. And yes, as you might suspect, the head was wagging at that one too.

The Convent of Saint Mary Magdalene lay only about half a mile east of the castle, and perhaps a bit less than a mile east of the town of Caerleon, so I had a short walk when I left the castle gate and turned left. It being late morning, the drawbridge was down and folk were leaving and entering the castle with regularity, going about their normal business. I looked up into the barbican as I passed through, wondering whether Robin was on duty. As I didn't hear any mocking calls of recognition, I assumed he must be off at the moment and would take a shift later in the day. As commander of the watch, he generally reserved the night shifts for himself, those being the most crucial to the protection of Camelot.

The road was easy and the sun was shining, and though it was autumn and the temperature was quite brisk, to me it felt almost like a spring day. I suppose part of the reason for that was that Rosemounde's eyes and the mocking twist of her mouth hung in the air before my eyes the entire trip to the nunnery, so that before I even realized that I had been walking, I was standing before the gate into Saint Mary Magdalene's. I wasn't sure how long I'd been walking or what time it might be, but as a servant woman opened the gate to me, I heard the bells ringing sext. The servant, dressed in a light brown smock that had seen better days and a small nondescript hood covering her hair, was a peasant with rough features who might have been anywhere between thirty and fifty years old. She was employed, I supposed, as a general household servant by the nuns, and one of her tasks was apparently acting as porter. Surely the convent did not receive a large number of visitors, but there must have been enough traffic with the world that the woman was kept quite busy. That might explain her haggard look. And living with nuns who, for most of the day, went about trying to keep a rule of silence might explain the servant's very taciturn demeanor.

I greeted her warmly enough. "Good morning, mistress, and how are you this lovely morning?" All right, as I said, I was feeling pretty good at that point.

"Your business?" she responded, without changing her expression.

"I am here on the king's business, actually." That, I thought, would give her a jolt if anything would. But her eyes didn't even blink at the mention of the king.

"And it is?"

"Yes, well, I'm investigating a mysterious death at the castle." Death, I figured, would impress her. But she only stared blankly, waiting, I assumed, for me to explain my business further.

"The death of Sir Patrise. Perhaps you heard about it?"

Nothing.

"Well, the fact is, the king has asked me . . . that is, has asked my lord Merlin, with me as his assistant, to look into the murder of Sir Patrise, to try to discover the truth behind the murder."

She still stared at me blankly.

"Right. Well, it seems one of your nuns here at Saint Mary Magdalene's—a Dame Agnes, we think—was seen in the castle on the day of the murder. We believe she may have some information that will help us. So Merlin has asked me to come here to see her, to find out, you know, what she may have seen. That would help us."

I began to think that the servant woman had been carved out of stone, and that those few words I had thought I heard her speak earlier must have been figments of my imagination, for she continued to stare at me with an expressionless face.

"So I'm wondering if I might be allowed to speak with her. Dame Agnes, that is."

"Not without permission of the prioress."

The fact that she finally spoke startled me so much that it took a moment for her actual words to sink in. Finally I responded, "Fine. Might I be allowed to see the prioress, then?"

The servant let out a long and disgusted sigh and turned slowly. I assumed I was to follow her. "They're at the office now. The refectory after. I'll tell Madame Hildegard you're here. You wait in her quarters."

Pleased at her ability to string a multitude of sentences together when necessity warranted it, I followed the servant silently across the open yard that separated the gate from the main buildings of the nunnery. I had visited the convent on a few occasions before and could find my way round in a pinch. Saint Mary's was not a large convent, but it was a healthy size, with at least thirty nuns in residence. As with most nunneries, the high wall that surrounded the yard enclosed a garden and small orchard and even a fishpond, as well as several outbuildings including a stable, a mill, and a granary. The important main buildings were closer to the gate. The church with attached cloister sat to my far right, where I could hear the nuns finishing the office of sext. The refectory next to that was where the nuns ate, and it had an attached kitchen where I assumed Dame Agnes must work. A dorter in the middle contained the sisters' individual cells where they slept. They held convent meetings in the chapter house, which also contained a small library. It was in the chapter house, for lack of another space, that the nuns who worked on manuscript copying set up their work stations during those six hours a day the nuns were expected to work. Behind the chapter house was a small infirmary for ill or aged members of the community.

Finally, on the far left, were the prioress's quarters, separate from the rest of the sisters' cells and somewhat less ascetic, for the prioress was expected on occasion to have dealings with visitors from the secular world.

The servant woman showed me into the foyer area of Madame Hildegard's quarters, where she kept visitors waiting. The servant nodded to a small wooden chair in that outer hall, and as I sat she volunteered, "I'll see the prioress," and left.

It was a bit awkward waiting there alone, wondering when or if the prioress would make time for me, wondering whether I would ever actually get to see Dame Agnes at all, wondering whether she would have anything to say to me if I did get to see her, and wondering underneath all the while what the Lady Rosemounde's sweet coral lips would taste like if I were to . . .

Now hold on. I mentally slapped myself. Concentrate on the task at hand. I wondered whether even thinking about such things in a place filled with virgin women dedicated to prayer was by itself a deadly sin.

But my theological speculations were interrupted by the servant woman returning. She had with her a plate with a piece of bread, a few vegetables, and a small helping of fish that I assumed she had brought from the refectory where the nuns were now having their midday meal. I realized when I saw it that my stomach had been growling all the time I was sitting there, and I took the plate from the woman thankfully.

"Dame Hildegard is on her way. She wants to be rid of you before she eats."

I thanked the servant for her hospitality and began to make quick work of the food she had brought. I was just finishing the last of the fish when the inner door to Madame Hildegard's apartments opened and there stood the prioress herself. She must have come from the refectory and entered the house by a different door. Tall and imposing in her black Benedictine habit, she stood and looked down her beaked nose at me imperiously.

"You are the boy from the court?" she asked rhetorically. "Come in. Sit down. I'm not sure how much I can help you. What exactly is it you want?"

I was beginning to suspect that Saint Mary Magdalene's was not really a very friendly place. Madame Hildegard showed me into the room, which was simply furnished with three wooden chairs, a wooden writing desk, and a large trunk in the corner. The only ornamentation in the stark room was a small tapestry on the wall that depicted the Magdalene herself, weeping and dressed in a hair shirt. Farther in, behind this room, was another room—apparently the prioress's sleeping quarters—to which the door stood slightly ajar. The prioress sat in the chair next to the writing desk and I faced her from the other chair.

"What I want is to speak with Dame Agnes. As I assume your servant told you, I'm helping Merlin investigate the murder of Sir Patrise. Now we suspect that whoever killed Sir Patrise had been in the kitchen at the castle. Dame Agnes apparently brought some spices over to the kitchen on the day Patrise was killed, so we need to know what she might have seen when she was there. Maybe she saw something or someone and can help us find the killer."

Madame Hildegard's eyes widened at this bit of news, but she only said, "If she saw anything important, she would have told me. I really don't think she can help you at all." The prioress was a woman in her fifties, though she seemed to have a strong constitution. Her green eyes looked sternly at me and her wrinkles bent down her face in what seemed like a permanent frown. "Besides, she cannot be seen right now."

"I realize that your schedule is very strict, but I understand the sisters are eating at the moment. Couldn't her meal be interrupted to help with the king's business?"

"The king's business does not take precedence over God's," Madame Hildegard corrected me. "Our midday meal does not simply provide nourishment for the body. It also gives our nuns food for the soul. Each day we read from important works of theology or Saints' Lives to educate and inspire the women here, as St. Benedict intended. But that is not really the point here. Dame Agnes is not in the refectory. She is confined to her own cell."

"Confined? Why? You mean she can't see me under any circumstances?"

"Dame Agnes is being disciplined for a serious infraction of the rule. That is all you need to know. In addition to corporal punishment, she has been assigned to keep to her cell for another week—until next Tuesday—with one daily meal of bread and water, there to pray and to contemplate her sins."

At that point, quite without warning, a small dog ran in from the other room and jumped up on Madame Hildegard's lap. It gave a small "Yip!" and then settled down comfortably, snuggling its head into her black robes. "Augustine!" she cried in surprise, and for the first time her face softened and was lit up with a broad smile that showed the prioress still had a good number of her own teeth. "Such a naughty doggy-kins!" she said with mock anger, and continued speaking in baby-talk: "Mommy told you to wait inside! What am I going to do with such a naughty, naughty baby-kins?"

I realized after a moment that my mouth was hanging open. I shut it quickly and hoped the prioress's change of mood could be turned to my benefit. "Uh, Madame Hildegard, perhaps you can at least tell me something about Sister Agnes? I mean, when did she come here? Where is she from? Who is her family? That sort of thing."

"She came from Wales, joined the convent about five years ago, as I recall," the prioress told me. She was distracted, looking down at Augustine and scratching his belly, much to his delight. Focused on the dog, she had become almost chatty.

"Dame Agnes was the youngest daughter of a minor Welsh nobleman who hadn't the wherewithal to find her a husband. I believe there was something about a love affair that had turned out badly as well. But he provided her with a small dowry and sent her here as a postulant when she was seventeen. She took her vows about three years later. Didn't she, snookie-kins?"

The dog did not answer, other than to roll onto his back as if to ask for more tummy-petting, so I responded for him. "And Dame Agnes is what? The cook here?"

"Dame Agnes is the deputy cellarer. She reports to the cellarer and helps her with her duties. Dame Agnes is chiefly responsible for tending the garden, planning the menus for the meals, and overseeing the kitchen. We do have servants who do most of the cooking. Oh, and she also deals with some of the patients in the infirmary. She came to us knowing a great deal about herbs, and so knows something about which ones are useful for medicine. We don't have a real apothecary so Dame Agnes fills that role. She's a very, very valuable member of our community, yes she is!"

That last sentence, of course, was addressed directly to Augustine, for the dog, annoyed that Madame Hildegard was not paying him the attention he firmly believed he deserved, had stood up on her lap and begun to bite and tug at her rosary hanging from the girdle around her waist. He made a small circle and settled back down once she returned to her baby-talking.

My ears naturally pricked up when I heard about Dame Agnes's aptitude with herbs. If we suspected Sir Palomides because of his amateur's interest in herbs of all sorts, why not suspect this nun? Especially since she had the opportunity, having been in the kitchen that day. But what could be her motive? There was no reason to think she had any contact with Sir Patrise or knew him from Adam. Or from Augustine, for that matter. Was there?

"Madame Hildegard," I asked as she seemed about to stand up and bring the interview to an end. "I realize that you are busy and need to rejoin your sisters. But if I could ask you one more thing: Do you know whether Dame Agnes was acquainted with any of the knights in the castle? Or whether she had ever known Sir Patrise? Or . . . has she ever been in Ireland? Or perhaps the Holy Land at the time of the crusade?"

The prioress lifted Augustine and placed him gently on the floor, where he began to run in circles and yip at her. She drew herself up to her full height once again and stared down her beaked nose with those penetrating eyes boring a hole in my skull. "Young man," she began. "That was not one more thing. It was four. You must learn to ask your questions one at a time and in a more organized manner. How can I possibly respond to such an undisciplined rash of inquiries? To my knowledge,

Dame Agnes has never been to any of those places. She came to us at a fairly young age, and I am relatively certain she had never been outside of Wales before she joined our convent. For that matter, she has never left Saint Mary Magdalene's since her arrival here, except to go to Caerleon or the castle or a neighboring town within a day's ride. As for her acquaintances, I cannot say whom she may have known before coming here. I believe her unfortunate love affair was with a knight, but he is most certainly not at Camelot or I would know of it. Now if you will excuse me?"

"Wait! Before you go, can you tell me what Dame Agnes is being disciplined for?"

"I have given you all the information I can, young man," she replied as she made her way to the door I had come in. "Have a pleasant walk back to Camelot."

"But can I come back and talk to her when her discipline has ended?"

"Our convent welcomes strangers. Good day to you." With that she disappeared into the courtyard and began to walk purposefully back toward the refectory.

I got up myself and walked much more slowly through the door. I shuffled back to the gate, where the same gregarious serving woman held the gate open, eager to close it quickly on me and the rest of the outside world once I had removed my polluting presence from the sanctuary.

During the slow walk back to the castle, I turned over new questions in my head: Did Dame Agnes's knowledge of herblore include a knowledge of poisons? What motive could she have had to want Sir Patrise dead? Was there any connection between them that the prioress had not precluded by her comments? Did she know Sir Palomides or know of Patrise's service in the Holy Land? Did she know Sir Ironside or any other knight in the castle? And how soft would the Lady Rosemounde's cheek feel pressed against my own?

CHAPTER ELEVEN:
STROLL AROUND THE GROUNDS

After my visit to the convent, I didn't know much more than when I'd left. I also felt a little thwarted since I hadn't actually had a chance to speak with Sister Agnes, so I really wanted to talk to Merlin. But by the time I had got back to the queen's chamber in the castle, Merlin was no longer there. I was a little bit disappointed, but I was also encouraged by that fact. It meant he had come out of his melancholy enough to rouse himself and leave the room. Whether he was about the castle somewhere or back in his cave, I had no way of knowing, but either way he was back in touch with reality and for that I had to be grateful.

But I had promised to visit with the queen when I returned from the nunnery, so I took a look into the inner chamber to see whether she was there yet. The first thing I felt when I poked my head around the curtain was a cold tongue slobbering on my cheek. I stood up sputtering and put out my hands, saying "Down girl, down!" It was Dido, one of the queen's greyhounds. Obviously the boy from the kennels had brought them here to be ready to greet Guinevere when she returned from her Norwegian dinner, but by the look on Lady Vivien's face as she held them by their leather leashes, the ladies-in-waiting had not anticipated that Aeneas and Dido would be paying them a visit in their own quarters.

The ladies Anne, Elaine, and Rosemounde were sitting in the far corner of the room, looking quite cross and holding nose-

gays before their faces. Lady Vivien's own nose was wrinkled in
disgust, and as I came in she quickly handed the leashes to me,
saying, "Gildas! The queen said you were to accompany her on
her walk with these great beasts. Take them, will you? Just get
them out of here." She made little dismissive gestures with her
hands as if to say "Out! Please!"

I laughed as Dido ran back and forth, trembling with the
excitement of "walk." Aeneas stood more regally, almost
stoically, as befitted his namesake. I was well acquainted with
both dogs from prior hunting days in the queen's company, and
I petted them both on the head and gladly took the leashes. I
thought I would take them out of those quarters and wait
outside for the queen, when I heard the outer door open and
the dogs began barking uncontrollably, catching a new scent.

When Guinevere walked in, Aeneas lost his reserve and both
dogs began leaping around her in ecstasy at the sight of their
master. "Down! Down!" she told them in a voice of command,
evidently a bit worried that they might get dirty paw-prints on
the long patterned surcote she wore over her royal purple gown.
Her blond hair, braided and twisted up, was conservatively
covered by a round linen headdress with a barbette around her
chin in a manner, I supposed, that suited the stodgy Norwegian
ambassadors. But I had never seen her with her hair confined in
that way. She looked almost unnatural. And her face betrayed a
kind of morose discomfort, as if things had not been going at all
her way so far today.

"Good dogs, good dogs! Yes, I do love you." And she bent
down to allow each one of them to give her face a bit of a kiss.
"Ah, Gildas," she said, turning to me, "is there anything more
comforting than the love of a dog?"

In my mind I began to count up a number of things that I
found more comforting, but I thought, given my reading of her
present mood, it was probably best just to agree with her and

move on. I even thought to share with her a bit of my episode at the convent.

"Everyone seems to like dogs," I agreed, glancing as I did toward the women hovering in the corner with their nosegays. "Why, even the prioress at Saint Mary Magdalene's has a little dog, a small spaniel or something like that, that comes to her and lies in her lap."

"Ach." Guinevere wrinkled her nose and shook her head. "I can't stand those little rat-dogs. I don't want to have to bend down to pet a dog. I mean really," she went on as she continued vigorously to pet Aeneas and Dido. "If you want a rat, get a rat! Don't get a rat and call it a dog. I've got no use for people like that."

And with that, she turned and motioned for me to follow. "Let's take a walk. I need the air and exercise after that meal." I followed her through the outer door with the dogs, and had to stop as she spoke with Sir Gaheris. She grabbed the leashes from my hands and shoved them into Sir Gaheris's, saying, "Here, nephew! As long as you're going to be following me anyway, make yourself useful! You can take the dogs. And see that you follow a good distance back. What I want to talk to Gildas about is a very private matter!"

Talking to a knight of the round table in that fashion was not exactly the height of courtesy, but Sir Gaheris, who was nothing if not a paragon of chivalry, merely bowed in assent and followed the queen's whim. The queen and I walked down the corridor and then out onto the staircase that led down into the courtyard of the lower bailey. Guinevere glanced back over her shoulder and smirked at the sight of Sir Gaheris at the top of the steps, fumbling with the leashes and trying to disentangle himself as Aeneas and Dido tried over his objection to bound down the stairway.

The queen ignored the muttered curses coming from the

direction of Sir Gaheris, and turned left at the base of the steps to stroll clockwise along the buildings and the outer wall of Camelot. We were passing the kitchen and the great hall on our left before she spoke to me, out of a seeming reverie.

"Ah, Gildas! To be fifteen again!"

"My lady?"

"Your age, I mean. Fifteen and back in my father's castle at Cameliard. In my memory it is always spring there and the place is always green. I want to wear flowers in my hair on May Day and have every young bachelor in the county vying for my attention. To be young and beautiful again. That's the last time I remember being happy." She ended with a sigh.

I don't need to tell you I was pretty taken aback by this attitude. I'd never seen the queen like this before. But then, I had seen her assume a variety of roles—most recently with Sir Bors—that were calculated to elicit a desired response, and I wondered if she was playing to me at this point. "My lady!" I answered her. "You could not possibly be any more beautiful than you are. Why . . . when you enter a room, knights stand astonished. I—I myself—I am, well, in awe of you . . ." I didn't know what else to say, and I'd begun stammering anyway, so I stopped, embarrassed.

The queen took my arm and smiled as we walked. "Awe is not the same thing as passion, my young Cornishman. How would you say my beauty rates next to that of . . . oh, I don't know, let's say our young Lady Rosemounde?"

Now my embarrassment was crossing over into mortification, and I could feel the hot blood rushing into my face. I knew that a more experienced courtier would have found the right words, would have given the queen a smooth compliment without in any way diminishing the other lady's legitimate beauty. And believe me, when I thought about it afterwards, I thought of many more and better responses I could have made. In fact, here's what I decided in retrospect I probably should have said: "My lady, each star in the heavens has its own undeniable beauty, but none can compare to the day star, whose brightness drowns out all others. So it is with my queen." And I kicked myself several times for not thinking of that on the spot.

What I actually said was this:

"Rosemounde! Oh, but she's so much younger . . ."

I honestly believe I could have cut myself on the keen glare directed at me from Guinevere's eyes.

I found myself wishing for a convenient hole to open up someplace where I could jump in and cover myself up.

But after a moment that seemed like a century or two, the queen couldn't hold her stare any longer and burst out laughing. "Oh, my, Gildas, you've got a long way to go before you can call yourself a courtier. Hasn't anybody taught you yet that the lady you're with is always, always, always the most beautiful one in the world? You've got to throw her all kinds of flattery. You know, hair like finely spun gold, eyes like sparkling gems, lips like coral, skin like alabaster, all that kind of crap. For crying in a bucket, don't you ever listen to those troubadour songs? How are you ever going to woo the Lady Rosemounde if that's the best you can do under pressure?"

By now I was thoroughly shamed and hung my head stuttering, "But . . . but . . . Lady Rosemounde . . . I don't . . . I mean . . . how do you . . . ?"

"Put your head up and stop that spluttering, boy. I've got eyes, don't I? A woman knows these things. I can see you fancy her. And there's no doubt in my mind that she has her eye on you."

"Really?" This conversation was not turning out so badly after all.

"Well what do you think? So help me, sometimes I think men are about the stupidest creatures God ever put on this earth.

Why do you think she giggles her fool head off every time you come in the room? Why do you think she teases you every chance she gets? Ye gods and little fishes, what does it take to get through to you? My dogs could have figured this out months ago." With that she looked back to see how the dogs were fairing with Sir Gaheris. He was still struggling with them, some ten or fifteen paces behind, as they strained to pull him along and catch up to the queen and me. "I'm almost certain those dogs are smarter than Gaheris," she added. "Another man."

"Well, what should I do, then? Should I fully admit my ignorance and throw myself at your feet, begging that you show me the way to secure Lady Rosemounde's favor?" There was enough irony in that, I hoped, to assuage the queen's insulted pride and get me into her good graces again.

By now we were passing the lesser hall and turning right at one of the guard rooms in the northeast tower on the castle wall. The queen took my arm again and mused, "Don't let someone else marry her, for one thing. There are those who say that marriage should be no real impediment to true love, but those people have never really been in love and married at the same time."

I didn't see what sense she was making, or understand how what she said applied to me and Lady Rosemounde. "Well, I know that she is of marriageable age. For myself, I'm still a page and have little means of support for a wife . . ."

"And you're too damned young, Gildas, I don't care what the law says. Look, you can't be a page all your life, and it's time you got moving toward knighthood. I think you're worthy. But you'll never learn what it takes to be a knight by staying in the service of the queen, even the queen of Camelot."

"My lady!" I was afraid of her tone. "You aren't going to cast me off from your service? Please, lady, not now! You are my sovereign lady. All that I do, I do for love of my queen. Have I displeased you in some way? Have I—"

"No, you silly goose, shut up. Don't you see what I'm saying? To be a knight, you need to enter a knight's service. You need to graduate from page to squire. It's time. Past time, really. You should have done it last year. Especially when you have the Lady Rosemounde to please. You cannot allow some young bachelor to speak to her father and snatch her away from you, and from Camelot, before you have a chance to win her yourself. And besides"—now she turned deadly serious—"in a week's time, you may have no queen to serve. I try to turn my mind's eye away from the stake, but I can't quench the fire that keeps burning in my imagination."

"Sir Bors will not let you suffer that fate, my lady. He will prevail. He is as doughty a knight as any in Camelot."

"Sir Mador de la Porte will strike with the fury of righteous anger. He will be more than a match for a reluctant Sir Bors, I fear. I know of only one knight who would be certain of winning the day against Sir Mador."

"And he is not here," I said, completing the thought. And she nodded in silence.

"Lancelot!" The queen scoffed at the name and let go of my arm, striding forward more purposefully. I quickened my pace to keep up. "I almost wish the fires would consume me while he's off philandering. It would serve him right!" She punctuated those last few words with stabs of her forefinger, as if she were arguing with some unseen audience.

"My lady, that would be something like using a battle-axe to kill a fly."

She sagged, deflated, and I feared she was about to cry. The only tears I had ever seen in the queen's eyes in three years of service were of the crocodile variety she had sprung on Sir Bors. Her healthy sense of irony had kept any real tears at bay—at least under normal circumstances. But Guinevere now faced murder charges, and her day of reckoning was hurtling forward. That was enough to play havoc with the strongest fortification.

I understood that the queen was having a true crisis of spirit, and that she had chosen me over any of her ladies-in-waiting as the one to whom she could unburden herself. And wisely, too. Tell any one of the four ladies, and it was the same as telling all of them, and after that, who else might know? Tell me and I would be as silent as the tomb. The queen knew my loyalty and love for her. I was the right choice.

"How lucky you are, Gildas, to be young and in love. The world opens before you like a bounteous new Eden, and anything seems possible. What happens when you are past the prime of your beauty, when husbands and lovers turn away and you have nothing left but the hollow shell of a life that you need to keep living?"

"You are the queen, my lady. Queen of the greatest realm in Christendom and consort of the most worthy king in all of human history. Surely there is something to be said for that?"

"Public life is no substitute for personal happiness, boy. Keep that in mind and your life will be more worthwhile. Consort you say? Have you ever seen him consort with me? You've slept in my outer chamber for three years. Tell me, young Gildas of Cornwall, how many nights in all that time has King Arthur visited his queen's closet?"

I knew the answer to that without having to do the math. It was exactly zero.

"But surely the king loves you," I forged ahead, ignoring the question. "He moved to protect you from Sir Mador's vengeance. He sent Gawain to find Lancelot. He wanted you to approach Sir Bors. He set Merlin to find the killer. All has been done at his command."

"He could have been my champion himself. His own knighthood gives him that privilege. Why not defend your own wife? He could have dismissed the charges. He is King, is he not? Justice is what he says it is. The laws are his and he can make or break them at his whim."

I thought about that for a moment. "That might be true," I answered slowly, "but I'm not sure we would want to live in a kingdom governed in that way. I heard Father Ambrose say once that the world is governed by laws set up by God—the law of Nature. The laws keep the world in order and keep all things in their place. If God were to break the laws of Nature, it would be—"

"It would be a miracle." The queen completed my sentence. We both fell into silence as we turned westward, passing another guard tower on the southeast corner of the castle wall and began making our way along the outer wall toward the keep. The keep, the inner fortress and final defense of the castle, was the tallest in Europe: a circular stone tower some fifty feet across and ninety feet high, with stone walls three feet thick at the base. The only windows in its brown-gray walls were long strips through which defenders from within could shoot arrows. The tower loomed above us, blocking the sun from view, as Guinevere resumed her reverie, speaking not so much to me as to some nameless force in the air around us to whom she felt she needed to justify herself.

"When he came to my father, I was only fifteen myself. He had been King of Logres for three years, during which he had beaten down the rebellion of King Lot and expelled the Saxons from his kingdom. He was well on his way to becoming the grandest king in Christendom, and he was young and handsome. My father, Leodegrance, was Arthur's ally and I was his only daughter. Arthur arrived at Cameliard with King Ban and King Bors, his Gaulish allies, and chased off King Rience of Ireland, who had besieged Daddy's castle. Daddy thought he was doing me a great favor when he struck the bargain that wed me to the king. I brought with me my inheritance as my father's only daughter—that is, the entire kingdom of Cameliard. Daddy got a powerful ally and a sum of twenty thousand marks from Arthur in exchange for me and my estate. And me? I got to be queen."

"Arthur loved you then, didn't he? I've heard stories that he fell in love with you at first sight when he saw you in your father's castle, and so defeated the army of King Rience for your sake and then immediately begged Leodegrance for your hand."

The queen smiled wanly. "A rather romanticized version of it, I'd say. As far as I could tell, it was a business deal pure and simple. I was just thrown in to clinch it."

"So you believe that the king never loved you?"

Guinevere shrugged. "In his own way I suppose he did. The 'love at first sight' thing has a ring of truth. But listen, Gildas, don't ever let yourself get carried away by that idea. You can't really love somebody at first sight. Maybe you like something about them—their eyes, their hair, something about the way they smile—but that's not going to get you through the long years. You've got to know somebody before you can ever love her.

"A man whose love is based on a pair of eyes that strike him suddenly through the heart is one whose love will change with the seasons," the queen continued. I thought of Sir Gareth and his sudden ensnarement by the Lady Lyonesse, and how that affair seemed to have remained fresh for years.

"Can't love deepen from that first kindling, my lady? Can't beauty be the flame that draws the moth, and personality be the net that captures it forever?"

The queen gave me a puzzled look. "Not the most attractive metaphor, Gildas, but what you say is exactly the case. Acting upon one's 'love at first sight' before knowing whether it will deepen into the lasting kind is the most serious mistake people can make."

Knowing that the queen was speaking generally but thinking about herself, I figured what she really wanted me to do was give her an opportunity to open up. Looking back, it might not have been the smartest thing for me to do. What she was revealing to me were not simply snatches of her private life. She was a queen. She had no official private life. Everything she revealed to me was a matter of national security. Maybe it was even dangerous for me to hear it. In fact, there was no maybe about it. She was setting me up for treason just by telling me. The question was: how much did I love the queen?

I didn't have to think very hard about the answer. I asked the simple and inevitable question. "You're talking about the king. When did his affections wane?"

Guinevere sighed from deep in her heart. She gave a quick glance over her shoulder to see just where Sir Gaheris was—he was now some twenty steps behind us, pulling on the dogs' leashes as they strained to bark at a handful of guards coming out of the keep. We were now crossing the middle bailey, passing the well on our right. Satisfied that only I could hear her words, she began to pour them out through her tears.

"It doesn't just happen. There's no point at which you can say, 'here it is' or, 'this was what came between us.' To start with, I don't think I could say he ever really made an effort to know me, to understand me. I was always simply his beautiful appendage—the world's most beautiful queen who decorated the arm of the world's most eminent king. We had little time together without courtiers around, endlessly. That and he was always away, what with the Irish war, and then the Gaulish war. How could we build intimacy if there was never time to be intimate? How could he ever know *me* when he spent all of his time creating *himself?*"

I walked with my head bowed, studying the earth and trying to understand problems I was too young to have ever experienced, but that I was mature enough to sympathize with. "Were you never happy then, my lady?"

She snorted again. "Oh, I certainly thought I was. All the great clothes I could ever want and a hundred courtiers bowing to my every whim at any given moment. But no private moments with *him.* And that's what I needed.

"Oh, I know what you're thinking. I'm not talking about the bedroom," she asserted bluntly as I felt myself crimson. "God, you men are all alike. No, we had a fair number of those intimate moments the first few years. But when I failed to get pregnant, those trickled down to nothing. I don't know how many years it's been since we've had *that* to share."

"But the king still needs you. He still has you sit with him at important court functions, like the Norwegians' visit today, for instance. Who else could he trust to do that?"

"Oh, nonsense, you foolish little page. He could just as well have commissioned a bust of me to be made and sat it at the table today. I was there as the ornament of his court and nothing more. I made pleasant conversation about the rainy weather in Logres this time of year, about Norwegian fjords and salmon, and listened to a very dry monologue concerning Norwegian shipbuilding by the fellow on my right who didn't know when to shut up. Do you have any idea what a clinker is?"

"No, my lady. But surely Arthur wanted you there because he values your charm, and knows that you are his dearest asset and ally in building relationships with foreign powers. And he doesn't just value you for that. Listen, the night of the unfortunate dinner, I saw his face. The thought that you were in trouble pained him deeply. He called Merlin out of the cave of his exile to prove your innocence. Is that the action of someone who doesn't care?"

"The actions of someone feeling regret. Maybe feeling some guilt. Maybe knowing how much of himself he should have given me and never got around to it. I don't know. Perhaps he cares. But not enough to truly be my husband. You know, your Merlin once told me, long ago, that in the old days the king actually went through a ceremony in which he was married to the land. It's Logres that must be Arthur's first love and his first concern. I'm only a second wife. That's all I'll ever be as long as Arthur rules this kingdom."

We were passing the barbican now at the end of the upper bailey, and we turned north to walk past the gate. Robin saw us from the gatehouse above the portcullis and doffed his hat and bowed to the queen. She nodded, and when she had put her head down again he mouthed to me something like "toady" and laughed silently. I unobtrusively threw a "fig" gesture at him and walked on just behind the queen. Sir Gaheris followed behind, still a good twenty paces back, but walking more easily now, as it seemed Aeneas and Dido had worn off their excess energy and were trotting along nicely on either side of him.

Finally Guinevere broke the silence with the one thing I was hoping she wouldn't say: "That's why Lancelot was so important to me."

"My lady," I began, hoping to beg off, "perhaps there are things that it would not be wise to confide in me about—"

"Nonsense!" She opened her eyes wide in order to cast on me her most imperious gaze. "You've gone this far, boy, you're not going to pull out now and leave me high and dry! Hear it you will! Lancelot has been my *lover.* There, I've said it aloud." She breathed a monstrous sigh of relief, and then words rushed forth as if a dam had burst and set free her years of silence.

"It was as if I had been buried alive, you understand? The mindless cipher of Arthur's queen, trotted out on state occasions to smile and act as a display case for all the expensive clothes and jewels in the kingdom—riches he got as tribute from conquered lands or from allies courting his favor. Hang them on Guinevere, that's what she's good for. But nothing more. Nothing intimate. Leave her to her rooms and her ladies and let them spin and weave and read romances and stay in their little corner until it is time to trot her out again. The endless horror of that kind of life, Gildas, is more than I can describe. And it promised to go on and on forever.

"Then he came to Camelot, the handsome, noble Frenchman. And nobody could beat him in the field, you understand? Nobody could unhorse him. He was the best. The best anyone had ever seen. The best there will ever be. Strong. Skilled. Courteous. The paragon. And he loved *me*. You see, Gildas, he loved me in a way that the king had never learned it was even possible to love. He was not interested in showing me off to visiting dignitaries. He was interested in showing me how much he loved me by doing anything I wanted him to do. He won his tournaments and gave me the prize. If I wanted him to lose the tournament he would drop out and let Sir Tristram or Sir Lamorak have the victory. If I had wanted him to bring me the tongue of a dragon he would have done that too. Don't you see what that meant to me? *I* was his priority. *I* was the most important thing in his life. Without *me* his life would have been meaningless."

"I understand it all, my lady." At that point I was hoping she would stop, or at least would talk more quietly. Sir Gaheris was still his preferred twenty paces behind, but we were passing by the stables, and I could see Taber coming out the door leading a brown palfrey. He nodded to us and I returned the greeting, hoping he hadn't been able to hear anything that the queen was saying.

"Gildas, it was as if I were fifteen again and happy. Here was the young gallant falling all over me again. Oh, Gildas, I loved him for it."

"Yes, my lady, but it may be prudent of you to keep your voice down right now. It certainly wouldn't do for you to be heard speaking of such things. Personally, I'd like to keep my head where it is, at least for a few more years."

"You're right, of course. I'll try to be less boisterous. But that won't be hard, since now things are clearly not as they were."

"Well, I meant to ask, lady, why exactly is Lancelot not here in Camelot now? Certainly if he were your champion there would be no question of your safety. He would die defending your honor and he is the greatest knight in the world."

The queen hung her head, and for the third time I saw tears moisten her eyelashes. She batted them away and continued resolutely. "Seventeen years he has been my secret lover." I flinched. She looked over at me and growled, "Hear it you will! Seventeen years. But the past two he has been gone from Camelot for longer and longer periods of time. What am I to make of it? His love to me cools, I swear I feel it. I was jealous. I am positive he has been unfaithful to me with Elaine, the daughter of King Pelles. I know that for a fact, because I had it from Sir Lamorak before he died, and he'd heard it from some Welsh lover of his. I threw these things up to him, wanting to have it out with him there and then. I was not going to be left dangling, like a used sock. He swore all was false and that he loved me as much as ever. But then he told me that there were suspicions among the court—that Sir Agravain and that young brat Mordred, in particular, were spreading rumors about us, and he did not want to make it appear that the rumors had any validity. So he was avoiding me for my own sake, he claimed.

"Well, damn it, Gildas, if I wanted to be avoided, I could be avoided by the king himself. Why did I need his upstart sycophantic French courtier to do it for him? I told Sir Lancelot that he was a false recreant knight, that he was a common lecher, and that he was to void my sight. I discharged him from the court and said that upon pain of his head he was to see me no more."

I stared at her, thunderstruck by her words. She looked over at me and shrugged, a small twisted smile on her face. Taking that as my cue, I offered "Well, that might explain why he hasn't been here to take up your cause, my lady." Then, thinking a little further, I said, "It would also explain why Sir Bors was rather reluctant to champion you as well, for Lancelot's sake."

"Yeah, well, to hell with him if he can't take a joke."

At that we both laughed heartily. Gaheris, behind us, perked up, and Aeneas and Dido followed suit, sensing something amusing was going on. But the queen continued, "So you see, Gildas, I don't hold a lot of hope that Lancelot will come to save me. And I don't know how much I can count on Bors to fight for me. I do know I am innocent of that man's murder, but there are times when I feel as if this life is too painful to continue on my present course. Without Lancelot, what have I got to live for?"

"My lady, never say so! There are those who love you too much to think about not having you with us. Even the king, and I tell you true, was ready to weep at the thought of the flames touching your beauty."

The queen sighed again. "Oh, I'm not ready to give it all up yet. But I'm afraid it will have to be you and Merlin who save me. So good luck with your nun, and anybody else you have yet to question. Merlin truly needs to work magic for me now. The days are running out."

"We're doing everything we can, my lady. Merlin is the smartest man I've ever seen. If there's anyone in the world can solve this mystery, I swear he's the one." If we can ever get him up out of his fetal position and back on the case, I added to myself.

And then, silly as it sounds, and corny as it may have seemed to the queen herself with her streak of detached irony, I felt myself overcome. I went down on one knee there in the grass of the lower bailey where we had returned, and grasped Guinevere by the hand. She looked at me with a startled yet bemused expression and cocked her head to one side. I looked up at her and made my vow:

"But Merlin or no Merlin, Lady Guinevere, I will save you. I swear it by all I hold dear Yes, I swear it by the Lady Rose-mounde's eyes, if that will suit you. I shall not rest until I have found the real killer and set you free. I cannot speak for King Arthur or Sir Lancelot, but here is one man whose love you will always have. I pledge to you my life, my honor, and my service." And with that I kissed her outstretched hand.

Exactly what her expression would have been at that point I can't say, because at that very instant Aeneas and Dido, seeing someone on the ground at their level, assumed that I was there for the express purpose of roughhousing with dogs. In their ecstasy they dragged Sir Gaheris forward until they were able to jump all over me, licking and snuggling and wrestling me all the way to the ground.

There was a burst of laughter from the queen and a surprised shout from me, followed by a mumbled curse from Sir Gaheris as he tried to disentangle the leashes and separate the dogs. When things had settled down I stood up, a little sheepish at having my grand gesture trampled by greyhounds, but the queen touched my shoulder.

"Gildas," she said, "I take back what I said earlier. You need no lessons in courtesy. You are courtesy itself. But remember, I am serious about your becoming squire to some good knight, and I shall give it some thought over the next few days. If nothing else, it will take my mind off my own dilemma," she added in an aside. "You must become a knight, for only a Sir Gildas of

Cornwall will hold any chance of winning the fair Lady Rose-mounde.

"As for the other, I accept your offer of service, and look forward to the successful completion of your quest. You have my blessing—and thanks.

"Nephew!" She barked out as a command. "We are nearly back to the entrance to my solar. Turn the leashes over to Gildas and he will return the dogs to the kennel. You will need to follow me back up to my rooms so as to guard against any sudden urges I might have to run naked through the halls of Camelot. Guard my door well tonight. I might just get crazy!" And with that she turned and walked calmly up the steps leading into her part of the castle.

Sir Gaheris looked at me, rolled his eyes, and sighed like one long suffering. Without a word he handed me the leashes and marched dutifully after the queen. I did hear him mutter under his breath, "One more hour until Gareth's shift."

Left alone with the dogs, I had time to think about what had just happened. I had done little thinking during the long conversation with the queen, only a lot of reacting as she took me through her emotional tempest. I walked slowly back toward the kennels, which were close by the stables back in the upper bailey. The queen had just confided in me every private feeling she had had in the past twenty-five years. She had revealed to me her affair with the king's greatest knight, making me a party to adultery and treason. In the assumption that I would never reveal any of her secrets to a living soul, she had also promised to find me a squire's position in preparation for my becoming a knight. And in return for these considerations I had vowed to serve her, to devote my life to saving her. And to top it all off, she had wept three times. The only time I had seen her do anything like that before was when she was trying to manipulate someone into doing what she wanted him to do.

At that thought I stopped and jerked my head up. Was that what had just happened to me?

CHAPTER TWELVE:
KNIGHT HAWKS

"Up boy, let's go! God's feet, we're burning daylight!"

I woke very slowly as the old pair of hands gave me a good shaking, and I looked up through sleep-fogged eyes into a pair of overgrown gray eyebrows about four inches from my own. "Merlin! Where the devil have you been, old man?"

"Back in my cave resting, of course. I told you it took me days to recover from those visions, didn't I? Well, I'm recovered. Let's go."

Without looking back he flipped me a piece of bread and headed out the door. I pulled on my hood and stumbled after him. Sir Gareth barely had time to ask as we rushed down the corridor, "Hey! Where're you off to in such a hurry?"

"We're going hawking! No time to chitchat!" Merlin called back and took me out the same door and down the steps I'd strolled along yesterday with the queen, at a much slower pace.

"Hawking? Don't we have a killer to catch?" I responded between mouthfuls of bread.

"Don't be obtuse!" Merlin chastised me, back to his old self. "Do you think killers wait around in their homes waiting for us to come and fetch them? The Red Knight of the Red Lands is out hawking today. We're going to get a few horses and ride out to find him. We'll act as if we happened to meet there by accident, and try to make pleasant conversation with him."

"Sure. Pleasant conversation like, 'Sir Ironside, I hear you hated Sir Patrise. Wanna tell us why you murdered him?' "

Merlin shrugged. "Stranger things have happened. Anyway, he'll be off guard. But the clock is ticking on the queen's trial, and we need to talk to as many people as we can. And we need to *think*." The old man pointed to his head, as if he wasn't sure I knew which part of the anatomy was used in the thinking process.

"Well," I answered, "I *think* we're going in the wrong direction. Aren't the stables the other way?" We were just coming to the kitchen.

"Roger!" Merlin called. The cook poked his head out the door. "How about a little drink to wash down our breakfast? We have a dry ride ahead of us."

"Right!" Roger obliged, ducking back inside the kitchen and emerging a few seconds later with two cups of watery beer.

"Ah!" Merlin smacked his lips. "That should do it."

"Found anything out about this killin'?" Roger asked in his slow drawl, wiping the sweat from his brow with his sleeve. Even this early in the morning—it must be barely prime—I could feel the kitchen was beginning to heat up.

Merlin took a long swig of his beer and then wiped his mouth on his own sleeve. "We're getting closer," he answered evasively. "We've been talking to the folks you said were here the day of the unfortunate dinner. They've given us a great deal of information and we're trying to see how that all fits together."

" 'Aven't got a clue, 'ave ya?" Roger asked.

Merlin shook his head, shamed into honesty. I just kept drinking my beer. "You're sure you only remember those two visitors that day? Sir Palomides and Sister Agnes?"

"Agnes? That her name. is it? Well, I never knew what to call 'er. So I guess you've found somethin' out anyway! Naw, nobody else to speak of. Just, like I said to ya afore, the queen 'erself and then Kay. Course, Kay was with other knights every time 'e was 'ere."

Merlin's head jerked toward Roger and his eyes flashed with shock and disbelief. "What! God's shinbones!"

Unable to restrain myself, I caught Merlin's tone and cried. "You mean there were other knights in the kitchen that day with Kay?"

Merlin had recovered enough by then to finish my question. "How many?"

"Well, that's 'ard to say, bein' as 'ow I didn't pay an' 'ole lot of attention 'cause it was Kay, you know. The boss. But they were with 'im, so I figger it's 'is job to watch out for 'em, see. Anyways, they were with 'im the 'ole time, far's I know."

"When did they come in with him?"

"Well, lemme see." Roger took off his hat and scratched his chin. "Seems like Kay was alone the first time 'e come in early in the morning. Then Palomides and the nun was there later. An' then Kay come in again, and that was with them other knights like I says."

"Do you know who they were? Any of them?"

Roger scratched again and shook his head. "Not by name. An' I didn't look real close. Seems to me at least one of 'em I've seen with Kay before. Sorry, can't tell ya anything else."

Merlin, clearly fuming but keeping his temper in check, said quietly between clenched teeth. "I do wish you had mentioned this when we talked with you earlier."

Roger merely shrugged and reached out for our empty glasses. "Thanks for the drink," Merlin said measuredly. "If you can think of anything else—like the names of those knights— you'll let me know, won't you?"

"Oh, right! Anything to 'elp, old Mage." And with that Roger turned back into his kitchen to begin preparations for the mid-day meal.

Merlin turned and stormed off in the direction of the stables, muttering to himself about dimwitted cooks and soft-headed seneschals. "And a week full gone that could have been spent searching out those other knights."

It was Wednesday. We had one more week to solve the case, and the heavenly spheres were ceaseless and unrelenting in their forward movement. But I wasn't sure that this new wrinkle was as significant as Merlin seemed to think it was.

"But the knights were with Kay the whole time, according to Roger. I don't see that any of them could have done anything with Sir Kay with them all the while they were in the kitchen," I babbled from behind, trying to keep up with Merlin. For an old man he moved pretty swiftly when he had a mind to.

"In case you haven't noticed, my good young page, Sir Kay could not find his own behind with both hands. He's an incompetent blusterer who likes to be in charge because it gives him prestige, but whose greatest contribution to leadership is staying out of the way so that somebody with some sense can get something done."

As a matter of fact, I had noticed, as had most folks who stayed long enough in the castle. "Do you think that one of the knights with Kay could have been Sir Ironside?" I asked.

"Ah!" Merlin turned around briefly—though he kept walking backward—and raised an index finger into the air. "*That* is the question, is it not? For we think he had a motive. Sir Patrise's dalliance with his wife, if rumor prove true. And his being with Kay would provide him with clear opportunity."

"What about means?" I asked, ticking off in my mind Merlin's three criteria for finding the killer.

"That," the old man said turning back around, "we'll have to find."

"Couldn't we just ask Kay who was with him that day?"

"We could indeed," Merlin replied thoughtfully. "But first I'd rather ask Sir Ironside himself. It might be instructive to see how he reacts if we catch him off guard."

We were crossing into the upper bailey and I could see Taber standing with two brown palfreys at the stable door. Merlin must have been up and about very early this morning, so as to have already visited with Taber about having our horses saddled and ready for us when we arrived. At that moment, at the idea of horses saddled and waiting, something clicked in the back of my mind—but then it faded and I couldn't quite put my finger on it. I knew I was forgetting something. I just couldn't remember what it was.

"Thanks, Taber," Merlin said as he took the reins from the stable hand. "We appreciate your being so willing to get them ready for us on such short notice."

Taber, stooped and scrawny, bowed his head slightly so that his thin, greasy brown hair fell forward into his sooty face. When he opened his mouth to say "Just doing my job, sir," I noticed he had but few teeth left. He bowed again and added, "Enjoy yer hawking, good sirs," before he ducked back through the stable door.

Merlin swung into the saddle and I stepped into mine a bit more gingerly. If I was ever going to be a knight indeed, I had to learn a good deal more about horsemanship. "But we'll talk to Kay before long," Merlin told me, continuing our conversation as if there had been no break. "First, though, I need to find out from you everything that happened at the nunnery. You did go there to visit Sister Agnes, I understand?"

"I went there for that purpose, yes," I told him as our horses moved at a trot and I struggled again to keep up with him. We passed quickly through the gate and over the drawbridge almost, but not quite, too fast for Robin, who was able to shout out one small insult to me as I trotted past the barbican: "So they found you a horse, Master Gildas! Now all you've got to do is stay on her! Don't worry. Pretend she's a young damsel!"

I took a moment to flip Robin another fig for him to see over my receding horse's rump, even as I began to tell Merlin about my experiences at the Convent of Saint Mary Magdalene. He listened intently as we rode north into the fields, and then began musing aloud.

"If Sister Agnes is in charge of the garden at the nunnery, and if she provides herbs and concoctions to the infirmary there, then she's quite likely to be acquainted with the foxglove herb that we know poisoned Sir Patrise. She would know more about such things than Sir Palomides ever could have picked up by loitering around kitchens between here and Jerusalem."

"But what possible motive could a nun have to kill Sir Patrise?"

"She wasn't always a nun, you Cornish dunce. You said something about a love affair gone bad or some such thing. I don't understand it, but I have heard that love sometimes compels people to do things they would never have done otherwise."

"You don't understand it? You, locked in your enchanted cave by the nymph Nimue?"

"I've told you before not to burn me with the facts," Merlin chided, though his eyes danced with irony. "In any case, my point is that Sister Agnes may very well have been holding a grudge for years. Perhaps she finally saw her opportunity to settle a score, or avenge a wrong, or whatever she thought she was doing."

"But how could she know exactly when she would have the chance to get her vengeance? How would she know to bring the poison just at the time she did?"

"Precisely the correct question, my lad. How indeed? She had to have an accomplice within the castle walls who knew not only that the dinner was to take place, but also that Sir Patrise would be there. We've already talked about there being more than one person involved in this crime. Now it appears we were right."

"If Sister Agnes is guilty. Do we know that for sure?"

"We don't know anything for sure, dunce!" Merlin looked back to me, exasperated. "But we'd better start getting some facts soon. Sister Agnes was confined to her cell, you say, for violations of the rule? What might those violations have been?"

"I guess probably murder would be a violation of the rule. I don't think Saint Benedict put that on his list of things to do in cloistered life: Lauds—rise and pray; Lauds to Prime—breakfast and private devotions; Prime—sing holy office; Prime to Terce—murder some knight; Terce—sing offices again—"

"Are you still talking?" Merlin shot back. "Clearly the abbess would have done more than confide her to her cell if she thought Sister Agnes had committed murder. This kind of punishment probably had to do with some more minor infraction, but more serious than, say, talking during periods of forced silence, or forgetting the words to one of the offices. We need to find out just what Sister Agnes did."

We rode on in silence for a few moments, through the fields where now only weeds and the stubble of harvested crops remained as autumn wore on. There was a cold nip in the air again this morning, and I was glad I had been able to snatch my hood before we left the castle. We began to travel northwest, straight across the fields and toward a corner of the wood where apparently Merlin thought he would find Sir Ironside and his falconer hunting. Finally I spoke up and broached a subject I'd been thinking about for the past two days.

"Merlin, when you had your . . . attack or whatever it was
. . ."

"Vision," he said simply.

"Yes, well, vision then. When you had it, do you remember what you said?"

"I never actually remember. Someone will write it down and tell me afterwards, but it never really does me any good. It's one of the things I've become known for, and it amazes people that they can see my 'prophesies' come true. But as I told you before, the predictions never make any sense to me—or to anyone else, for that matter, until they think about them after the fact. And now I suppose you're going to tell me what I said, and want to know whether it means anything to me."

"Wow," I teased him. "That's exactly what I was going to do! You really *can* predict the future!"

Merlin leaned back from his horse and tried to cuff me around the ears, but I ducked away. "Little scamp," he grumbled, not terribly angrily. "I ought to knock a hole in that silly Cornish pate of yours. It'd probably improve your brains if I aired them out a bit."

"What you said," I continued in earnest, "was something about a great bear being brought down by a bunch of dogs. Or curs, I think you called them. And then you said 'Listen to the Lion.'"

The old necromancer shrugged. "If that's what you say I said, I'll have to believe you. But it really means nothing to me. As for interpreting its meaning, your guess is as good as mine. Well, probably not *as* good, but close."

"But they are all symbols. Do you think they might have something to do with heraldic symbols? Should we think about knights' coats of arms?"

"If you want to think about it and try to put it together, be my guest. But I've wasted enough time trying to figure out those riddling prophecies in the past, and it's always been a waste of my time. I'm going to focus on trying to find Sir Patrise's killer, and I'm going to start by questioning that gentleman right up ahead there."

I hadn't noticed that we were coming up to a lone knight, Sir

Ironside, on horseback precisely where Merlin had expected
him to be—here in the open field some hundred yards south of
the edge of the wood where Merlin had his cave. The Red
Knight of the Red Lands was uncharacteristically dressed in a
green surcote, with a black cloak and hood against the chill of
the morning. A smaller palfrey stood some twenty yards off, his
reins tied to a bush of stubble. Standing next to Sir Ironside's
horse was Muggs, one of the falconers from Camelot, whom
Ironside had paid to train the expensive new gyrfalcon he had
imported recently from breeders in Iceland. A magnificent bird,
she must have weighed nearly five pounds. She was beautiful
with her almost snowy white plumage. This was the first time
they had brought her out to engage in a hunt. Muggs held her
on his wrist, and she still wore a leash attached to a long slender
cord, or creance, that Muggs held in his other hand. He and
Ironside looked up as we approached and the Red Knight gave
us a surly greeting.

"You're stirring awfully early this morning, aren't you old
man? You've nearly spooked my Hippolyta!"

"Well, we'll keep the hood on her for a few more minutes,
and she'll be all right," Muggs told him. "So long as you talk
softly, and as long as you two don't go riding off suddenly after
I unhood her."

"Sure, easy does it then," Merlin said. "We'll all keep very
calm."

Sir Ironside looked at him suspiciously. "So what are you doing here, Merlin?" he asked in a very low voice.

"Oh, we are out and about on the king's business."

"Are you sure you don't mean the queen's?" Even in such
low tones it was possible to distinguish a bit of a snarl in Sir
Ironside's voice. He had thick black hair that resisted any attempt to tame it, and a dark black beard as well. His complexion

was sanguine, and his fierce eyes burned like black coals in that sea of red.

"Indeed," Merlin reminded him, "the two are one flesh, being man and wife as well as king and queen. Her unfortunate position resulting from Sir Patrise's death has sent us on this quest to find the truth behind that murder."

The Red Knight snorted and burst out, somewhat louder than he had intended, "Sir Patrise. Humph! That Irish bastard."

At the noise, the falcon jumped, and Muggs put a finger to his lips in irritation as he stroked Hippolyta gently and whispered to her through her leather hood.

"You seem to have rather strong feelings about Sir Patrise, my lord," Merlin probed. "Was there some bad blood between the two of you? Some unresolved matter—"

"That would make me want to kill him?" Sir Ironside finished the sentence for him. "You're damned right there was. That son of an Irish whore was trying to make a cuckold of me. You understand? He was trying to bed my wife."

Merlin raised his bushy brows high and he said quietly, "The Lady Catherine? My lord, many a man has suspicions, but most are merely insecure. For yourself, I understand that you keep your wife in a well-guarded castle several leagues from Camelot. Why do you think someone has been able to penetrate the defenses of that castle? Do you have proof?"

"The rumor is rampant," Sir Ironside growled through clenched teeth. "It merely confirms my suspicion about the *Lady* Catherine as you call her. And I can't say I completely trust the guards I've placed around the castle. My experience has been that where there's smoke there's fire. The rumors would not exist if there were not some truth to them."

"And my experience has been," Merlin went on coolly, "that if you are always expecting the worst out of people, you will generally get it. If you refuse to trust your wife, how can she act in a trustworthy manner? And why would she want to?"

"My wife is mine and I will deal with her as I see fit. That she is a slut of the first magnitude I have no doubt. If you want to know why, peruse this letter." With that the Red Knight reached into his right boot and pulled out a piece of folded parchment. With a quizzical look, Merlin took the letter and unfolded it.

Meanwhile, Muggs handed the gyrfalcon over to Sir Ironside, and untied the leash and creance. Sir Ironside held the bird gingerly on his left fist, the bird perching on his leather gauntlet to protect the knight's hand. Slowly and carefully, the Red Knight removed the hood from the bird's eyes. Sir Ironside, watching the sky, waited motionless.

In a moment, I saw what they had been waiting for: a small wedge of geese, inspired by the cold autumn weather to turn south, honked overhead. I saw Hippolyta's head jerk up at the sound, and almost simultaneously Sir Ironside made a casting off gesture with his fist. The falcon took off, soaring overhead in pursuit of the geese. Her wingspan as she began to climb into the heavens must have been nearly five feet, and she continued to climb until she looked like nothing more than a speck against the gray clouds, soaring high above the vee made by the geese.

I looked over to see whether Merlin had taken note of the falcon's flight, but the old man was absorbed in the parchment the Red Knight had given him. His face remained expressionless, but he handed the note over to me grimly when he had finished. I looked at it. It was another poem. This is how it read:

To Catherine:

The sun that warms the tender plants
Also warms my soul,
And Love awakens in my tender heart.
I think of him who keeps us torn apart

That jealous fool,
Who never gives our love a chance.

I long to spend the night with you
To hold you by my side,
And take the fruits that love can give.
Without your love I fear I cannot live,
And after I have died
You'll see that my pure love was true.

But he who guards you night and day
Has put up heavy walls
That serve to keep you in and keep me out.
And with no word from you I'm forced to doubt
And loneliness galls.
I cannot eat and fear I'll waste away.

Defy the jealous one and come
To me your truest love!
For all his spying make his eyes go blind
Escape from those cruelest ties that bind
And with me move
To where true love may find a home.

"But why are you so certain the poem is from Sir Patrise? It has no name on it. It could have been written by almost anyone, I should think," Merlin asked, still keeping his voice quiet and calm, though with the bird in the air, there seemed to be no further reason for it.

"Oh, it's from him all right. I made sure of that. Let's just say I persuaded the *Lady* Catherine, as you call her, that it was in her best interests to give up her lover."

"You mean to say you beat your wife until she confessed to you?" I burst in. Merlin put a calming hand on my arm but I had heard all I wished to from that smug, red-faced bully. "Is that what a courtly gentleman does with his own lady?"

"Hold your tongue, boy, or I'll cut it out and feed it to my birds. She is indeed my own lady, and who are you to question what I do with my own? Who are you to question anything I do, you upstart son of a Cornish ragpicker? If you were a knight I'd have you in the lists today and cut out your heart. Mind him, Merlin. He'd better not cross me a second time." His eyes blazed at me. His enraged face grew even redder as he leaned toward me, and his hand went down to rest on his sword hilt.

Merlin, placing himself strategically between the Red Knight and me, continued calmly, "The page is the queen's and he is under my protection and the king's. You were better pacify your ire or face the full wrath of King Arthur. Now you were saying you forced your wife to implicate Sir Patrise. But how can you be sure she was telling the truth? Wouldn't someone in that situation say anything to appease her tormentor?"

"I don't like your tone either, old man," Sir Ironside grumbled. "But rest assured, she told me the truth. She knows how badly it would go for her if I found she ever lied to me. And I'll tell you something else." He was close enough to Merlin's horse to plant an index finger on the old man's chest. "It will be a long time before any man looks at her with pleasure again. I made sure of that. Her face will be a long time healing." And with that the Red Knight smiled a brutal grin.

Merlin, unimpressed, pressed forward to the most important question. "Are we to believe that your vengeance stopped with the Lady Catherine? Isn't it true that you would have wanted to exact vengeance on Sir Patrise as well?"

"You're damned right I would have. I told you already. But poison? I'd never do it that way. I'd have had him in the lists and cut him to pieces. Then I'd have stripped him of his armor and hung his pathetic body up to rot, until the crows had picked his stinking bones clean."

All through his last comments he was looking skyward, watching Hippolyta gliding high overhead. I looked up as well, in time to see the falcon tuck in its enormous wings and begin a powerful dive. The geese, sensing what was coming, split from their wedge and flew in several different directions, but one of the trailing birds, a smaller and weaker young goose, seemed to react too late. That was the bird that Hippolyta had chosen for her target. I watched in shocked fascination as the falcon struck hard into the other bird, her talons tearing the flesh and her curved beak breaking the neck of the weaker goose, while staying in full flight. As the two birds fell to the ground, Muggs ran over to retrieve Hippolyta and her quarry.

Sir Ironside looked at Merlin with a satisfied smile and said, "I like the thrill of the kill. The struggle of the pathetic victim as I wrench his life from him. It would have been a particular pleasure to disembowel that Irish bastard."

Merlin looked into his face, paused for a moment, and then nodded. "Right. Well, we'll trouble you no more. As I say, we are on the king's business and can't delay too long about it. Nice chatting with you, but we really can't stay any longer. Good day to you then." And with that he turned his horse back in the direction we had come and began trotting off. Sir Ironside, caught off guard by Merlin's sudden departure, merely stared after him with an open mouth and a puzzled look in his brutal eyes.

My own face almost certainly bore a similar expression. "Merlin!" I called to him as I trotted all the faster to try to keep up. "What in the world was that all about? I think we had him there. He all but admitted he was the one who killed Sir Patrise! What do we do now? Shall we go to the king and get an armed guard to arrest him?"

"Then we'd be arresting an innocent man," Merlin stated

flatly without turning his head.

"Innocent! Him? He brutalized his own wife. Gareth knows he killed forty knights. If he's innocent, Satan's a choirboy."

"He killed the knights in single combat according to the rules of chivalry. As for his wife, he has certainly broken the rules of courtesy in his treatment of her, but those rules do not have the force of law. There is no law in Logres that allows the king or his representatives to interfere in the private affairs between a man and his wife."

"Well, there should be a law that protects her."

"Until there is, he is innocent before the law. He did not kill Sir Patrise."

"What? Why, because he says he didn't? Why should we believe him?"

"Because he has always killed within the code of chivalry. And he has never hidden any of the violence he has committed. If he had killed Sir Patrise, he would have no qualms about telling us so."

Realizing Merlin was right, I slumped in my saddle. I had thought our quest was at an end. But it seemed we were right back where we had started from. And besides all that, the Red Knight would go free after all, and would not have to pay for his crimes. It was all too depressing. "So we're out of clues," I ventured.

"Not quite," said Merlin. "Do you still have that parchment?"

Suddenly remembering that I was still holding the poem that Sir Ironside had shown us, I handed it over to Merlin and said, "Yes, here it is. But what good does that do us? It's Sir Patrise's poem, and Sir Patrise is dead."

"It's not Sir Patrise's poem," Merlin said, riding on without taking the parchment from my hand. "Look at it again. The rhyme scheme. The meter. The language. They are identical. There's only one person that could have written that poem."

I looked at it again as I trotted along, and then looked up with a start. Merlin was right.

"Sir Palomides!" I exclaimed.

CHAPTER THIRTEEN:
THE OUTCAST

It was well after sext and Merlin and I had been able to grab a smaller-than-usual midday meal before getting on with the most important task at hand: finding and confronting Sir Palomides about the poem to Lady Catherine.

We had heard that some of the knights had set up a quintain in the lists and were practicing their jousting maneuvers there, so we headed in that direction, across the middle bailey and behind the keep. Here there was a large door that opened into a long, narrow area between the inner castle wall and the outer crenellated wall that stood above the moat. This area, some twenty yards wide by a hundred yards long, was the practice lists for the castle. There was another area outside the castle walls that served to house tournaments and had rooms for spectators to stand and for the gentler folk to sit and watch the spectacle. But the lists between the castle walls were for more serious work that prepared a knight for combat.

The door was open, and we entered gingerly, having no desire to be run down by a charging warhorse in full barding. But we needn't have been quite so cautious. There were indeed two large brown destriers there, on which knights and squires were taking turns charging the quintain, but neither men nor horses wore armor.

On one end of the lists stood Sir Tristram, Sir Bleoberis, Sir Brandiles, and his young squire, Colgrevaunce, holding one of the great horses. On the other end were Sir Palomides, Sir Breunor ("La Cote Male Taile"), Sir Ywain's squire, Thomas, and, mounted on the other great horse, Sir Gawain's son and squire, Florent.

Florent held a lance and glared grimly at the wooden quintain some fifty yards before him. I couldn't help thinking how much he resembled his famous father as he sat on the horse, his red hair flowing, his brown eyes bent fixedly on the target. The others all shouted encouragement to him as he began to urge the horse forward. Florent held the lance taut, couched against his saddle so as to put all the weight of horse and man behind the thrust, and he reached the top of his gallop just as he drove the lance into the wooden dummy. As it spun on the post, he sped by quickly enough to avoid being struck from behind by the weighted sack from the other side of the post as he was passing.

A cheer went up from all the witnesses, and Merlin took that opportunity to make his way quickly across the area toward Sir Palomides. Colgrevaunce was mounting the other charger in the meantime, and steadying his own lance for the charge, receiving advice all the while from Sir Brandiles. When Sir Palomides saw Merlin approaching, he rolled his eyes and then took a defiant stance.

"What do you want now, old man? Haven't you disturbed me enough already?"

"No," Merlin answered frankly. "Not nearly enough. You lied to us, my Lord Palomides. And I want to know why."

In rage his blood rose to darken the Moor's complexion. He barked angrily, "You're mad, man. What are you talking about? If you give me the lie, I shall have to challenge you, old man or no. Prove your words or face my sword." Out of habit his hand reached to his belt, but to Merlin's good fortune the Moor had come unarmed to the list area.

Merlin, however, kept his voice low and steady, saying, "This way, my lord. What I need to ask you is private." With that he drew Sir Palomides aside so that no other knights were in range of his voice. As he did so, a thunder of hooves told us that Colgrevaunce was charging, and the laughter that followed told us without our bothering to look that the squire had missed the quintain altogether in his assault.

"Why did you lie to us about knowing Sir Patrise?" Merlin put it to him bluntly.

"I never did so!" Sir Palomides ranted. "I told you that I did not know him before, and I . . ." But Merlin had taken the parchment with the poem to Lady Catherine from his sleeve where he had kept it, and held it open before Sir Palomides's eyes as he raved. The sight of the poem made the words catch in his throat. Sir Palomides's brazenly defiant pose evaporated and he looked like someone had knocked the wind out of him. Still he was not about to admit anything. "What's this?" he asked, as if confused. "A love poem? What does it mean to me?"

"You don't recognize it?" Merlin pushed. "Look again. Look at the pattern of the stanzas. Look at the rhyme scheme. Look at the phrasing and the images."

"Pah. All these love poems sound the same. Always the wound of love and the lady is the healer. Always the prisoner of love and the lady holds the key. Always the unattainable lady and the servant lover."

"But not always the six-line stanzas with the long rhyming couplet in the middle—that's unique. *That,* my lord, is *yours.*"

Sir Palomides sighed and raised his eyebrows as a sign of concession. "The verse form imitates the wheel of Fortune, do you see? It begins with the 'a' rhyme, rises to its climax with the couplet in mid-stanza, then falls again to end where it began at the 'a' rhyme. Each stanza repeats in its very structure the rise and fall of Fortune's wheel. It's a comment, you understand? A comment on love and on lovers, who subject themselves to the fickle whims of Fortune when they turn their eyes from the highest good and chase after their lovers, the baubles of this world."

"A bauble you've been chasing yourself for quite a few years," Merlin reminded him.

"Ah, yes." Sir Palomides sighed again. "The fair Isolde. But Fortune keeps me pinned at the bottom of her wheel, I'm afraid. I cannot rise up but I cannot let go of the wheel."

A sudden groan exploded from all others in the lists, and we looked up in time to see that Colgrevaunce had not only missed the quintain altogether with his lance but had run into it with his shoulder as he rode by. Trying to recover his balance on the charging warhorse, he had slowed down enough that the weighted bag on the other side of the quintain had spun around and struck him from behind, knocking him off of his horse. Sir Bleoberis and Sir Ywain came running to help him out of the dirt while the horse stopped and looked back at him with what I could swear was a disgusted look. Colgrevaunce, drooping his arms around the two knights' shoulders, limped off with a very red face and downcast eyes.

"When Fortune's wheel spins and casts you down, you fall with a crash," Sir Palomides observed. "But what is it you think you know, old man? That I wrote this poem to the Lady Catherine? And what if that is true?"

"It *is* true, of that I have no doubt. And I don't think it was out of love for the lady herself. I'm sure that in your wish to prove your true devotion to the Lady Isolde, you would never dally with any other woman. Whatever else you may be, you are not a false lover."

Sir Palomides nodded to Merlin with a slight bow of acknowledgment. "Thank you, my lord. I take that as the highest compliment."

Merlin had only been thinking out loud, and was interested

only in stating the facts, not giving out compliments. "So that means," he continued undeterred, "that you wrote this poem at the request of Sir Patrise, to help him woo the Lady Catherine. You lied about not knowing him. In fact you knew him well enough to be his go-between in this love affair."

Merlin was way ahead of me with that leap, but I caught up quickly and saw that he must be right. And when I did, I lost control and burst out, "He trusted you! Why would you betray him and kill him?"

"Gildas!" Merlin glared at me, and I could feel the fire behind those dark eyes.

Sir Palomides actually laughed. "That's far too great a conclusion to jump to, my cheeky young page. I have betrayed no one. I have murdered no one. I have written a love poem at the request of a poor, inarticulate Irishman whom I befriended as a fellow alien in the court. Beyond that there is nothing I am guilty of."

"Except lying," Merlin reminded him. "When you lie to someone investigating a murder, it means you have something to hide. It means we can't be sure that anything you say is true."

Sir Palomides scoffed. "Pah. Hear this, for you can be sure *it* is true: all our lives are a fabric of convenient lies. The Christians who slaughtered the 'infidel' of Jerusalem said they did it as God's will. That convenient lie made it possible for them to live with what they had done. And here in Camelot? What lies make it possible for the queen to live with King Arthur? Or for Sir Bors to defend her 'innocence' for the sake of Sir Lancelot? Or for Sir Gawain and his brothers to live undisturbed at court? Or for Sir Ironside to sweep forty dead knights under the rug? Or what about yourself, old man? Besotted of a water nymph, you spend all of your time isolated in a cave? Why? Because you are 'enchanted'? Please! Without convenient lies, our entire society would collapse. Mine was as harmless a lie as you will find in Camelot. Tush. Don't chastise me with trifles."

"None of that answers the question, my lord. I am investigating the murder of a knight of the round table. At least one other life is at stake, and I will not allow a murderer to run free in Camelot. You lied to me about knowing the murder victim. That puts you under grave suspicion. It's time for you to tell me the truth or I will bring you before the king himself, and he will have the truth out of you in more unpleasant ways than our conversation."

Sir Palomides only laughed again. "Stop trying to frighten me, old man, I'm beyond that. Do you think after what I've seen in my life I fear the rack? Or for one minute believe that King Arthur would stoop to use it? He is, of all men living, the least likely to resort to such methods. But for my honor's sake I will tell you what passed between the Irish knight and me."

He glanced toward the lists again, where now Thomas, the other squire, had mounted and was galloping toward the quintain. He struck the dummy, but at a slant with the lance, and so the lance glanced off and shot from Thomas's hand, flying end-over-end through the air to come down some thirty feet away. Thomas stopped his horse in bewilderment, and while he sat there the weighted bag swung around and glanced off his skull. He trotted bewilderedly back to the side he had started from, rubbing the bump on his head and looking lost.

Sir Palomides shook his head. "He has a long way to go, that one. But Sir Patrise . . . let me see. I first approached him a few weeks after he had arrived in Camelot, when I heard that he was of a noble Irish family. My Lady Isolde is daughter to the Irish king, and I was certain he must have known my lady, and would be willing to talk to me about her. You know yourself that a true lover is always and everywhere beset by thoughts of his beloved, and is always looking for reasons to talk about her."

I had to admit there was some truth in that part of what Sir Palomides had to say. Certainly since I'd become aware of the beauty of the lady Rosemounde, her image had been dancing across my field of vision wherever I went. And I had to admit that discussing her even that brief moment with the queen had been the most pleasant thing I'd done in the past two days. Admittedly, most of what I'd been doing was decidedly unpleasant, but still, the vision of Rosemounde was the bright spot in every waking moment.

"So . . . you talked to him about Queen Isolde?" Merlin prompted.

"And beyond my wildest imaginings, I found that he was in fact second cousin to my lady. His mother, the Lady Deirdre, was the daughter of the Earl Robert, second son of King Conchobar and the current king's grandfather—"

Merlin shook his head. "Spare me the details. Go on."

"Well, he was more than a confidante to me. He told me what he knew of the lady Isolde's childhood and life in Ireland before her marriage to King Mark. Told me how she had met Sir Tristram." With that, Palomides jerked his head across the lists to where Tristram stood, oblivious to his envy, watching Thomas arm himself for another go at the quintain. "Told me too of all her likes and dislikes, her favorite flowers, scents, animals, everything I could use to woo her. Not that any of it ever did me any good, or made her think of me in any way like she thinks of *him*." The head jerked again.

"So why, if you spent so much time with Sir Patrise, was your friendship with him not so well known in Camelot? Why did no one tell me that if I was looking into Sir Patrise's murder, I should talk to his good friend Palomides to find out whether he had any enemies?"

"Our friendship was not common knowledge around the castle. We met in out of the way places or at odd times of the night. In the first place, while there are several who know of my love for the lady Isolde, it is still important that such a love not become open and public. She is the queen of Cornwall, wife of King Mark. Courtesy forbids making such a lady's name a common word among the vulgar."

"And the other reason no doubt had to do with the other lady's name, then?" Merlin went on.

"Precisely. What Sir Patrise wanted in exchange for his gossip about the lady Isolde was my help in wooing Lady Catherine. My own great success as a lover must have prompted him to seek my advice."

I snorted at the heavy irony in his voice.

"Particularly, he wanted help with poetry?"

"Yes. You know the cliché among lovers: the truer the lover, the greater the poet. The greater the poem, the truer the love. Only Patrise, true as he was to Lady Catherine, had a tin ear for poetry and no tongue for it at all. So I helped him out. He was grateful. I was content. Where was the harm?"

"No harm," Merlin answered. "Until somebody killed him."

"Not I, certainly! Why would I kill my lady's own kinsman, especially one who was helping me to woo her?"

"Why would you lie about your relationship with him?"

"Who wouldn't have lied under the circumstances? I did not know until the funeral that Sir Patrise had been at the siege of Jerusalem. I can add two and two as well as you, old man. I knew where the first suspicion would fall: here is Sir Palomides. He is an outsider, a Moor. And he has a strong motive. He must be the guilty one. If you knew of anything that connected me with Sir Patrise, it would be I, not the queen, on trial for my life. Is that where you intend to put me now?"

Merlin shook his head. "Your explanation satisfies me for now. I do not really believe you killed Sir Patrise."

"What of your young friend there, who was so quick to judge

before?" Sir Palomides glared at me with his wide black eyes again.

"Well, maybe I jumped a little too soon," I admitted. "I'm reserving my judgment. For now."

Sir Palomides gave another of his hearty, booming laughs. "But now that you know of my intimate relationship with the Irish knight, are you going to ask me whether he had any enemies?"

"Of course," Merlin looked at him shrewdly, knowing what was coming. "Enlighten us, if you can."

"Sir Ironside hated him with the coldest of passions. He would have killed him without hesitation if he'd had the chance."

"Hatred or no hatred, Sir Ironside is not guilty of this crime."

"Indeed?" Sir Palomides looked at him wide-eyed. "Are you so certain of his innocence?"

"As certain as I am of yours," Merlin told him.

Sir Palomides was as well aware of the irony in that statement as I was, but he made no comment. In fact, the lists suddenly became completely silent. Every knight had stopped talking and all were facing in the same direction, toward the gate from the middle bailey through which Sir Bors had just come, accompanied by his brother, Sir Lionel. Sir Bors carried a helmet under his arm, while Sir Lionel held a long lance in one hand and the reins of Pegasus, Sir Bors's great brown destrier, in the other. Evidently they had intended to get in a little practice with the quintain today with an eye toward the battle Bors must do one week from today as the queen's champion.

Bors and Lionel stopped immediately when they came through the door. Every eye was on them but not a word was spoken. No one uttered a word of greeting, no one approached them in fellowship, no one even smiled. Lionel turned red, his black beard shaking with bridled rage as he glared around at the other knights, daring them with his eyes to say something against his brother. Bors himself remained stoic and expressionless, though he too looked around the lists to see whether he had any friend in the group. As soon as he met the knights' eyes, they turned away. Bors ignored them, and he and Lionel walked toward the side of the lists at the far end from where Merlin and I still stood with Sir Palomides.

At their approach, Thomas quickly dismounted and nearly ran to the other side of the lists. More slowly, Sir Tristram and the other knights moved off, so that by the time Sir Bors and Sir Lionel had reached their position, everyone else, including both other horses, was at the opposite side of the field.

Sir Bors appeared not to notice. As Lionel held his mount, Bors eased himself slowly into the saddle and held his helmet aloft. He brought it down over his head, covering his nut-brown, oval face so that nothing was visible but the eyes through a cross-shaped slit in the iron face. Bors reached down and Lionel handed him his spear. As he backed off, Bors gave Lionel a silent nod of thanks and then stiffened. His body formed a solid mass of concentration as he leaned forward, lance poised, focused and deadly.

Then, with a sudden flick of his heels against the horse's flanks, Sir Bors was off, charging toward the target. The hoofbeats of the great warhorse pounded the turf, picking up more and more speed as he charged, and I could see the explosive tension in the muscles of Bors's right arm as he aimed the lance expertly at the quintain.

With a thunderous crash of released fury, Bors, Pegasus, and the lance struck the unresisting quintain dead center so hard that the wooden dummy flew into a thousand pieces. The watching knights gave a collective gasp and stared in slack-jawed disbelief at the remains of the shattered jousting dummy. Pegasus galloped a few yards past the quintain and then slowed to a walk and stopped. Sir Bors pulled the helmet off and looked back to study the scene. When his face turned forward again, I thought I saw the left corner of his mouth twist upward a bit with satisfaction.

Unable to restrain my admiration, after a moment's shocked paused I threw my right arm into the air and whooped a cheer for the greatest feat of knighthood I had ever seen on the practice field. Sir Lionel cheered more loudly than I, and he was joined by Colgrevaunce and, in a subdued manner, by Merlin himself. But that was all. Even though clearly none of the other knights present had ever seen such a feat, they were still not willing to acknowledge anything accomplished by the pariah Sir Bors had become.

Bors dismounted, looked at Lionel, and shrugged, as if to say, "That's all we can do here." They turned and began to leave the area.

I felt ashamed at what I saw as a lack of courtesy by the knights present in the lists, and leaving Merlin to finish any business he might still have with Sir Palomides, I rushed to follow the brothers. "Sir Bors!" I called to him as I followed him out the gate. "A word, please!"

Bors turned to look at me. His face remained expressionless, but I saw in his eyes a small glint of irritation. Sir Lionel did not conceal his annoyance with me.

"You!" the black-bearded Frenchman bore down on me. He came toe to toe with me, glowering down from a height at least a head taller in stature and at least two strata higher in social rank. His face red with fury, he bore down on mine and he took no care about letting me feel his full wrath. "It's that witch of a queen you serve that's caused all of this, boy!" he barked in my face. "My brother can't even be in the same room with any noble knight in Camelot! They shun him and heap abuse on him behind his back. They call him the queen's minion and the puppet champion. They make up rhymes to mock him."

"Rhymes?" I asked bewildered. "What do you mean?"

Sir Lionel screwed his face into a disdainful knot and curled his upper lip, and in a high pitched voice sang

> *"Queen Guinevere sat down one night*
> *With a dozen men or two;*
> *When she stood up she'd killed a knight*
> *Could've been me, or you!*
>
> *Now she's thinks she's got a plan—*
> *'For help I'll ask Sir Bors!*
> *'Cause I can tell he's the kind of man*
> *Who likes to help us whores!'"*

"That is what they are singing behind his back. Some even go so far as to gossip among themselves that Sir Bors conspired with the queen to kill Sir Patrise. They are calling him what they are calling her: a destroyer of good knights! As for you, I suggest you leave us alone. Being seen with the queen's boy can do Bors no good at all. Get out of here! We don't want anything to do with you!"

By now Sir Lionel's exasperation had grown so great that he almost shouted his last words. Sir Bors placed a hand on his elbow to caution him. "Whatever has happened, it does not give us the right to speak or act discourteously to a courtier of the queen, brother," he said with his even, impassive voice. "Young Gildas has done none of the things you castigate others for, and desires only our welfare. He is not to be blamed for trying to help his liege lady. And in truth, if he is successful in finding the true murderer of Sir Patrise, he will clear my name as well. It will then become clear to all that the cause I championed was right before heaven, and I will be vindicated."

"And if he and the old necromancer fail to find the killer? Or if the killer turns out to be the queen after all, which I tell you by God I would not rule out, what then?"

"Then I will be no worse off than I am now. And in any case our young friend here cannot be blamed for his loyalty, which in courtesy he owes to his lady under any circumstances."

Both Sir Lionel and Pegasus let out a snort at that, but Lionel, straining a bit under the bridle, gave me a slight bow of the head and said through clenched teeth, "My words were spoken in anger, Gildas, and out of concern for my brother. I pray you give me your pardon for courtesy's sake."

Having a knight apologize to me put me on unfamiliar ground, but I bowed slightly in Lionel's direction and mumbled some kind of acceptance, just as Merlin came out of the gateway from the lists to join us. The old man was the first to speak.

"Good Sir Bors, your treatment by the other knights is unconscionable. You are doing the right thing, I assure you, yet they can't seem to understand that. I will try to set it right with any knights I speak to."

"Don't bother, old man," Sir Lionel interrupted. "The knights think at least as badly of you as they do my brother, for helping the queen in your own way. They all think she is guilty and they think anyone who helps her must be guilty as well."

"It's true that I'm shamed before my peers," Sir Bors acknowledged. "But I am not completely abandoned. My kinsmen stand by me." And he reached out to touch Sir Lionel's shoulder. "And Sir Gareth has been kind. Sir Ywain has spoken kindly to me. But the others do indeed shun me. I sleep alone in a corner of the great hall, since none will share sleeping quarters with me. When I sit down to a meal the other knights suddenly lose their appetites and rise, so I've taken to begging scraps from the kitchen rather than be shamed in that manner. It is as you say. In courtesy I can do no less than I am doing for my queen. But the blow to my honor is almost more than I can bear."

The words were spoken out of a sincere pain, but still Sir Bors's brown face remained almost expressionless. Had he been as emotional as his brother, many a knight of Camelot would have been challenged in the lists and would perhaps be bereft of arms, legs, or lives by that time. For though Sir Bors suppressed his rage at his situation and his tormentors politely in conversation, he clearly channeled it all into the strength of his arm in combat, as just evidenced by his shattering of the quintain in the lists.

"It's Sir Kay who's the worst," Sir Lionel broke in. "Him and that little band of sycophants that's always hanging about him—Sir Brandiles, Sir Breunor, Sir Pinel, Sir Dinadan, that group. They're the ones who made up that mocking song, and they were the first to shun Sir Bors in the court. As he is the king's seneschal, the other knights believe this is the proper way to act toward my brother."

"Well," Merlin said, trying to be encouraging, "by a week from today, it will all be over, and our lives will get back to normal."

"I think not," Sir Bors told him. "If I lose the battle, it will be clear that I championed an unjust cause. If I win the battle, the knights will say that I labored to let a murderer go free. My shame is assured no matter what. No, my only hope is that you prove the queen's innocence. I pray that she is innocent. I pray that you are a clever enough mage to prove it."

"You have my word," Merlin said, with more respect than I'd seen him show anyone else on our investigation. "I will not rest until I have found the truth of this matter."

"Come," Lionel said to his brother. "We need to get out of Camelot. Let's you and I take the dogs and go hunting. We can hunt until we have to come back for the battle. It will get you away from this shame."

Bors nodded, then with a bow to Merlin and to me, walked

slowly off with Lionel leading Pegasus. His head was held high as he walked across the middle bailey, but I noticed that no one who was about any business in the yard greeted him, and many changed the direction they were walking in order to avoid coming anywhere near Sir Bors as he strode through the courtyard.

"Come," Merlin said as we watched the two brothers leave. "Let's you and I do some hunting as well."

CHAPTER FOURTEEN:
A GAME OF CHESS

It was Sunday evening. It must be around vespers time, I guessed. We sat together in Merlin's cave, melancholy and discouraged. Every moment that passed was another moment closer to the queen's trial, and we were still nowhere closer to solving the murder of Sir Patrise than we had been the night of the unfortunate banquet. Except that we had eliminated some suspects. At least, we thought they were eliminated. Or we were pretty close to eliminating them. Oh, let's be honest. We hadn't really eliminated anybody, and we had more suspects than we had begun with.

We'd spent the last four days talking to every single knight in attendance at the queen's dinner. Had they seen anything suspicious? Had they heard anything suspicious? How well had they known Sir Patrise? Had they liked him? Not much new information had surfaced. We had a picture of a knight who kept a very low profile in Camelot. A relative newcomer to the court whose cousin, Sir Mador, was his closest companion. A knight who liked hunting and hawking—along with every other knight at court—who went to mass almost daily in the palace chapel with Father Ambrose, and who could trace his noble Irish ancestry back six generations.

Though I knew the knights were aligned against Sir Bors because they thought the queen was unquestionably guilty, I hadn't really fathomed the full extent of their animosity until we were actually out among them. The queen's insistence that

Sir Patrise take one of the apples—her near command, as they saw it, to the newly arrived knight that he taste the fruit—was to most of the knights all the evidence they needed to convict her of murder in their own minds. Merlin was able to convince them to talk to us only by reminding them in not-so-subtle ways that it was by the king's command this investigation was proceeding, and to refuse to answer his questions was tantamount to treason.

But the information we were able to get from them was lean at best, useless at worst. Sir Tristram was suspicious of Sir Palomides. Sir Safer, of course, defended his brother but suspected Sir Ironside, and Sir Bleoberis remembered Sir Ironside's tirade against the Irish. Sir Pinel suspected Sir Gawain because he had left so fast. Sir Agravain had never liked Sir Kay, and figured he was capable of anything, including this. Sir Kay, when asked which knights were with him when he visited the kitchen, was no help at all, grumbling that it "could have been anybody" and that he "couldn't remember that far back." His theory was that Sir Bors must have had something to do with it because, after all, he was helping the queen, who was obviously guilty.

Since we had for all practical purposes decided that there was no point investigating any of these knights further as suspects, it appeared we were back to square one.

Which is, I suppose, why Merlin decided it was time to take a break from the investigation and teach me how to play chess.

It would be a chance, he reasoned, to get his mind off the investigation and let him come back to it with a clear head, perhaps able to look at things in a new light that would help him get somewhere. I prayed he was right. For myself, I was getting more and more confused as the queen's guilt seemed more and more unshakeable.

So for three solid hours, Merlin and I had been at the game. The old necromancer had checkmated me six times in a row, of course, but I was getting to the point where I was able to hold my own for a relatively long time. I had actually put him in check three times in the last game, so I had high hopes that I might be able to beat him, or at least fight him to a stalemate, sometime soon.

We sat at a small table in Merlin's dry, snug cave. His fireplace was putting out a comfortable warmth but not much light, so a candelabrum stood on the small table over the chessboard. I leaned back against a woven tapestry of St. George and the dragon that hung from the cave wall and watched Merlin lean his head morosely in his hand, resting his elbow on the table. Then I leaned forward and made my opening move.

"Queen's pawn to queen three," I said, moving my white piece ahead.

"Being the queen's pawn yourself, I suppose that's the natural opening for you," Merlin commented, his mouth turned up with a hint of irony. But then he quieted down, and seemed deep in thought behind those huge eyebrows.

Merlin was beginning to muse over his pieces, no longer able to keep his mind off the problem we faced. "Twenty-four knights at the table, and the queen makes twenty-five. Everyone but Sir Patrise himself, I suppose, must be thought of as a suspect."

"And the servants? And the kitchen help?" I added. The list of suspects was as long as my arm.

Merlin sighed. "It's true. They must be considered. Let's think this through. The kitchen staff themselves seem an unlikely group. They are the same people who prepare every meal for the castle. Nothing of this nature has happened before or since, and we have had the same set of cooks and scullery folk for several years. Roger seems to know his crew and has given us no reason not to trust them. Besides, no one in the kitchen would have had any idea who would be eating which particular fruits. If anyone from the kitchen had done this, it would have been as a purely random act of destruction: send poison to the table and see who is unlucky enough to eat it. And someone that unbalanced would certainly be identified by Roger at some point as untrustworthy. No, I'm really not suspicious of anyone in the kitchen."

"Merlin, I've been thinking. Suppose the whole thing was an accident? Suppose someone in the kitchen mistakenly poisoned the apples, and this was not murder at all?"

Merlin shook his head vigorously. "No, Gildas. This wasn't a simple case of food poisoning or some such thing. Foxglove is never used in cooking. It is occasionally used in small doses medicinally, for someone with a bad heart, but never in the preparation of food. The kitchen would have none of the herb there. Someone had to have brought it in with the deliberate purpose of causing the death of whoever ate those apples. We are definitely dealing with murder."

"Right." I said. After a moment's pause, I finally reminded him, "It's your move, you know. Are we going to play anymore or not?"

"Oh, uh, all right," he mumbled absently, and moved his own queen's pawn to queen four.

"So what about the servants? The squires and pages who poured the wine and carved the meat? Aren't we under suspicion?"

"I'm fairly sure I can rule you out as a suspect," Merlin told me.

"Thank you for your vote of confidence," I answered sarcastically. "But what about the others? Florent was there. I'm trying to remember others—I'm pretty sure Colgrevaunce was around, but I didn't pay much attention to them. I was concentrating on the table so that I could gossip with the queen later on."

"One of the squires or pages certainly could have had something to do with the murder. Remember, we know there were two people involved somehow. The killer almost certainly had to have an accomplice who found his way into the great hall after the murder to take away the evidence. So it's certainly possible that the accomplice was a squire or a page. The knights had been ordered to void the room. They would have been watching one another very, very closely after the dinner, so we can assume most definitely that whoever came into the great hall that night was not a knight. Ergo, it very likely was a squire or a page, but he would not have been the chief culprit. He would have only been doing what his master encouraged him to do. The person behind this murder is almost certainly a knight, and I'd venture to say it must be one of the knights at the table with the queen and Sir Patrise—someone who was on hand to watch and make sure his scheme did not backfire. But who? Which one?"

"Someone who hated Patrise enough to kill him," I stated the obvious. "And who hated him more than anybody? Sir Ironside?"

"Motive, Gildas." Merlin assumed his professorial voice. "Who would have been most pleased, or have benefited the most, from Sir Patrise's untimely demise? Sir Ironside certainly is someone with a motive. But did he have the means and opportunity? We have no knowledge that Sir Ironside knows anything about herbs or medicinal plants. Actually, we have no knowledge that Ironside knows anything about anything at all other than hawking and killing knights. But he also does not seem to have had the opportunity to get at those apples."

"Unless he was one of those knights who were with Sir Kay when he visited the kitchen earlier that day. Roger couldn't tell us which knights they were."

Merlin pursed his lips. "Sir Ironside is a loner. He does not socialize with many of the other knights and is not one of those you see hanging about Sir Kay, trying to curry favor with the seneschal. Besides, while his temperament would not stop him from killing Sir Patrise if he had the chance, all of his other murderous attacks have been on the field of chivalry. He would have done it with a sword, not poison, if he were the killer. But we've gone over this ground before."

"Yes, we have. It's like an echo in here. Here, king's pawn to king four." But I kept my finger on the piece. It seemed like a bold move. I was attacking his queen's pawn. Of course, I wasn't really thinking of taking it, since he'd take my pawn with his queen and then his queen would command the middle of the board. Obviously, he could take my pawn where I was moving it. But then I could take his pawn. But that would mean he could swoop down and take my queen. But then I'd take his queen, so he wouldn't do that. So I decided it was all right and took my finger off the pawn.

"What about Sir Palomides? Are we eliminating him from consideration?"

Merlin shrugged, looking at the board but, I thought, not really seeing it. He leaned on the table with his right elbow and rested his chin in his right hand. With his left hand he drummed the table with his fingers. "Sir Palomides had means and opportunity. We know he was in the kitchen that day. And we know he knows a great deal about herbs, at least for cooking. It's not unreasonable to assume he might know something about plants to avoid while cooking. That is, unless you want to poison your guests. And it's certainly possible his motive could be Sir Patrise's taking part in the massacre at Jerusalem. But their connection seems to have been friendly, and he does not seem to have known anything about Sir Patrise being with the Frankish crusaders until after he died."

"So he says. Nobody else even knew about their friendship, so we only have his word for it. Are you sure we can trust him?"

Merlin let out a sigh and raised his formidable brows. "I'm

not sure of anything. But I'm willing to trust him for now. He's an unlikely murderer."

"What about the nun?"

"Sister Agnes is a puzzle. We still don't know how deeply she is involved, if she is. We know she also had means and opportunity. We don't know anything about her connection with any of the knights, or with Sir Patrise in particular. But we've got to get in to see her. Tomorrow if possible."

"Dame Hildegard said she was confined to her cell until next Tuesday."

"I could get the king to send an armed guard with me to the convent. But that would probably not be good politics, would it? Today begins the new week. I hope we can wait until Tuesday to find out what Sister Agnes knows. Queen's bishop's pawn to queen's bishop three, by the way."

Hmph. Well, I thought, that protects his queen's pawn, so that if I take it he won't necessarily have to move his queen if he doesn't want to. He seems to be playing more defensively than he has in the other games.

"But if Sister Agnes is involved, she still has to have an accomplice here in the castle. Someone had to be at the banquet to see that the scheme went according to plan," Merlin interrupted my train of thought.

"If she's the one behind the poisoning, then couldn't the accomplice be one of the squires or pages in the room, rather than one of the knights?"

"Back to that again, hmm?" the old enchanter mused again. "I still don't think so. Their entire position at court is based on their relationship with their masters, the knights. Jeopardize that and they lose their livelihood and their entire future."

"If they hated Sir Patrise enough, don't you think they might risk it?"

"Anything's possible. But if we're thinking about Sister Agnes as the prime mover in this plot, then she would be the one with the severe hatred, and would have had to convince one of the servants on the inside to join her. No, my hunch is still that we're probably looking for a knight. But who's left?"

"Roger said that when Kay visited the kitchen, he had some other knights with him. But who? And how many?"

"Surely no more than two or three, I should think, or Roger would have made more of a point of telling us about it the first time we talked to him. Now it's not likely to be any of the most respected knights, since they are generally aware of what a useless tub of chicken fat Sir Kay is. So you will never see Sir Tristram or Sir Ywain fawning around Kay. Nor would it be any of the king's nephews, who wouldn't need to court Kay's favor even if they were inclined to do so. Nor is it likely to be any of Sir Lancelot's kinsmen. And we know it was not Sir Palomides, so we can almost certainly eliminate Sir Safer as well."

"And Sir Ironside is friendly with no one, as we've already pretty much established. So who do we have left?" While Merlin considered my question, I moved my own queen's bishop's pawn to queen's bishop three. I couldn't go wrong if I copied his moves, right? Anyway, that gave my queen two nice diagonal paths to venture out into the fray.

"There was Sir Breunor, La Cote Male Taile, correct?"

"Yes, and he was sitting next to Sir Pinel. Then there was Sir Galihud and Sir Galihodin on the other side of Sir Patrise."

"That makes four," Merlin said. "Sir Blamor and Sir Bleoberis are relatives of Lancelot, but not in his inner circle. I suppose they might benefit by playing up to Sir Kay."

"Yes, and they were there too. Bleoberis was next to the Red Knight. Tristram was next and then Sir Brandiles. But then came Ywain and Palomides. So of all those knights, only Sir Brandiles is likely to have been with Sir Kay."

"That makes seven of them. Any two or three of them could

have been with Sir Kay when he visited the kitchen. Do we know anything about them that would connect them with Sir Patrise?"

"Well, Blamor and Bleoberis de Ganis are kinsmen to Sir Bors—second cousins or some such thing. They're from Gaul and have been here in Camelot for years. No reason for them to have known Sir Patrise. Although they would have been here to fight in Arthur's Irish war, wouldn't they, some eighteen years ago? Could there be a connection there?"

"Sir Patrise was in the Frankish army during the time Arthur was at war in Ireland," Merlin figured, counting again. "I can't see that there could have been any chance to have met the knights on Arthur's Irish venture." He looked down at the chessboard, deep in thought, and moved his king's pawn to king four.

Very well, now *his* queen had two clear diagonal paths to swoop down. But I couldn't see any way that he was threatening me right now. He just seemed to be going through the motions with the game.

"Well, Sir Brandiles and Sir Galihud have been in Camelot for years, too. They were both rescued from Sir Turquin by Sir Lancelot not long after Lancelot came to Logres," Merlin continued. "I don't see any connection there either."

"Um . . . Sir Pinel is from Wales, and has no connection with Ireland that I know of."

"And Sir Galihodin is actually a king within the country of Surluse. No connection to Ireland. And what motive would a king have, after all?" Merlin mused. "Then there's Sir Breunor le Noire, the knight of the ill-tailored coat. Another Frenchman and another knight who's been in Camelot for years. If any of those knights is guilty, there are things we don't know about them."

That seemed so obvious I wondered if Merlin was getting

overtired again. I hoped he wasn't going to drift into another one of his dark moods. I looked at him carefully, studying his face, which appeared as impassive as a stone.

"King's bishop's pawn to king's bishop four," I said, hoping to rouse him. I was attacking his king's pawn, and right now he had no way to defend it. And if he took my pawn, I could take him with my bishop. Not a bad move, I thought to myself. Then I thought that maybe we could take a different tack. "Is there anything your 'vision,' or whatever you call it, can tell us? What was it again? A bear eats a wolf and a lion talks about it?"

"No, you dunce!" Merlin livened up now. As I knew he would if I botched it up well enough. "No. The great bear is killed by dogs, isn't it? And then 'listen to the lion.' "

"So is Patrise a bear somehow? His killers dogs? Who is the lion?"

"The only lion I know of is the one that belongs to Sir Ywain," Merlin said, thinking out loud. "That might mean the vision is saying that Sir Ywain knows something."

"We talked to him, though, when we talked to the others. He didn't seem to know anything more than any of the other knights. Hmm. He's the son of King Uriens of Gore. No connection with Ireland. Unless he's hiding something."

"So we don't know anything about a motive for him. And we don't know of any opportunity that Sir Ywain might have had to poison the apples. He's Sir Gawain's best friend. He never associates with Sir Kay, so he certainly would not have been one of the knights in the kitchen with Kay."

"So he's out? But what else could the lion be?"

"Nobody's out," Merlin replied. "We need to have a longer talk with Sir Ywain. If Sister Agnes was the poisoner in the kitchen, there's no reason Ywain would have to have been there."

"But if that's true," I reasoned, "there's no way to rule any of the knights out, whether they were with Kay or not."

"Precisely," Merlin answered and looked at me with a smile of grim irony.

I sighed. "We just keep going round and round and getting nowhere." I thought for a moment. "What if Sir Mador de la Porte killed his own cousin for some deep reason only known within their family? And accused the queen to throw suspicion off himself?"

Merlin smiled. But all he said was "King's bishop to queen's bishop four."

Now what was he doing? The bishop was there, pretty much commanding the center of the board for now, and actually attacking my king's knight. But if he took the knight, I could just take his bishop with my rook, and he wouldn't gain anything by it. Besides, he was leaving that king's pawn unprotected completely. But I didn't want to be too hasty. I thought about it for a moment longer.

"Sir Mador de la Porte," Merlin began, as if there had been no gap in the conversation, "has put his life on the line in the belief that the queen is guilty. He will be doing battle with one of the most formidable knights in Arthur's kingdom, but has so much faith God will protect the right that he hasn't shirked from the confrontation. It's not a case of someone trying to throw suspicion off himself by accusing someone else. This is a man who believes in his cause.

"But you make me smile, young Gildas. I once told you that you didn't ask the right questions, but you're showing the proper instincts, I think. It's time for us to start thinking in new ways. What we've been doing so far has got us nowhere, and we need to think of any alternatives we can."

"Right. Pawn takes pawn," I said to him decisively, moving into his king's file.

"So who are some other suspects we haven't thought of?" he asked, ignoring his loss completely (and robbing me of the chance to gloat). After a pause Merlin suggested, "How about Sir Safer? We never really thought of him, did we?"

"No. It was Palomides who knew the herbs and had been in the kitchen. But Sir Safer was at Jerusalem too, so he had just as good a motive to want Sir Patrise dead as his brother had. Sure! Maybe they worked together!"

"I don't think so." Merlin shook his head, tiredly I thought. "I believe Palomides is telling the truth when he says he knew nothing of Patrise's involvement in that crusade. But you know, that doesn't mean that Sir Safer hadn't known about it long before Sir Palomides found out."

"And how do we know that Sir Safer wasn't one of the knights with Sir Kay when he visited the kitchen?"

Merlin shook his head. "Sir Safer is a Moor. He would have stood out as different from the other knights. It's a detail Roger would have remembered."

"Maybe," I said, not completely convinced. "Or maybe it's just another detail he conveniently forgot to tell us."

Merlin had no answer to that, other than to move his king's knight to king two.

What was the point of that? He couldn't move it anywhere else from there. Two of the spaces were blocked by his own men, and the other would be directly into the one spot where my pawn could take him. And besides, he was blocking his own queen's path. When I thought about it, I realized he was clearing the way for himself to castle, but still it seemed like a weak move to me, and I worried again that he was tiring too much and that he was about to descend into one of his spells.

"Let's keep Sir Safer in mind to question further," Merlin said. "Still," he sighed again, "if Sir Safer knew about Sir Patrise and the crusades, he'd have told Palomides about it, I'd wager my head. In honesty, I believe he is the sort of person who lives to follow his older brother's lead and would never do anything without Sir Palomides's knowledge or approval."

"Like Sir Ector de Maris, or Sir Lionel. Or, for that matter, Gawain's brothers. Except for Gareth. But that reminds me. What about Sir Gaheris as a suspect?"

"Gaheris!" Merlin exclaimed, genuinely surprised. "Why would we suspect him, of all people? The king's own nephew?"

I moved my queen's knight to queen's rook three. Sure, it was in the path of his bishop, but I didn't think he'd want to exchange pieces, and I planned to attack the bishop with my queen's knight's pawn on the next move. Then I answered Merlin. "Sure, Gaheris. You know he's capable of murder. Look what he did to his own mother."

Another look of surprise raised Merlin's massive brows. "You've heard that story, have you? What have you heard? From whom?"

"I heard it from Sir Gareth himself, that night you fell ill with the 'vision,' as you call it. I'm sure he ought to know the truth."

"I'm not saying it isn't the truth, I'm asking what you've heard. Are those not two different things?" He was getting even testier. I began to go beyond worry to certainty that he would be flat on his back before the night was over. I began to make a mental list of the people I needed to talk to tomorrow if Merlin was incapacitated. There was Sir Ywain and Sir Safer—and Dame Agnes, absolutely, on Tuesday. Meanwhile, I answered him.

"Gaheris found his mother, the Lady Margause, in bed with Sir Lamorak. He took a sword and in a fit of rage cut off his mother's head. I was almost sick when I heard it. Somebody capable of something like that is capable of anything, isn't he?"

"King's knight to king's rook three," Merlin said, disagreeing with me.

"You don't think so?" I asked.

"You said it yourself. It was a fit of rage. Gaheris was

209

overcome by passion and committed an act that any rational man would shrink from. But he was not a rational man at the time. His passions had transformed him into a beast."

"I'll say," was all I could answer. "So?"

"*So*," he emphasized, "this murder was an act carefully planned out. It was not an act of hot passion but cold calculation. The Sir Gaheris I know would not have done this. He would have been incapable of it. His crime was a bestial one. He forsook his God-given reason and debased himself. The murderer we are seeking perverted his God-given reason and turned it into something evil. This crime is demonic, not bestial. And that's much worse."

I'd never thought about it that way before, but I considered it now as I looked down and studied the board. All Merlin had done was copy my move, as I had copied him before. Oh wait. I saw now that he was protecting his bishop. But I could still move ahead with my attack. I'd be glad to trade a pawn for a bishop any time. "Queen's knight's pawn to queen's knight four," I said. It attacked his bishop. It stopped him from attacking my knight, and it forced him to retreat from the center of the board. I thought I had him on the run now.

"Well, if not Sir Gaheris, try this one," I said, brainstorming. "What if Sir Ironside's wife is involved in this? I mean, you know, she had a motive, didn't she? Ironside was beating her up, all because Sir Patrise was sending her these love poems. As far as we know, she didn't want anything to do with him. Or even if she did, she'd have been too afraid of her husband to take Patrise as her lover. For her own safety and peace of mind, she could have wanted him out of the way!"

Merlin pursed his lips and looked at me approvingly. "Plausible. Very plausible. She could have been the one on the outside. But again, she must have a knight as her accomplice."

"Or Sister Agnes. Maybe they were in contact?"

"Certainly another question to put to Dame Agnes when we see her . . ." Merlin's voice trailed off.

Oh dear, I thought, he's almost gone. Better go and let him sleep. Maybe he'll be a little stronger in the morning.

"All right, I'll just do this," Merlin said, moving his bishop down the diagonal to take my king's knight.

"Oh, Mary!" I exclaimed, not without a little anger at myself for forgetting about that possibility. "All the time I thought you were after my one knight, and it turns out you wanted to get the other one!"

There was a long pause as Merlin stared at me, his mouth wide open and his dark eyes piercing me under brows raised as high as he could get them. Finally he said in a soft voice, "Say that again?"

"I said, all this time I was thinking you were after my queen's knight, but as it turns out you wanted the other one all along."

"God's kneecaps!" he shouted, leaping to his feet and knocking the table over, sending the chess pieces flying all over the cave. "How could I have been so blind? Such a complete imbecile?"

"Merlin, what on earth are you talking about?"

"The knight—Sir Patrise—all this time we've been thinking the murderer was after him, but the target must have been someone else all along!"

I shook my head, still not seeing what Merlin was trying to tell me.

"Don't you see, Gildas?" Merlin was up waving his arms and pacing the cave excitedly. His voice rose higher and higher with every pace. "All this time we've been looking for the murderer of Sir Patrise. We've been following the path Sir Mador set us on. But think, boy, think! The only reason to believe someone was out to kill Sir Patrise is that the queen insisted on his eating the apple. Which makes the queen the number one suspect. But if we assume the queen had nothing to do with the murder, then isn't it obvious that the target was not Sir Patrise at all? This whole thing was a conspiracy to murder someone else at that table, a plot that went terribly awry and landed on Sir Patrise, a perfectly innocent bystander—"

"And implicated the queen, another perfectly innocent bystander, in poor Sir Patrise's murder." The full enormity of the plot that had been hatched at that banquet was now finally coming home to me. "But who was supposed to die?" I asked Merlin after taking a moment to get my breath.

"Only one possibility!" Merlin spun around to glare down at me, his dark eyes flashing, his nostrils flaring with the scent of the chase. "Who was the guest of honor at the dinner? Who was seated at the queen's right hand, sure to be the first offered the fruit in that bowl? Who is well known to be a great lover of fruits, especially apples?"

"My God!" I felt the blood drain from my face and became so light-headed I needed to hold onto my chair to keep from falling.

"Yes!" Merlin cried. "Sir Gawain himself!"

CHAPTER FIFTEEN: FLOWER OF THE WORLD

Knowing that Sir Gawain was the target of the murder attempt meant reorganizing ourselves completely. It meant that everything we'd found out up to that point was pretty much useless and we had to start over again, trying to discover who, if anybody, would want Sir Gawain dead.

Well, it's not quite true that everything we'd found out was useless. We still needed to know why Sister Agnes had been confined to her cell. She could just as easily have something against Sir Gawain as Sir Patrise, since we had no idea what her motive could have been anyway. And we still knew that Sir Palomides had been in the kitchen, as had Sir Kay and at least two other knights, probably from among that list we had generated. But we decided—or I should say that Merlin decided, because he was gung-ho to get an early start on Monday morning—to find out all we could from Gawain's son Florent and his brother Sir Gareth about Gawain's enemies. Who were they and why might they want him dead?

That's why shortly after prime on Monday morning we were stepping over the stretching, just-waking bodies of the squires and pages who all slept in the great hall of the castle. On a bench in the corner he had staked out for himself, we found Sir Florent, rubbing his eyes and looking dumbfounded as Merlin, speaking faster than most of us could think this early in the morning, shouted in his ear the news that Florent's own father had been the target of the murder attempt at the queen's banquet.

Florent had his father's flowing red hair and florid complexion, but his brown eyes had come from his mother's side of the family. At eighteen, he was at once handsomer and gentler than his father. He was nearly ready himself to be knighted. I'm sure Arthur was just waiting for the right time to make his grand nephew, Sir Florent, Knight of the Round Table. Of course, personally, I'd always found him a little dull, a little too prone to throw a wet blanket on any fun someone might be having— that someone often being yours truly. He certainly didn't take after his father in that way. However, having seen him taking his tilts at the quintain, I knew he was definitely his father's son in knightly skills.

At the moment, though, he sat in his chemise and hose with his back in the corner of the room, his legs splayed out in front of him as he tried to shake his head awake. He wore a puzzled expression, as if, in wakening, he wondered if the things Merlin was saying to him were part of a half-remembered dream or reality.

"Wuzzat?" he managed to murmur in a leaden-sounding voice. "My father is dead, you're saying?"

"No, no!" Merlin said, fighting back his impatience. He always had a little trouble accepting it when *other* people were slow to perk up. "I'm talking about Sir Patrise. I'm telling you that I am now absolutely certain Sir Patrise's death was the result of a botched plan to kill your father at that banquet."

The news was now slowly sinking through Florent's skull. "What? How do you know? Where did you find this out?"

Merlin shook his head and waved the questions away. "No time to talk about that. It's far too complicated to explain now." Seeing me look at him askance—there was nothing complicated about it; we had just missed the obvious up till now—Merlin shrugged a little for my benefit and went back to concentrating on Florent. "Let's move to somewhere we can talk a little more privately. I want to ask you some questions about your father."

Florent nodded gravely, pulled on a pair of leather shoes, and walked with us out of the great hall and into the passageway that led toward the queen's quarters.

As we walked Florent slowly down the corridor, Merlin on one side of him and I on the other, Merlin spoke quietly in his ear. "We need to know, Florent, about any enemies your father has. Anyone that you can think of who might have had something against him . . . who might have hated him enough to want to kill him."

Florent shook his head, a look of honest bewilderment in his young brown eyes. "Everyone admires my father. He is the premier knight of Arthur's court, and heir apparent to the throne. He's the model of courtesy for the court. How could he have any enemies?"

Good lord, Florent, I thought, are you really this naïve or are you just putting on a good show? "Somebody wanted him dead," I reminded him. "So there's at least one person out there who doesn't admire him so much."

Florent shook his head again. It was a real challenge for him to come to grips with the fact that the whole world was not in love with Sir Gawain. "Enemies of the king might see him as a likely target, I guess," he conceded. "I mean . . . I know that there've been threats from Morgan le Fay before, not only threats to Arthur, but to our whole family."

Merlin's tongue clucking made it clear, to me at any rate, that he didn't give too much credence to Florent's suggestion. "That old witch hasn't been particularly active lately. And of the people at the banquet, I can't think of anyone who would be a likely agent of hers. Although, I admit, poison would have been a preferred method of hers if she were after someone like

Gawain. But I can't imagine she would have left things so much to chance that the plot miscarried as it did. Let's think further about it. Your father must have other enemies."

"None he ever speaks of, at least to me." Florent shrugged. He was clearly shaken by the news but seemed sincerely stumped by the idea of putting his father and enemies into the same sentence.

By now we were nearing the turn in the corridor that led directly to the queen's chambers. As we came in view of the door, we saw Sir Gareth standing guard, as usual, before the queen's rooms. When Florent caught sight of Gareth, he ran to him crying "Uncle! They say that my father is in danger!"

The words transformed Gareth's visage from the gentle, kindly face I had grown used to into a stern front, ready for battle if need be. His right hand went to the hilt of his sheathed sword while his left grasped Florent's forearm.

"Gawain in danger? From whom? Where are my brothers?"

"No, Beaumains, put up your sword. The danger isn't immediate. Florent is talking about the queen's banquet."

Less tense but more confused, Gareth relaxed his grip on his sword, and on Florent's arm, and turned to Merlin. "The banquet? What has that got to do with my brother?"

So Merlin explained to him again what we'd already been through with Florent: that Sir Patrise's death was an accident resulting from a plot against Sir Gawain that had gone wrong. "But rather than stand here in the corridor, why don't we step inside the door, where we can have a little more privacy. Sir Gareth, you won't be deserting your post, since you'll be right inside, and no one will be able to get in the door without your challenging them immediately."

We all saw the sense of that and slipped inside, to the outer chamber where Merlin and I had been sleeping the past several nights. The four of us sat on the two straw mattresses on the floor, Merlin and I on one mattress facing Florent and Gareth against the wall on the other.

"Sir Gareth," Merlin began. "We are trying to learn what enemies Sir Gawain might have. Who might have reason to want him dead. I'm afraid Florent is drawing a blank. His only suggestion has been our old friend Morgan le Fay."

Gareth snorted. "Good old Aunt Morgan. What a lovely woman. My mother's sister has always hated Arthur—jealous of his power I suppose. And she's never been one to let a little bit of family sentiment toward her nephews stop her from using them to get at the king. You think she might be behind this, old man?"

Merlin shook his head. "It doesn't seem to be her work. For one thing, she loves to take credit for everything she does that causes the king distress, and she hasn't owned up to this murder yet."

"I suppose that could be because it failed," Sir Gareth suggested. "Besides, the queen has been accused. It would serve Morgan's purposes, wouldn't it, to bring the queen to disgrace or even to death? That would be the surest way to strike at Arthur's heart. Even surer than the murder of his heir apparent."

"And if the target was my father to begin with," Florent jumped in, "she is the only enemy I can think of."

Sir Gareth looked at Florent with a bit of surprise, and then cautiously began to correct that notion with Merlin. "Well, there are a few more who would not be overcome with sorrow to see my older brother poisoned. Keep in mind he had quite a reputation as a ladies' man in his youth. When the king of South Wales found him in bed with his daughter, he swore to have his revenge. That was years ago, but there have certainly been others with similar complaints. Forgive me, Florent. This is a time for truth, and we need to explore all options, not tell gentle lies."

Clearly Florent had never heard any of those kinds of stories about his father, and the blush in his cheeks was as red as his hair. He looked at the floor and breathed heavily. If it weren't his favorite uncle saying such things, I suspect he would have challenged him in the lists for shaming his father's honor.

"Poisoning seems too sneaky for a king or an angry husband," I chimed in. More and more I was feeling the need to ignore Merlin's orders to keep my mouth shut. But he didn't seem to mind this time. "I mean, wouldn't you want to challenge him to defend the lady's honor if you felt he'd damaged it? So why resort to poison in that case?"

"Young Gildas is right," Merlin floored me by saying. "This doesn't appear to be the work of some jealous husband or lover, or some noble father feeling his daughter's marriageable market-ability had been damaged by Gawain's premature testing of the goods. There's something more devious here, and more hateful."

"All the more reason it could be Morgan le Fay," Florent insisted.

"There is another possibility. The house of Pellinore harbors a strong hatred of our entire family, most particularly Sir Gawain, and for reasons you well know," Gareth told Merlin. He did not specifically mention the murder of Sir Lamorak, and I took his cue that it was something he still would rather not discuss in front of Florent. He had tarnished Sir Gawain's reputation in his son's eyes enough for one day. It was painful enough to witness the undermining of the idol Florent had made of his father in his own mind, without seeing what happened when that idol shattered completely.

Merlin nodded fiercely. "That is precisely the sort of offense that would breed the kind of hatred capable of this murder."

Florent nodded as well, in the kind of self-deceived misunderstanding that no one cared to tell him was a misunderstanding. "I know the descendents of King Pellinore have a running feud with the Orkney clan. Something about some unresolved quarrel between Pellinore and old King Lot. But how many of them are left?"

"Well, there's Sir Agloval. But he lives in Wales. He hasn't been seen in Camelot since his brother, Sir Lamorak, was killed. And there's the youngest son, Perceval."

"Perceval?" Florent was taken aback. "But he's a friend of my father's. I've seen them together. My father was one of his only supporters when he first came to Camelot. I remember. It was not many months ago."

"But Perceval is the son of King Pellinore," Merlin reminded him. "It's true, he was raised by his mother in a remote part of Wales after his father died and never knew anything about the feud. Never even met Sir Lamorak, as I understand it. But the call of the blood to avenge a kinsman is a call that few men can resist, even those as basically decent as young Perceval. But Perceval has been off seeking adventures for months. If he is behind this, like Agloval, he's doing it from afar."

"Well that's that, then," Florent commented. "None of them sound very likely."

"Unless we haven't exhausted the list of enemies. It may be that there are other, less directly related, members of the Pellinore clan we aren't aware of. Or are there other enemies we haven't mentioned?"

Gareth shifted a bit on the mattress, looking uncomfortable. "I understand the gravity of this investigation," he began, "and otherwise would say nothing about this. But in the interest of completeness, and our need to look at every possibility, I do feel like I've got to say something. My brother Gawain is head of our family since King Lot died. We all defer to him and abide by his decisions, even when some of us disagree with them. But two of my brothers, Sir Agravain and the youngster Mordred, have quarreled with Gawain about a number of things recently. On more than one occasion I've seen them nearly come to blows over issues that Gawain had decided for the family. In all honesty I cannot say that either of my brothers would be above using poison to achieve a desired end."

Merlin looked skeptical. "Even on their own brother?"

"I'm not saying it's likely. I'm only saying that if we need to look at all possibilities, we shouldn't ignore that one."

"Well I for one won't even hear of it," Florent broke in. "My uncles are honorable men, and I cannot believe they would stoop to anything as low as what you are suggesting."

"Your uncles are my brothers, and I know better than you just what kinds of things they will stoop to," was all Gareth said in answer.

At that point a head poked out from behind the curtain, and I had a sudden feeling of vertigo as my heart dropped into my shoes. Her head was uncovered, and her dark hair fell in untamed tresses around her shoulders as her wide, dark eyes penetrated my soul and her mouth twisted into its familiar smirk. It was Rosemounde.

"Gildas!" she called. "Come here, please!"

While I could think of nowhere else on earth I would rather be, my legs felt heavy as I moved toward her, as if I were wading through waist-deep water. When I reached her she took me by the arm and led me behind the curtain.

The other ladies sat in the middle of the room working on their embroidery. An empty chair that would have closed the circle marked where Rosemounde had been seated before she came to get me. The queen was not present, and I assumed she must be sequestered behind the closed door to her private closet. The women were talking and laughing, and I noticed that they seemed to be asking riddles of each other. But Rose-mounde pulled my attention away from them as she held on to both my arms and looked earnestly into my face.

"The queen has asked me to learn where you stand with the investigation," she said in tones low enough not to be heard by the groups on either side of the curtain. "She is becoming more and more distraught, and refuses to come out of her room today. She asked me to find out what you have learned. You and Merlin, I mean."

I lost myself in those grand dark-brown eyes, like two black pearls set in the alabaster fairness of her face, until I remembered that she expected me to answer.

"Oh . . . uh . . . you can tell my lady the queen that we have had a breakthrough. We are certain that the murderer never meant to harm Sir Patrise, but intended all along to poison Sir Gawain, but the plot fell apart."

Lady Rosemounde's eyes grew round with surprise, and she was about to whisper something back to me when Lady Vivien, in a loud voice, asked her next riddle.

"What is it that people love more than life and fear more than death? The poor have it and the rich need it. The contented man desires it, the miser spends it and the spendthrift saves it, and all men carry it to their graves?"

"But how do you know? I mean, how did you find out?" Rosemounde asked me quietly.

"The answer is *nothing!*" Vivien's voice broke in again. "See? People love *nothing* more than life, a miser spends *nothing,* men carry *nothing* to their graves. Get it?"

As Lady Elaine and Lady Anne nodded their assent and murmured in approving tones, I answered Rosemounde. "It was easy to figure out, really. Once we stopped thinking in terms of the queen making Patrise eat the apple, we realized that Sir Gawain had to be the target. Well," I admitted, ashamed to meet her eyes, "Merlin figured it out, really."

"Oh, I've got one! I've got one!" Lady Elaine cried. "Listen to this. This is a curious thing that swings by the man's thigh, below his belt, and it hangs beneath the folds of his clothes."

There were some shocked gasps from Anne and Vivien, followed by uncontrollable giggles. Lady Rosemounde looked mortified and turned a bright shade of red. Now she was the one not meeting my eyes.

Lady Elaine continued, "It's stiff and thick but it swivels around, and it has a hole in the front end. When the man wants to use it, he lifts his garment and puts this thing into a familiar hole, and puts the whole length of it in. What is it?"

"I'm sure you know far better than we do!" Lady Anne chided her, then poked Lady Vivien. and they both burst out in boisterous roars.

"Give up? Give up?" Lady Elaine demanded. Then she shrieked out, "It's a *key*! Get it?" And the other two answered her with shrieks of laughter.

"They would not dare be so raucous if the queen were with them," Rosemounde explained, her eyes aimed at the floor. "They are somewhat unruly today because the queen has chosen to remain in her closet."

Sensing the depth of her mortification, I suggested, "Why don't we take a short walk in the bailey? We can talk of these matters without interruption."

I saw a wave of relief pass over her as she moved quickly to grab a blue ribbon from a nearby chair to keep her hair in place. "The best idea I've heard all day!" she whispered. "Let's get out of here!"

As we passed through the outer chamber, Rosemounde quickly tying her hair back with the ribbon, Merlin was just finishing his conversation with Gareth and Florent. "Then this is the plan, as I see it. Sir Gareth will discuss the matter with his brothers to glean what he can from them. Florent will talk to the other squires to learn what they know about their masters' origins and their whereabouts on the day of the banquet. Meanwhile Gildas and I will be checking with Sir Kay and anyone else we can think of who might know the ancestry of the knights currently in the castle. If we find a connection with the Pellinore clan, we may have our suspect."

As I held the door for Rosemounde, I told Merlin, "I must speak to this damsel on the queen's business. I'll catch up with you later." The old wizard drew himself up to his full height and looked down his nose at me with eyes wide in bemused surprise. I ignored him and followed the Lady Rosemounde out the door.

I watched her as she descended the outer steps into the lower bailey. She wore a fine woolen tunic of robin's egg blue, belted at the waist and sporting sleeves that widened extravagantly at the wrists. She looked up at me as I hurried down the stairs to her and offered my right arm for her to hold onto as we walked. A stroll to the barbican and back should give us plenty of time to discuss the queen's situation—and anything else that might come up.

She batted her lashes at me a moment and then looked away demurely. As we began to walk I noticed the left corner of her mouth twist up slightly again, as it had a habit of doing. "Now, Gildas of Cornwall, senior page to Queen Guinevere, give me some words of comfort I can use to assuage my lady's anxiety."

"We have had a breakthrough, as I told you, Lady Rosemounde," I began, sounding, I thought, like someone in control—like a man in charge. "We know now that Sir Gawain was the intended victim. And we are narrowing down the number of suspects to those knights at the banquet who had reason to want Sir Gawain out of the way. The list of suspects is getting much smaller. Perhaps," I added on a sudden inspiration, thinking to impress the lady with my manliness, "we shall put the few suspects to the rack, and force the truth out of them, if they cannot be persuaded to talk any other way."

I knew immediately by the look of horror on her face that I had made a miscalculation. "Oh, don't worry, my lady," I said, suddenly flustered, "I doubt it will come to that. Merlin is a great persuader, and too kind to impose that kind of questioning on men. I . . . I said it merely to try to alleviate your fears, to convince you that we were doing everything we can to find the killer and to free the queen. Believe me, I love the queen as much as you do, Lady Rosemounde, and would die before I let harm come to her."

"Then I pray you tell me the truth instead of feeding me what you think I want to hear," she told me, her dark eyes driving the point home, but her lips dancing with amusement as usual.

"Forgive me, my lady. In my courtesy, I have always been told to tell women what they want to hear. Truth is sometimes a casualty in such conversations, I'm afraid."

There was a long pause as we continued to stroll, past the castle keep in the middle bailey. It appeared that Rosemounde was trying to find the right words to answer what I had said to her. Finally she broke her silence and said, quietly but firmly, "Let there be no such casualties between us, Gildas. You and I must always deal in truth."

There was no smile or smirk to those coral lips now, but only sober gravity as she looked directly at me in undisguised fear. "The truth is," she continued, still looking straight into my eyes, "that I am not concerned solely for the queen. It's true that I care for her and do not want to see her shamed, or worse. But my own situation disturbs me just as much."

Now I was all ears. I hadn't thought about it before, but the queen's disgrace must needs have some effect on her ladies-in-waiting. What that effect might be, I hadn't stopped to consider.

"To be honest," I answered her in kind, "I can't promise you anything as far as the investigation goes. It's true that when we realized the target had to have been Sir Gawain, it was a breakthrough, and we're really on the right track to solve this thing now. And I think if anybody can figure it out, it's Merlin. But whether he's going to find the killer before Wednesday and the queen's trial, I just don't know. It's going to take some luck, I think."

Rosemounde sighed and we walked more slowly, now in the upper bailey and toward the front gate and the barbican. I felt her left hand tighten on my arm. "You know that my father, Duke Hoel of Brittany, sent me to King Arthur's household in order to learn the manners of court and the behavior befitting a grand lady."

I hadn't given the matter much thought. But as I walked with her there and considered what it meant for her to be the daughter of a duke, the Lady Rosemounde at that moment seemed even more unattainable than she had at any time before. "That is, as I understand it, the general practice among the daughters of noble houses like yours," I answered her noncommittally.

"Yes. Learn courteous behavior and how to run a household, and find a husband. That is what my father expects from my time at Camelot."

I gave another neutral grunt, though I was beginning to sweat and feared I might hyperventilate.

"But Gildas." She stopped and peered earnestly at me again. "If the queen is shamed, I will not be allowed to stay here. My father will bring me home, and then ship me off to another court, probably in Wales or Ireland, or even Gaul. I would never see Camelot again. And I'd be expected to ensnare a likely husband in whatever new place I'm planted."

"That . . ." I paused, weighing my words. I didn't want to

make a complete fool of myself, but I didn't want her to think that I was at all indifferent to this new revelation. Then I continued, "That would be a dark day for Camelot."

"Then you are saying it would grieve you to see me leave?"

It was as direct a question as I was ever likely to get. And she had just told me that, no matter what, we needed to be truthful with each other. I looked into those deep brown eyes and lost myself in them. "It would be . . . more than my heart . . . could bear . . ." I stammered.

By now we had reached the gate, and stood directly under the barbican. We stopped and she looked up at me again, but now her earnestness was gone and she wore the old playful, teasing smirk as she looked me in the eye. "Gildas of Cornwall, I'm fifteen years old. Every other girl I know who's my age is already promised in marriage, unless, like Elaine and Vivien, they're second or third daughters whose fathers haven't got dowries left to lure the best husbands. But my father wants to announce my betrothal before the year is out. And when he does, it will be to a landed knight of my own class. If what you say is true and your poor heart can't bear the thought of me leaving, then you need to get moving, boy! I need a knight! If you waste any more time, then *I'll be gone*." And she punctuated the last three words with her index finger poking into my ribs.

"Well I . . . certainly I want . . . if you just wait for . . . look, I'm going to try to . . ." It was as if English were not my native language, and I had trouble forming coherent sentences in it, but Rosemounde understood the gist of my meaning without needing words and, giving me that sly grin of hers, she suddenly undid the ribbon from her hair and thrust it into my hand. "Keep this for me," she whispered, and then, even more startling, she leaned forward and kissed me full on the lips. Before I had time to react, she had skipped off back toward the lower bailey and was gone. And I was left speechless and astonished.

The memory of the warm touch of her soft lips on mine, and of the scent of her perfumed hair as she leaned close to me, had my head spinning and my knees wobbling. It must have been several minutes before I remembered to breathe. The Lady Rosemounde, the Rose of the World, was willing to entertain, even to welcome, my courtship. But unless I began to make serious progress toward full knighthood, I would lose her.

But that had never been my strongest desire. My talents, and my interests, lay more in the area of letters than in lists. I had much rather study books than battleaxes, or spend my time with texts than with quintains. When I saw my future self, it was more as Merlin's replacement than as Lancelot's.

But then, it wasn't Merlin who got the girl, was it?

I thought about Merlin, rejected by Nimue and living alone in a cave; and then I thought of Lancelot, lover of the most glamorous queen in the world. Then I thought of Rosemounde. And the choice became suddenly very clear. I must become more like Florent. I must devote myself to learning the knightly skills and to training my mind and body for the shock combat of the mounted knight.

It certainly wasn't going to be easy, not the least because I had neglected those arts for so long. Besides, I didn't have the advantage of a famous father like Florent did, to help teach me the basics. If I was going to learn knighthood fast, I needed to become squire to a great knight. And I could only do that with the queen's help, as she had already promised.

Help she couldn't give if she were burnt. All the more reason for me to redouble my efforts to find the killer and clear her name. I vowed not to sleep until we had found him and brought him to justice, whoever he was. I was impatient with Merlin for being so methodical. I wanted to return to him and get him up and going right now!

"Well, wasn't that a touching scene." The voice directly behind my right ear nearly made me jump out of my hose. It was Robin.

I spun around to see him standing, hands on his hips, with the familiar sarcastic expression twisting his lips. His head was uncovered and the breeze tousled his long blond hair. A hearty laugh shook the breast below his dark green tunic as he said, "Such goings on! Young Gildas the investigator takes time off from his quest to find the murderer in our midst in order to fondle the prettiest of the queen's ladies-in-waiting!"

"Oh, Robin, get your head out of the moat. She's just concerned about her mistress, and I had some good news for her. So she's grateful, and gave me a kiss in friendship."

"Oh, yes, I'm sure you're good friends. I'm sure you're just like a sister to her. But back up, Gildas. You say you had good news for her? Do you mean to say you and that old charlatan have stumbled on the murderer after all?"

"Well, not quite. Not yet, anyway. But we did have a breakthrough yesterday. We now believe that the murderer was not trying to kill Sir Patrise at all, and that it was all a plot to get at Sir Gawain, but the poison never reached its intended target. So we need to find out who has a grudge against Gawain."

Robin snorted. "Who doesn't? He does have a lot of enemies in court. But that reminds me. Did you ever find out why his horse was already saddled and ready to go that night of the banquet? Wasn't that kind of strange? Do you think it had anything to do with the murder attempt?"

I stood for a moment, dumbfounded, then smacked myself in the forehead with an open palm. "That's what I was trying to remember to ask about at the stables! That's got to be an important clue! I've got to tell Merlin!" And without any more ceremony, I left Robin scratching his head and smiling at my haste as I ran, still clutching the piece of blue ribbon, at full speed back to meet Merlin at the queen's chamber.

Chapter Sixteen:
Listening to the Lion

The remainder of that Monday proved of little use. Merlin wasn't sure what could be done to find out about Sir Gawain and his pre-saddled mount, though we did visit with Taber at the stables. He confirmed that Sir Gawain had come to him shortly before the queen's banquet with the request that Taber have his warhorse saddled and ready to ride immediately at the conclusion of the feast, when Gawain planned to excuse himself and come to the stable for a quick getaway. Where he was going or why he needed to leave so suddenly, Gawain had not confided to Taber. The stableman would say only that the knight seemed anxious, as if he was riding to a destination that he had no desire to find. For now, that was all we knew about the horse.

Gareth had reported to Merlin that evening that his brothers were as genuinely upset to hear about the plot on Sir Gawain's life as he was, but had no additional ideas about motives or about possible suspects. Nor had Gawain confided in any of them his intended destination for the evening after the queen's banquet. Florent had fared no better in his probing of the squires and pages present at the queen's banquet.

Colgrevaunce, he reported, had noted a few sparks flying between Gawain and Sir Bors during the banquet, but I remembered something like that myself, and saw nothing in it but Sir Gawain's usual teasing of the stolid knight. No one who knew him could seriously suspect Sir Bors. And even if it were possible to have suspicions, his going out of his way to draw the criticism of the other knights to himself by defending the queen made no sense at all if he wanted to cover up his own guilt.

As for our own mission to Sir Kay, that had been a waste of a good three hours. Kay was more than willing to discuss the pedigree of different knights of the round table, but none of his information was valuable or even particularly interesting. We decided not to tip our hand by letting him know we were looking for relatives of Sir Lamorak. Kay could never be trusted to keep a secret even if he wanted to, which was unlikely. He was really too stupid to keep a secret from anyone who desired to wheedle it out of him. So we hinted that we were interested in the pedigrees of knights associated in any way with Wales, and off he went.

It was grueling to sit for hours listening to him drone on through those thick, pouting lips, details like, "And Tristram's father was Meliodas, the king of Liones. Now Tristram's mother was Elizabeth, the Welsh sister of King Mark of Cornwall, who died giving birth to him. The boy was named Tristram because it means 'sorrow' in the Cornish tongue, and he was named so to commemorate the death of his mother. Well, the boy was abandoned by his father and raised in secret by Governal. When he was fifteen years old . . ."

We had to abandon Sir Kay and try to think of a better plan.

Meeting back in the queen's outer chamber, the four of us compared notes and tried to decide what to do next. We were getting nowhere fast, and the queen's trial was the day after tomorrow.

"The one witness I am certain can give us some real information is one we haven't talked to yet," Merlin said as Gareth, Florent, and I sat gloomily on the straw mattresses across from him. "But tomorrow, Gildas and I will head for the Convent of Saint Mary Magdalene, where we'll have the whole truth out of Dame Agnes, or bring the wrath of King Arthur down on that prioress. Sister Agnes was here that day, and she's been hiding from us. And now it's time we knew the reason."

That was all we could do today, and though I was anxious to break down all barriers between us and the murderers *right now,* the only sensible thing to do was to turn in for the night and to get a fresh start in the morning when we were rested and thinking more clearly. Gareth stepped outside the door to relieve Sir Gaheris, who had been on duty all day while Gareth helped us with the investigation. Florent decided he might as well sleep here in the queen's outer chamber rather than go back to the great hall, so we blew out the candles and he, Merlin, and I settled in to our respective mattresses and tried to sleep. But I did have one question to whisper to Florent before we nodded off.

"Florent!" I hissed.

"Hmm? What is it, Gildas?"

"I . . . uh . . . I was wondering . . . that is, when this is all over and we've caught your father's attacker . . . I need a few lessons. I mean, really intensive lessons, in jousting and swordplay. I, uh, I've been too lax in my training for knighthood and, well, I notice that you've picked up those skills pretty well in a fairly short time. So what I'm asking, I guess . . ."

"Sure, Gildas," Florent said, turning over and facing the wall. "If you want a crash course in knighthood, I'll be glad to help you. You help find my father's would-be killer, and I'll make a knight out of you. Now let's get some sleep."

I rolled over myself, musing that it was gratifying to know help was there for the asking. I burrowed into the mattress and thought about Rosemounde's soft lips again as I tried to drift off. But before I did, I heard Merlin, through his rhythmic breathing, softly mutter *"Mulier est hominis confusio."*

★ ★ ★ ★ ★

Tuesday morning we were up and about before prime, stopping by the kitchen for a roll and cup of ale from Roger before starting out for the convent. I realized I was pinning all of my hopes on Sister Agnes, and had no idea what our next step would be if she didn't give us the information we needed.

We had planned to skip mass out of necessity in the morning, feeling pressed by the increasing urgency of the queen's position. But as we were passing the chapel on our way toward the barbican, I noticed Sir Ywain coming toward us, heading for mass. He was dressed simply in a dark green surcote belted over a brown tunic and hose. He had a blue cloak but he had not pulled the hood over his head, so that his long brown hair stood out shaggy, not unlike a mane. The brown beard and dark brown eyes made him resemble even more closely his famous leonine companion. The sight of him jogged something in my brain: the knight of the lion. Listen to the lion, Merlin had said. And the great bear is attacked by the pack of dogs.

What was the connection with Sir Gawain?

I suddenly knew: it was Lamorak.

In bringing down Sir Lamorak, one of the three greatest knights of Arthur's table, hadn't Gawain and his brothers acted something like a pack of curs? That had to be what Merlin's vision was about, didn't it? What did Ywain know about that incident?

"Wait!" I cried, a good deal louder than I had intended. Merlin started and glared down at me along his beaked nose. Sir Ywain stopped and looked quizzically at me. Six other people in the vicinity stopped as well to find out what I was shouting about. "Uh . . . sorry, we just need to talk to Sir Ywain here. Sorry." I nodded to everyone else—Lady Elaine and Lady Vivien, a page of Sir Tristram's, and Robert, squire to Sir Bedivere, along with Sir Dinadan and Sir Pinel, who raised an eyebrow at me and moved off slowly. The others all followed Sir Pinel and left me standing in the lower bailey with a bemused Sir Ywain and a rather irritated Merlin.

"We need to talk with Sir Ywain?" Merlin chided me when we were alone with him. "And just what is it we need to talk with Sir Ywain about, boy?"

"I'm curious about that myself," Ywain added. "I've already talked to you about whether I was in the kitchen, and whether I knew Sir Patrise before the banquet, and a dozen other things that had nothing to do with me. I don't know what else I can help you with."

"No, listen," I said excitedly. "Merlin can tell you that we now believe that the target of the poison was really Sir Gawain, not Sir Patrise. It was a plot that went very wrong."

"Gawain!" Sir Ywain opened his eyes wide at the thought. "That puts a new light on things altogether." Ywain's thoughtful expression made me certain he knew something about Gawain that no one else did. As one of Gawain's best friends in Camelot, Ywain was privy to aspects of Gawain's life secret even from his brothers.

"You know something?" Merlin prodded, forgetting that he had chastised me for stopping the knight in the first place.

"Perhaps," Ywain said, still thoughtfully pulling on his beard.

"The vision, Merlin!" I exclaimed. "Think about it. Sir Lamorak is the great bear. Gawain and his brothers are the pack of curs. Listen to the lion. Sir Ywain must be able to tell us something."

Sir Ywain put his hands on his hips and shook his shaggy head. "What you seem to know about Sir Gawain and Sir Lamorak already is surprising, since it is certainly not common knowledge. Sir Gawain is my friend. I would not say anything to you or anyone else to dishonor him. If that is what you are asking, then I'm afraid I can tell you nothing."

"It's not Gawain we're after, you great lunkhead, it's the person who tried to kill him!" Merlin exploded, exasperated. "God's nostrils, can't anyone here think past the end of his nose?" Merlin, whose own nose extended a good ways farther than most, waved his hands in frustration. "Can't people see that in not talking to me, they're protecting a murderer? Out with it, man. What do you know about Sir Gawain?"

Sir Ywain looked toward me and raised his eyebrows quizzically, as if to say, "I've got a tame lion at home, but I'm not quite sure how to deal with this kind of beast."

"Look," I told him frankly. "It's been a long two weeks, and we're pretty frustrated right now. There's a murderer on the loose, and the queen is about to go to trial for her life for something she didn't do. So anything you can tell us that could help, we'd be really grateful for."

"Gawain was spared this time, but those who failed to kill him at the banquet are certain to try again. They must be caught and stopped," Merlin added, "before there are more lives destroyed. Lives you will be partly responsible for if you have evidence you refuse to share with us." Merlin's voice had become almost threatening.

But he needn't have gone so far. Sir Ywain was willing to talk. Now that everyone else who was stirring at this hour had gone to mass in the chapel and the bailey was deserted, Ywain was more willing to speak. "I'll tell you what I know," he began. "Just promise me that it goes no further than this."

"I can't promise that," Merlin told him. "If we need the information to prove to the king who the guilty party is, we'll have to use it."

"All right," Ywain relented with a sigh. "But use only what you have to, won't you? There's no reason that a worthy knight should be made the object of common gossip."

"Fair enough," Merlin agreed. "But what is it you know?"

Shrugging, Sir Ywain answered, "What don't I know? Sir Gawain, you know, is my cousin. His mother, Queen Margause, was my mother's sister. Queen Elaine. We didn't know each other well growing up, but when he found out I was at Camelot, he made it a point to take me under his wing.

"I suppose you've heard about the magic fountain and all that. How I killed the guardian of the spring that protected the Lady Alundine's estate? He attacked me when I took water from the spring, and after I had wounded him I chased him right back into Alundine's castle. I was trapped there when the portcullis closed on me and crushed my horse. But Lynette, her lady-in-waiting, gave me a magic ring that made me invisible and saved my life when all the guards came out to protect their master."

The bit about the magic ring was a little hard to swallow, even from a guy who kept a pet lion, and Merlin and I exchanged skeptical glances as Ywain told his story.

"So this knight I had wounded ends up dying, and I'm still hanging around the castle, invisible. But Lynette is bringing me food and things so I don't starve. She convinces the grieving widow to marry *me* so that I can protect her. Obviously I've proven to be a better fighter than her ex.

"All right, it seems like a crazy plan to me too, but who can understand the quagmire of women's minds? The word comes to the Lady Alundine that King Arthur himself is heading that way with an army. The lady can only assume her ex, in his rather insane habit of attacking anybody who drinks out of their spring, has whacked one of Arthur's favorite knights and the king is coming to take revenge. So Alundine takes Lynette up on her proposal and voila! Next thing you know I'm married to the lady of the house. Which was not such a bad thing. I had my own estate I was likely to inherit from King Uriens, but in marrying her I stepped into another good-sized estate with a pretty formidable castle. And a really nice magical spring to boot. Not to mention the lady herself, who was a fine-looking woman. Though to tell you the truth, I was a lot more attracted to Lynette. But you take what life gives you."

"I'm sorry," I interrupted. "What does any of this have to do with Sir Gawain?"

"Getting to it, getting to it. Anyway, so as the new Lord of Alundine's castle, I rode out alone to face King Arthur's army. Lady Alundine and Lynette and their castle guard thought I was crazy, or the bravest man they had ever seen. Of course, I was neither. I just knew the king a lot better than they did.

"Well, the king and his knights got to the spring and the king drank from it, which was my cue to ride up and challenge them. I was in the armor of Alundine's late husband, so nobody recognized me, but I challenged the king to let me fight his chief knight. If I won the battle, they were to depart and never bother the Lady Alundine again. If the king's champion won, then the spring would become the king's property.

"It might have seemed a lot to risk, but think about it. What other choice was there? I couldn't fight the whole army, and without that agreement, things could have gone even worse for the Lady Alundine than losing her magical spring.

"But I had hopes that things would turn out even better. Naturally, I knew the king's champion would be his nephew, Sir Gawain. And I knew that if Gawain once suspected it was me he was fighting, he would out of courtesy yield to me. So the thing for me to do was to put on a good show at first and then, well into the fight, reveal my true identity. And that's what happened.

"We broke a few lances through charging each other's shields, and then dismounted and brought out the broadswords. After a few whacks with those, I called for a breather and stood aside, leaning on my sword. Gawain, panting a bit from exhaustion, lifted his visor and said to me, 'Sir Knight, you fight with the strength of a bull. Tell me your name, I pray. A knight of such gifts should stand with the king, not against him.'

"At that, huffing and puffing myself, I lifted my visor and surprised them all. 'It is I, your cousin Ywain,' I told him. 'I've married the lady of the castle and am honor bound to defend her lands and spring against all comers, even my lord the king.'

"Well, you should have seen the look on his face. Gawain was struck dumb. He looked back at the king in wonder and exasperation, and then made the ultimate gesture of courtesy. He went down on one knee before me and said, 'My Lord Ywain, the spring is yours. I know you would not defend an unjust cause, and it is no dishonor to acknowledge you as victor. Indeed, it would be to my shame if I were now to continue our duel. If my lord the king agrees, we will recognize the Lady Alundine's sovereignty over the spring.'

"King Arthur certainly knew what Gawain would do once he saw whom he was fighting, and raised no objection. But for my own courtesy, I was not to be outdone. I dropped to a knee myself and held Sir Gawain's gauntleted hands in my own, and said. 'For my part, I acknowledge Sir Gawain as the superior fighter. Rather than accept his withdrawal, let me propose this: that the Lady Alundine become vassal to the king, and that she hold her lands, castle, and spring in perpetual fiefdom from the king, accepting and supporting him as her liege lord.' "

"Wouldn't the lady have been pretty angry about your giving away her sovereignty like that?" I asked.

"That was the beauty of it," Ywain continued. "She really wasn't giving away anything. She would hold sway over her lands. She simply owed the king allegiance, that is, support in his wars or advice in his government. Since I was one of the king's knights already, Alundine was supplying the king with both by letting the king have me. And now the king was obliged to protect her from any threat, since if any brigands attacked her or her lands, they were in effect attacking the king himself. The Lady Alundine came out of that stronger and more secure. And I came out of it owing my life and my happiness to Sir Gawain and his courtesy.

"There's a lot more to the story. After that day, Gawain challenged me to go on a quest for adventures, and we spent a year traveling around together, competing in tournaments and winning honor. You've probably heard about how my lady rebuked me and cast me off, sending Lynette to get the magic ring back from me and denounce me for not keeping my word to come back within the year. I admit I was wrong and neglected her. But I realized then—which I hadn't before—how much I loved and needed her, and had lost her through my own carelessness. As a result, you have probably heard I went mad for a while. That's when I met my lion and befriended him. But you don't want to hear about those adventures. You want to know about Gawain."

"That was the idea, yes," Merlin said, a little impatiently. "We don't need to know about everything you ever did with Sir Gawain. We just need you to tell us what you know about his enemies, and what happened on the day of Sir Patrise's murder."

"I know, I know." Ywain closed his eyes and held up his hands. "I only wanted to make sure you understood why my friendship with Sir Gawain is so strong. And so that you understand that he is the paragon of courtesy. This business of Sir Lamorak . . . all I will say about that is that he has suffered inwardly these six months since it happened. I'm sure I'm the only one he's talked to about it. His brothers cannot be trusted."

"Even Sir Gareth?" I countered.

"Sir Gareth condemns the action out of hand and refuses to listen to anything about it," Ywain replied, shaking his head. "Sir Gareth has cut himself off from his brothers as much as he has been able to since the event. He is civil to Sir Gawain, but will not discuss the matter. As for Gawain's other brothers, they had no compunction in killing Lamorak and do not regret it now. The only reason they want to keep the murder quiet is to avoid suffering the consequences for it. Sir Gawain keeps the secret out of shame."

"If he is so ashamed, what led him to ambush Sir Lamorak in the first place?" Merlin pushed him.

"The ties of blood. You know that the feud between the houses of Pellinore and of Lot has never been settled. Both sides will continue the senseless bloodshed until there is some kind of mutual satisfaction or renunciation of the violence. Sir Gawain gave in to his brothers' demands for vengeance and, as head of the family, led the assault on Sir Lamorak. It was discourteously done, and Sir Gawain is his own severest critic. The act was a betrayal of Gawain's own truest character, and he suffers for it. But I will not betray him, or stop reminding him of that true courtesy to which he owes his allegiance. Nor will I desert him when he needs friends."

"All quite admirable, I'm sure," Merlin answered, becoming more impatient. "But what happened that day?"

"Why was Gawain's horse saddled and waiting for him?" I asked again.

"On the day of the queen's banquet," Ywain began in a quiet voice, finally getting to the point, "Sir Gawain received a written challenge. He found it among his clothes when he dressed for the day that morning. It was written in a fair hand on a scrap of vellum—he showed it to me after chapel that day. It read something like:

'*Sir Gawain—know that I hold you the vilest of creatures. You are a recreant knight and a destroyer of good men. You murdered Sir Lamorak like a coward and a thief, and I throw his murder in your teeth. He was a courteous and honorable*

240

knight and was worth a hundred of you and your base brothers.

Therefore I challenge you to the utterance: on Wednesday evening, at the hour of vespers, meet me in the clearing in the woods two miles north of Camelot—you know the place well. Come and come alone, alone, or be known as the shameful coward you are.'

"And that was all. There was no signature. I told him I would ride there with him, that he couldn't go alone, for it was most certainly a trap. I knew it was. What better place for an ambush than that clearing surrounded by trees?"

"What did he say to that?" I asked.

"He said he knew it was an ideal spot for an ambush. He knew it because that was the spot where he and his brothers had ambushed Sir Lamorak. That was what the note meant when it said 'you know the place well.' Gawain was going into a trap and he knew it. But he said if he was killed, it would be just punishment for his sins. And if he lived, he would ever think of his battle there as his penance to atone for Sir Lamorak's murder. Either way, he felt he would be rid of his guilt and shame after that night."

"But he seemed so relaxed at the dinner, as if he hadn't a care in the world," I remembered.

"That is Gawain's gift. As paragon of courtesy, he is at his most charming in social situations like the queen's banquet. If anything, stress makes him all the more talkative and witty in a crowd. I think it's what helps him put the anxiety out of his mind."

"So are we saying," Merlin said thoughtfully, his chin in his hand and his index finger tapping his nose, "that Sir Gawain went to this evil tryst that night? And if so, since we have heard nothing of him since, might he have been killed there?"

"Or did he decide to ride directly to find Sir Lancelot, as the king asked him?" I put in.

"If he went to the clearing in the woods first, then it's not likely he ever rode after Lancelot," Merlin conjectured. "And that means that there is no hope that Lancelot will come by tomorrow to fight as the queen's champion."

That had not occurred to me, and I suddenly felt a sinking sensation in my stomach. More bad news for the queen.

But Ywain was more optimistic. "If the king bade him search for Lancelot, then any business Gawain had of his own would have been set aside. Challenge or no challenge, Gawain would have seen his first duty as obedience to his lord the king. I haven't been worried about him since that night, because I was sure he hadn't gone into the ambush. He would have done as the king commanded."

"Unless," Merlin suggested, "Gawain realized immediately what was going on. Surely he alone of anyone at that feast—anyone, that is, except the murderer—would have seen the whole picture, or at least suspected it. He knew there was a trap laid for him that night, and he must have realized that the poisoned apples were intended for him, guest of honor at the feast and known for his love of fresh fruit. To save the queen, he might have thought it was better to confront his attackers and bring back to Arthur the real assassins than to spend time look-ing for Lancelot to fight an unnecessary duel on the queen's ac-count."

I thought back, but couldn't see it Merlin's way. "He sure didn't act like he suspected anyone other than the queen when we stood before King Arthur."

"Perhaps not. Perhaps the connection between the events didn't strike him until later. Or perhaps they never struck him at all."

Ywain had gone pale and his eyes had taken on a sudden fearful glow. "But if he did put the two together," he began slowly, "then he would have gone straight to the clearing. And if

242

he did, then he hasn't come back. He may be lying there now, murdered by these cutthroats!" His last words were almost lost in a kind of frenzied cry as he turned suddenly and began to run toward the stable. "I must find out!"

"Wait!" Merlin shouted after him. "We're coming with you!" And we followed quickly after him, Merlin looking awfully spry for an old man.

Taber and his stable hands helped us to grab three mounts as hastily as possible, and before I'd had much time to think, we were mounted on three swift palfreys and cantering out the castle gate, with Robin giving us a puzzled look as we passed.

We bore north and broke into a gallop. Ywain, his face frozen in deep concern, had to be distressed at his sudden realization that, despite his conviction to the contrary, Sir Gawain might very well have been lying dead in the woods these ten days and more, and the trail of his killers grown cold with time. He seemed to want to make up for all the lost time right now, on this ride, and he galloped at breakneck speed through the late autumn field north of the castle.

When he plunged into the woods, he was forced to slow his pace a bit, but he urged his horse on, ever faster, along the beaten path through the woods that led in the direction of the clearing. We passed the turnoff to Merlin's cave and the horses splashed across the cold brook, but Ywain outpaced us impressively and had reached the clearing well before us.

By the time we arrived at the spot, Ywain had already dismounted and was searching the area closely. The clearing was roughly circular, with about a thirty-yard diameter, so there was not a very large area to search. But it was overgrown with tall grass, except for a trail through the middle where horses had worn a dirt path. Dead leaves and branches also cluttered the area, making it difficult to see what might be lying about.

Merlin and I dismounted to help, and Ywain finally spoke for the first time since we'd left the castle.

"Look through the grass on either side of the path first. If Gawain was ambushed, he'd have fallen from his horse and would be lying directly off the trail."

"But if that were the case," Merlin reasoned, "passersby would have seen the body and reported it at the castle. There are at least a few travelers who pass this way every day. If the murderers wanted to hide their crime, they would have moved the body, perhaps closer to the trees, and covered it with branches or leaves. They may even have buried it if they had enough time."

"Burying it would have given Sir Gawain more respect than they were likely to have shown. But you're right. They probably would have tried to hide it," Sir Ywain conceded. "Let's spread out and look closer to the perimeter, then under the branches. We can work inward from there, toward the trail."

Merlin and I grunted our agreement and I split off to the right side, moving to the line of trees and kicking through the grass and dead leaves as I slowly traced my way along the circumference of the clearing. But I had only been at that a few minutes before I heard a call of dismay from Sir Ywain on the other side of the clearing.

"Here!" his anguished cry rose above the trees. As Merlin and I rushed quickly to his side, he fell to his knees and began throwing off leaves, grass, and branches that were covering the body.

It lay on its belly in the grass. Protruding from the back was an arrowhead that had pierced the body completely through the heart. Another arrow had entered the right temple and so stuck out of that side of the head like quill in an inkstand. The cold, dry weather had kept it from deteriorating much for the past two weeks, and no doubt the foliage that had buried it had kept the carrion birds and beasts from attacking the corpse. As a result, even the black habit that clothed the body was still almost completely intact.

Sir Ywain, still on his knees, rolled the corpse onto its back. I gasped audibly when I saw the face.

"My God!" I exclaimed. "Dame Agnes!"

Chapter Seventeen:
The Second Nun's Tale

At least, I assumed it was Sister Agnes. The face was not particularly well preserved and all I had to go on was the glimpse I had had of the young nun in the back of the cathedral at Sir Patrise's funeral. But who else could it be? What had happened to her, that she should be lying here well outside the walls of her convent, a convent in which the prioress had told me she was confined to her cell for her serious breach of the strict Benedictine Rule? And if it was indeed Dame Agnes, then it seemed that the one witness who might have put all the pieces of this puzzle together was now forever silenced.

"We need to get her back to the convent," Merlin said sensibly. "They must know what has happened to her."

"Throw her over my horse," I offered, knowing it would be expected of me anyway, being the youngest and least in rank. "I'll lead the horse back to the nunnery."

Sir Ywain, his stoic features betraying no special disgust at touching the young girl's corpse, bent down and lifted the slender body and then placed it gently across the saddle of my palfrey, so that the arms hung down one side of the horse and the legs the other.

"Use her wimple to tie her hands and feet together, to prevent her from slipping off the horse," Merlin advised.

Ywain tenderly pulled the white scarf from around the head and neck of the nun, and as he did so, a flood of golden curls cascaded down, hanging below her motionless head like moss from a dead branch. We were all taken aback by the length and beauty of the hair. Certainly it tokened a nun not particularly comfortable within the strictures of the rule, harboring a secret vanity of which her prioress was almost certainly unaware. Hanging from the tresses was a long green ribbon, embroidered with flowers that she must have used to tie her hair back. The ribbon proved a more convenient cord than the wimple, and Ywain gently pulled it from the tangle of curls.

When Ywain had tied her hands and feet together, we began the slow amble back toward the convent. It was a somber ride and none of us had anything much to say. I watched the ground as I led the horse back along the path we had just ridden so rapidly only minutes before. Though my back was to the corpse, I could not get the image of those flowing blond curls out of my mind. This was not simply a cog in the wheel of God's Church I was leading. It was someone who had been a unique individual—a young girl, disappointed in love, whose dreams of marriage and secular success had been thwarted by economic realities, and who believed she could make a worthwhile life in the Church, vain about her hair and individual enough to disobey the rule when she thought she had to. I didn't know why she had come out to this place. I didn't really understand why she had been killed. I just knew that she was a girl not much older than Rosemounde, and perhaps as silly and as exasperating, and therefore perhaps loved once by someone like me. Now gone forever. Why?

Perhaps Merlin was reading my mind. At any rate, he began slowly to speculate about some of the things I'd been pondering. "Sir Gawain had indeed been summoned to an ambush. Two archers lay in wait in the trees, expecting Gawain to come charging into the clearing on his warhorse. But he never came. He had gone off in the other direction, following his king's command as a true vassal must, rather than attending to his own business, despite its importance. But Sister Agnes somehow knew that an ambush would be waiting for him. She rode out here to try to stop Gawain, or to try to stop the murder if Gawain had already made it this far.

"It was well after vespers when the meal was over. Perhaps she was waiting and saw Gawain leave. Or perhaps she left before he did, to try to head him off and prevent the attack. Either way, when the archers who lay in wait for Sir Gawain heard hooves pounding rapidly toward them, they notched their arrows and drew back their bowstrings. As soon as the figure on horseback broke into the clearing, they let the arrows fly. It was too dark to see it was the nun, and they needed to fire too fast to make sure of their target. When they saw what they had done, they dragged the body away and hid it as best they could, and probably went back to wait in ambush again. But the real target never came."

"That must have been the way of it," Ywain nodded. "But poor Sir Gawain. He was the unwitting cause of the deaths of two innocent people on the same night. Talk about bad luck."

"I'm not convinced Sister Agnes was completely innocent in all this," Merlin replied thoughtfully. "How would she have known about the ambush if she were an innocent bystander?"

"Perhaps a conspirator having second thoughts, then?" Ywain conjectured.

"What I don't understand," I began, still unclear about the details, "is that if Sister Agnes was killed on the night of the banquet, then who was it I saw in the cathedral at Sir Patrise's funeral? And why did she look so distraught?"

"Questions we're going to need answered before we leave the nunnery," Merlin replied. "This all revolves around our nun here. I have a feeling this dead body will liven up the tongue of that tyrannical prioress."

★　★　★　★　★

The rough-faced peasant woman answered our knock at the convent gate in the same surly manner as before, demanding, in a tone that was not encouraging, that we state our business. But when she saw what I had draped over my horse's saddle, her eyes popped and her jaw dropped to her chest. Not surprisingly, she said nothing, but covered her mouth with her hands and backed away in horror and disbelief. Merlin, as usual, took charge.

"Don't just stand there gaping, woman, go and get your prioress. One of her brood has fallen from the nest and died."

At that she nodded and ran off to fetch Madame Hildegard. Meanwhile Ywain and Merlin dismounted and we led our palfreys through the gate and into the convent yard, where a stable boy, wearing the same shabby clothes and the same blank look as the porter, ran up to take our horses. "Must be the woman's son," I conjectured to myself. My own horse I still held on to, not sure of what should be done about its cargo.

It was a matter of moments before Dame Hildegard came hurrying out of the refectory toward us, with little Augustine trotting along at her heels and half a dozen other nuns behind her. Two other male servants brought up the rear.

As they drew near the corpse, I could see signs of recognition on the sisters' faces followed by great cries of distress and fear. A few of them dropped to their knees and began praying "Ave Maria" before three others began chanting a slow dirge.

Augustine ran up to the corpse, yipping, standing up on his hind legs, the better to reach Dame Agnes. But when he caught the scent of the corpse, he backed down, his tail hanging limply, and slowly trotted back to the security of his mistress. It was a somber-faced Madame Hildegard who bent down to pick up the whining dog.

"Andrew! Matthew!" she called to the two servants who stood

outside the circle the nuns had made around me and my horse. "Please take Sister Agnes into the chapel. Sister Frideswitha! Sister Deborah!" The two older nuns who had been praying on their knees looked up. "Please fetch some water and follow them. Prepare the body for burial as best you can. Dame Alice!" One of the chanting nuns stopped and looked expectantly at the prioress. "Please run and fetch Father Bernard. He must prepare the funeral mass. And it must be done quickly. Our sister has come home to us."

Those she had addressed leapt immediately to carry out her commands, and the body was lifted from my horse and carried toward the chapel by the two servants. The stable boy had come back and now took my horse as well.

The prioress held her dog close as she barked out the orders, and her voice maintained its tone of authority. Her face, though, twisted into a mask of sorrow, the pain in her eyes like that of a mother who had lost a child.

So it was indeed Dame Agnes we had found in the woods.

But as I looked into the faces of the three sisters who remained, clustered now around their prioress and sobbing without shame, I clearly recognized one of them, a young and pretty nun, no more than nineteen certainly, with deep brown eyes and a thin, hooked nose. The same face I had seen so deeply moved at Sir Patrise's funeral. Perhaps it was her youth, but she seemed now as well to be the one most distressed by Sister Agnes's murder.

"My Lady Prioress," Merlin began, gently but firmly. "We now have two dead bodies on our hands. Unless we find out why these two died, a third innocent life may be lost: that of the queen."

"None of us is innocent," Madame Hildegard reminded Merlin, absently petting Augustine. "Well," she added after a moment, "perhaps the beasts . . . and the children . . ." With that, she glanced over her shoulder at the young nun weeping behind her.

"I'm not here to debate theology, Madame Prioress. Or even morality," Merlin told her. "I am here to get to the bottom of these murders, and I must speak with any of your sisters who knew Dame Agnes well. I must do it tonight, or all may be lost."

Sadly, but with no less authority than ever, the prioress answered, "First we must commit our lost sheep to God and to the grave. Then we will talk. There will be time," and with that, she turned to go to the chapel.

Before she could turn and follow her prioress, I reached out to seize the young nun's sleeve. "Sister!" I addressed her quietly.

She looked over her shoulder at me, a certain amount of fear and even annoyance showing through the sorrow in her dark brown eyes. "Yes?"

"How may I call you?"

"I am Sister Blanche," she answered. "What is it you want? I must go and mourn my sister."

"Dame Blanche, please talk to us after the mass. We have a lot of questions for you—I saw you at Sir Patrise's funeral."

With more fear than annoyance or even sorrow, Sister Blanche pulled her sleeve away from me and walked off to the chapel, without giving me an answer. Madame Hildegard, looking straight at me as she looked back, called out again, with more authority and less sadness, "There will be time after the funeral. We must prepare. There's an end of it."

With that they all walked away, and Merlin, Ywain, and I were left staring at each other, looking in vain for answers. Merlin's lips were pursed and his eyes followed the prioress into the chapel. "Come, then," he said as he started after them. "Somebody here knows something, and we're going to find out what it is tonight."

We stood in the back of the chapel as Father Bernard, the priest attached to the Convent of Saint Mary Magdalene, said the requiem mass. Dame Agnes's face and body were covered by a shroud, so that the mourners could not dwell on her decaying earthly remains but rather the immortal part of her that now claimed her eternal reward in the bosom of Abraham. But had Agnes died in a state of grace? If she was mixed up in Sir Patrise's murder, it could hardly be so. Yet when the choir of nuns sang, Sister Blanche's pure soprano rose above the others, like the voice of an angel, and somehow beyond all reason I felt that Sister Agnes must even now be hearing notes like those from another heavenly choir.

It was a feeling that lasted only until the end of the mass.

The service ended quickly, and Andrew and Matthew lifted the shell of Dame Agnes from her bier, carrying her behind the chapel, where Father Bernard would say a short prayer over the grave and the nun's body would be speedily put under the earth, for the two weeks of lying in the woods, even in the cold weather, were now noticeably taking their toll on the remains.

As the service broke up and the nuns left to go to their work, Madame Hildegard motioned for us to follow her. She took Sister Blanche by the sleeve as she walked out the chapel door. Merlin, Ywain, and I followed the two nuns across the courtyard to Madame Hildegard's private quarters, where I had met with her before.

There were only three chairs in the sparsely furnished room, and the prioress sat in one of them, motioning for Dame Blanche to sit next to her. "My Lord Merlin, please be seated. I do not apologize for my lack of furnishings, but I hope your two servants will not object to standing during our conversation."

I stifled a laugh, but noticed that Sir Ywain was turning red and scowling from where he stood on the other side of Merlin's chair. The old man corrected her quickly: "You mistake, my Lady Prioress. In the turmoil of our arrival, I neglected to introduce Sir Ywain, Knight of the Round Table, and Gildas of Cornwall, page to my Lady Guinevere, Queen of Logres."

Ywain and I nodded courteously to Madame Hildegard, and she unceremoniously waved her hand. "My error then. Yes, I recall the page from his visit last week."

I was about to speak when Merlin prevented me. "And you were not very forthcoming at that time, by his report," he said. "Perhaps now you will be more candid about Dame Agnes and her involvement in these killings? You said at that time she was being confined to her cell. Quite obviously, she was not in the cell at all, but by that time had been slain. Why did you lie to Gildas then? Surely there is no longer any reason for secrecy. The girl is dead."

The small white dog came prancing out of the prioress's private cell and leaped again into her lap. Madame Hildegard stroked him absently as she answered Merlin's charge.

"There is certainly no longer any need to protect Sister Agnes. She is beyond mundane pain or suffering now. But when the page came to me earlier, we did not know where she was. We knew she was missing and had not returned. It wasn't until after I had talked with your page, when the horse she had taken returned riderless, that we feared the worst."

"But why not ask Gildas for help in searching for her, if you were concerned that she hadn't returned to the convent?"

"Because he was from the castle. Sister Agnes had left during that Wednesday morning after a messenger from the kitchen at Camelot arrived asking for some spice or other. I granted her permission to go. But when she had not returned, Dame

Blanche confided to me her concerns for Agnes. There was a certain knight from the castle who had visited Agnes twice in the last week, the last time on the day before her disappearance. Blanche told me Dame Agnes was in a very agitated state after the knight's last visit, and was just as agitated when she left that morning to run to the castle kitchen. We did not know whether any visitor from the castle could be trusted, or whether those visits had to do with Sister Agnes's disappearance."

During the last part of the prioress's disclosure, Sister Blanche had broken down in sobs. Now her face was buried in a handkerchief that she pulled from the sleeve of her habit. It was a bad time, but Merlin had to find out what it was she knew.

"Dame Blanche, I apologize for making you talk with us so soon after the shock of Sister Agnes's death, but we must learn what evidence you might have that can help us catch these killers." The old man began very gently, "Please tell us, first, how well you knew Dame Agnes."

Dame Blanche half-composed herself, and, interrupted by occasional sobs, began her story. "Sister Agnes was my closest friend here among the sisters. We arrived at Saint Mary Magdalene's about the same time, and at the time were the youngest postulants in the convent. We were really close. We used to spend all of our free time together talking about what our lives were like before coming here. I didn't have much to tell. I was fourteen and my father had already married off three daughters. He never thought he'd have a dowry for me, so he tried to make sure I got an education. The nuns at Winchester taught me grammar and rhetoric and logic, and they taught me to sing. They told my father that I had a voice like a nightingale." With that Dame Blanche reddened with modesty. "And that he should be able to marry me to the church without much dowry. And so I came here when I was fourteen, so as not to be an old maid."

My heart sank at that, when I thought of my Lady Rose-mounde, already past prime marriageable age, and me without any way to claim her. I hoped fate had something in store for her other than the veil. But I fought off those thoughts and tried to focus on the matter at hand.

"Sister Agnes was seventeen when I arrived. She was so kind to me . . ." Blanche broke off again, and we had to wait a few moments while she wiped the tears from her eyes and composed herself so she could go on speaking. "She used to tell me all about her life in Wales before she joined the convent."

"We're very interested in hearing about that, Sister," Merlin said encouragingly. "Especially about the love affair that we understand ended unhappily for her. Can you tell us anything about that?"

"Her father was a minor Welsh nobleman called Geoffrey of Milford," Blanche answered, nodding. "I understood that she was betrothed to a celebrated knight of Wales when she was twelve. It was to be a great step up for her and for her family, and everyone was envious of the match, she said. Her father had been a loyal retainer to King Pellinore, so to reward him for his years of faithful service, Pellinore wanted to marry off his eldest son to Geoffrey's daughter."

"You're saying that Dame Agnes was once betrothed to Sir Lamorak?" Merlin cried, astounded. Dame Blanche had said it casually, but this was the link that bound together everything else we had been seeking for the past two weeks. Dame Agnes had been in the kitchen. She was an expert in herbal lore. And her former lover had been murdered by Sir Gawain and his brothers. Here were means, motive, and opportunity.

But how, then, had she ended up dead herself?

"Sir Lamorak, yes, that was the name." Sister Blanche seemed surprised that we knew it. "He was dashing, handsome, romantic, and twelve years older than Agnes. But she fell madly in love with him at first sight. She said he always treated her courteously, like she was a grown woman and not a twelve-year-old, and she appreciated that in him. He gave her a gift when they first met, an embroidered green ribbon for her hair. He told her anyone with golden curls as beautiful as hers should never cover her head. I think she still had the ribbon. She kept it with her always."

Madame Hildegard frowned but said nothing. I looked at Ywain, who stared at the floor.

"King Pellinore and Sir Geoffrey had agreed that the wedding would take place at St. David's on Agnes's fourteenth birthday. But that day came and went and Agnes was still an unmarried virgin."

"Sir Lamorak had reneged on his pledge?" Merlin probed.

"So it seemed to her and her father. Lamorak had left Wales and was off seeking adventure. By that time King Pellinore had been killed, so Sir Geoffrey had no one to complain to. And rumors were reaching Wales from the north that Sir Lamorak had found a, well, more mature woman to be his paramour."

"Queen Margause of Orkney," I blurted out.

"Why . . . yes." Sister Blanche looked at me, and then at Merlin and Ywain, with eyebrows knit together, puzzled at our knowing so much of her story already. "So, angry at the way he and his daughter were being shamed by Sir Lamorak, Sir Geoffrey wrote Lamorak a letter, to be delivered to the castle of the late King Lot of Orkney. In the letter he called Lamorak a false knight and challenged him to single combat if he did not return and honor his pledge to marry Geoffrey's daughter. But no answer ever came."

"Was he sure the letter ever reached Sir Lamorak?" Merlin asked.

"There was no way to be sure. But one thing they were sure

of: Sir Lamorak had deserted Agnes, and there would be no wedding. Agnes pined away, rejected any other suitors, and ended up here when her father despaired of ever marrying her off."

"So she didn't exactly come to the convent with a profound vocation," Merlin commented.

"She came as a postulant, of course, and unsure of her vocation," Madame Hildegard broke in. "But she learned to love God and to desire to do his work. She learned to work hard in the kitchen and in her herb garden, and to pray sincerely. I was never unhappy with her vocation once she had committed to our order."

Merlin bowed in deference to her. "I must accept your word, my Lady Prioress. But her hair . . . the ribbon . . . It would appear that she never completely renounced the world."

"One can only *completely* renounce the world when one is dead," the prioress answered, stroking the dog in her lap. "We are all perpetually on the road to perfection, but the destination is achieved in another world."

"Right," Ywain muttered. "Even our pure and innocent lamb, Sir Lamorak, slain without provocation by the merciless Gawain, seems to have had a long way to go on that road, wouldn't you say?"

Merlin glared at him and muttered, "That's not really helpful right now." He turned back to Dame Blanche. "Now this is very important, Sister. You said that a knight had visited Dame Agnes twice the week before her disappearance. And that she had been distressed. Did she confide anything to you about who this knight was or why his visits upset her?"

Dame Blanche shook her head thoughtfully. "She never said why, but she was very anxious after the last visit. I do remember that during his visit the two of them went to the apothecary storeroom. I thought she was showing him where she did much

257

of her work. The time before—it was perhaps two or three days earlier—she had visited the scriptorium with him. She was not so anxious after that visit. She seemed, instead, very . . . I don't know, energetic and distracted, but not upset. Anyway, those weren't the only times I had seen her with this knight."

"He had visited her before?"

"Once before, probably six months ago. When he left she was crying. I tried to comfort her, but she was inconsolable."

"I remember her behaving in a distraught manner some months ago," Madame Hildegard agreed. "She would not tell me what was troubling her, though she did confess several times to Father Bernard in that time. She soon recovered, and I attributed it to the fact that young girls are often emotional, and so forgot about it. But she confided in you, Sister Blanche?"

"She did." The younger nun was tearing up again but pressed on. "She told me that the visitor was a knight of Arthur's court, and had come to tell her that Sir Lamorak, her former lover, was dead. Even though she had now dedicated her life to prayer and holy pursuits, she was devastated by his loss. The priest consoled her that she would see him again in heaven. I hope that is what is happening now. But she bore an unrelenting hatred toward Sir Lamorak's killer, whoever he was. The knight had told her that the body had been discovered, but that the killer had never been found."

Sister Blanche paused. She wiped her eyes again and took some deep breaths. As tenderly as he could, Merlin urged her just a little further. "Now Sister, this is very important. Did Dame Agnes ever tell you the knight's name, or anything about his parentage? And can you tell us anything about the way he looked?"

"He was Welsh, first of all. From near Dame Agnes's hometown. I never knew his name," she replied, "but I could easily recognize him again. He was not very big for a knight—

thin and not very tall. His face was lean and bony, and he had small, dark, close-set eyes. When you looked at his face, his features seemed kind of squeezed together, like a prune."

Merlin kept gazing at Dame Blanche impassively, but I could tell by the tone of his voice that he was becoming more and more excited as her description continued. He clearly had someone particular in mind when he asked "And do you remember what his hair looked like?"

"He nearly always wore his hood," Blanche answered. "But I did see him once with his hood down, and I remember that his hair was brown and straggly, and very thin."

"Thank you," Merlin said, his eyes closed and a kind of relief on his face. "You've been most helpful, Sister. Please accept my condolences for the loss of your friend and sister, and I apologize to both of you"—he sat back and bowed his head to include Madame Hildegard as well—"for disturbing you at this difficult time."

"May I ask one thing?" I interrupted. Merlin looked at me in annoyance, but I pressed on. "Sister Blanche, why were you at Sir Patrise's funeral, mourning so visibly in the back of the cathedral?"

"It was not for Sir Patrise that I was crying," Dame Blanche replied, her head bowing low. "I had heard of the death of a knight at Camelot, on the same day that Sister Agnes had failed to come home. I remembered how fretful she had been before she left, and after the Welsh knight had left her the day before. I thought there might be a connection between the two things. Perhaps, I thought, Dame Agnes would be at the funeral. Perhaps the knight was her Welsh knight, and her distress had to do with her knowledge of his impending murder. I needed to see for myself. But of course, I was wrong on both counts, as it turned out. I wept out of concern for Sister Agnes, and prayed that we would see her again. I'm afraid I prayed very little for

Sir Patrise's soul."

"Now if there is nothing else," the prioress said, rising dismissively and ignoring Merlin's courtesy, "we must be about our business. Ritual does provide a network of comfort when all the world seems to be crashing down," she confided in us quietly, then added in a much louder and authoritative tone, "and we must prepare for vespers. I trust you can show yourselves out? Fine. Good day to you."

Madame Hildegard and Dame Blanche left the house without another word, though Blanche did nod politely to us as she left. Augustine returned to his lady's chamber. And Ywain, Merlin, and I were left to fend for ourselves. "Well, how do you like that?" Sir Ywain grumbled as we exited the prioress's quarters and headed for the convent's stables to pick up our horses. "Never even a thank you for bringing their prodigal daughter back to them."

"No one will ever accuse the nuns of Saint Mary Magdalene's of being overly hospitable to guests," I agreed, recalling my last visit to the convent.

"It's a difficult time for them. Perhaps we shouldn't judge," Merlin corrected us. The comment seemed uncharacteristically generous of him. But I noticed he had a very satisfied expression on his face.

"You know!" I exploded. "You know who the murderer is!"

"Don't you?" he asked me.

"I know who the description reminds me of, but I still can't figure out what exactly Sister Agnes's role was in the whole thing."

"It's just a matter of making the right deductions, boy."

"And what would those be?" Ywain asked, more lost than I was.

"We need to piece together exactly what Sister Agnes was going through first," Merlin said, his pontifical voice in rare form.

"Six months ago, she receives a visit from our Welsh mystery knight, who tells her that Sir Lamorak has been murdered. Agnes is devastated, but has no concrete target for her anger because no one knows who Lamorak's killer is."

"That much is easy enough," Ywain told him.

"Right. But now, months later, the same knight returns. This time he has found out who the killer is: Sir Gawain. He tells Dame Agnes that he will avenge Lamorak's murder by meeting Gawain at the site of the atrocity and slaying him there. She agrees to write the challenge to Sir Gawain in her own hand, takes our knight to the scriptorium during the hours of rest for the convent when no one else will be around, and pens the challenge we heard Ywain tell us about."

"And that's why she seems all excited afterwards." I followed Merlin's drift. "And when the knight comes back two days later, she gives him the poison. That's what they went to the apothecary house for."

"True. Only Sister Agnes would have had the knowledge and skill to provide the distillation of foxglove needed for the murder."

"So she poisoned the apples?" Ywain asked.

"Roger said he had seen her handling the fruit, didn't he?"

"Yes, she handled the fruit, but no, she did not poison it," Merlin replied with confidence. "Remember that she was particularly agitated when the knight left her the second time. He must have revealed to her a change in plan. There were to be two traps laid for Sir Gawain: the poison at the meal and the ambush in the forest. If one failed to do the job, the other would make sure of him. Nothing would prevent Sir Gawain's death. Agnes, the avenger of her lover's murder, hated Sir Gawain and wanted to see him dead. She was happy to support the idea of killing him in combat at the scene of his own foul crime. But Dame Agnes, the holy sister, recoiled from the thought of poisoning an unarmed and unsuspecting victim. Her hatred allowed her to provide the Welsh knight with the poison, but her conscience would not let her rest. She agonized over what she had done until the call from the kitchen the next day gave her the opportunity to visit the castle—and, she hoped, to prevent the wrong she had helped to plan."

"Then she was looking at the apples because . . ."

"She was checking to see whether they had been poisoned. Apparently there was no trace of the poison at the time she examined them, so she went off without saying anything to anyone about the plot."

"Went off where? She never returned to the convent," Ywain asked.

"She must have stayed in the castle until evening, perhaps praying in the chapel or some other out-of-the-way place. But she needed to see what happened at the banquet. Our Welsh knight, no doubt accompanying Sir Kay on his visit to the kitchen, poisoned the apples after Agnes had examined them. Agnes must have been keeping a close eye on the great hall to determine what happened at the dinner. When the commotion ensued afterwards, she would have known that the poisoning had occurred. It was she who crept secretly into the great hall to retrieve the poisoned apple and remove the evidence."

"How can you know it was her?"

"It had to be someone other than one of the knights. They and their pages and squires had been told to void the great hall for the evening, you remember? None of them would have been able to sneak back in without his absence being noted by some of the others, and they would have told us when we interviewed them. It had to be an outsider who removed the apple."

"But why would Dame Agnes have tried to prevent the murder but then cover up the evidence afterwards?" I asked.

"Guilt and shame were the reasons for both. She felt guilty at having supplied the poison, so tried to prevent its use. But once it had been used, she needed to make sure it would not be traced back to her."

"But how did she come to be killed in the woods, then?" Ywain asked.

"She would have learned from the buzz around the castle that it was Sir Patrise who had died and that the queen was accused of the crime," Merlin explained. We had reached the stables and the dull stable boy was bringing out our horses. "She knew Sir Gawain was still alive and that her accomplice was not under suspicion. And that meant Plan B, the ambush, was still in effect. This was where the conscience of the nun overcame the urgings of the bereft lover, and she determined to stop that murderous ambush at all costs. She may have seen Gawain ride his destrier through the gate and assumed he was going to the secret tryst. In any case, she mounted her own horse and rode to the spot where she knew the assassins were waiting."

"But Gawain never got there, and when Dame Agnes rode in, the archers shot first and looked at the victim after," I finished for him. "But Merlin, what I don't understand is why Robin never said anything about Sister Agnes leaving the castle in such a hurry that night. When I passed the gate headed for your cave, he told me only that Sir Gawain had galloped through. He never mentioned a young nun."

"He may not have thought it was important. Or perhaps she hadn't left yet. It's something we need to ask him. But I think it is also important to find out whether all of his archers are accounted for. Anyway, we need to get back to the castle." Merlin swung himself into the saddle of one of our palfreys.

"Do you want me to talk to Robin?" I asked as Ywain and I mounted our own horses. "I know him well."

"That might be best," Merlin said. "I'll take Sir Ywain with me and try to track him down as quickly as possible tonight."

"Track *who* down?" Ywain asked, bringing up the rear with his horse. "The killer?"

"Sir Pinel!" Merlin and I answered in unison, and spurred the horses on toward Camelot.

CHAPTER EIGHTEEN:
THE STAKE

"I can't believe I didn't see it!" Merlin was worrying as we rode back to Camelot, the sun setting at our backs. "Right under my nose the whole time, and I didn't see it. But Pinel is not the sort of knight you really notice, is he? Still, he fit every profile we had of the killer. He's Welsh. We all knew that. It's just that no one really knew his parentage. He was at the dinner sitting right next to Sir Kay, you told me. He was always with Sir Kay. Of course he *had* to have been with him that day when Kay visited the kitchen. He should have been on top of our list of suspects the whole time."

"Everything looks clearer in hindsight," Sir Ywain agreed. "But you were looking at other leads. They seemed legitimate at the time."

"Wild goose chases!" Merlin snapped. "We weren't even looking for enemies of the right victim. I pray we can get things straightened out in time to prevent any more deaths."

"Don't blame yourself," I tried to console the old man. "I was fooled the whole time. Now that I think of it, it was Sir Pinel who was with Kay that morning I ran into him at the stables, and Pinel kept going on and on about how Sir Palomides was such a connoisseur of herbs and such. That was what made me suspect Palomides of the poisoning to begin with. And I remember now, it was Sir Pinel, too, who stood behind me talking to Sir Breunor about the Red Knight of the Red Lands and his wife! He was always trying to put suspicion on somebody else! I feel like such an idiot!"

"That's because you *are* an idiot!" Merlin snapped back at me. "God's elbows, why didn't you at least tell me who it was you were getting those false leads from? Oh, never mind," he told me as I started to sputter. "Why expect you to notice Sir Pinel any more than anybody else?"

Darkness was beginning to shroud the castle—it was certainly nearly compline—as we clambered over the drawbridge, and I looked up as we passed under the high window of the barbican to call out, "Robin! Are you up there, Robin?"

An unfamiliar voice answered back, " 'E's not up 'ere now. Not 'is shift."

"Do you know where he is, then?" I called back.

"Gone off to sleep in the keep, I expect. You 'ave business with 'im, then?"

"I do. I'll look for him up there." And I trotted after Merlin and Ywain to the stables. Taber, prevented from going off to his own bed by the lateness of our return, grumbled a bit at us, but we had more important things to worry about.

"Right," Merlin said. "Ywain and I will go to see whether Pinel is sleeping in the great hall. We'll find him, wherever he might be. You go talk to your friend Robin."

"I'm on my way," I called as I started off toward the castle keep.

The keep was already dark when I arrived. There were candles burning just inside the door and I took a candelabrum with three candlesticks in it to light my way. It was unfamiliar ground for me. The keep was strictly a military structure and housed the castle garrison—archers and guards like Robin, not the knights who made up the mounted cavalry. The walls were three feet wide at the base, tapering to eighteen inches at the top, and the round tower was fifty feet in diameter and rose to a height of ninety feet. The walls were bare stone inside, and even in bright daylight it was dark within, the only breaks in the wall being cross-shaped slits through which the artillery could fire arrows to defend the tower from attack. The keep was designed as the last refuge if the castle was under siege and the outer walls had been breached. It was designed to be impregnable.

I scaled the stone staircase to the second floor of the tower, where a dozen men lay on benches along the wall. As quietly as I could, I tiptoed from one sleeping form to another, holding the candelabrum near enough to each to enable me to study their features. I got several curses and a promise to show me another use for the candelabrum before I finally shone it in the face I recognized as Robin's.

He wasn't asleep yet, and when the light struck his face he sat bolt upright and squinted at me through the dark. "Gildas? Is that you, boy? What are you skulking about the keep at this hour for? I may be mistaken, but I believe the ladies-in-waiting all sleep over in the queen's quarters. That's where you want to go if you want to start bothering people in their beds."

"Stop your jests and listen to me. I'm serious," I told him.

With that he stood up and looked at me intently, the flames of the candles flickering between us in the dark. "What then?" he asked, suddenly all business. "Something to do with your investigation? Because it's high time you and the old charlatan came up with something, or the queen may burn tomorrow."

"We know who the murderer is," I told him. His eyebrows raised and his deep blue eyes got bigger, each of them reflecting three flames back at my eyes. The deep shadows cast by the candlelight in the dark keep gave his face a formidable sternness as I gazed into it. His nose seemed lengthened by the shadows, and his eyes seemed to glisten from within deep black caves. His blond mustache appeared dark in the shadows, but his strong chin protruded into the light. His blond hair, too, lay in the shadows and looked dark as well. He wore it long, shoulder length, and it was to a great extent his vanity. But now it was tangled into a bush, since I had got him out of his bed. Hmmph. Master Kempe is unkempt, I couldn't help punning to myself, in spite of the seriousness of the situation.

"Well *who* then, damn your eyes?" Robin cried, tired of waiting for me to continue. He said it loud enough that several other sleepers grumbled and cursed at him to shut his trap, it was late.

"Wait," I said, suddenly cautious. "First I've got a question for you. On the night of the banquet, when I left to go and fetch Merlin, you told me I had just missed Sir Gawain, galloping off on the king's business, right?"

"Of course. And you were on foot, and told me the same, and I gave you a little bit of guff about not believing you and all. Said I was the Emperor Lucius, if I recall, and then you buggered off. What's your point?"

"You never told me, or anyone else, about the nun who left on horseback as well."

That comment hit him like a brick. His head went back as if I'd punched him. He didn't seem to know just how to respond. After a moment's pause, he asked quietly, "How'd you know about *her*?"

"We know about her because we found her dead today in the forest."

Robin's face fell, rearranging the shadows of the candlelight into a much grimmer pattern. "Dead! By accident or . . . ?"

"If you call two arrows through her body accidental, I suppose it was by accident. No, Robin, she was murdered, and right in the clearing where a trap had been set for Sir Gawain. This was all connected."

"Sir Gawain? Someone was out to kill him as well?"

"He was always the target," I told him, taking a deep breath.

It looked like I was going to have to start at the beginning. "Look, Sir Patrise was killed by accident. He was just in the wrong place at the wrong time. This was a plot to assassinate Sir Gawain, by a Welsh faction that wanted revenge on him for the death of Sir Lamorak."

"Sir Gawain was responsible for the death of Lamorak?"

"Just listen, will you? It was Sir Pinel, the Welsh knight, who was behind it all. He's the one who poisoned the apples, and he's the one who laid the trap for Sir Gawain in the forest. But the nun, Dame Agnes, was his accomplice. She mixed the poison and she wrote the note challenging Gawain to a showdown in the woods. But she had a change of heart, and rode to the clearing in the woods to stop the murder—"

"And ran right into it instead," Robin followed me to the inevitable conclusion. "Poor Sister Agnes."

"But why didn't you tell us about her leaving that night? We would have found out about the plot much sooner if you had only come forward."

"She asked me not to," Robin admitted, shaking his head at his own gullibility. "I knew her by sight. She was no stranger to our kitchens here and entered the gates at least a few times a week. I used to joke with her about how it was a great waste that someone as young and pretty as she was had taken the veil, and as to how if she ever wanted to give up her vows she should look me up first. That sort of thing. Didn't mean anything by it, you know. She'd just laugh at me."

Somehow that was easy to believe.

"So when she says 'Master Robin, please don't tell anyone you saw me leave at this time. It's really important that nobody knows I was here tonight,' well, I figure she just didn't want to get into any trouble with her prioress for violating the rule and all, so I tell her it's all right, her secret's safe with me. Well, I'm buggered. I never figured a nun could have been involved in all this."

"Well, Master Robin Kempe, you're a great lunkhead, aren't you?" I asked him.

He shrugged. "Guilty as charged, your honor. But listen now. If Sir Pinel was sitting all innocent like at the banquet, then who was it sitting out in the woods waiting to pick off poor Agnes when she rode in? I smell a rat, and one that's close by, I think." He began to shift his eyes to the other sleeping forms in the keep.

"Exactly," I agreed. "There were two archers, and they were well trained. They picked off Sister Agnes, galloping into the clearing on her horse, with one shot apiece. There's only one place they could have got that kind of training."

"Right here," Robin agreed. "And I know who they are. Two Welsh archers, Owen and Harry. They weren't on duty that night and didn't come back to the castle until the next day. I thought they'd been to the stews in Caerleon. Yes, don't look so shocked my young page, some of the soldiers go in for that sort of thing. But that story won't hold up to a little aggressive questioning."

"Not too aggressive," I urged. "We want to get at the truth."

"I'll get at the truth," Robin muttered. *All right, listen to me!* He called in a huge voice. "Everybody up! We have traitors in our midst! I want you to arm yourselves and find me Owen of Monmouth and Harry of Haverford. Arrest them and bring them to me. They are wanted for the murder of a nun and conspiracy to murder Sir Gawain. Consider them armed and dangerous!"

In the meantime, as I learned later, Merlin and Ywain were rousing the sleepers in the great hall to search out Sir Pinel. Merlin thought it best not to raise a general alarm, so that Sir

Pinel might be taken unawares—and so that allies of his might not rise up to defend him with arms and turn the whole thing bloody.

Like most of the knights and squires, Pinel slept generally in the large open space of the great hall. Some of the greater knights—Sir Kay, of course, Sir Gawain and his brothers, Sir Lancelot and his kinsmen, Sir Tristram, Sir Palomides and Sir Safer, and Sir Ywain himself, for instance—had separate, more private quarters, not unlike the queen's chamber but not as large. But most knights slept in the great hall or in the smaller lesser hall, those being the two largest spaces in the castle. Yet tonight Pinel was not to be found there. Speaking privately to Florent, Merlin left instructions that Sir Pinel was to be detained if he did show his face in the hall, and Florent agreed to call for his arrest if Pinel showed up.

Snatching a torch from its holder near the door, Merlin pressed onward to the lesser hall. Once again, he and Ywain were disappointed. There was nothing to do but appoint another deputy from those sleeping in the room. This time Merlin asked Sir Breunor to raise the hue and cry if Sir Pinel was spotted. The search party moved on to explore other rooms in the castle.

And so it continued well into the night, Merlin and Ywain searching unsuccessfully for Sir Pinel, Robin and his men turning the keep upside down searching for the two Welsh archers. And nobody having any luck.

The bells of Saint Mary Magdalene's were chiming matins when the two parties came together in the middle bailey for a conference.

"This search is useless in the dark," Ywain complained. "An army could hide in the shadows of the castle and we'd never know it in this gloom. Unless we raise a general alarm, I don't see how we can find Pinel, or the two archers, by dawn."

"I still advise against the general alarm," Merlin said.

"There'll be so many people milling about that Pinel could lose himself in the crowd and slip away. Or worse, he could raise other knights to his side and vow to fight his way out. We've had two deaths already. We don't want any more innocent blood spilt over this."

"Neither he nor the archers can slip away with the gates closed and my men on guard," Robin disagreed. "But I'll grant you we don't want this turning nasty."

"It still could," Ywain reminded us. "If Pinel and those archers get together, there'll be hell to pay when we try to arrest them."

"Owen and Harry are definitely not in the keep," Robin reported. "I've had the whole garrison turned out to look for them in every corner. My guess is they're not in the castle at all."

"Escaped?" I asked.

"Not bloody likely, unless it was sometime during the day. I'm guessing they went into town for the night. They're probably completely unaware we're looking for them."

"Well, if we don't find them, can we still stop the trial by combat in the morning?" I asked. "We know what happened. We know the queen's innocent."

Merlin hung his head, his protruding eyebrows screening his eyes from me, and he shook his head from side to side. "All we have is our word and our deductions. We don't have actual hard evidence that Pinel is the guilty party. Without that, the queen still stands accused. Sir Mador will never withdraw his accusations without proof, and the king will not stand in the way of justice in the queen's case, and so destroy his reputation for integrity and truth."

"Then unless we can find Pinel or the archers and get them to confess, Sir Bors may be killed and the queen burnt at the stake. Or, if they are spared, Sir Mador may be killed for trying to avenge his cousin."

"Indeed," Merlin answered me. "That is precisely the case. And further, even if the trial ends well for the queen, many in Camelot will still doubt her innocence without a confession from Pinel."

"Then we've got to redouble our efforts to find them," Robin asserted pragmatically. "Here's what we'll do. I'm going to send a dozen of my men into Caerleon to search the inns and brothels for Owen and Harry. Five to one we turn them up there. We double the guard at the gate, so that in the morning, when all leave the castle to attend the trial, the guard can look carefully at anyone who leaves, and we'll nab Pinel then if he tries to get away. Meantime, I'll have another dozen men left here and, with us four, we'll go over every inch of this castle until we turn up the bugger. Right?"

And that was that. Robin gave commands, and the garrison followed his lead. We went back to searching, quietly and systematically, and continued to turn up nothing. It wasn't long before the castle began stirring, first the fires in the kitchen, then the stables, kennels, and mews, the servants fetching water from the well, the priest heading for the chapel. And the light burst over the horizon, giving us a silent ally in our search and making it much harder to hide in the shadows.

People streamed through the gates, heading for the lists, the site of the trial, which was to take place shortly after prime. While we were no closer to success than ever, I felt there was nothing more I could do here, and that perhaps there was something I could do at the trial. That is, I could perform my duty as the queen's page and comfort her in her hour of need.

"Merlin," I said to the old man, "I am going to the queen."

He looked up at me and nodded. His face was grave.

★ ★ ★ ★ ★

In a meadow beside the castle, the king had caused an arena to be raised, with bleachers on the north and south sides of a space a hundred yards long and fifty wide. At the rear of the north bleachers, midway along the tilting field, were two covered boxes, each furnished with a single cushioned chair, one for the king and one for the queen. A short wooden barrier ran straight down the middle the length of the field, so that the knights could tilt with each other, riding their horses in one another's direction on either side of the barrier. On the east and west ends of the tilting field were broad open areas where Sir Mador de la Porte and Sir Bors de Ganis had pitched their tents, in which they had placed their armor and weapons for the joust.

But Sir Mador had ordered more than this. Behind his pavilion he had erected an iron stake, piled high with branches and tinder. Two of Sir Mador's pages stood with burning torches on either side of the iron stake, waiting for the trial to be over—waiting for the queen to be condemned. The sight made my heart sink in my chest, knowing that the queen must not only watch her fate being decided by mortal combat here in the lists, but must also have continuously and relentlessly in view the fire waiting to consume her flesh should her champion fail.

When I arrived at the lists, out of breath after running from the castle yard, I entered from the west, so that the first thing I saw was the stake and the fiery torches. Their heat sent a chill through me that no cloak could warm, and I rushed past into the arena. Already seated in her box in the north stands was my lady the queen. Sir Gaheris stood off to her right, armed and stoic. It would be his job, along with Sir Gareth, to escort the queen to Sir Mador's iron stake if the trial turned out badly for her, or if Merlin was not able to bring Sir Pinel in to confess in time. I ran up the bleachers two tiers at a time to bring the queen what news we had.

In defiance of her critics and detractors, the queen had come to the trial not humbly, in a poor smock, as one would have expected of the defendant in a murder trial, but rather decked out in her finest trappings of office. "Let them know who it is they are condemning!" she told me when I saw her.

Her head was uncovered, but her long blond tresses were enclosed in the back by a crispine, a fine gold mesh set with gems that hung from a golden fillet, a strip of metal encircling her brow. She wore a tight-fitting chemise of rich, olive-green satin, laced up the side and embroidered with gold filigree set with small emeralds. It was girdled by a gold belt with a tongue hanging down to her knees. Over this, in the cold autumn breeze, she wore a blue woolen garde-corps that reached to the ground. It had long, wide sleeves with arm-slits at the elbows. Sitting there in her private box, she looked for all the world like a reigning monarch rather than a prisoner awaiting condemnation. For monarch she was.

"My lady," I whispered, bending down to her ear. She held her head high in an attempt to brazen out the situation, but the intense look in her eyes betrayed her inner turmoil.

"Oh, Gildas," she whispered, her voice breaking. "Thank God you're here. You're the only person I can stand."

"Listen, my queen. We have news. We now know it was Sir Pinel who poisoned the apple that killed Sir Patrise."

Guinevere gasped in surprise. "And you have proof of this?" she wanted to know.

"No, my lady. Not proof that would establish your innocence in court. But we know that Pinel was trying to kill Sir Gawain. He also set a trap for him that ended up killing a poor young nun rather than Gawain. In that he had two accomplices, archers from the palace guard."

"Worse and worse," Guinevere tsked. "Bring the proof that will free me!"

"Merlin, Ywain, and Robin are in the castle even now, searching for Pinel and the archers. They will have the truth out of them, and that will free you!"

"Well, pray they do it before this battle begins. If we can avoid the bloodshed of good knights over nothing, by all means let's do it. But Gildas," she said, putting out her arm and touching my sleeve, "let it not come to trial for my sake. I fear Sir Bors wavers in his dedication to my cause. If he is beaten, I will burn. Gildas, save me from the fire."

"Exactly what we mean to do, my lady. Now if you'll excuse me, I must find Sir Gareth and enlist his help." I clambered down the bleachers back to the ground, for I thought I had spotted Beaumains standing on the far end of the lists, near the spot where Sir Bors was beginning to arm himself for the battle. I ran in that direction, past the stands filling with knights and ladies as well as townspeople, curious to see the outcome of this much talked-of trial.

Gareth was leaning glumly against a railing behind Sir Bors's side of the lists. He looked up at me and his face brightened. "Gildas!" he called. "What have you found out? Is my brother safe?"

"I can't tell you anything about Gawain, but I can tell you who tried to kill him. It was Sir Pinel. He poisoned the fruit and he set a trap to ambush Gawain. The ambush failed . . ." I reassured him as he started at my words. "It killed an unsuspecting nun instead."

"Cruel," Gareth muttered. "But you have him in tow, then? We can call off this charade and save Sir Bors the trouble of arming himself?"

"We haven't been able to find him anywhere in the castle," I admitted. "So we don't have any hard and fast proof of the queen's innocence. Unless we find him and force a confession from him, the trial will have to continue, I'm afraid. But I came to you to ask for your help. While Merlin, Ywain, and Robin search the castle, can you keep your eyes open here, and arrest Sir Pinel if you see him in the crowd?"

"I'll snare him like a cornered rat. Don't worry. If he shows his face here, it'll be for the last time. I see Florent off there to the right. I'll go and enlist his help. Between the two of us, Pinel will never get out of this arena."

The great destrier Pegasus stood already fully armed, his front hooves stamping nervously in the dust before Sir Bors's pavilion, pitched at one end of the arena's jousting area. A page held the horse while Sir Lionel, acting as Bors's squire for the battle, helped Sir Bors arm himself for the fray.

Bors stood in a brown, padded and quilted hacqueton that reached to his waist, wearing hose of double-woven mail and iron boots of the same mesh that he had donned before coming to the lists. A pair of golden spurs were fastened to the boots. On his head Sir Bors wore a padded skullcap to protect him from the chain mail that would cover all but his face.

I watched Sir Lionel help Bors into a long hauberk of the same highest-quality chain mail. A mail coif was attached to the hauberk that came up over Sir Bors's head, and sleeves extended over his hands to form a chain mail mitten with leather palms for grasping his lance. My own father, the Cornish armorer, would have been impressed by the mesh. No sword or lance could pierce that corselet, but it was still supple enough to allow Bors free movement of his arms, and even of his hands.

Over the hauberk Sir Bors put on a colorful surcote of red and silver that would match his shield. Around it Sir Lionel fastened, first, a narrow belt around the waist, and then a broader white sword belt with a scabbard reaching from Bors's waist to his feet. In the scabbard swung a great broadsword, a keepsake handed down from Sir Bors's father, King Bors de Ganis.

Around Bors's neck Sir Lionel hung his shield, blazoned with a field gules on which an ox argent stood rampant. Sir Gawain had always said that the ox was the perfect charge for Sir Bors, dull and stolid as he was. Though certainly nobody had ever seen an ox do what it was doing on Sir Bors's shield.

Over Sir Bors's head Lionel now placed a heavy, flat-topped conical helmet. It had slits for air in the front and a broader slit for his eyes. Breathing and seeing cannot have been easy in that thing, but saving the head from being cloven asunder by a broadsword blow, or pierced straight through by a lance thrust, were, for the next hour of Bors's life, a lot more important than breathing and seeing.

Finally, in Bors's right hand Sir Lionel placed a long spear of ash wood, tipped with iron, that would be his chief weapon in the upcoming joust. Sir Bors, now fully armed and ready for shock combat with a mortal enemy poised to fight him to the utterance, mounted Pegasus by means of a small stepladder. The some sixty pounds of armor and weaponry he now held would have made it almost impossible for him to swing into the saddle of his great warhorse in the normal way.

Mounted, Sir Bors looked down the lists at Sir Mador de la Porte, poised and ready on his own destrier at the other end of the lists. Sir Mador wore a surcote of black and green, and bore a shield blazoned with a field vert on which a hawk sable was displayed.

The two knights, in full battle gear and mounted for action, each rode slowly to the center of the arena. Their horses stood side by side and faced the royal box at the center of the north bleachers. Each of them had removed his helmet and held it under his left arm, while each held the iron-tipped lance in his right. By now the king was present, sitting in royal purple robes and holding his scepter, image of power, while he looked down at them and said in a loud voice, "Who is it has business before this court of the king's justice? Come forward and state your cases."

Sir Mador moved his horse forward a few steps and called out to the king in a voice audible to all present, "I, Sir Mador de la Porte, take my oath before the king and all these present, that the queen treasonously murdered my cousin, Sir Patrise. And moreover, I shall prove the truth of this charge with my body on any here that would maintain the contrary." With that he backed his horse up until it stood perfectly parallel to Pegasus again. As he did so, a loud cheer came from the greater part of the crowd in the arena.

But with that Sir Bors moved his horse forward, and shouted in a voice loud enough to stifle the cheers, "As for Queen Guinevere, I say that right is on her side. I will make her innocence good with my hands. She is not guilty of any treason in Sir Patrise's death, and of that I swear my oath before the king and all those here assembled." No cheers followed Sir Bors's declaration, but utter silence hovered over the crowd.

I glanced up toward the queen and saw her looking about, taken aback by her complete lack of support. I also noticed that one of her ladies-in-waiting was now standing directly behind her, leaning over and speaking in her ear. I began to make my way as quickly as possible back to the queen's box. The lady was Rosemounde.

With that, Sir Mador turned on Bors and said, "Come off, then. Get ready to fight, and we shall soon see which of us is in the right."

"Sir Mador," Bors told him, in a voice intended only for the Irishman's ears, but which I overheard as I crossed before them at ground level and began making my way up the stands. "I have always respected your prowess as a knight. And believe me, I understand your grief and anger at your loss. But I have promised the queen to do this battle for her, unless a better knight should arrive to take up the cause in my place. I believe in my heart that the queen is innocent of these charges, and I trust in God to be on the side of the right. So I will do this battle without fear. Take back your charges, before blood is spilt here unnecessarily."

"If you've got nothing more to say," Sir Mador shouted so that all the crowd could hear him, "come off and do battle or else yield to me."

"Take your place," Bors called back, abandoning his futile attempt to avoid the combat. "I'll answer your charges now." And with that, the two knights withdrew to their respective ends of the lists, and prepared to tilt at each other in mortal combat.

By then I had reached the queen's side. Rosemounde, her loose hair ringed by a flowered circlet, wore a simple blue linen gown with a jeweled belt and a dark brown cape. She looked up at me, fear in her big brown eyes. Her lower lip, so often twisted ironically at me, now trembled with pity and dread for her mistress's fate. I took her by the hand to comfort her, but the queen would have none of it.

"Belay that, Gildas. I'm the one who needs comforting. Lady Rosemounde, run back to the castle. Find Merlin and tell him to come to me. I want him here to persuade the king that what Gildas says is true, that Sir Pinel was the poisoner. Proof or not, the king will be swayed by what the old necromancer says. Quickly, go."

Rosemounde bowed and murmured some kind of assent to the queen's wishes. She brushed my hand lightly with her fingers as she walked past me, down the rows of seats to head for the castle. I put my hand on the queen's shoulder to comfort her as we prepared to watch Sir Bors joust Sir Mador for the lady's life.

The king had made his way down from his box to the edge of the field, where he stood holding Excalibur aloft. Sir Bors and Sir Mador faced each other from opposite ends of the tilting field. When the king dropped his sword, the combatants would spur their horses forward for the tilt. A breathless silence fell upon the crowd as every eye was on the king. His arm twitched and began to move.

Suddenly the unmistakable sound of thundering hooves broke forth. The noise startled the king because he had not yet given the signal, but neither horseman had begun his charge. The sound was coming not from the lists but from farther off. Confused, I looked in the direction of the sound and saw two riders approaching in a cloud of dust. Sir Bors and Sir Mador both removed their helmets and relaxed their postures, as the whole crowd gazed, bewildered, in the direction of the riders.

By the time they galloped straight past Sir Mador's stake and pavilion, directly into the lists themselves, we could see that the lead rider was Sir Gawain. When the queen saw him, she grasped me by the sleeve. "My lady, your prayers may have just been answered," I told her.

The second knight was in full armor and helmeted, sitting on a pure white horse. His surcote was a simple dark green, and the shield that hung from his shoulders was blank. But it was clear to me—and, by the tears in her eyes, to the queen also—and, by the look of relief that spread across the king's face, to him as well—that the knight in disguise was none other than Sir Lancelot du Lac.

"My Lord King," Sir Gawain called as he and the disguised knight faced their horses toward the stands in the same way that Bors and Mador had just done. "I have brought with me a knight of great prowess who has sworn to take on himself the defense of the queen. He has come a great journey over the past several days to be here for the trial. He prays that Sir Bors of his courtesy yield his position as queen's champion, and allow him to take up the quarrel with Sir Mador de la Porte over the queen's innocence."

Sir Bors rode back to the center and faced the king again, saying, "I swore to defend the queen to the utterance unless a more worthy champion could be found. I yield the queen's defense in the faith that this unknown knight is in fact more worthy than I to defend her honor. He may have this quarrel, and may God speed him." If anyone else in that arena recognized Sir Lancelot, it was certainly Bors de Ganis.

Sir Mador, who for his part had also ridden back to the center of the field, told the king, "I care not what champion the queen sends to meet me. I have the right and I will prevail. Let the battle begin!"

The king turned and looked at Guinevere to make sure that she agreed formally to the substitution. She merely nodded at him and waved her hand. The fear had gone from her, and there was a new confidence about her as well.

"Sir Knight," the king addressed the disguised Lancelot. "You have ridden a long way, and that fully armed. You, and your horse, deserve to have a short respite at least before plunging into battle."

But Gawain answered for Lancelot, "My lord, the champion requests that the battle begin immediately. He will not stand to have these false charges leveled against the queen for a single moment longer."

Arthur paused, looking at the helmeted knight and at Sir Mador, who had put his helmet back on and was brandishing his lance in anticipation of the fight. "Very well," the king relented. "Let the battle begin."

Sir Gawain and Sir Bors rode off together toward Bors's pavilion at the side of the lists, and Sir Mador returned to his position at his end. Sir Lancelot rode slowly and determinedly after Bors, holding out his hand to take the lance from his cousin's grip before lining his white destrier up to charge against Sir Mador.

With Lancelot in the lists, the outcome of the joust was no longer in doubt. Sir Mador was up against a machine-like efficiency that no human being could ever match or sustain combat with for long. The queen knew this better than anyone. Tears of relief were streaming from her eyes as she turned them to me and, with a voice that could now afford to be charitable, told me, "Run after the Lady Rosemounde. Tell Merlin we no longer need him for my sake. But tell him that my concern for Sir Mador de la Porte requires him to stop this battle if he can, as soon as he can. Go now."

Hoping to catch up with my Lady Rosemounde before she got back to the castle, I scampered down the bleachers and took off at a dead run toward the front gate. But she must have walked quite briskly, as I saw no sign of her. In no time I had crossed the drawbridge and dashed toward the middle bailey, where I saw Merlin waiting. But just as I reached him, everything changed.

We heard the muffled whimper before seeing the two of them. When I turned toward the keep, it was as if I'd taken a blow to the chest from Lancelot's spear.

He had Rosemounde.

Sir Pinel, looking unkempt, unshaven, wearing only his hose and unbelted gray shirt, was holding the Lady Rosemounde in front of him like a shield. At her throat he held a long dagger. Her terror-filled eyes met mine and held them, silently pleading. Her mouth moved, but all that came out was a low moan.

Pinel had his back against the wall of the keep so that no one could come at him from behind. "Nobody move!" he commanded as we all stood dumbfounded. "Stay where I can see you!"

There were only four of us in the entire bailey—Merlin, Ywain, Robin, and me. There were ten guards manning the barbican and another dozen sweeping the rooms of the castle. Otherwise, besides the dozen soldiers searching the city, everyone else was at the joust, and we could hear occasional cheers and groans from the crowd watching Lancelot and Mador's duel. But it wouldn't have mattered if we were four or four hundred; there was no question of rushing Pinel and disarming him. The tender flower of Rosemounde's life hung by a thread and the murderer Pinel held the shears.

"Now all of you cooperate, and this sweet young thing may live out the day," Pinel growled. "You, boy," he called to me, "go and fetch me a horse from the stables."

"Not I," I responded instantly. "I will not leave the Lady Rosemounde." I could see by the relief in her eyes that I had made the right choice. I knew she was terrified, but my being there somehow made her less afraid to face this ordeal.

"Well, somebody had better bring me a horse or this girl's blood will be on your heads!"

"I'll go," Ywain said, nodding to Merlin and dashing off toward the stable. Perhaps it would have made more sense for me to go, Ywain being the one person there on our side trained in single combat, but combat did us no good as long as Pinel had the girl. I wanted to calm her.

"Rosemounde," I said, as if we were the only two people there. "Keep looking into my eyes. I will not let you go. Nothing will come between us."

"Very pretty," Pinel roared in disgust. "You'd all better do as I say or these young lovers are going to have a very tragic story. When that horse gets here, you're all going to stand back while I mount it with this little slut in front of me. Then you, Master

Robin, are going to command the garrison at the gate to let me through. Then you're going to lie down in the dust while I gallop off. If there is any pursuit, I swear to God you'll find this little tart's carcass along the way."

"How do we know you'll let her go at all?" Merlin asked him. "You've already killed two innocent people. Why should you blink at a third?"

"After all," Robin added, "you can only hang once." All the time we were gradually moving closer to him, waiting for the opportunity to disarm him, should it arise. All the time I kept my eyes on Rosemounde's.

"Give us assurance we can trust your word," Merlin said. "A place and time where you'll drop the girl off safely."

"I'm making the demands here!" Pinel bellowed. "Now back off! You get the girl when I say you get the girl. If you don't like it, try me now. I'll slit her throat like a fatling pig."

"And then you'll have nothing to bargain with," Merlin reminded him. "What makes you think you'll ever get away with this? Who are you to defy the entire kingdom of Logres, try to assassinate the king's nephew, put his queen in danger of burning? You think that King Arthur, master of all Christendom, will blink at this?"

"Ha!" Pinel spat on the ground. He pulled Rosemounde closer to him and motioned with the dagger as if to pierce her.

She cried out and I soothed her again. "It's all right! He's not going to do it!" I told her.

"The hell I'm not!" Pinel cried. "You, old man, what do you know about it? King Arthur blinks at his own queen's adultery. The king blinks at his nephew's brutal murder of Sir Lamorak, a knight more noble than any three of your Gawains, yea, or your Lancelots!"

"And what about Sir Patrise? And Dame Agnes?" Robin threw up to him.

285

"That foolish Irish knight blundered in where he didn't belong. I have no remorse for him. As for Dame Agnes, as you call her, that slut turned traitor in the end. She helped me plan the whole affair and then changed her mind at the crucial time. She got nothing more than her treason deserved. The only thing I'm sorry about is that the recreant Gawain is still alive. But not for long. I'll hunt him down and cut out his heart."

"You?" Merlin scoffed. "If you were half the knight Sir Gawain is, you'd have challenged him in the lists, instead of trying to kill him by stealth. But you didn't have the courage to do that, did you? Your way is poison, or ambush, or hiding behind the skirts of a woman because you're not man enough to do battle with a man."

It was worth a try, I'll admit it. Merlin was clearly trying to anger Pinel so that he'd let Rosemounde go and take the bait and attack us directly. But Sir Pinel didn't bite.

"*He* was the coward first. *He* was the one who ambushed Lamorak. He deserved to die in the same manner, the bastard!"

"Bastard?" Merlin caught at the term. "Sir Gawain is legally and officially the eldest son and heir of King Lot of Orkney. It is you, as I recall, whose parentage is listed by the castle heralds as 'unknown.' "

"I am the son of King Pellinore de Gales!" Pinel pronounced calmly and with assurance, as if he'd been practicing the announcement for years. "My father never claimed or recognized me, but my mother was lady-in-waiting to Pellinore's queen and told me it was the king had sired me. I grew up waiting for his acceptance, and I would have had it, too. He was about to legally acknowledge me when his life was cut short by King Lot. Sir Lamorak was my elder brother, the head of the family I should have been accepted in to. I have proven myself to be Pellinore's true child by what I have done, and I will avenge Lamorak's blood to the utterance when I next meet Sir Gawain!"

Merlin looked over to me. "Well, there's the motive," was all he said. By now, Ywain had returned with the horse. He rode it up close to the wall of the keep where Pinel was standing, then dismounted.

"Back off! Back off! Get way back now!" Pinel ordered us. He moved Rosemounde closer to the horse and told her, "You take the reins and hold the horse." He had the idea that he would quickly mount the horse and pull her up after him, without ever letting the knife wander far from her throat, or ever letting loose of Rosemounde's arm. It was a tricky procedure, and if we were going to do anything, this was the time.

Robin turned his back to Pinel and called out to the tower, "Matthew!"

"Sir?" came the questioning shout from the barbican tower.

"Sir Pinel and a young lady will be riding through the gate. There is to be no difficulty for them, understand?"

"Yes, sir," came the reply. But I noticed that, as his back was turned, Robin had taken an arrow from his quiver and notched it in the string of his bow. Pinel, preoccupied with watching the rest of us as he calculated how to mount the horse, paid no attention to Robin's hands. But Robin was ready to fire if he ever got the chance.

What happened next all happened so rapidly that no one had any time to think. Only to react.

To my far right, Merlin moved into action suddenly, as if he were about to throw a ball. His arm extended toward the horse and he called out in an unrecognizable voice the command, *"Incendia!"*

A great explosion of fire and dust burst in front of the horse, which reared up in fear. Pinel, one hand on the horse and the other grasping Rosemounde, was jarred backwards and released his grip on the girl. She raced forward at the chance and ran into my arms. Robin, given the split-second opportunity, brought up his long bow, took aim, and sent an arrow whizzing straight into Sir Pinel's naked throat. The renegade knight collapsed against the wall of the keep. He was dead before he hit the ground.

"You're safe, my love!" I said to her. Yes, I know it was cliché, but what else was there to say?

"Yes," she said. "We're all safe now." And with that, wouldn't you know it? She fainted dead away in my arms.

"Good shot, Master Robin!" Ywain complimented him.

"Nothing any of my garrison couldn't have done," Robin replied in a "just doing my job" kind of way. But then he turned to Merlin. "What on earth was that explosion, old man? Where did *that* thing come from?"

A small smile twisted the edge of Merlin's mouth, and he got the coy look on his face that meant he wasn't going to tell *all* his secrets. Finally he said, "I never said I *couldn't* do magic."

At that point a huge groan came from the crowd at the lists outside the castle. It tapered off into a chorus of a few cheers mingled with a much larger chorus of moans. The trial was over. Lancelot had made short work of Sir Mador. I only hoped he hadn't killed him, now that our investigation had finally made the entire battle meaningless.

Epilogue:
Saint Dunstan's Abbey

The old monk ceased. The half-dozen young brothers who had gathered round him for the duration of his story waited expectantly for more, but they were disappointed. Brother Gildas had apparently decided to leave it at that.

They enjoyed listening to Brother Gildas regale them with stories about the days of King Arthur, who was now nothing but a distant memory for the old man, and for them, a figure that had passed into legend and myth. They had no way of knowing how much of the story Gildas was simply weaving out of imagined romance, and how much might have held a kernel of truth. But whether skeptic or true believer, each monk there was rapt by the old man's telling, and encouraged him to give them another tale whenever he could.

The hour between vespers and compline was to be set aside for reading and meditation at the Benedictine Abbey of Saint Dunstan. But as often as not, a group of the newly tonsured would congregate at that time to hear Brother Gildas's stories. Today, a cold, brisk Monday in March, they were sitting next to the fire in the refectory, catching its last warmth as it began to die down with the day.

Forty years Brother Gildas had worked in the scriptorium here, in this out of the way Hereford monastery close to the Welsh border. His storytelling was a tradition in the house. The abbot generally turned a blind eye to this minor infraction of the rule. So long as the group of listeners remained quiet and attentive to Brother Gildas, they could be said to be in meditation, couldn't they? And he remembered being entertained by the old monk's stories himself years ago when he had first entered the abbey. But now it was getting close to the time when they would need to gather in the church to sing compline, so the old man had cut off his tale.

"But Brother Gildas," the young monk with the big ears asked. "Was the queen ever cleared?"

Brother Gildas looked at him and smiled, having expected that to be the first question they asked him. "Lancelot had beaten Sir Mador, so legally she was cleared. Mador was ready to die after Lancelot had beaten him, but the king ordered Lancelot not to harm Sir Mador. Still, there would have always been doubts about Guinevere's innocence. Merlin was so exhausted once Sir Pinel was killed that he went directly back to his cave, and lay there in one of his dark moods for days afterwards. Ywain and I tried to make our way to the lists, to give our evidence before the king dispersed the crowd. We wanted everyone there to know who had really killed Sir Patrise, and Dame Agnes too.

"But we were prevented. By the time we got to the arena, who do you think was there before us? It was the Damsel of the Lake, Nimue. I don't know how, but she had been keeping track of everything Merlin and I had been up to, and knew the whole story. She stood before the king and all the assembled crowd and revealed that it had been Sir Pinel who poisoned the apple that killed Sir Patrise, and that he'd also set a trap that backfired and killed Sister Agnes, and that both of these things were done in an attempt to murder Sir Gawain. Sir Pinel, she told them, was Sir Lamorak's half-brother, and so his motive was the ongoing feud between the houses of Lot and Pellinore.

"By then the only thing left for Sir Ywain and me to do was add the fact that Sir Pinel had been killed trying to escape, and that the garrison was even now trying to hunt down Owen and Harry, the two Welsh archers who had been in on the conspiracy to ambush Sir Gawain.

"Well, Sir Mador was mortified by that, and was actually shedding tears when he knelt before the queen and apologized for accusing her unjustly. He also apologized to the king, to Sir Bors, and to Sir Lancelot, who by then had taken off his helmet and showed everyone who he really was, to almost nobody's surprise. Everyone forgave Sir Mador, since it was easy to understand how he could get the wrong impression. Afterwards he caused a large monument to be put on Sir Patrise's grave, that read, 'Here lies Sir Patrise, knight of Ireland, who was poisoned at the queen's feast, of which murder the queen was falsely accused, but the murderer was found to be Sir Pinel de Gales, a son of King Pellinore.' Sir Mador always had this way of stringing out his sentences. But anyway, it was pretty ironic that in his death and because of his treachery, Sir Pinel finally got the recognition as Pellinore's son he had always craved."

"But what about the archers? Were they ever caught?" The handsome, blue-eyed monk wondered.

Gildas nodded and went on in the same manner as before. "It turned out to be just as Robin Kempe had predicted. His troops in Caerleon found them in one of the town's brothels. They'd had no idea what had been going on in the castle and were taken completely by surprise at their arrest. But it took almost no effort at all to get them to confess to Sister Agnes's murder and, by extension, the plot to assassinate Sir Gawain. They hoped for leniency, blaming it all on Sir Pinel, who certainly was the instigator, but who was conveniently dead and couldn't tell us what Owen and Harry's true part in the plot had been. So the king condemned the two of them to hang.

"But here's the unexpected part. Sir Gawain, of his great courtesy, stepped up at that point and interceded for the two archers. He said there had been too much bloodshed already in the feud between those two great houses, and that he would not see another drop shed if it could be prevented. Owen and Harry received a commuted sentence on condition that they swear never to bear arms against Sir Gawain or any member of his family again, and they were exiled from Logres.

"And even more than that, Gawain invited Sir Agloval and the young Perceval, the two surviving brothers of Lamorak, to meet him at Camelot and swear before the king and the court to foreswear all vengeance forever. Gawain and his brothers did so as well, symbolically laying down their swords. Not that there was ever any danger that Gawain and Perceval would fight. They were always the best of friends. But to have both houses give up the feud like that was an impressive sight to witness. I suppose it never would have happened if it weren't for Sir Pinel and his treachery. So some good came out of that terrible time after all."

"Some good," the blue-eyed monk conceded, "but three dead and many others put in danger. And two of those killed were innocent of any wrongdoing."

"Well," Brother Gildas conceded, "one was innocent. Dame Agnes was repentant, which is not exactly the same thing. But the Lord works in a mysterious way his wonders to perform, does he not? Who knows how many more might have died if the feud had continued?"

"Did Merlin stay confined to his cave after that?" the large-eared monk wanted to know.

"Ah." Gildas smiled at the memory of his mentor. "Merlin never got over his dark moods, but we were able to rouse him from his cave on a number of occasions after that, to be sure. It was quite some time, though, before I ventured to see him again."

"And you, Brother Gildas," came a voice from the back. It

was the thin-nosed, thin-lipped Brother Nennius of Kent. "Did you become squire to some worthy knight, then, as the queen had promised?"

"Indeed!" Gildas replied, with a note of worldly pride that would probably require some penance at his next confession. "The queen informed me shortly after her trial that she had arranged for me to become the squire of Sir Gareth of Orkney himself. Though I hated to leave the queen's service, I couldn't imagine a better master than Beaumains. Between him and his nephew Florent, I knew I could be made ready for knighthood in no time."

Brother Nennius followed up with the obvious question: "Then what became of you and the Lady Rosemounde? Did she indeed marry another before you became a knight? Or did her father finally approve of you as suitor to his daughter?"

"That," Brother Gildas answered, his face becoming impassive and his voice turning flat and expressionless, "is another story altogether. One that we don't have the time for this evening."

And as if on cue, the bells began to chime, calling the brothers in to the chapel for compline. The six young monks all rose immediately and started off. As they hurried away, Brother Nennius whispered conspiratorially, "Tomorrow after vespers?"

"Perhaps, perhaps," Gildas assented tentatively. "If God wills, and the abbot." He smiled and waved them off as he rose much more slowly to his feet.

He took a deep breath and paused. If he walked into compline a few minutes late, it would be no great sin. He might receive a stern look from the abbot or the prior, but he could always claim the infirmity of age—something he was taking more and more advantage of lately.

He stood for several moments, a solitary figure before the fire, whose dying light cast a red glow on his features and emphasized the shadows made by the age-worn crags in his weathered face. Anyone observing him would have had a hard time reading his expression. But there was no mistaking the sigh that issued when he let out his breath. In that brief moment before he turned from the fire and went in to compline, he reached into his robe and brought out a tattered piece of cloth that he wore pinned to his shirt, next to his skin. It was frayed with time and faded to a pale imitation of its original blue, but it was unmistakably a ribbon from a young girl's hair.

ACKNOWLEDGMENTS

I have set this story not in the sixth century, the time of the historical Arthur's career, but rather in the High Middle Ages (roughly the twelfth or thirteenth century), the time when the legendary Arthur flourished. Thus it is not exactly a historical novel, and that is my excuse for any anachronisms you might notice.

Although Merlin and Gildas do not appear in the original story, the tale of Guinevere, Sir Patrise, and the poisoned apple will be familiar to readers of Sir Thomas Malory's fifteenth-century *Le Morte Darthur*, which is the basis of most modern versions of the legend of King Arthur. Gareth's tale of Sir Ironside and the story of Gawain and his brothers' feud with Sir Lamorak also have their source in Malory. Sir Palomides's story of the fall of Jerusalem is compiled from texts that can be found in books like *The Crusades Through Arab Eyes* by Amin Maalouf (1984) and *Arab Historians of the Crusades* by Francesco Gabrieli (1984), which might be supplemented by Edward Peters's edition of *The First Crusade: "The Chronicle of Fulcher of Chartres" and Other Source Materials* (1998) and Caroline Smith's Penguin edition of *Chronicles of the Crusades* (2009).

Gildas is actually the name of a sixth-century monk famous for composing a history called *De Excidio et Conquestu Britanniae* ("On the Ruin and Conquest of Britain"), which is the first text alluding to battles between the Celtic Britons and the Saxons usually associated with the figure of Arthur. Nennius,

295

who is named as one of the monks in the concluding scene, was a Welsh monk and author of *Historia Brittonum* ("History of the Britons"), which names Arthur as the British war chief. In reality, Nennius and Gildas would not have been contemporaries.

Modern readers may be a bit confused by the use of canonical hours to report time in the novel. At the time in which the story is set, most people thought of the day as divided by the hours of divine office, which they could hear announced by church bells. There were eight of these hours or offices: Assuming a day in spring or fall, with approximately equal twelve-hour periods of day and night, the office of *prime* would occur around sunrise, about six a.m. according to modern notions of time. The next office, *terce*, would be sung around nine a.m., *sext* would be around noon, *none* at about three p.m., *vespers* at six p.m., *compline* about nine p.m., *matins* at midnight, and *lauds* around three a.m. These are the approximate times for events in the novel.

ABOUT THE AUTHOR

Jay Ruud offers this book as first in a series of Merlin mysteries. Jay is Chair of the English Department at the University of Central Arkansas. He is the author of *"Many a Song and Many a Leccherous Lay": Tradition and Individuality in Chaucer's Lyric Poetry* (1992), the *Encyclopedia of Medieval Literature* (2006), *A Critical Companion to Dante* (2008), and *A Critical Companion to J.R.R. Tolkien* (2011). He has taught at UCA for eleven years, prior to which he was Dean of the College of Arts and Sciences at Northern State University in South Dakota. He has a PhD in Medieval Literature from the University of Wisconsin-Milwaukee, has three dogs, four grandchildren, is a long-suffering Chicago Cubs fan, and believes that Lee Harvey Oswald acted alone.